WHITE SUN WAR

The Campaign for Taiwan

MICK RYAN

CASEMATE

Philadelphia & Oxford

First published in the United States of America and Great Britain in 2023.
Reprinted in 2024 by
CASEMATE PUBLISHERS
1950 Lawrence Road, Havertown, PA 19083, USA
and
The Old Music Hall, 106–108 Cowley Road, Oxford OX4 1JE, UK

Paperback Edition: ISBN 978-1-63624-250-7
Digital Edition: ISBN 978-1-63624-251-4

A CIP record for this book is available from the British Library

Printed and bound in the United Kingdom by CPI Group (UK) Ltd, Croydon, CR0 4YY

Typeset in India by Lapiz Digital Services, Chennai.

For a complete list of Casemate titles, please contact:

CASEMATE PUBLISHERS (US)
Telephone (610) 853-9131
Fax (610) 853-9146
Email: casemate@casematepublishers.com
www.casematepublishers.com

CASEMATE PUBLISHERS (UK)
Telephone (0)1226 734350
Email: casemate-uk@casematepublishers.co.uk
www.casematepublishers.co.uk

For Jocelyn, Dana and Kara

Foreword

Taiwan, officially known as the Republic of China and formerly called Formosa, is a small island that has seen a succession of rulers over its long history. It is originally thought to have been settled six millennia ago by Austronesian speakers who were the ancestors of indigenous Taiwanese. Successive waves of people have populated the island in the last several hundred years including the Chinese, the Dutch in the 17th century, followed by the Chinese again during the Qing dynasty. Thereafter came the Japanese in the 1890s, who used the island as a major base during the Second World War, and then the Chinese in the wake of the Pacific War. It became the final, and enduring, refuge of the Chinese republicans from 1949.

Therefore, the island of Taiwan is no stranger to invasion. Indeed, war has been an important part of its history. Interestingly, an invasion of Formosa was one of the options considered by Admiral Nimitz in 1944. Codenamed the *Causeway* Joint Staff Study, a massive force of American air and naval might would bombard the island before landing a force of over 236,000 soldiers and Marines to defeat the 98,000 Japanese defenders.

Operation *Causeway* never came to be.

Instead, the American Central Pacific drive focused on the seizure of Okinawa as a preparatory step for the expected invasion of

Japan. But, as the *Causeway* planning study makes clear, this was an operational problem that had both combat and logistic complexities.

However, this was not the only study of such an invasion. Between 1949 and 1951, the new Chinese Communist Party government in Beijing conducted intensive planning for a similar operation. Aimed to bring the Chinese civil war to a conclusion, successive iterations of the plan described the requirement to land nearly half a million Chinese troops in Taiwan and its outlying islands. The planning was well advanced when a combination of the outbreak of the Korean War, the 1950 unearthing of a massive Chinese spy ring in Taiwan, and the presence of the US Seventh Fleet postponed the operation.

The operational challenges explored by American and Chinese planners in the 1940s feature in the more modern arrival of invading troops told in these pages.

Initially, I was tempted to write this story as a historical tome. It would have been a book informed by years of research and hundreds of interviews. The book would have been rich in footnotes, maps, and direct quotes from participants. I would have undertaken a traditional book launch, done the normal speaking events at universities and war colleges, and then moved on to my next research project.

But something was nagging at me about this approach. Perhaps it was that most people no longer have much of an interest in history books and their arcane lexicon and pages of notes. Maybe it was the fact that we know more now about how people learn and adapt. Possibly it was my experience in using fiction to prompt different and more creative responses from my students.

It therefore occurred to me that there might be a better way to tell this story. A way that was accessible to many more people.

As a young man, I read and had immediately been impressed by Michael Shaara's *The Killer Angels*. Published in 1974, it won the 1975 Pulitzer Prize for Fiction for its depiction of the three days of the Battle of Gettysburg. It is a story filled with real historical figures, a character-driven narrative that explores the emotions and decisions of commanders on the field of battle over those three decisive days in 1863.

It was a hugely influential book, receiving multiple other awards besides the Pulitzer. *The Killer Angels* had a significant influence on how contemporary Americans thought about the Civil War and the Battle of Gettysburg. It shone new light on characters such as Joshua Chamberlain and James Longstreet, individuals whose deeds had either faded into history or who may have been treated unkindly by earlier historians.

I believe it was so popular, and influential, because humans respond much more powerfully to stories. It is hard coded into us. From the earliest development of language, humans have used storytelling to pass on knowledge—whether that has been the method to build a flint knife, sow crops, or govern wisely.

As Shaara wrote in his introduction to the book, "Stephen Crane once said that he wrote *The Red Badge of Courage* because reading the cold history was not enough; he wanted to know what it was like to be there, what the weather was like, what men's faces looked like. In order to live it he had to write it. This book was written for much the same reason."

Consequently, I decided that I would eschew non-fiction and instead write the history of the war for Taiwan as a novel in a similar vein to Michael Shaara's masterpiece.

My aim, beyond sharing the lessons of this conflict, and war more generally, is to demystify the reasons the belligerents went to war over this island off the coast of China. The book explores why so many young (and not so young) Americans, Japanese, Koreans, Vietnamese, Australians, and other nationalities volunteered, served, and sacrificed to preserve a young democracy. And why, over a longer period than anyone foresaw, a seesawing and devastatingly destructive fight on the ground, in the air, at sea, and in space and cyberspace was waged by humans, AI, and non-sentient machines.

The focal point for the story is the lead-up to, and conduct of, the Battle of Taichung. Of course, this city and the battle for its possession is now as well known as other historical battles in the 20th-century Pacific War. And while there were even more vicious battles in the campaigns that followed, the Battle of Taichung stands as an important turning point in the history of the campaign for Taiwan.

It became a strategic rallying point for the Allies in particular and was a central aspect of every information (and misinformation) campaign that followed. And it showed, as the Russo–Ukraine War demonstrated, that the power of the United States and the West more broadly was not in decline.

Like *The Killer Angels*, my book tells the story of war and its participants through the lens of a vital battle and the events that led to it being fought.

This book is a representation of several stories of those who fought in the battle. It is not designed as a fast-paced thriller, although I hope it is just as engaging. Instead, the narrative follows the tempo of a military campaign. It indeed has moments of high-tech wizardry and fast-flowing combat action. It has terror and bewilderment.

But it also has those quiet, and sometimes boring, moments before and between combat engagements, during which military and political leaders must discuss the purpose and conduct of war. These are the discussions that define strategy and the employment of the full array of national resources to achieve political objectives.

And in between the battles, the book explores the motivations and fears of the protagonists. How they dealt with the aftermath of battle and stinging losses of their people. And how they prepared for the next fight. And the next.

I hope that the reader will come to appreciate that, despite all the very best analyses, algorithms and calculations, humans are still immensely flawed beings. That our competitive nature, despite our other magnificent traits, continues to draw us into war despite our best efforts. Wars might start through the calculations of one side, but once begun, miscalculation, fear, and ambiguity reign.

Sometimes these things lead to noble actions and victory. Other times they lead to cowardice and loss. This is a persistent feature of war, something that the great Clausewitz wrote about in his masterpiece, *On War*. And while the kinds of tools we use to fight now might be different, the human emotions and motivations that Clausewitz described in his book remain a persistent aspect of war and human existence.

It is, as Clausewitz tells it, the enduring nature of war.

The war over Taiwan, and this book's telling of it, features all these elements.

Finally, it must be re-emphasized that wars are not fought by machines.

People fight wars.

Mostly, these are ordinary people, rudely drawn from their normal lives to take part in the most extraordinary and awful thing that humans can be engaged in. Every human response is present in conflict—fright, bravery, boredom, timidity, joy, sorrow, faintheartedness, and many others.

This story is one that is written through the eyes of the participants. It features characters from both sides and at many different levels of the military institutions they are members of. Some belong to the oldest of tribes in war: infantry and cavalry. Others belong to the newest of tribes and are experts in space warfare. Just as war features both change and continuity, so too do the various specialties—the tribes—of military institutions. This novel explores the impact of these changes.

I have included, where appropriate, maps that show an approximation of the positions at different stages of the war. The word "approximation" is appropriate; no single headquarters or commander can ever see the full picture in war. These maps, based on contemporary sources, reflect the known situation at particular times during the conflict.

I had the opportunity to interview many of the surviving characters who were featured in this story. For those who did not survive long enough for me to have interviewed them, I was given privileged access to their writings. This included their blogs, social media entries, online journals, and other communications with their closest relatives. The raw emotion that shines through their words is hopefully given its respectful due in this book.

But not only is this a story about the people who fought this war.

It is a story that I also dedicate to them.

Regardless of what they did, where they did it from, or where they are now, they were for this brief moment in human history a part of events that did indeed change the world. They served, and fell, in their tens of thousands, and deserve recognition—and our enduring gratitude.

I hope this story, called the *White Sun War* after the distinctive central feature of the Taiwanese flag, informs the reader about the trajectory of the war. I trust it helps readers to understand how this war started, how and why it was fought, and what we must all learn from it. It also tells the story of how the military services of many nations had to learn new ways of thinking about war and conducting operations because of the profound changes in technology over the past two decades.

White Sun War, and many of the historical examinations of the conflict that have preceded it, shows that those who were slow to learn about new technologies, new concepts of fighting, and new ways of organizing before the war often struggled to catch up during the war. Such was the pace of learning and adaptation once the conflict began.

But these are not new lessons. We have seen the same thing occur in the wars that were spawned during—and after—the last three industrial revolutions.

Finally, I hope this book shows that we human beings—despite our most noble of ideas and aspirations—are still capable of the most appalling miscalculations. And of the most terrible of atrocities against those who do not look or think like us.

As was the case in the first decade of the 20th century, many politicians, and academics early in the 21st century assumed that economic integration across the globe would prevent large-scale warfare. That enhanced connectivity through the internet and travel would allow better understanding of different cultures. And that our trade with one another would prevent us from fighting each other. They further assumed that it was not in the interests of their competitors to initiate large-scale fighting—especially ground wars—to achieve their national interests.

They were wrong.

Again.

The Russian invasion of Ukraine, and its enormous destruction and disruption of the global security environment, dissuaded many of this notion. The outcome of what Sir Lawrence Freedman called a "delusionary strategy" from Vladimir Putin, the Russians made just about every political, economic, and military mistake that it was possible to make over the course of their military campaign.

And then, within a few short years of this foolish and strategically inept Ukrainian conquest, the Chinese invasion of Taiwan.

So, we were wrong about war and its continuing grip on human civilization.

And we will be wrong again in the future.

Our best hope is to minimize these wars and ensure that they do not spill over into a nuclear—or even biological—conflict that could spell the end of humans on this planet.

We must study and understand such things if we are to have any chance of preventing such destructive conflagrations in future.

Mick Ryan
New Honolulu
June 2038

Preliminary Operations

Prelude

The Massacre

2 March 2028, 2230 hours
Tinian Island
West Pacific

"This is approaching mass slaughter, Captain," she heard through the earphones that were embedded in her combat helmet.

Mass slaughter was exactly what she had hoped for.

"Roger that, Sarge. Just as we planned," she responded.

Captain Dana Lee monitored her heads-up display, her arm screen, and other monitors as the butchery continued. The killer bots were working at peak efficiency and slaughtering the enemy with almost total abandon. That it was getting close to midnight, with no moon, and was pitch black made not the slightest difference. Even the old Second World War parallel airfields were hard to discern in the darkness.

"So far, so good," she continued over their vehicle's intercom.

Sergeant James sat up in his turret. He was commanding their armored vehicle, allowing Lee to lead their unit from the rear compartment. A little younger than the other sergeants in the troop, James had nonetheless brought with him a sterling reputation as a professional junior leader when he arrived in the unit just a few weeks before they left their home base in Colorado for this training mission. And while quiet and studious, James was able to hold his own with some of the rowdier senior non-comms in the troop.

Their adversaries had suffered massive attrition over the past two hours and were now showing signs of breaking. If they did that, then the slaughter would really go into overdrive. A fleeing enemy with a broken spirit and little remaining cohesion had no defense against a powerful, aggressive military force bent on their destruction.

Lee was no stranger to death. Her experience predated her time in the Army.

At twelve years old, Lee had lost her younger sister to leukemia. It had been a long and drawn-out death for a sister whom she had loved dearly. The vacuum it had opened within her had never really been filled. Even with loving parents, Dana had closed off a part of herself that she felt would probably never be reopened. It had hindered the formation of friendships, especially close ones.

She had also been exposed to death in training accidents. Armored vehicles were unforgiving beasts. Whether it was vehicle rollovers or other incidents, Captain Lee had become used to the fact that her profession was more likely than any other to expose her to, and in some ways insulate her emotions against, death.

Therefore, the killing that played out on the screens before her elicited minimal emotions from the young Army captain.

Such was the reality of war, from the time of the ancients, Lee pondered. Recently, she'd had more cause than was usual to muse on this topic. After assuming command of her cavalry unit just over a year ago, the ability of her unit to fight and succeed against a larger adversary had been a core element of her approach to training and leadership. Particularly with some of their new equipment, it was a very capable organization in the killing and destruction business.

Dana led a newly formed troop within a cavalry squadron of the US Army. The Army had set up several of these squadrons, each including five troops—the equivalent in size of an infantry company—which were a mix of human and robotic systems. A "mix" was perhaps somewhat of a stretch. For every human and armored vehicle in the new cavalry units, there were dozens, and sometimes hundreds, of different ground and aerial robotic systems. And that didn't include the multitude of bespoke algorithms that assisted them in surveillance, targeting, network security, logistics, personnel tracking, and tactical planning.

As a junior lieutenant, she had been part of one of the old-style cavalry scout platoons in the 1st Cavalry Division. Equipped with an old Bradley cavalry fighting vehicle, she had learned how to conduct missions such as reconnaissance and security, and to lead her soldiers. That was at a time when the cavalry organization, its equipment, and its modes of operation would still have been recognizable to previous generations of cavalry soldiers. Not so with her current unit.

Three years ago, with the Army finally understanding that its current organizations and missions were becoming less relevant in the Pacific theater, a slew of old organizations had been adapted to be more lethal. They were re-equipped with longer range weapons and reorganized to be able to deploy more quickly around the large swathe of the earth that was the Pacific Ocean. Infantry, armor, cavalry, aviation, engineers, communicators, logisticians, and many other elements of the Army had been forced to quickly adapt how they fought and how they were organized. More importantly, they had begun to change how they *thought* about fighting.

The drivers of these changes were twofold. First, the People's Liberation Army (PLA) had begun to widely deploy a range of ground, air, and naval unmanned combat systems that had greater survivability than most crewed fighting systems. Massive numbers of autonomous munitions, which could loiter over a battlefield for hours, were now available to every nation on earth. It made 21st century battlefields much more deadly to all combatants. It meant that, without significant structural and conceptual change, the Army would be taking a knife to a machine-gun fight against the Chinese (and any others) if they went to war.

The second forcing function was energy. New developments in energy storage, using carbon fiber structures, had resulted in batteries and other storage devices having an exponentially greater storable energy supply. This meant that both crewed and autonomous systems could stay on mission, and at greater distance, than had ever been possible before.

And of course, the Army loves a slogan. So, Lee's unit was part of the "Cavalry 2030" program. In essence, the old six-Bradley structure of the cavalry troop had been expanded to eight vehicles. But the vehicles were very different. Externally, they looked like familiar cavalry fighting vehicles. But inside, they had been totally stripped and refitted with an all-electric drive system, vehicle mounted counter-drone systems, and AI-driven secure communications networks.

The backend of each vehicle, where previously the human scouts had been carried, was vastly different. The rear of each of these vehicles carried just two people. But they also transported dozens of different uncrewed ground-combat and surveillance vehicles, as well as a variety of small unmanned aerial vehicles (UAVs). Some of the autonomous systems were even a mix of the two, with mid-size ground vehicles toting small UAVs.

All this meant that cavalry officers such as Dana had to rethink how they scouted and fought on the battlefield. They had to accept that the lethality of enemy systems sometimes required humans to hold back further from the front line. The PLA uncrewed ground and aerial vehicles were so fast and so lethal that it was sometimes untenable for humans to get too close to enemy formations.

Close combat was beginning to be dominated by the myriad of uncrewed systems that Dana's unit operated. Linked by high-security networks back to their parent combat brigades and divisions, they permitted the new-era cavalry units to conduct reconnaissance missions and survive. This would provide the early warning that allowed Dana's commanders the vital seconds and minutes to make decisions influencing success or catastrophe on the battlefield.

The current engagement was a case in point.

Lee's unit was on a security mission, protecting the right flank of her parent brigade's advance. One of their small Black Hornet UAVs, launched from a medium uncrewed scout vehicle, had detected the exhaust signature of a Chinese medium tank. Using the bespoke AI that coordinated the air and ground autonomous scouts in that area, two small Gnat UAVs had been dynamically re-tasked to confirm the signature. Concurrently, multiple micro and small ground uncrewed scout vehicles had begun seeking out other Chinese vehicles, UAVs, autonomous ground sensors, and communications networks, using an established doctrinal template for the deployment of a Chinese combat unit.

It took less than ten seconds for Captain Lee's network of uncrewed ground and aerial scouts to map out the locations and strength of one of the reorganized PLA mix-mechanized brigades. Comprising stealthy Type 99 medium battle tanks, Type 94 wheeled infantry fighting vehicles, and a variety of networked autonomous air and ground vehicles, the Chinese made an inviting target.

But not just yet.

Lee's network of sensors and autonomous vehicles remained in stealth mode while they communicated this back to Lee's vehicle. She monitored the developing situation while checking the different settings that ensured data was passed up the line to her higher headquarters. It was not a constant flow of information, however. Data was shared in rapid micro-bursts between nodes which then disconnected to prevent hacking or compromise of their network.

Within microseconds, a short-term connection was established and the targeting algorithms in the fire coordination center at brigade headquarters were presenting options to the brigade commander for the destruction of the PLA unit. These algorithms also pinged Lee and her unmanned systems, giving a warning to clear certain areas that would be shortly under attack.

Seconds later, as the ground and aerial uncrewed systems quickly withdrew away from the Chinese vehicles, long-range precision rockets and artillery began to pour down upon the Chinese formation.

The rain of fire that was engulfing the PLA brigade was tightly synchronized. First, the long-range artillery cannons procured by the Army in the last three years fired a mix of high-explosive shells and precise anti-vehicle rounds. Then, once the PLA brigade had begun to respond to the incoming fire, the loitering munitions and uncrewed ground combat vehicles in the area unmasked from their camouflage and electronic stealth modes and began to engage light vehicles and dismounted humans.

The investment in unmanned ground combat vehicles (UGVs) over the past half-decade was finally paying off, Lee thought. Her unit had been the beneficiary of many upgraded systems. She particularly liked the M5 *Ripsaw* autonomous combat vehicle, and its more recent upgrade, the M5 Mark II *RipShark*. While both were highly lethal, the Mark II *RipShark* (she loved that name) was also designed with higher levels of protection against electronic interference and electromagnetic pulses. These lethal ground combat vehicles were complemented with several autonomous logistic vehicles that automatically assessed levels of ammunition and serviceability, and then deployed to those UGVs most in need of assistance.

At the same time, all of their counter-autonomy systems came online and prepared for any Chinese counterattack. A range of different electronic attack, cyber, and hard-kill counter-UAV and counter-missile systems had been rapidly developed and introduced into service over the last few years. But, as Lee pondered this, her mind shifted to her favorite anti-missile and anti-drone system, which was being procured from the Israelis.

They called it "Iron Beam." It was, at long last, a cheap laser protection system that could shoot down missiles, artillery, mortars, and UAVs. All at about two bucks a shot. It was accurate and being deployed across the whole Army. And, as the Army liked to do, it had renamed this laser system for American use.

They called it "ALPS"—Army Laser Protection System.

Lee thought it was a pretty lame term.

But she had more to think about right now, and her attention was drawn back to her command screens.

Lee's unit began to map the communications networks across the PLA formation as they lit up with different autonomous systems communicating with each other. Panicked human operators, reporting up and down the chain of command, allowed the electronic warfare personnel that were part of her unit to confirm the locations of the various enemy headquarters. These locations included the brigade headquarters as well as its superior divisional headquarters. These were then targeted by long-range precision weapons, including precision strike missiles, which they just called "Prism," as well as land-attack variants of the Navy's SM-6 missile (also known as the "Standard Extended Range Active Missile") that was part of the new Army "Typhoon" ground offensive system.

The link analysis provided by the cyber and electronic warfare teams, supported by the work being done by bespoke algorithms, traced the military chain of command for this Chinese brigade up through its division, corps, and joint command headquarters.

This information was then also added to the rapid joint-targeting cycle that sat well above Captain Lee's unit. Against these enemy headquarters' locations, the full effect of Air Force and Navy long-range traditional and hypersonic weapons was brought to bear.

At the same time, the electronic warfare UAVs were conducting counter-autonomous systems activities by jamming communications among the Chinese crewed and autonomous elements as well as spoofing the PLA units with fake locations of the American forces. Other electronic warfare elements, with their sensors on satellites and in small autonomous ground vehicles, measured all the electronic emissions of the PLA force for use in future engagements. The sensors and human operators were supported by advanced algorithms and high-security cloud-based data analytics for real-time analyses and targeting support. Electromagnetic maneuver warfare had become a staple of Army units over the past several years, and they were good at it. Almost as good as the Russians. At least as good as the PLA.

Other counter-autonomous systems closer to Lee's position were monitoring the air and ground for any PLA systems that might have "leaked" through Lee's sensor network that emanated in concentric layers from her small unit. Hard and soft kill systems, including electronic pulses, lasers, and mini versions of the naval close-in weapon systems, stood ready to identify and kill any of the Chinese autonomous systems that might approach.

Finally, the information and influence team were busy recording the engagement and then streaming different video compilations onto the Chinese social media known to be frequented by middle-class families who provided their only children as soldiers. The key message of the videos—which edited out anything too gory—was that the Chinese Communist Party's illogical expansion beyond its usual borders was resulting in the unnecessary deaths of their children. The intention—because these tactical influence

10

activities were nested within a national information and influence strategy—was to shift public opinion in the People's Republic of China and force the president and his cronies in the Politburo to focus more on domestic concerns.

The overall result on the ground, however, was the slaughter that Captain Lee was now seeing on her screens. Her command vehicle, which was swiftly moving cross-country in anticipation of other Chinese PLA units in the area, would have previously bounced her command pod around violently. But the stabilized platform upon which her command suite sat kept her almost unnaturally stable.

While Lee's armored vehicle was different and tactical information was shared differently, some things in warfare stubbornly remained the same, such as half-drunk coffee and cold Meals Ready to Eat—also known as MREs—on the move. It wasn't very advanced but it sustained them.

While she kept one eye on the current engagement between the combat units of her parent brigade and the Chinese, she kept her other on a portion of the map 10 miles away: her next objective, and a fine location to rendezvous with all her returning uncrewed systems. This site would be where the UAVs and UGVs would meet her troop in a stealthy hide to replenish fuel and munitions. She would then be able to plan in detail the next phase of their operation.

Lee found herself smiling.

Who would have thought, just a few years ago during her time as an economics student at Columbia University, she would end up here? Certainly not her parents. Her father, who managed his own hedge fund in Manhattan, had always expected Dana to follow him into "the business."

Her mother, a lawyer who also worked in Manhattan a few blocks from her father's firm, had been more open-minded about her oldest daughter's future. She understood that while Dana adored her father and was studying economics to please him, her daughter was different. It was probably why Lee had followed an old boyfriend into the ROTC program while she was at Columbia. The program she had attended was actually run at Fordham University, which meant she had become expert at juggling her time. It was a skill that now served her well.

The boyfriend was soon history, but she had persevered with the military training program, despite it being physically and emotionally draining. And while her mom had understood Dana's desire to branch out from the family business, her father had taken a little bit longer to come around. But he had, eventually. And he had been there, beaming proudly, at her commissioning ceremony. After commissioning, she had eventually ended up earning her Stetson in the cavalry.

A short, sharp *ping* brought her back to the present. Suddenly, all the screens in her command pod went blank, as did her heads-up display.

The displays of maps, data, crew, and vehicle locations all vanished. Their many different colors faded to singular black screens. All that remained was the display on her arm screen. It was connected only to data sources such as her physiology or internal data repositories like the *Encyclopedia Militaria*.

The busy radio chatter that passed through the headphones embedded in her helmet ceased. The sudden lack of chatter and banter between members of her troop came as a shock to someone accustomed to this almost constant source of information.

Within a second, a new display appeared on her previously blank screens.

ENDEX

The exercise scenario was over.

Lee slowly removed her crew helmet. Sweat had soaked through her short hair and dripped down the rear of her neck and the side of her face. Her first thought was of her vehicle crew commander, sitting in the turret of the vehicle.

"Hey Sarge, how you doin' up there?" Dana called up through the back of the turret.

"Ma'am, from my display up here, it looks like we cut up that enemy brigade real bad. Lots of letters home to families after that one," James replied. There was little sense of joy in his voice at having successfully destroyed an enemy unit and hundreds of human beings. But there was a tone of professional satisfaction.

"You know, it probably won't be that easy in the real thing. Fighting algorithms is hard, and their programming has come a long way. But once we are fighting humans, it will be harder. They will do things that we just won't think of. It will hurt for real, not just virtually. Anyway, how about I put some coffee on?"

James finished, and there was momentary silence on the net. Like Lee, James was a serious scholar of war and fighting. It was not just his job but his profession. He understood what caused people to fight, and how once fighting started, it could head in very unexpected directions.

This was especially the case if one was fighting in a military institution for a nation that didn't have an overall strategy or a clear theory of victory. They had both experienced this in Afghanistan.

Lee regularly scheduled professional development sessions with her junior officers and non-commissioned officers to discuss these matters, as well as the latest developments in manned-unmanned teaming tactics, and enemy technological developments. It made for a hectic life.

After a moment, James came back up on the radio to break the silence.

James continued, "One other thing, Captain. I just received a call on the squadron command net. They want us back at the headquarters location as soon as possible."

Lee nodded to herself, silently acknowledging the order to move. It was normal for the different elements of the cavalry unit Lee was part of to meet after training missions to conduct debriefs and discuss what they had learned. Such meetings were very useful— Lee and her troopers were also fortunate to have a lieutenant colonel in command of the squadron who allowed them to fail in training if it meant learning.

Not all her previous bosses had been like that. She was pondering this when James spoke again. This time, his words did surprise her.

"Apparently, we are being detached from our squadron. And get this. The rumors say that we will be going to work for the Marines."

Phase I

1

Flood and Fire

1 May 2028
Federal Emergency Management Agency (FEMA) Headquarters
Washington, DC

Dammit, thought FEMA Administrator Diane Keene.

Keene stood at a raised central command node in the midst of a whirl of activity at the FEMA headquarters emergency management center. A large room, its floor was covered in curved flatscreen monitors, at which sat operators from a myriad of national and state agencies. The floor was already littered with the detritus of those who had worked multiple long shifts monitoring the current weather emergencies taking place across the continental United States.

The screen in front of Keene was displaying the latest track for the hurricane that had already ripped its way through the Caribbean. Named Hurricane Jo by the National Hurricane Center's naming convention, it had already outstripped the 2005 record-breaking Hurricane Wilma—at that time, the most intense storm ever recorded in the Atlantic. With wind speeds over 180 miles per hour, it had caused carnage, killing dozens of people. It had also resulted in billions of dollars in damage, as it worked its evil way through the Caribbean, Florida, the east coast of the United States, and even as far north as Nova Scotia.

The monster that Keene was looking at on the screen was worse. Much worse.

June hurricanes were unusual. Normally, June saw hurricanes only every other year. And they normally had reasonably predictable paths—forming in the Gulf of Mexico and tracking either through the western Caribbean toward Texas, or on a more easterly attack across Florida.

This hurricane was acting more like a July hurricane, forming in the eastern Caribbean and moving westward across the Bahamas. But, unlike other July hurricanes which hit the Carolinas, this one was tracking for a direct hit on the city of Miami.

Historically, the vast majority of hurricanes in the Atlantic and Gulf of Mexico had occurred in the months of August, September, and October. Either side of those months, hurricanes occurred, but nowhere as frequently. At least, that had been the case until the last several years. The past three seasons had not only seen more powerful superstorms. More hurricanes were occurring earlier, even in May. And the season had extended well into November and even December.

Over 6 million people lived in the Miami metropolitan area and its immediate surrounds. The city also had a significant number of high-rise buildings, with over 300 of these multi-story concrete and steel structures reaching ever higher into the skies.

Hurricane Jo had already caused catastrophic damage as it rampaged north through the Caribbean. Puerto Rico was a major disaster area, although damage and death reports were still coming in since it hit there 24 hours ago. So far, it looked like the death toll there would be at least in the hundreds and that infrastructure had been devastated. The Dominican Republic had likewise suffered terrible damage and a huge loss of life.

Some of the smaller Caribbean islands had suffered even worse. Saint Barts, Antigua, Nassau, and Grand Bahama had essentially been erased from the map. High winds and storm surges had combined to destroy large proportions of buildings and other infrastructure. There were currently no communications with any of these islands, so the death and injury toll was unknown.

Keene pondered the events of the past 24 hours as she looked at the screen. This was probably just a preview of even worse to come, she thought, as Hurricane Jo powered toward Florida and the densely populated areas around Miami. On average, the city was only 6 feet above sea level. This meant that many areas were low lying and vulnerable to flooding if there was tidal surge accompanied by heavy rain.

Already a Category Five storm, the aftermath of this hurricane might result in a reassessment of the system to include a new category that covered even more powerful super hurricanes that had emerged over the last several years.

With the average temperatures of the ocean still rising, the amount of energy available to fuel these storms was increasing. Last year's hurricane season had been bad enough, Keene thought, with two hurricanes that had set records for their intensity and wind speeds. This hurricane was looking to be even worse. It was a calamitous start to the season.

Miami had about eight hours to prepare for the landfall of this hurricane. Of course, long before the massive storm crossed the coast of Florida, it would be taking its toll on land and at sea. But on making landfall, Keene and her team at FEMA expected a truly awful toll in human lives and damage to property.

She would almost despair if she wasn't distracted by another pressing emergency.

On the other side of the country, wildfires were spreading in California, Oregon, and Washington state. Like the hurricane season, the wildfire season now extended much longer than had been the case even a decade ago.

Keene again pondered the latest report from the Intergovernmental Panel on Climate Change. Like the IPCC's previous report in 2021, the 2026 report had been pessimistic about the impact of rising global temperatures. The unequivocal nature of its findings about human activity warming the atmosphere, ocean, and land were enough to deeply concern even those with a smattering of scientific understanding.

But like its predecessors in 2021 and 2016, the most recent climate change report had been paid lip service by most of the major carbon-emitting nations. The ratchetting up of tensions between China on one side, and the US and its allies on the other, had only made things worse. While China had continued to churn out propaganda about its green energy initiatives, at the same time it had continued to pump massive amounts of carbon into the atmosphere. The continuing slowing of its economy, and the credit crunch of the past several years, had slowed investment in renewables and green energy.

So, the earth continued to warm. The fires burned longer and hotter.

Keene, who was conservative by nature and had served a stint in the Army three decades before, was by no means "green" in political orientation. But the scientific evidence, and the changes in climate, had her convinced. Unlike many colleagues in her party, she was constantly amazed at the cognitive dissonance of many of today's politicians and business leaders. But, regardless of whose brand of political party was in charge, the hurricanes continued to increase in intensity. And they were emerging over a much longer period with each successive year. It did not bode well for the future.

Keene sighed. She was fretting over things that were entirely outside her power to control. She had to turn to solving problems that were within her power, and that she was resourced and authorized to resolve. And her problems were truly mammoth.

On the east coast, she had a massive hurricane bearing down on one of the most densely populated and low-lying urban conurbations in the United States. Hurricane Jo was already predicted to be the first hurricane to cause over 100 billion dollars in damage. *Lord knows how many people would lose their lives*, Keene thought.

At the same time, across the western states, she was dealing with the largest and most destructive series of wildfires in United States history. Already, more than 5 percent of California's land had been burned, more than the previous worst season back in 2020. And that was just California. Oregon had turned into a hellscape, and Washington state was seeing wildfires in areas that had rarely burned before.

These fires, occurring across a longer period each year, had even been given new classifications by Australian researchers. Now, a fire that burned over 100,000 hectares was called a "mega fire." One that burned a million hectares was called a "giga fire." Even the descriptions for these events were unprecedented.

To make matters even worse, many of the usual supporting agencies were either not available or were severely limited in their capacity to assist FEMA. The National Guard, which would normally be used during disasters, had been nationalized and was unavailable. In response to growing Chinese provocations, the president had ordered a mobilization of the military, and large parts of American industry, to ensure that he and his cabinet had more options to consider, should things with the Chinese really start getting difficult. It meant that many of the troops, vehicles, and aircraft that would normally be on call to respond during natural disasters were no longer available.

There were some other military assets—such as Air Force transport aircraft—still available. But even they had become scarcer over the last six months.

The president and his national security advisers had hoped that by mobilizing the National Guard, it would send a message of US resolve to the Chinese and their Communist Party overlords in Beijing. The theory was that it would supply an additional deterrent effect against any Chinese move against Taiwan. *Good luck with that*, Keene thought.

For several years, the Chinese president had been giving speeches about the importance of reunifying China. Hong Kong and Taiwan, in the Chinese president's view, were integral elements of China.

The expectation among the senior bureaucrats that Keene associated with, and the occasional senior military officer that she met, was that Taiwan was next. But as Keene and everyone else knew, Taiwan was only 110 miles across the Taiwan Strait from the Chinese mainland. The US was much, much further away. And while the government's narrative was that they would not let a democracy fall prey to the predations of the authoritarian Chinese Communist Party, geography would get a big vote if the Chinese were to move against Taiwan.

It was always about the geography, thought Keene. No matter the emergency that her agency was responding to, geography shaped how they responded. Distance between points decided how quickly they could respond. Swollen rivers or closed mountain passes could limit access to disaster sites. Geography could hinder fires and floods and it could also help them.

She returned to the problems at hand: Florida and the west coast.

Both, individually, were catastrophes on an unprecedented scale. Together they posed an overwhelming challenge, and not only for

Keene's FEMA personnel in the various regions. These were disasters that would necessitate a mobilization of resources from across the nation. It would take her country years to recover.

Already, the president—despite his many other distractions and continuing focus on his own media image—had met with his cabinet that morning to discuss areas of federal spending that might be cut to pay for these calamities. But with the increases in military spending over the past two years, there was little fat to be found. And even if there was, they would need to get Congress to agree to allocate additional funding. *Again, good luck*, thought Keene.

Just this morning, the president's Chief of Staff had called and informed Keene that she would need to reallocate funds from other parts of her budget to deal with the west coast fires. There would be no extra funding for these so-called "blue states"; the president had little empathy for the majority of his western citizens who routinely voted against his party.

Keene noticed someone from the emergency operations center running towards her. Normally, the operators here would report to supervisors, who would then report to the center commander. Only then would scraps of information be passed to her.

As the person approached, Keene realized that they were wearing a military uniform. It was her liaison officer from the Pentagon, a young Army major who insisted on being called "Hal"; he had been detailed to her office a year before to ensure that FEMA had another flow of information to keep the Administrator informed quickly about strategic decisions and to work around the military bureaucracy when requesting military assets for disaster assistance.

He was good to have around. Not only was he well connected into the Pentagon bureaucracy, which was resistant to all outsiders, but he was good natured and happy to take on additional tasks to assist the Administrator.

The look on the face of her military liaison told her nearly everything she needed to know. Keene frowned. *This cannot be good*, she thought.

"What is it, Hal?" Keene asked, when the military officer was within hearing distance.

He did not stop but walked directly up to Keene. He moved his head close as he spoke quietly to the Director.

"Ma'am, the Chinese are moving into the early stages of another large-scale exercise, similar to last year's scare. While last year's maneuvers didn't result in the invasion, the Joint Chiefs and the national security adviser are a little worried that this year they might proceed with an actual invasion. The president has therefore just moved us to DEFCON 3 in anticipation. We are on high alert for military action from the PLA. We are to expect cyber and other attacks in CONUS if hostilities break out."

Hal stepped back.

Keene nodded and tried to keep a neutral expression as she pondered the extra stress this added to her already heavy load of responsibilities. *Well*, she thought, *today is now just totally fucked.*

2

The Successor's Dilemma

3 May 2028
Zhongnanhai, Beijing

President Zhang growled at the members of the Central Military Commission. The meeting had continued well into the evening, and he was yet to eat. Despite the late hour, there were still unresolved issues that the president, also chairman of the Central Military Commission, found quite unsatisfactory. Although he had only been president for a little over a year, he still could feel time and opportunity slipping away.

Much had already been achieved in the previous years to drag these old military fossils into the 21st century, the president knew. When he assumed the presidency, the various services and military regions had been forced to continue adapting to what the president viewed as imperatives of 21st-century war and competition.

And to ensure that they learned the many lessons from previous conflicts including the American invasion of Iraq, the Russian conquest of Ukraine, and the Iranian incursions into Afghanistan just a couple of years before, the PLA had delivered several briefings to the Commission on their lessons from these 21st-century wars. These observations had been an important part of the planning that had ultimately led to this meeting. But there were other important issues that had consumed the president's time in the previous year. The president interrupted a long monologue from someone sitting off to his right.

"The most vital imperative remains loyalty to the Party. We have seen Chinese academics at the PLA National Defense University suggesting that the PLA should be disassociated from the Chinese Communist Party. Worse still, some have advocated for removing the military from the control of the Party altogether and placing it under the state. If we are to move forward in this great endeavor that we are gathered here to discuss, we must assure the purity of the PLA and ensure its loyalty to the Party."

The president had overseen the completion of reforms to the PLA command structure and replaced hundreds of generals and admirals believed to be corrupt or ideologically compromised. In practice, this was often the same thing. The purges, begun by his predecessor, had ushered in a new generation of more conformist and ideologically reliable senior leaders in the PLA. This reliability was much more important than old notions of military competence.

"Reliability ensures competence," the president informed those in the room.

He reflected on these purges and smiled at the thought of one notable general from the People's Liberation Army who had foolishly spoken to a confidant about aspirations to be a member of the Politburo and eventually become president. He, and his family, had perished in a very unfortunate aircraft accident during the reforms in the mid 2020s.

One more rival removed from the board, the president thought.

Even this august committee, traditionally the preserve of the most senior and powerful military leaders, had not escaped the attention and transformative zeal of President Zhang's predecessor. First, the chiefs of the Army, Navy, and Air Force had been removed, and directed to focus on commanding their respective forces. The Central Military Commission —what the generals called the CMC—had also been reduced to just seven members. This ensured that its focus was less about the political power of the PLA and more about the melding of the various arms of the Chinese military so they could operate together as a joint force.

More importantly, the different elements of the PLA needed to work with the other arms of the Chinese Communist Party (CCP) to achieve the late president's aspirations for his nation. China would become a strong, modern, and prosperous nation with a formidable military capable of operating wherever the president and the Central Military Commission required. He had spoken on this topic numerous times over the years, and he had chosen senior military leaders who would carry out his will.

American military operations over the past three decades had demonstrated just how powerful a more collaborative and unified military organization could be. If the Army, Navy, and Air Force could be cajoled or forced to work together, who knew what magnificent achievements they might be capable of? So, with energy, and not a little arm twisting, the president's predecessor had begun a concerted effort to modernize the PLA, its weapons, how it trained and educated its people, and how it was commanded.

Now, many of the reforms of the past decade were reaching fruition. The three military services were much better at cooperating to undertake joint operations. That didn't mean they no longer hated each other—they did. But they had become much better at camouflaging such bickering. And they were more effective, and easier to control, because of it.

The removal of military regions and the formation of the five theater commands had helped. The military service chiefs no longer directly commanded their forces, except for what the Western military leaders often called "raise, train, and sustain" functions.

The theater commanders, with their joint headquarters and support from the Beijing-based Joint Staff Department and the Strategic Support Force, made all the major decisions about the deployment of PLA forces as well as the planning for current and future military operations.

Over the past ten years, the Eastern and Southern Commands had received the most attention. While the Western Command was important in dealing with the various problematic ethnic groups, and the Central Command was essential to securing Beijing, it was the commands that looked out on the South China Sea and across the strait to Taiwan that absorbed the majority of the Party's focus.

These two commands were key parts of his predecessor's plan to unify the nation once again under a single flag and a single leader. As the late president had made clear, the current situation with their rebel province was untenable. It could not continue from generation to generation. And just as Tibet and Hong Kong had been brought under the governance of the Chinese Communist Party, so too would Taiwan. Despite the peaceful efforts to do so in the last few decades, it was increasingly likely that the current situation would remain a source of instability unless decisive measures were taken to resolve the issue.

The president and the other six members of the Central Military Commission were ensconced in a hyper-secure meeting room. Swept regularly for any form of monitoring device (except those placed by the Party, of course), it provided the most secure location for their sensitive discussions. While there were view screens on the wall, and AI-scribes embedded into the tabletop, the room was designed to permit no electronic signal to come in or to emerge from its steel, copper, and timber walls. It was, for all intents and purposes, an electronic black hole, which the American, Japanese, or any other national spy agency would be powerless to penetrate.

The room was part of a secure and hardened facility that had been excavated deep beneath the ground of Zhongnanhai in Beijing. Formerly an imperial garden, Zhongnanhai now housed all the most important agencies of the Chinese Communist Party. It had been used for government functions as far back as the Qing Dynasty. It had seen its importance grow after Chairman Mao Zedong had moved into the complex upon the formation of the People's Republic of China.

In this facility, the most sensitive of meetings related to the security and stability of the Chinese nation took place with the president and his core advisors and most trusted confidants. It was here that the direction had been given to have the PLA armored formations suppress the protestors in Tiananmen Square in June 1989. Here too, a different president had chaired meetings in those calamitous few weeks following the outbreak of coronavirus in Wuhan in the second half of 2019, which would become a global pandemic. Now to today.

"Comrades, we have a decision to make of the utmost importance to our nation," the president continued. In some respects, the president knew that this was the day that his whole life had been preparing him for. His privileged early childhood, followed by his time in the provinces and then his redemption and return to Beijing—all of it had provided the foundational knowledge and internal courage to make the decision he was about to make. He would have to give the most serious order that any Chinese leader had issued since the formation of the People's Republic in 1949.

The president mentally shook himself out of his reflections. He needed a sharp mind. He needed to focus. And he needed some final pieces of information that would inform his final directions for the forthcoming operation.

The president spoke to the one of the large screens before him. "General Tsung, please give me your assessment of the current situation in the South China Sea."

"Yes, sir," came a curt response.

The military officer on the screen then launched into his prepared briefing. It was short, just 20 minutes long. The president had made clear, early in his tenure after he had secured control, that he had no patience for long, technical briefings. Such blathering seemed to be the special province of senior military officers and was often made more confusing by their arcane jargon and lengthy explorations of side issues.

The president looked around the room to see if there were any questions from the other members of the CMC.

Silence.

They were stoic, ready for what was to come. They had been planning this day for the past three decades. Ever since the two American aircraft carriers had sailed up the Taiwan Strait and humiliated the Chinese people, the PLA had begun to modernize and prepare for what would occur in the coming days. These final updates from the military commanders were more of a formality than anything else. After years of preparations, secret rehearsals, AI-assisted computer simulations, diplomatic maneuvering, information operations, cyber-attacks and the coercion of different nations and Western corporations, they were confident in the plan that was about to be unveiled.

Those assembled in the room were also probably most interested in another military officer on the second large screen before them. Admiral He Wang, Commander of the Eastern Theater.

The admiral had the most important military appointment in all the People's Republic. His command—one of the new joint theater commands established several years before—was responsible for operations in the eastern part of the country. Admiral He was also answerable directly to the CMC—and therefore the president—for operations in the East China Sea, and for Taiwan.

"Sir, we have just completed a final series of simulations with our latest generation of AI-driven wargames. These are the most realistic simulations ever devised. With the Americans distracted by their elections, and two major natural disasters, their strategic decision making is the most degraded we have ever seen. If we combine this with our current force overmatch in the western Pacific and favorable geography, our simulations indicate a better than 95 percent chance of securing the main island in under one month." He paused, allowing the president and the other assembled personages in the room to consider this information.

After a moment, Admiral He continued his briefing. "All units are in high readiness. Our holdings of ammunition, precision weapons, fuel, and other logistic necessities are at maximum levels, with sufficient reserves to account for any delays in the forthcoming operation. Our autonomous systems are networked, secure, and ready to commence the first phase. We have conducted years of cyber reconnaissance and know the appropriate civilian and military networks inside out—they will be easy to compromise, at least for the time we need. We believe we are well capable of securing the island and installing our own government before the Americans and their allies can respond in force. This is despite their mobilization efforts of the past year."

Admiral He stopped there. He understood that the president and the other members of the Central Military Commission were well acquainted with the forthcoming operation. There was no need for more detailed explorations of what was to come. He decided to conclude his brief.

"Sir, our forces are ready. The correlation of forces between us and the Americans will never be better than they are now. They have still not completed their transition from Middle East ground warfare to what is required in the Pacific. However, in a few years they will be much more formidable. Now is the time to strike." Admiral He paused and then finished with a single sentence. "We will play our part in reunifying our nation once again under a single red banner."

President Zhang nodded. His face remained expressionless, as always. It was a skill that had served him well throughout his career. He would not be dropping his guard now, just at the moment when the People's Republic was about to achieve its greatest victory.

It had not been entirely smooth sailing when he achieved the presidency. Indeed, until 15 months ago, he had been just another member of the Politburo of the Chinese Communist Party. Not that he was any ordinary member, of course. He had been a part of the smaller Standing Committee of the Politburo, which with its weekly meetings, held the reins of power on behalf of the president. And while his predecessor, with his large-scale purges of the senior bureaucracy throughout the land, had trimmed the power of the Politburo, the standing committee still retained a huge amount of power over the day-to-day lives of all Chinese citizens, and how resources were used across the country.

It had been during one of their weekly Standing Committee meetings that he had been informed about the assassination of his predecessor. A senior member of the president's elite protection team, supposedly the most loyal soldiers in the party, had drawn his weapon and fired a single bullet into the brain of the president.

Apparently, her motivation had been the COVID deaths of family members in Shanghai during the 2022 and 2023 reemergence of the pandemic. She had waited a long time to achieve her vengeance. But the guard's motivation was unimportant. Her actions defined her as a murderer and an enemy of the state. Other members of the president's close protection team had quickly dispatched her.

What *was* important was the choice of a new leader who would keep the nation stable during the transition period—and not allow the outside world to know too much about that transition, including the manner of the president's passing.

Zhang leaned back in his chair, pondering the events of that night and the potential for calamity to befall the Party and China if they could not manage a smooth transition of power. So, in an all-night session in which several members had canvassed for support among their peers, the Politburo had eventually chosen him as president.

He had to make many big decisions in the first 24 hours. Most important was to deploy the cover story for the death of his predecessor. There was no good to be had in telling the world of the assassination. That would only give hope to those who sought the downfall of the Party, both within the borders of China and beyond.

Zhang had personally overseen a new narrative about his predecessor succumbing to overwork on behalf of the Party and the Chinese people. And while he was almost certain that the intelligence agencies in America and Europe had their suspicions, by and large it had been a story that had been lapped up by journalists and politicians around the globe.

The other significant decision was the operation that they were gathered here to discuss. In a secret session of the 20th Party Congress back in October 2022, the Politburo had agreed on a plan, put forward by Zhang's predecessor, to reunify the nation by the end of the decade. They had agreed in secret that peaceful reunification with the rebellious Taiwanese province was less likely as each year passed.

They had considered many different approaches to the reunification effort. The use of economic means over the last several decades had clearly failed. They had also considered a blockade of the island, but given the stakes for American alliances in the region, it was highly likely that American military intervention would eventually occur.

No, the reunification and Taiwan had to be accompanied by breaking the trust between the Americans and their allies in the western Pacific. The only way to do this was to strike at Taiwan and the Americans at the same time, and to destroy as much of their fighting forces, logistic support, and bases as quickly as possible.

33

The Committee understood that speed was of the essence; the military operation would need to be conducted quickly, before the US and its allies could assemble to assist the island.

And the Taiwanese leader, who arrogantly called herself a president, must be killed. Quickly. Despite the power of their military, even China could not afford the global influence that might be achieved by a latter-day Zelensky broadcasting speeches and sending tweets from the island.

"You must strike rapidly and with great force," Zhang informed the military commanders present. "And I do not want the leader of this rebellious island to be left alive." He paused for a moment to let that sink into those around the table and on the screens at the front of the room. "Kill her, and those around her, as fast as you can."

3

Lethal in the Littoral

3 May 2028
Guam

Mud clogged his nose and mouth. Colonel Jack Furness lifted his head out of the mire. He looked up, then left and right. He was on the ground, surrounded.

His Marines, conducting their morning physical training session at their Guam barracks, were similarly facedown ready to commence another set of pushups. A passing rain squall had turned the grassy field into a quagmire, which would ensure their morning exertions were slippery and that they would emerge soaked and filthy.

At least this kind of wet and mud was better than what was happening back home on the east coast. The storms and flooding there were catastrophic. Furness had no doubt that the east coast Marines, based at Camp Lejeune, would be providing disaster relief over a wide swathe of the east coast states.

Their green t-shirts and shorts were now uniformly brown. Furness, like his Marines, was covered in the rich tropical mud that resulted from the frequent downpours this time of year. Luckily, however, the ambient temperature was still warm. Sliding around

35

in the mud and shallow puddles during their PT session actually provided welcome relief from the tropical heat and humidity that was the norm here.

The morning routine for his regiment dictated that physical training continued regardless of weather. If they had to be prepared to fight in the rain (and other unpleasant weather), they could damn well train and do PT in this heavy downpour as well.

Furness normally did his physical training with his Marines. He preferred the camaraderie of collective physical endeavor with one of his rifle squads rather than running with his sergeant major like other regimental commanders. It was just his way, and had been since he had commanded his first platoon of Marines, a junior lieutenant just out of training, all those years ago.

After graduating from the Naval Academy, Furness had been sent to Quantico. First, he had completed the 28-week basic officer course at the Basic School in Camp Barrett. Immediately afterwards, he had attended the shorter infantry officer course. Through these experiences—the academy, the Basic School, and the infantry course—he had acquired essential knowledge that had served him well in his first regiment.

Each subsequent appointment, whether it was in a Marine regiment out on the west coast or in Hawaii, or a training job at Quantico, and even the staff jobs at the Pentagon, had broadened his experience and his intellect. But his current job, commanding this new regiment, would take every bit of experience and leadership acumen that he possessed.

The alarm on Furness' wristwatch sounded just as the squad leader yelled out a halt to the session. It had been a good hour of training, but it was now time to turn to other pursuits. Furness had a hectic day ahead, a day which would mainly be focused on an operational problem that his divisional commander had sent him via the SIPRNET, their secret-level email system, the day before.

An hour later, showered, scrubbed clean, and in his Marine Corps combat utility uniform, Furness settled back in his desk chair, took a sip of his steaming hot black coffee (no sugar), and contemplated the day ahead. The email from his divisional commander the previous day had led to frenetic activity in his headquarters. While the contents of the email were focused on training, the problem itself was one that Furness was sure would actually occur at some point in the near future.

Taiwan.

Furness and his regiment had been tasked by the divisional commander to develop a plan to move his Littoral Regiment—the first of its kind, formed in Hawaii back in 2022—to Taiwan's western coast and establish a defensive posture against a Chinese invading force. While this was an entirely fictional scenario, it provided Furness with a good opportunity to test the capacity of his planning staff at the regimental level as well as in his subordinate units.

The regiment that Furness led had four major components, each of which would be tested by the training scenario.

The first was his Littoral Combat Team. This was essentially an infantry battalion with an attached long-range anti-ship missile battery. It could fight on the ground at close quarters while reaching out with its long-range missiles to target enemy vessels at sea.

Next, his Littoral Logistics Battalion provided all manner of support to his Marines, including food, ammunition, fuel, equipment repair, and other basic services to get the Littoral Regiment where it needed to be, and to support it while it was there.

The third component of his regiment was the Littoral Anti-Air Battalion. This unit was a recognition that, unlike the wars in Afghanistan and Iraq, if American forces were to fight in the Western Pacific, they would likely have to face large numbers of enemy aircraft. It had been nearly eight decades since American military forces had needed to worry about attack from the air.

But the lessons from recent conflicts showed that the threat from the air—from both crewed and autonomous aircraft—was now very significant. And very lethal. If they were to face off with the PLA, the Marines would need to step up their capability to defend themselves against aerial threats. And therefore, each Marine Littoral Regiment contained this battalion that provided surveillance, early warning, support for Marine aircraft, as well as short- and long-range defensive missiles.

Just recently, their capacity to undertake reconnaissance and strike had been augmented with the cavalry troop from the US Army. The unit, led by the very capable Captain Lee, had proved itself during a series of exercises in the last two months.

Finally, Furness' headquarters made up the fourth and final major part of his regiment. It provided the brain and leadership for the regiment's operations, and contained the normal staff branches such as operations, planning, personnel, and logistics. But in recognition of changes in 21st-century warfare—and PLA capabilities—the regimental headquarters also possessed very capable human intelligence, cyber, and information warfare units.

It was Furness' job to orchestrate the planning, actions, and operational outcomes of all four elements. With two thousand Marines, and a huge quantity of complex weapons, vehicles, and communications systems, this required detailed planning, constant training, teamwork at every level, and good leadership.

All this passed through Furness' mind as he considered the day ahead. The pending exercise would ensure that he brought all elements of his command together and that they were orchestrated in a way that would achieve the stated intent of his divisional commander. It was demanding, and he was required to brief his plan to his boss in just over 24 hours.

But his current assignment was no more demanding than any of the problems that he and his classmates had tackled during his time at command and staff college, or the following year at the USMC School of Advanced Warfighting, or any of his numerous operational deployments. He was pondering those wonderful years at Quantico, devoid of any responsibilities other than his growing family (now four boys) and his own professional development, when a knock at the door drew him away from his memories.

It was his executive officer, Lieutenant Colonel Nick Eyre. A sharp officer who had only just joined the regiment after a tour at Quantico teaching on the Marine Staff Training Program, he was responsible for ensuring planning at the regimental level took place in accordance with the direction of Furness.

"Sir, the planning staff from HQ and the battalion COs are assembled in your conference room."

Furness smiled at Eyre. He then thanked his XO, drained the last of his coffee, and rose from his seat. They walked together down the hallway the short distance from Furness' office and into the crowded conference room.

"Colonel, I heard your son made the middle-school baseball team back at base. That's great news."

Eyre, a fine XO and a good conversationalist, could always be relied on to have family news from back at their home station on Oahu. He stayed in regular contact with his wife, who provided detailed insights into what was happening with the families in the regiment.

"Yes, I got a short note from him in the secure email dump late last night. We are very proud of him. With that and his grades, he is tracking well for college," Furness responded.

Eyre nodded, knowing they were about to enter the briefing room. He had the staff assembled and ready to brief the regimental commander.

"Room," Eyre called as Furness passed through the doorway from the corridor.

As the assembled Marines in the room rose to their feet, Furness quickly waved them back into their seats. He had little time for many of the formalities expected by other senior officers. Furness preferred that his Marines be respectful but focused on being excellent at their combat responsibilities. That included being able to work together collaboratively in planning sessions such as the one he was about to discuss.

"Good morning team. That was a heck of a PT session this morning. XO, please pass my compliments to Corporal James—he certainly gave this old Marine a good workout in the mud," Furness said. He gave those in the room a wry grin and then turned to his XO.

"XO, can you please show the first slide."

Furness turned to look at the screen behind him. On the screen appeared a map of an island. It was a narrow, long island with mountains on its eastern side and large cities in its north and south. Its western coastline featured a dense road and communications network, numerous rivers running east to west, multiple population centers.

Taiwan.

"Ladies and gentlemen, our planning problem today, on which we will back-brief the Division Commander tomorrow, is the deployment of our regiment to defend against a PLA invading force. Of course, we will be part of the 3rd Marine Division, but we will be the leading unit to arrive. Subsequently, additional Marine and Army units will arrive to help the Taiwanese defend their island."

Furness paused. This was not the first planning problem his team had faced in the past year. The faces around the table showed determination and a resolve to produce the best solution of all the Marine regiments in the Pacific that had been tasked with a similar operational problem.

At least once a month, these kind of planning problems were dispatched to all the Marine units across the division. It was a method used by the Division Commander to keep planners on their toes, and ensure they constantly thought about how they might fight and win against the PLA. More importantly, these activities, with different regiments competing against each other for the best solutions, generated the competitive tension that produced new and original thinking about their most difficult operational challenges.

Furness loved competing against his fellow regimental commanders. They were all his friends, and some were his classmates from Quantico. But he, like the rest of them, knew that competing against each other was a vital part of honing their Marines, their warfighting capability, and their capacity to think laterally, to a fine edge. It would pay off at some point in the future.

Furness continued addressing those assembled in the room.

"Before we get into my detailed planning guidance, let's hear the latest estimate on PLA intentions from the regimental intelligence section."

A young Marine captain, who had been seated along the wall of the room, and not at the table, then stood and moved to stand beside the screen at the head of the room.

"Good morning, Sir. Good morning, everyone. This is our estimate of the current situation and PLA intentions."

Captain Leah Kahn, a ground intelligence specialist in the Marine Corps, was a frequent briefer of these planning sessions and other regimental meetings. A confident and experienced analyst, prior to arriving in this regiment two years ago, she had been on the joint intelligence staff at the Headquarters of Indo-Pacific Command in Hawaii. Kahn possessed a deep understanding of the PLA, its operational concepts, the geography of Taiwan, and the capabilities of the Taiwanese military. She paused briefly for effect and then launched into the main body of her brief.

"We know, from the statements of the previous Chinese president as well as his more recent replacement, that the Chinese are becoming more impatient to get Taiwan back. While these kinds of statements go all the way back to Mao, in the past several years China's military capabilities have begun to match their strategic intentions. Over the last three to four years, we have seen a massive stepping up in the air and sea activity by the PLA Air Force and PLA Navy all around Taiwan. The expansion of the Navy, especially their Marine Corps and amphibious lift capability, has been quite impressive. Despite this, the Taiwanese people and their government have made it clear they do not want to be the next Hong Kong, Macau or Xinjiang. We should be in no doubt that at some point in the short to medium term, the Chinese will try to return Taiwan to the People's Republic of China.

"Of course, it would be very difficult for even the Chinese to hide a major buildup of forces prior to an attempt to take Taiwan. While there are dozens of bases and seaports from which they might mount a large-scale invasion, from Yantian in the south to Wenzhou in the north, we believe that the signature of such a massive force would be very hard to conceal," the captain continued. She then paused and looked around the room.

"So we assess that any lead-up to such an operation would be preceded by strategic-level activity to distract the United States. That would not be difficult. With this being an election year, and with the massive storm and flooding catastrophes on the east coast and fires out west, our government already has a lot on its plate. The Chinese Communist Party has a lot of different options to make our lives even harder, and these include collusion with the Iranians to step up aggression in the Gulf, and an increase in Russian activity in Ukraine, the Black Sea, or Syria. It is also almost certain that large-scale exercises, like last year's massive amphibious space and rocket-launch training activity, would provide cover for the assembly of aircraft, ships, armored vehicles, troops, and rocket forces for an invasion.

"Finally—and probably the best indicators of an attack—would be a takedown of US and Japanese satellites and undersea internet cables. Concurrently, we would see a range of sabotage activities and discreet assassinations across Taiwan to cut communications and main logistic supply routes, and to disrupt the cohesion of their government and military decision making."

Furness looked around the room. This was not the first time many of the participants in this exercise had heard this information. They all knew that understanding the strategic context for their mission—even if it was just an exercise—could help in developing an effective operational solution for their regiment.

Furness then spoke.

"Captain Kahn, thank you. Can you now give a quick summary of Chinese options for seizing Taiwan? When we discussed some of your analysis last week, I thought your latest considerations on how the Chinese might plan an invasion were leading-edge stuff."

Kahn suppressed a smile at the praise and changed the slide on the screen next to her before leaping back into her briefing. She liked working for Furness. He was professionally demanding but always quick to acknowledge the efforts of his subordinates.

The screen at the head of the room now showed Taiwan. There were multiple arrows leading from the Chinese mainland, all pointing to different parts of Taiwan.

4

A Knife in a Space Fight

3 May 2028
3rd Space Operations Squadron
United States Space Force

Technical Sergeant Kara Hickling reclined her gamer's chair and adjusted her headset. The virtual reality in which she was immersed had come a long way since the simple games she had played at college even a few years ago. The technology that underpinned VR, including computing power, data analytics, eye-tracking software and ultra-resolution displays, meant that what she saw while wearing this headset was nearly indistinguishable from the world outside. Nearly.

Even with the most expensive headsets and their extraordinary displays, she still knew she was in an alternate reality. But it was an alternate reality in which she could control real-world actions and outcomes.

The 16K displays for each eye, with almost zero latency, were the result of years of technological breakthroughs in civilian tech companies. And now the technology had been appropriated by the US Space Force for many of the personnel in its Space Deltas.

The Space Deltas were what the force called its different functional commands. A range of different missions, all related to space capabilities, were distributed across the many Deltas of the Space Force. The term itself had led to some derision from those in the other services. But it was a means to an end. The 21st century was seeing new technologies and different kinds of people entering the military. The leaders of the Space Force knew that different thinking, and more imagination, was needed if they were to survive the coming decades. The term "Deltas," and a range of other initiatives, was designed to foster different ideas, different organizational approaches, and different pathways to mission success in military operations.

Hickling had transferred from the US Air Force, and into the Space Force just over six years ago. After several years of hard work and dedication, she had become frustrated by the disinterest and inattention of her Air Force commanders. That, and a divorce, forced her to reassess her priorities and what she wanted to do for the remainder of her life. She had been 24 years old, in a job she didn't particularly like, and on the other side of a not-so-successful marriage.

So, after moving into a new apartment and adopting a tabby cat that she adored, Hickling had become one of the first to transfer into the nascent Space Force. It was an act that would have upset her father to no end. He had been a senior non-commissioned officer in the Air Force, and after twenty years of service, had reached the rank of Chief Master Sergeant. Unfortunately, around the same time her marriage crumbled, her father had been diagnosed with late-stage prostate cancer. Four months later he was dead, and her mom had moved back to live with family in Seattle.

The long and the short of it was that she was no longer an airman. She was a space professional, a member of a new part of the profession of arms—a Guardian. The new and different approaches to military activities offered by the Space Force had been attractive to Hickling from the first time she had heard about the raising of the new force. She was fascinated by everything to do with space. The organization had met her expectations, and more. Even the leadership styles were more open and trusting than she had been used to in the Air Force.

In the Space Force, everyone knew that they were part of a small, technologically advanced organization, upon which the entire US military—and many of their allies—depended. They were the smallest US military service, still only around 15,000 people. But each day, they supported the United States Space Command to provide assured communications, missile warning, space surveillance, precision navigation and timing, space weather reports, and a range of other services to enable military operations.

This distinction between the Space Force (the institution that Hickling was a member of and that developed space capabilities), and Space Command (which conducted space operations, such as missile warning, precision navigation and timing, satellite comms, and human spaceflight) was sometimes confusing to outsiders. And it required a great deal of collaboration between the two entities.

But for Hickling and her day-to-day activities, she was not terribly concerned by which space organization was giving her orders. What she was focused on was the offensive space missions that she and her team were directed to undertake in support of military missions around the world.

Her squadron was part of Space Delta 9—the most secretive of all the Deltas. Hickling was a member of the Delta that was one of the most sought-after assignments for Guardians, both officers and enlisted.

Orbital warfare.

Their mission was to protect and defend American and allied space-based assets, while deterring and attacking the orbital assets of adversaries. To do this they were equipped with some of the most advanced technology that had ever been developed for use in space. This included the newest version of the Orbital Test Vehicle, previously known as the X-37, but now called the S-38: the *Stiletto*.

They also used all kinds of technologies to build and maintain awareness of what was occurring in space, including the locations of satellites, spacecraft, and space junk. This included closely monitoring space weather, particularly the prediction of coronal mass ejections, which released massive amounts of plasma and an embedded magnetic field that could play havoc with the earth's satellites and electrical grids.

That was bad. Very bad. Therefore, Hickling's first task every morning, before she even had a cup of coffee, was to check space weather. Generally, she had found that this was the best indicator of whether she would be having a good or a bad day.

The Geostationary Operational Environment Satellite series of satellites, operated by the US National Environmental Satellite Data and Information Service and launched in the last two years, fed Hickling real-time information on space weather. Their mission was reliant on the earliest information possible about electromagnetic radiation and charged particles released by the sun's solar storms. These presented dangers to all of the Space Force's satellites, especially those that provided communications and precision navigation and timing. But their spacecraft were also vulnerable. Thus, early warning of solar storms was vital to Hickling's job.

She quickly scrolled through a variety of menus in her VR environment. The sensors on their satellites, including ultraviolet imagers and magnetometers, were all displaying normal readouts. Space weather was not going to ruin her mood, or that of the Space Force—today at least.

Hickling then turned to the next part of her normal morning routine. She scanned the morning intelligence reports, especially those that updated her on Russian and Chinese anti-satellite operations and co-orbital maneuvers. She examined the latest reports about the disasters on the east and west coasts in the US. Things were awful in those areas. Luckily, she was from the Midwest and had no family or friends in those areas. But many of those she worked with did.

Hickling then turned to peruse a variety of strategic news reports, which lately were focused on the South China Sea, Taiwan, the Senkaku Islands, and the Malacca Strait. In the South China Sea, the Chinese Coast Guard, working in concert with the PLA Navy, had sunk yet another Vietnamese Coast Guard vessel. This time the sinking was brazen, having taken place inside Vietnam's 12-mile limit. *This is going to raise some hell*, Hickling thought. The Vietnamese were tough. They had fought the Chinese before and had beaten them. Now, they were beginning to show signs that they might be willing to do so again.

Next, the Chinese Communist Party was continuing its charm offensive with the Europeans. While there had been some rocky times in the relationship over the past several years, the allure of the Chinese consumer market seemed to insulate European minds against the more unattractive aspects of CCP governance and conduct.

In the Senkaku Islands, the PLA Navy continued its ongoing presence patrols which had been undertaken without cease for nearly three years. While some analysts believed it foreshadowed an eventual move to seize the islands, others postulated that it was designed more to wear out the Japanese Maritime Self-Defense Force in its constant responses to Chinese incursions. It wasn't working yet—the Japanese had commenced a naval, cyber, information operations, and air force buildup several years before—but eventually the strain would begin to bite on the smaller Japanese military.

Last but not least, Hickling turned her attention to the strategic situation in Taiwan. The pressure on the Taiwanese government through Chinese information operations was unrelenting.

Whether it was using sympathizers in Taiwan to spread discord, covert cyber-attacks against government, infrastructure and corporate targets, or daily incursions into the Taiwanese Air Defense Identification Zone, the Chinese Communist Party was employing an ever-evolving series of tactics to influence the Taiwanese people. The Chinese also wanted to build a perception in the international community of the inevitability of Taiwan returning to the Chinese fold.

It clearly wasn't working, given the recent statements of the Taiwanese president. Her resolute stance in the face of the Chinese behemoth was as inspiring to Hickling as it was frustrating to the Chinese Communist Party leadership.

Reports read, Hickling could finally move on to the most vital element of her morning routine: coffee. Her VR setup allowed her to order a coffee at the small café that had been established just outside the secure zone of the building that she worked in. The technicians in the next office had somehow jury rigged an algorithm that allowed Hickling and a select few members of her team to place their orders for coffee with a few eyelid movements and then make their way outside to the café to pick up their morning fix.

"Not bad coffee this morning, Tech Sergeant." It was one of the new junior officers, who had accompanied her immediate boss, Captain Marcus, down to the coffee cart.

Marcus, probably the most mature, intelligent, and engaging commander she had had, now joined the conversation.

"Always good coffee here. By the way, Tech Sergeant Hickling, how is that new VR simulation coming along with the *Stiletto*? I watched some of the reviews last night and was impressed by your skill maneuvering the vehicle. It looks like we are ready for the live mission."

Hickling, having just picked up her morning brew and savoring the first mouthful, nodded enthusiastically. "Sir, I think we are good to go. That *Stiletto* is a great upgrade to the old X-37. We have worked hard in the sims and ironed out a lot of the early kinks in the system." She was excited about what lay ahead today.

"Well, I look forward to observing the mission. I have full faith in your team. See you up there shortly," Marcus responded. He then turned and re-entered the building.

Hickling checked her watch. Time to get back to her VR rig and conduct final preparations for the next few hours.

Five minutes later, Hickling was back at her station and immersed once again in her VR mission-world. It was time for the main game for today. A task that she had been rehearsing with her team, as well as with others in several of the Space Force Deltas. They would be repositioning the S-38 for a sensitive on-orbit mission. For real.

She recalled her first classified briefing on the spacecraft almost a year earlier.

"The S-38 Orbital Vehicle—now called the *Stiletto*—is an improved version of a previous orbital test vehicle that has been conducting classified space missions for the US military since 2010. But the newer model is a whole new ballgame," Captain Marcus had said. He delivered this briefing to all those who were given access to the Special Access Compartment that covered the operations of the orbital warfare team.

"It is much larger than its predecessor. That gives it more payload capacity, but also a greater fuel load that could be used for maneuvering the vehicle in space. And a greater endurance for its top-secret missions."

After some more technical data on the *Stiletto* and its supporting systems, Marcus had concluded the briefing.

"The other big improvement is that it is much stealthier. With the right radar, the old X-37 could be tracked by various nations trying to figure out exactly what the vehicle was doing. The *Stiletto* employs faceted panels—flat sections of external skin that can reflect away radar—as well as radar-absorbing material to achieve a very small radar cross-section. In fact, it has a smaller profile than the vast majority of the hundreds of thousands of pieces of space junk that currently orbit the earth at different altitudes. This makes it almost impossible to track by earth-based space surveillance systems—something you will see in the simulations in the coming weeks."

Hickling smiled to herself, recalling how many *Stiletto* missions she had completed since that initial briefing session. Returning to the present, she contemplated the mission before her.

Hickling could maneuver the *Stiletto* very close to the satellites of their adversaries (and even their friends on occasion). Once proximate to these satellites, they could examine them remotely or disable them through electromagnetic pulses or lasers. On several occasions, the *Stiletto* had even been able to "acquire" some of the smaller satellites owned by the Russians and Chinese and return them to earth for detailed examination and exploitation by Space Command and other US government agencies. Of course, the Chinese and Russians suspected the whereabouts of their missing satellites. They had even made discreet inquiries, and some accusations, to the Americans. But their accusations, lacking concrete proof, had always fallen on deaf ears. The S-38 *Stiletto* was too stealthy and the orbital warfare team too cunning to be caught in the act of appropriating the property of another nation in space. Such was the nature of Hickling's mission today.

The target satellite was an extraordinarily sensitive capability for the Chinese. Called *Jinan 1* and launched back in 2022, it was the second Chinese satellite designed to support quantum-encrypted communications networks. A major improvement on its predecessor *Micius*, *Jinan 1* had demonstrated its ability to undertake entanglement-based quantum-key distribution—which underpinned unbreakable encryption methods—during several experiments. Unbreachable quantum communications were one of the holy grails of 21st-century warfare. And while the US national security community and the Defense Advanced Research Projects Agency, known as DARPA, were reasonably certain that America still held a narrow lead over the Chinese in quantum technologies, they could not be absolutely certain. Thus, the Americans devised a plan to acquire *Jinan 1* and find out just how advanced Chinese, and PLA, quantum technologies were.

But this was no simple snatch-and-grab operation. It had begun months beforehand, with careful intelligence collection and plotting the path of the satellite. The intelligence effort also included collecting data on the various experiments conducted by the Chinese with the satellite in the preceding years.

Then, a ruse was required, one which the Chinese might even believe for once.

A purpose-designed micro-satellite was launched by a civilian space launch company with no links to the US military. The microsatellite, described in company brochures and media releases as a new type of weather satellite, was placed in a similar orbit to *Jinan 1*. A week ago, that civilian micro-satellite had unexpectedly exploded. Media releases by the company described an "unexpected collision with a small piece of orbital debris."

The reality was quite different. The microsatellite had been designed to disassemble itself, forming multiple smaller parts that each were on a trajectory to intercept the *Jinan 1* satellite. Of course, the Chinese would attempt to maneuver their valuable "bird" to avoid a collision. The Americans knew this; they had been monitoring communications at the Chinese satellite control station for years.

The Space Force therefore knew what the Chinese engineers on the ground saw, thought, and discussed. The Americans also knew about the Chinese intentions to correct the orbit of *Jinan 1* to ensure it was not destroyed by debris from the "exploded" American micro-sat. Enter Hickling and the other members of Delta 9 of the US Space Force. Before the Chinese could move it, the Americans would steal it in a space heist.

An important part of this plan was knowing exactly where all the key elements of the plot were. The Space Force's Geosynchronous Space Situational Awareness Program had lofted several satellites into orbits between 2014 and 2022. Known by space experts as "neighborhood watch birds," this spacecraft allowed the United States military to detect and monitor objects at various orbits around the earth. Importantly, they helped in protecting American satellites in geosynchronous orbit. Some of the most crucial satellites for national security sat in this orbit, at 22,200 miles above the earth. This included communications satellites and missile warning birds. So, utilizing the space awareness feed from these satellites, they knew in real time the positions of *Jinan 1*, the parts of the micro-sat, as well as the *Stiletto*.

Hickling heard a familiar voice through her headset: Marcus.

"Your challenge this morning is to maneuver the *Stiletto* close to the Chinese satellite, disable it with a brief electromagnetic burst, secure it on the payload bay, and then swoop away before the sections of the other American micro-satellite intersect with their orbit. Then, as the *Stiletto* carefully thrusts off, it will release the small radar receptors designed to replicate a debris field. This will provide a new radar return for Chinese space awareness radars, hopefully convincing them that their satellite had been destroyed in a collision with the debris from the American micro-sat. Over."

Hickling acknowledged Marcus' direction. He liked to give a precis before they executed each mission. It was his thing, thought Hickling. The *Stiletto* would slip in, complete its mission, and just as quietly slip into another orbit before returning home in a week or so. And hopefully, the technology it revealed upon arrival in the United States would prove invaluable. At least, that was the plan.

They had rehearsed the mission all through the previous months. It required precision timing and maneuvering from Hickling and the rest of the command. In multiple simulations—or what they called "rehearsals"—the *Stiletto* had either arrived too early or too late. Sometimes it had failed to secure the Chinese satellite in its payload bay, and on several occasions, the simulated S-38 had been destroyed by the American micro-sat.

But eventually, after dozens of rehearsals, they had perfected the timing, the maneuvering, and the space domain awareness reports that would be needed to successfully complete the mission. Today was the day for Hickling's team to finally go live and acquire the Chinese quantum sat.

"Tech Sergeant Hickling, you can proceed with the final approach. 1st Squadron have provided a pathway to your objective that is clear of space junk. Commence on my mark."

Hickling's boss, Captain Marcus, spoke into her ear again through the VR setup. If she wanted, she could have had a 3D representation of the captain actually appear before her in the virtual environment, but she preferred the vocal cues instead. She wanted her full attention on the mission at hand. The captain began a countdown from ten.

"... three, two, one, mark. Commence maneuver," Marcus continued.

Hickling, using eye blinks as well as a virtual glove that appeared in the high-definition display all around her, began to move the *Stiletto*. As they had rehearsed, Hickling had to be extraordinarily precise in her movements and timing.

The *Stiletto* conducted a series of short burns with its maneuvering thrusters to first enter the same orbit as the *Jinan 1*. Having achieved that, it slowly approached *Jinan 1*.

The American spacecraft, as it slowed its approach, also opened the doors to its payload bay. Similar to the layout on the old space shuttle, the two doors swung open from the top of the *Stiletto* to reveal a large, vacant space. The only equipment in the payload bay was an articulated grappling arm, which was mounted against the port inner side of the bay.

The arm design was based on that of the old Canadian arm that had been used over the life of the Space Shuttle program. It was smaller, of course, but contained many of the same (if updated) features. Its main component was the manipulator arm, with several joints similar to a human arm. Where the arm was connected to the *Stiletto* was a joint permitting pitch and yaw. There was also a small explosive charge that allowed the emergency disconnection of the arm if needed. Further along was an elbow joint and then a joint that resembled a human wrist with multiple directions of movement. At the end of the arm was a grappling fixture that could use magnetic and mechanical ways of securing an object.

Hickling began unfolding the arm. It was something she had rehearsed many times in the lead-up preparations to this moment. The arm was slowly extended to its full length. At the same time, the *Stiletto* slowly continued its approach to the Chinese satellite.

Hickling's VR showed her the full 3D picture of what was occurring several hundred miles above her in space. She could zoom in or out or view the approach of the small shuttle to the *Jinan 1* from multiple angles.

After nearly an hour of maneuvering, Hickling was ready for the next phase. The *Stiletto* had matched the Chinese satellite's orbit and was in the correct station to begin recovery using the arm. The arm, now extended, was just a few feet away from the satellite, ready to snatch it into the payload bay of the *Stiletto*. Hickling, only slightly nervous, began to move the arm and its grappling attachment toward the *Jinan 1*.

The first finger of the grappling hand reached the satellite. It made contact. And then everything went black.

5

Plum Blossom

3 May 2028
Zhongnanhai, Beijing

President Zhang felt a change in the atmosphere in the room. His direction on the future of the current president of the rebellious island had been ruthless. But necessary.

"Have we attended to concurrent challenges that might impact on this operation?" Zhang asked those in the room.

Admiral He spoke up before others around the table could contribute. *He is a bold and ambitious one*, thought Zhang. *He will bear watching in the future.*

"Mr. President, our Russian partners are conducting a large-scale exercise near the borders of Finland and the Baltic states, as well as naval exercises in the Black Sea and in the Baltic. Both open sources and our sources inside European governments tell us it is causing significant unease there. To our south, the Indian front is largely quiet. We do not expect the Indians to undertake any military operations that are a threat to us while we are distracted with other activities in the coming months. Just in case, we have placed units in our Western Command on a higher level of readiness."

The admiral paused, looking around the room before turning back to the head of the table.

"Finally, the Japanese will be offered a non-aggression agreement just before we launch our operations. The diplomats in Tokyo and in Beijing believe this has almost no chance of success. However, it will be made public by us and hopefully cause disruption in their domestic politics and in their relationships with the United States, Australia, and others."

Zhang nodded. There remained many unknowns in the relationships between the Americans and their partners. He addressed the assembled group again.

"How the Americans and their allies will react to the Chinese operations in and around Taiwan remains to be seen. Making commitments before conflict and undertaking joint exercises is one thing. Committing forces and thousands of military personnel to operations is another matter entirely. Despite the speeches of their political leaders, every measure of their societal capabilities and commitment indicates that the people of America and their key partners have little interest in fighting for a small island that is a very long way away from them. Or to lose thousands of their young people doing so."

Zhang understood the debates, both here and overseas, about the theory of decline in Western democratic nations and fractures in their societies. There were many different interpretations, but Zhang firmly believed that the irreversible decline in Western capabilities and influence was an opportunity for his nation.

Coupled with the modernization of the PLA, and ongoing distractions of the American politicians and media, China would have a window of opportunity in the coming years to undertake such an operation to forcefully reunify the Taiwanese people with their mainland cousins.

But it would be a narrow window. Despite its impressive progress over the last four decades, China was still reliant on world trade and imports of key necessities.

Zhang turned to the man on his immediate left. The premier of the State Council, also known beyond China as the premier, was traditionally the chairman's most senior civilian advisor. The incumbent was a holdover from his predecessor. However, Zhang had seen no reason to dispense with the experience of the man. He was no threat to Zhang, but was a source of excellent advice on finance, trade, and the Chinese economy. The premier was not normally a member of the Central Military Commission. But this was far from a normal meeting. And any military campaign that was as vital as Taiwan, and which would generate the ire of the Americans and their friends, needed input on strategic economic and trade impacts.

"Premier, please provide us with your insights on the probable impacts to our nation from an economic perspective," Zhang ordered in a quiet but firm tone.

The premier turned to his audience. One of the screens displayed charts that presented figures about imports into China.

"Chairman, as you know, we have been stockpiling those items which are likely to be interdicted or cut off by the Americans in the event of any action against Taiwan. We also observed the impacts of the American sanctions against Russia. Our focus has been the major import categories, especially crude oil and petroleum products, which represent over 15 percent of total imports. Most of these arrive by sea from the Middle East, and we are assuming that route will be cut off by the Americans and Indians. We have built a strategic reserve sufficient for six months' normal usage but could stretch that with land exports from Russia and domestic rationing. Rationing, however, would impact on manufacturing industries.

"Our other major import category is integrated circuits. We have managed to establish fabrication enterprises that produce a proportion of domestic demand; we won't need to scavenge chips from washing machines like the Russians. However, the best circuits must still be imported from South Korea, Taiwan, Malaysia, Japan and the United States. We have a small strategic stockpiling of these more sophisticated chips. But this will only last for several weeks of normal use."

There was a soft murmuring around the table. The admiral on the screen made to speak but was cut off by Zhang.

"The fabrication facilities in Taiwan will be a priority for our forces. We will be prioritizing their capture so they cannot be destroyed."

The premier nodded and then continued his briefing to Central Military Committee members.

"Imports such as iron ore and cars can be covered from our strategic reserve. We possess around six months' worth of holdings for iron ore. And for cars, this is a low priority, and we will be able to undertake an acceptable level of substitution with domestic production."

The screen changed to show a list of countries with percentage figures next to them.

"Finally, foreign direct investment represents over 150 billion US dollars' worth of investment in our manufacturing and technology industries. Much of this, however, flows through Hong Kong. We should assume that the uncertainty in the global environment that might result in military action in Taiwan would cut off most of this foreign investment in our country.

"On the export front, over 25 percent of our current exports by value go to the US, South Korea, and Japan. We can assume that these markets will be closed to us if there are hostilities over Taiwan. We earn over 400 billion dollars each year from our exports to America alone. This will hurt us much more than it does the Americans."

Zhang held up his hand. He had heard enough from the premier. The economic statistics were useful. However, his main aim of having the premier conduct this briefing to the Central Military Commission had not been to fill their heads with trade and economic data. No. His key objective was to ensure that the military commanders, in Beijing and the Eastern Theater Command, understood the need for a rapid conclusion to their invasion of the rebellious island province. While their nation would be able to continue operating for the next six to twelve months, any prolonged military operations after that would begin to significantly hurt their country.

"Thank you, premier. You have provided us with very useful information that has strategic importance for this campaign," Zhang said. "You have also highlighted that our military campaign is not open-ended. We must act with haste to hold off American and Japanese support, while at the same time securing the entire island and providing a new and legitimate government." Zhang looked around the table, and at the screen containing the face of Admiral He, to see nodding heads.

Despite the detailed updates from the premier and the military officers, thereafter there was minimal debate. Some of the older members had advised caution. They still feared the American ability to leverage its advanced technology and latent industrial capacity into an unbeatable war machine. Others had proposed that, despite American reticence to engage in a ground war again after twenty years in the Middle East, they could not afford to let Taiwan fall. Because of this, the Americans would be a much more dangerous foe than the war planners inside the PLA had predicted. The general idea from these members was that America remained a slumbering giant whose wrath they were best to avoid.

But, in the main, the members of the Politburo had agreed to the aims of the plan and its timeline. Zhang's predecessor, with his purges, had guaranteed a mostly compliant Politburo. It was now a group that was less imaginative and less willing to challenge the ideas of the new president. The little debate there was among Politburo members was overshadowed by the overwhelming sense that there might never be a better time than the present to confront America and remove its influence from the Western Pacific.

The case put forward for such an audacious strategic objective was multifaceted. While the reunification of all of China's territory under the red banner was a vital national goal, there were other important reasons for the timing. Zhang decided to summarize these for all present before announcing his decision.

"The Americans, after decades of lethargy in the Pacific, are beginning to show signs of building a force that might be able to successfully intervene in any military operations around Taiwan or the South China Sea. For years they have postured and debated but done little to develop the kinds of technologies and long-range expeditionary forces that would be needed to deter us from reunifying Taiwan with the mainland. American operations in Iraq and Afghanistan have been a useful two-decade distraction, from our perspective. But in the last few years, this has changed. Our PLA strategic analysts believe the correlation of forces in the Western Pacific is starting to shift back toward the Americans."

The president considered this for a moment.

The PLA was very powerful and currently had many technological and geographic advantages. But that was expected to change with developments in the American—and Japanese—militaries from around 2027 onwards. And now that the Party leadership had constructed this magnificent new PLA, the people expected that it be used.

Zhang then laid out the logic for what would be one of the greatest military operations in history.

"Our economy has been underperforming for several years. While we are now a wealthy nation, 1.4 billion people are very expensive to support with infrastructure, healthcare, and other services. The military, and other security services such as the People's Armed Police, are steadily spending more of a national budget that is not growing as quickly as it had a decade before. The percentage of older people has grown while the population has decreased, and they are expensive to look after! It is unlikely that we can sustain our current level of investment in the PLA beyond the late 2020s." Zhang paused for a moment before continuing. "Diplomatically, the years leading up to our 21st Party Congress in 2027 have been difficult ones for China and for our Party. The direction to diplomats to be more assertive led to a wolf warrior culture developing among diplomats that had until then prized quiet, competent, step-by-step maneuvering. There have been some successes, but generally the new aggressive approach has been met with various levels of resistance from close neighbors and nations further away."

Zhang knew that the reality of the situation must be acknowledged, but he still had difficulty understanding how the many small nations of the world thought they could prevail against a country as colossal as China. Even Europe, which had been reticent to risk its trade links with China, was thought to be rethinking their strategy for interaction and technology-sharing with the nation. Party strategists believed that these diplomatic headwinds, combined with the restrictions on technology-sharing and the reaction of many countries to the emergence of a global pandemic from China, would eventually begin to strangle its growth as a global power. And probably in the next decade, or sooner.

Zhang's tone grew more optimistic as he continued to speak.

"Finally, there is the impact of the events of the last several weeks in the United States. It has been battered by multiple catastrophic weather events demanding a massive response from US state and federal authorities. The military airlift and logistics capabilities, some of which have been withdrawn from the Western Pacific, are now being redirected to support the tens of millions of Americans affected by these disasters on the west and east coasts. And the stark political divide between red and blue states has only made matters worse for them."

Zhang pondered just how serious things were at the moment in the American polity. The Republican National Convention was likely to confirm the nomination of a presidential candidate who was willing to make a strategic deal at the right price.

"These developments should be viewed as a historic opportunity. It is an opportunity to act if we are audacious and well prepared. It is an opportunity to fundamentally shift the balance of power in the Western Pacific and beyond."

They *were* well prepared. For the past two decades, the PLA had been developing the weapons, the joint forces, the logistics, and other capabilities that would give them the best chance of seizing Taiwan if they could not be coerced into returning to the People's Republic. Their policy of intelligentization had impacts across the depth and breadth of the PLA. It was an advanced, hard-hitting, and strategically deployable force. As a consequence, the PLA was now very big and very capable; it possessed quality and quantity.

As the military men had often briefed him, the PLA had the advantage in localized command of the sea, command of the air out to and beyond Taiwan, and a massive advantage over democratic nations in the exploitation of information. These three factors alone significantly reduced the cost of military action against their rebellious province across the strait.

And while the generals and admirals had faithfully promised that such an operation to reunify Taiwan with the mainland would only take weeks—months at most—Zhang preferred to think worst-case. The wars of the 20th century with their concepts of rapid decisive victory had led to long, drawn-out wars of national attrition. And a fight over Taiwan could also result in a protracted and expensive conflict between China and the United States, despite their best preparations. It was a scenario which should give even the most belligerent PLA members cause to reconsider.

However, the new president, like the others in the room, had been conditioned by decades of Party doctrine. He had seen the rebirth of his nation and its rapid economic growth over the past two decades. He had witnessed the stunning rapidity of the modernization of the PLA. And he knew that if they could get ashore, they could overwhelm the Taiwanese on the ground. To think that they might regain that renegade province without putting their troops, and governors, on the ground was foolish thinking. So very Western. And if America insisted on putting ground troops into Taiwan, Zhang was confident they could bleed the Americans until their domestic population called for a stop.

Having outlined the situation, Zhang returned to the matter at hand and addressed the group. "No," Zhang continued, voicing his thoughts. "A long-drawn-out war is not what the Americans want. Democracies have grown tired of lengthy military commitments. They lack the cohesion and commitment to endure such wars. They prize individual lives too highly. It is a decisive advantage that we have over the nations in the West. We cannot, must not, allow the unresolved situation with Taiwan to fester any longer."

The other members of the Central Military Commission were all looking at him, their expressions somber and expectant. The six other men, all veterans of the Party, were waiting on his command. A command that they and their predecessors had been waiting on for decades. Since 1949, in fact.

Zhang stiffened in his chair. He would not give such a momentous order while slouching. He looked into the face of each man sitting around the table. They all knew that this was the operation it had been their destiny to lead. They all knew that the window of opportunity was closing for China to regain its rebellious Taiwanese province. The 2028 presidential election candidates had both flirted with declaring independence. This was intolerable. With that thought in mind, Zhang made his final decision.

"Since the beginning of our Party last century, when confronted by a mounting threat to our interests, we have not waited to be attacked," he said. "We have struck first to gain the advantage of surprise. So too must we forestall the growing external threat to our people and the potential for an independent, American pawn just off our eastern shore." He paused a moment, contemplating the irony that the massive operation his words would unleash was named after the national flower of Taiwan.

"Launch Operation *Plum Blossom.*"

6

Fortuna Fortes Juvat

3 May 2028
Guam

"In any operation, the Chinese will seek to achieve information dominance." The intelligence briefing from Captain Kahn continued. "It is a feature of all their operational concepts, and includes denying us information through cyber-attack, information operations, deception, and the achievement of operational and strategic surprise. Their concept of systems destruction warfare will drive their operational and tactical activities—they will seek to break down our capacity for unified operational effects. Finally, they will implement a national approach using joint military operations that are integrated within an information, cyber, diplomatic, and economic offensive at a time when they believe the United States is least able to respond. The upcoming election may be one such opportunity, although there is already considerable distraction in the lead-up to the November election."

Kahn paused to collect her thoughts before continuing. "At the next level down, there are four broad courses that are open to the PLA to launch an attack to seize Taiwan. First, they might envelop the island from the sea and air, as well as in cyberspace, establishing a cordon through which nothing can penetrate in either direction. This is coercion at its most brutal, and we believe that China might be capable of doing this with their large naval and Coast Guard fleet, integrated with their short-, medium-, and long-range sensor networks and their rocket forces. The problem, however, is that if the Taiwanese hold out, it will be a very difficult operation—and tough on ships and aircraft—to sustain over the medium term. It is unlikely the US would acquiesce to such a situation. We assess this as a less likely option, and the intelligence staff at Division and Indo-Pacific Command support this assessment.

"A second option is that the PLA conducts a semi-envelopment of the island, sending invasion task forces to the north and south of the island to attack on the east coast. This is quite audacious, and they have the strategic sensor network, ships, and long-range fire support to make this a feasible option for PLA planners. The real problem with this, however, is logistics. If they establish beachheads on the eastern part of the island, they must also establish secure lines of communication from China to the eastern shore, and use hundreds of ships and aircraft. This would require covering considerably more distance than landing on the western shore would, and there is a paucity of major ports on the east coast to unload ships efficiently. Finally, any force landing on the eastern shore would then have to fight its way across the mountain range that separates the east coast from the more populous western coastline. They could easily become bogged down. Notwithstanding the audacity of such a plan, the complex logistics—and greater vulnerability to attacks by the US from the east—dictate that this is an unlikely option for PLA leaders to want to execute."

She let that sink into the participants in the room. Even a cursory review of the map of Taiwan indicated that there were few beaches suitable to amphibious operations on the eastern shore. Those that were suitable would be easily targeted by the

US Navy and Air Force units that would inevitably stream west from Japan, Okinawa, Guam, and from across the Pacific as the Chinese launched their invasion.

Listening intently to the briefing, Furness had to agree with the captain. *No*, he thought, *even the Chinese would not do that.* They could not afford to be unsuccessful in their invasion. And for the Chinese president, failing in such a military adventure would literally be the death of him. Furness did not believe he would expose himself to such risk.

"Carry on with the next option, please," said Furness.

Captain Kahn nodded. "A third option is a single narrow thrust across the strait, direct to the western shore. This would probably feature landings at several beachheads in one region, either the northern, central, or southern parts of the island. It allows for a concentration of land combat power in a single area, assuming they can land it. It also gives the PLA a smaller part of the strait to clear and protect, and would ease the way for them to secure the invasion fleet, follow-on forces, and the necessary logistic elements over days, weeks, and months of an invasion campaign.

"But there are also disadvantages to this approach. It would mean assembling the invasion fleet and logistics in a small part of the Chinese coast. Not only would this be a complex undertaking, even for the Chinese, it gives us a nice and concentrated target which we could attack. It also telegraphs to us their main effort quite early on and allows US forces to develop plans to focus on a small part of the campaign area.

"A fourth and final option for the PLA—and one that the staffs at higher headquarters all think is most likely—is a broad-front invasion involving multiple landing beaches in the south, center, and north of the island. It is a complex undertaking and requires excellent operational and strategic orchestration. But its advantages far outweigh any challenges, and it is likely to be the preferred approach for the PLA theater commanders and the Chinese Communist Party Military Committee."

Around the table, heads nodded. Those assembled—battalion commanders and planning staffs—were experienced, and had explored multiple operational problems in different parts of the Western Pacific. For most around the table, the assessment by Captain Kahn had a strong military logic.

Kahn continued with her briefing to the officers assembled in the packed and increasingly stuffy conference room.

"In this broad-front approach, the Chinese would establish invasion 'lanes' to the north, aimed just south of Taipei, at the center of the west coast as well as in the south. This would allow them to hedge their bets in case one of the lanes was temporarily closed through our efforts. It would also allow the PLA to weight effort in that part of the island where they experienced the most success. The challenge is that it would require the PLA to secure the entirety of the Taiwan Strait. This is a massive undertaking, but we believe they have the ships, submarines, aircraft, strategic sensor network, and long-range missiles to pull it off."

She paused for a moment. Before she could continue, the plans officer from his regiment's logistics battalion interjected with a question.

"Okay, I understand that. But this is really a sea and air fight, isn't it? If the Chinese can secure the sea, air, and underwater areas you just briefed, isn't it then all over? I mean, all the clever analysts and think tankers back in DC seem to think that only the air and sea battle matter."

Furness had also pondered this question over the preceding months. He nodded to the captain, indicating silently that he would answer the question.

"There is a lot of logic in the arguments that any battle over Taiwan would be determined by sea, air, cyber, and info fights.

But these assume that the fight will be over quickly, within weeks, and that the US and other nations are not able to respond quickly. We also know that the Taiwanese people would probably put up a long and difficult fight against the CCP if there were no Chinese boots on the ground. The Chinese have to land troops, and lots of them. It is the only way they can hope to seize control," Furness said. "That makes it ultimately a ground fight. And the Taiwanese have agency. Don't forget that. If they fight, and we expect they will, it will be a very tough ground campaign for the Chinese."

The room went quiet as Furness and the others around the table pondered the nature of modern ground combat. Furness knew that it was something that the politicians back in CONUS, and in the capitals of their allies, had avoided speaking about publicly. In the 21st century, he thought, surely politicians and senior military leaders wouldn't repeat the mistakes of the previous century—namely the misguided thought that new technologies could avoid bloodshed on the ground. The pre-Second World War airpower theorists, who desperately tried to shore up support for nascent air forces, had convinced many that airpower would allow the avoidance of the horrible slaughter of the Western Front. The disasters of Poland, France, Schweinfurt, the many islands in the Pacific, and even Ukraine demonstrated that this was only true up to a point. Eventually, someone needed to fight and seize ground. After all, humans didn't live in the sea or in the air. Military organizations needed to seize and hold the ground where the enemy lived, whether mountains, plains, or cities.

That is where Furness, his regiment, and his beloved Marine Corps came in. The ground in Taiwan was difficult, a mix of mountain ranges, coastal plains crossed by rivers, and high-density towns and cities. The nation also had several offshore islands. Defending the country would be challenging.

Furness leaned forward in his seat, ready to give his commanders guidance for the planning that would take place in the wake of the intelligence brief. Just as he placed his elbows on the table in front of him, he felt a slight vibration in his pocket. Normally, he would have left his phone back in his office when attending a planning activity such as this. However, the scare of the previous year, when the Chinese looked like they might conduct a major operation against the smaller Taiwanese and Philippine islands, meant that they were all now at high readiness. Thus, he always kept the phone in his possession.

He drew the secure phone from his pocket, the screen bright with a message from his division commander, who was based in Okinawa. It was not a formal military message. In fact, it was just three words. Furness knew exactly what those three words meant. The last time he had read them, his division commander had been his battalion commander. He had used the same message to let Furness know that their battalion was deploying at short notice for operations in Afghanistan.

It had been the start of a personal and professional journey for the younger Furness. He had learned about war through the constant fear, uncertainty, and threat to his Marines. He had come to appreciate his own strengths, and his weaknesses, in the dusty brown hills, mud-brick villages, and green zones of Helmand province.

And he had learned about death.

He had lost several Marines on that first deployment. Some had been killed in action, whether it was through Taliban bullets or improvised explosive devices. But these were not the only ways to die in that awful place. He had lost two Marines in a vehicle rollover one dark evening, and another Marine killed herself after her boyfriend back home dumped her. His memories of Afghanistan were rarely positive. In fact, it was a place he preferred not to think about at all. And this time, Afghanistan was not on the cards. A new deployment was pending.

The room around him grew silent. They had been anticipating Furness speaking to them to provide detailed guidance for the planning of their Taiwan problem. The interruption provided by the phone meant that the air in the room was charged with anticipation.

Furness leaned back in his chair and looked up at the ceiling, a small smile forming on his face. He then looked back down at his phone at the message.

"PACK YOUR SHIT!"

And while he would need to use his more secure communications to verify what was afoot with his boss, he knew it could only mean one thing: Furness would be deploying his regiment, and at short notice. Almost all their deployment plans were focused on a single scenario. And the strategic situation in the Western Pacific had been getting worse for the last five years. There was only one place they were likely to be headed.

In Portuguese, it had been known as "The Beautiful Island." To Furness and his Marines, it was called Taiwan.

7

Stormfront Approaching

5 May 2028
Indo-Pacific Command (INDOPACOM) Headquarters
Honolulu

This looks suspiciously like last year's exercise, thought Admiral Jon Leonard as he focused his attention on the massive viewscreen before him. The screen, depicting western reaches of the Pacific Ocean and extending well into Southern and Southeast Asia, was a mass of red icons surrounding an island near its center. The center point, as had been the case for the past two months, was the island of Taiwan.

Leonard, a former attack submarine captain, had spent several years of his life commanding attack boats in the Pacific. And while it was an exaggeration to state that he knew the western Pacific like the back of his hand, he did possess an intimate knowledge of its waters, geography, and political fault lines.

As a junior officer, he had earned his dolphins on a Los Angeles-class boat out of Pearl Harbor. Subsequent sea tours, punctuated by the necessary evils of shore staff appointments, were spent deploying on attack boats out of Pearl Harbor and San Diego. He had passed months at a time in the narrow confines of the submarines, learning his craft and slowly progressing to command his own boat, the USS *Chicago*.

The early part of his career was spent learning about Soviet submarines, both their attack boats and the massive boomers with their lethal load of intercontinental missiles. With deployments in the northwest Pacific, it had been a constant battle between Soviet and American boat skippers to outthink and outwit the other side. Through all of it, he had gained a grudging respect for the Soviet boat skippers who were well trained, crafty, and when required, aggressive.

The games of cat and mouse with the Soviet boats had all but ceased in the wake of the dissolution of the Soviet empire. The Soviet submarines had mostly returned to their ports, and many of them simply rusted out alongside their similarly aging piers in naval bases around the old Soviet Union. With the increased wealth provided by energy exports, and the leadership of Putin, the undersea contest had re-emerged in the 2000s. But it did not have the same urgency, sense of imminent threat, or scale as had been the case before 1991.

But as the 2000s turned into the 2010s, a new threat had emerged in the Pacific. Chinese submarines, largely relics of the Soviet submarine construction programs, had been plying the near waters of China since the 1950s. Originally employed in a coastal defense role, the more recent development of indigenously designed and built nuclear attack submarines and ballistic missile boats had given the PLA submarine force longer reach and a more strategic role in achieving the aspirations of the Chinese Communist Party.

The initial classes of Chinese nuclear attack boats had been no match for the larger, quieter, and more capable American Los Angeles- and Virginia-class submarines. But the Chinese had demonstrated a knack for learning and continuous improvement in the design and employment of the nuclear—and conventional— submarine fleets. Their new Sui-class nuclear attack boat and Yuan conventional submarines were advanced, and more than capable of giving American submarine skippers a headache in the waters of the western Pacific.

The underwater domain was just one of the many challenges that Leonard was pondering as he refocused his attention on the screen before him. He was attending his routine morning briefing, and a middle-aged Navy captain at the front of the conference room began with an update on operations across the Indo-Pacific Theater.

"Sir, since March we have been tracking the PLA preparations for another large-scale exercise that will involve both their Eastern and Southern Theater Commands. We expect that they will continue to be guided by the new 2027 Military Training Regulations, which were signed by the new president last year. As you know, the timing is entirely dictated by the weather; from August, the typhoon season prevents any realistic military training activities."

The navy captain paused his monologue, waiting for the massive screen to zoom into the area covered by Taiwan and the PLA Eastern Theater Command. Leonard, who was very familiar with the geography of eastern China and the locations of ports, airfields, and headquarters, quickly scanned the growing concentrations of Army, Navy, and Air Force units at various locations. The newly zoomed-in section of the map was thick with red icons representing a variety of Chinese bases and units.

Leonard looked back at the captain, nodding that he wished him to continue.

"In a similar vein to last year's exercise, over the past two months we have seen a significant buildup of ground, air, and operational logistics units in the Chinese Eastern Command's bases. We have also seen a commensurate increase in traffic across their command-and-control networks. This includes their maritime, cyber, land, air defense, and conventional missile command sub systems. Some of these we have been able to break into; however, other systems have the new quantum encryption technology, and we just cannot get into those. At least, not yet.

"Accompanying the military buildup has been a ratcheting up of information operations and psychological warfare against the government and populace of Taiwan. Concurrently, the PLA Strategic Support Force's space systems division has been targeting all of our space-based sensors that have coverage of the eastern seaboard of China. They have had minimal success thus far, but they have also not used their most aggressive or destructive counter-space capabilities. The use of these, we believe, would be an important indicator of any real-time move against Taiwan and our allies in the region."

Leonard nodded and made a note on the secure e-pad in front of him. He would need to speak to his US Space Command counterpart about their on-orbit capacity to assure friendly space-based assets, and their readiness to support short-notice rocket launches for the replacement of the most vital communications and sensor payloads.

"Please continue," Leonard said.

Several long yellow rectangles now appeared on the large map in front of him.

"Sir, these represent the most likely amphibious landing sites on the main island of Taiwan. From the north, beaches around Taoyuan City are suitable for landings. These beaches are also close to airfields and to the capital, Taipei. Also in the north, but on the eastern coastline, the area around Toucheng is suitable notwithstanding the fact that it is much further from embarkation points than landing sites on the west coast. In the southwest, two main areas around the Tainan Gold Coast, and south of Linyuan, are suitable."

Large red arrows now appeared, originating from embarkation areas on the Chinese coast and leading to the four anticipated landing sites.

"We estimate the Chinese would use at least two of these landing areas, and as many as four. Each has proximity to a major port—should they be able to seize them—and would likely be supported by airborne operations inland. We also expect that we would see a significant amount of special operations across the island to destroy power and communications and create disorder, while also assassinating government and military leaders."

Leonard leaned forward in his seat. He had participated in multiple wargames that examined the many options open to PLA leaders if they decided that a successful invasion was a high probability. Contrary to newspaper reports in the past few years, the Taiwanese and American defenders had not lost every military wargame that examined this particular challenge. But they had lost enough to worry political leaders in Washington, DC. This had led to rapid investment in new technologies—some of which were so sensitive that even Leonard had not been briefed on them.

The wargames of the previous years had also led Pentagon planners to dust off old mobilization plans and update them for the 21st century. Not only might they have to draft in hundreds of thousands of new military personnel in any conflict with the Chinese, but the Americans would also need to rapidly expand the capacity to manufacture everything from high-end precision weapons, to ships, aircraft, and land combat vehicles.

Just yesterday, Leonard had participated in a top-secret VR conference led by the Vice Chairman of the Joint Chiefs, General Mary-Ann Scott, to receive an update on the very rapid, but also very quiet, mobilization planning which had recently been completed. Scott, who had been made the central authority for all US military mobilization activities, had led a small interagency and defense industry team over the last year to produce the mobilization strategy. In the previous month, it had been briefed to the president, the National Security Committee, and the congressional leadership.

Funds had been allocated, and the next mobilization phase—manufacturing expansion—was about to commence.

I hope we can step it up enough to outproduce the Chinese, Leonard thought as he pondered the VR conference that had taken place the previous day. While his nation had achieved extraordinary feats of industrial and national mobilization in the past, it was a different world now. And their political system was much more fractured.

An uncomfortable silence descended in the room. The Navy captain, noticing Leonard's distraction, had paused speaking and was waiting to regain the attention of his commander before continuing.

"Sorry about that. Just thinking through some industrial issues. Please continue," Leonard said.

"No problem, Sir," countered the captain before he resumed his briefing. "Chinese short- and medium-range ballistic missiles, as well as their suite of advanced and hypersonic cruise missiles, would be able to target Taiwan, as well as US and coalition forces throughout the western Pacific. The PLA has continued to expand the size of its missile force. Despite the developments made to our countermeasures in the past several years, these weapons are a significant threat to our deployed major fleet units as well as air and logistic bases throughout the region. High-value targets in Guam, Okinawa, Japan, and even Hawaii and northern Australia are likely to be on the PLA's target list."

Leonard nodded. The threat posed by the wide variety of Chinese missile systems was sobering. But he was also aware of several classified programs designed to counter this threat. The refocus on the western Pacific several years ago had focused the minds of the folks at DARPA and in the wider defense industry on countering this multilayered missile threat from the PLA. Between deception, spoofing, hard and soft kill options of sensors and missiles, as well as cyber disruption of sensors, networks, and Chinese manufacturing capabilities on the mainland, Leonard felt that the US military might have developed a systemic approach to minimizing the PLA missile forces. Maybe.

"Let's go through the correlation of forces again, please," Leonard asked. It was a weekly undertaking, where the staff compiled a comparison of Chinese and Taiwanese forces, and then in stages added in US, Japanese, and other potential coalition contributors at different times post invasion.

"Roger, Sir. The current Taiwanese deployed force, which includes the small mobilization in the wake of last year's scare, sits at 200,000 ground, air, and naval forces. Their reserve forces, we estimate, could mobilize around another 1.5 million, although that would take time and logistic support that might not be possible once an invasion commences. Given the extension in time for national service to one year in 2024, we expect the quality of these reservists to be good. Any mobilization of reserve forces is also likely to be disrupted by Chinese misinformation, sabotage, and missile strikes.

"While their forces are concentrated around the four key land sites I just briefed, large reserves are kept in the eastern part of the island and in underground air bases on the east coast. On the basis of these figures, we estimate that the PLA will focus on one main landing area in the south and one in the north. It would have to put ashore—in the first wave—at least 50,000 troops in each area, secure beachheads, airfields, and ports, and then commence landing troops for a second phase that would include ground operations to seize the key cities and strategic locations.

"While the PLA Navy has built a significant amphibious capability over the past two decades, they need to carry a large landing force—and its supplies—to multiple locations while also retaining a reserve of ships. Because of this, we think two landing sites is the most feasible option operationally and logistically for the Chinese. We expect that operations in Taiwan and its vicinity would represent the 'close' battle for the Chinese. They would also undertake 'deep-battle' operations to destroy or disrupt the capacity of our forces, and the Japanese, to come to the aid of the Taiwanese. This would include cyber operations against strategic targets around the world as well as strikes against our bases and deployed forces in the western Pacific."

Leonard acknowledged the information he had just received. But the correlation of forces wasn't complete just yet.

"And how are our allies?" he asked.

The captain signaled for the next transition on the map to commence. This time, the map zoomed out and showed a large swathe of the western Pacific from Japan in the north to Tasmania in the south.

"Well Sir, the Japanese are solid. Their efforts to increase spending in the past decade, and resolve some tricky constitutional issues, mean that they are well placed to secure their own territory, provide a solid northern flank for any operations in Taiwan, and provide a range of other strategic supporting capabilities, including space and cyber operations, for any large-scale US movement into the western Pacific. Their large, modern fleet of destroyers and submarines will be invaluable, as will their ground and air forces. And their politicians, while not seeking a fight, know that if it comes to them, they cannot shy away from it."

Leonard acknowledged this with a slight nod. He had worked with the Japanese submariners on multiple occasions. He knew of their capacity to build excellent conventional submarines. Their new Taigei-class attack boats, with their advanced energy storage and sonars, were probably the best anywhere in the world. And Japanese submariners had generations of experience.

"How about at the other end of the Pacific, down south in Australia?" Leonard asked.

The captain, until now confident and forthcoming, appeared reticent. After a short silence, he replied.

"Well Sir, they produce good soldiers, as we know from the last century. But their political class is reluctant to commit combat forces. They are still running an old fleet of Collins subs, which may be of some use in peripheral areas. Their messing about with different submarine programs in the past 15 years has led to nothing but old boats, lots of expenditure, a lack of investment in other more important military capabilities, and upset allies. Similarly, their Anzac class will be useful missile sponges, but they have been very slow to introduce new and improved frigates. While they will provide some useful bases and strategic support and are able to generate a larger army in a short period if required, it is unlikely the Australians' small defense force will be much use to us if anything happens in the coming months."

Leonard sighed. He knew many of the Australian senior leaders and had frequent discussions with their Chief of the Defence Force. He liked them a lot and they were always excellent hosts when he visited. But despite large investments in their Navy and other services, they were still only capable of providing small, one-shot task forces.

And their government had not paid enough attention to their own backyard, the south Pacific. The new base being developed in the Solomon Islands was a problem, Leonard thought.

"Anything else?" Leonard probed.

"They are beginning a mobilization process, so I expect their available forces will expand in the coming months. Their expanding Army will be what we will need most if the Chinese come ashore in Taiwan, or conduct other operations as feints in southeast Asia. The bright spot down under is the northern Australia strategic bastion. Over the last decade, we have been working with them to develop the Darwin area and its bases and logistics facilities as a secure strategic bastion for alliance aircraft, ships, ground forces, and logistics. We have excellent missile defenses in place, as well as hardened, secure communications. The bastion now includes a rocket launch facility that is part of our new alliance responsive launch initiative. We are looking at using this as a model for developing other strategic bastions in Guam and Japan in the coming year."

The captain had finished his brief and was quiet.

"Thanks. I would like an update on the alliance strategic bastion concept at some point in the next couple of days. It will be important moving forward, and I would like to look at options for accelerating the development of the bastions in Guam and Japan, as well as continuing to expand our ship repair facilities and cyber-assurance capacity in the Darwin strategic bastion," Leonard responded.

Now that this part of the brief was over, Leonard knew it was time for him to brief his staff on recent developments from Washington. In the past 24 hours, the president had met with his principal advisers in the National Security Council twice. The only topic on the agenda had been Chinese aggression against Taiwan, and the likelihood that this year's exercise would remain just that. Or, as a worst case, shift from a large-scale joint exercise to a full-on invasion of Taiwan.

During the Cold War, both NATO and the Warsaw Pact had conducted annual large-scale exercises on land, in the air, and at sea. The lead-up to, and conduct of, these exercises had featured intensive intelligence collection by both sides to confirm that what was taking place was truly just a drill. The scale of some of the exercises—involving hundreds of thousands of troops and the large-scale movement of ground, land, and naval units around Europe and across the Atlantic—sometimes spooked the other side.

Leonard began to speak to his assembled staff.

"In 1983, NATO undertook one of its largest ever exercises in Western Europe. Called *Able Archer*, this not only tested the strategic and operational maneuver of large-scale military forces; for the first time, it also included new types of coded radio communication as well as the participation of political leaders. The exercise was so realistic, several members of the Soviet Politburo were convinced it was a ruse for a NATO-initiated war with the Warsaw Pact."

Leonard paused, knowing many of the officers in the room had studied Cold War history to apply its lessons to the current competition with China.

"We now know that this Cold War exercise came close to generating a Soviet response that might have eventually led to a nuclear exchange. Because of this, many back in DC have compared last year's Chinese joint exercises in the Taiwan Strait to *Able Archer 83*. It literally scared the shit out of many of our political leaders. And it set in train the funding increases and mobilization activities of the past year."

There was a soft murmuring around the room. Many of the staff had watched the massive PLA exercise the previous year that had convinced many in the West that a Chinese invasion of Taiwan was imminent. While that did not happen, many analysts in Washington, Tokyo, Canberra, and beyond now believed that the scale and geographic scope of the annual PLA joint exercises were able to provide an excellent deception plan for the buildup before any real invasion.

"When we detected the movements of joint forces, missile organizations, and logistics units earlier this year, we had to once again ask ourselves: is this another large-scale PLA exercise, or just a ruse to cover for a grab for Taiwan by the Chinese?"

Leonard let that question hang in the room for a moment before continuing.

"Our national leadership is concerned that the current Chinese activities could get out of hand. At yesterday's National Security Council meeting, the president decided on a proposal put to him by the secretary of defense and secretary of state that would give the

Chinese leadership something else to think about. And hopefully, deter them from going ahead with any invasion."

At this, an aide to Leonard who had been sitting against the back wall stood up and walked around the table handing out red-colored binders. Each binder, the words "Top Secret" emblazoned on its cover, included a slim written brief containing maps, diagrams, tables, and deployment timelines.

"Ladies and gentlemen, before you is the plan to deploy US forces to Taiwan as a deterrent against this year's PLA joint exercise becoming a real invasion. While we have always provided military equipment under the Taiwan Relations Act, and in recent years provided more extensive training teams, we have not before deployed large forces to the island. Until now, doing so would have been seen as a provocation to the Chinese, and would undermine our policy of strategic ambiguity about whether we would defend Taiwan.

"The president and his advisors have decided that we need to take the initiative on this issue. In consultation with our Japanese, Korean, and Australian partners, we will deploy a force to Taiwan that we hope will be seen as a tripwire by the Chinese leadership. If they attack Taiwan, they will also be attacking American forces. We know the Chinese leadership believes that if they can seize the island before US intervention, the American people may not be willing to shed blood for us to take it back. But the president and his advisors reason that if any attack automatically endangers American service personnel, it might provide enough of a deterrent—at least for another year or two.

"At the same time, we don't want the Chinese to pick up that we are sending large forces to Taiwan until they are already on the ground. It could provoke them into launching a preemptive invasion. We need to lodge our initial force in secret. Once they are on the ground in Taiwan, our analysts and AI simulations back in the Pentagon have shown a very high probability that this will be a sufficient deterrent for the Chinese. At least for now."

This news caused some eyebrows around the room to rise. But no more than this. The military officers, conditioned by military service and multiple operational deployments in the past two decades, took this news in their stride.

"Warning orders have already been dispatched to the units involved."

Leonard looked across the table at the Commander of Marine Forces in the Pacific, a wiry Marine infantry general named Joe Bateman.

"Sir, the first of our new Marine Littoral Regiments will begin embarkation on the transports in the next few hours. It will take with it one of the new Army cavalry units with all their autonomous air and ground combat systems. They should be on the ground in 72 hours, and the follow-on regiments will arrive at 48-hour intervals. Our 3rd Marine Division headquarters should arrive within the week."

Leonard nodded at Bateman. They had spoken by secure VR last night, straight after Leonard had received word from the Chairman of the Joint Chiefs about the plan to deter Chinese aggression. Bateman had immediately set the wheels in motion with his Marines. Leonard then addressed the remainder of the assembled Army, Navy, Air Force, Space Force, and Coast Guard senior officers in the room.

"The directive in the binder in front of you confirms the force flow for the initial Marine contingents to Taiwan, and then several branch plans and decision points depending on the Chinese response. While these are similar to many of our wargames of the past few years, there have been modifications to take account of revised PLA dispositions and some of the new US and allied units, logistics, and manufacturing capacity that have become available in the past year."

The mood in the room, always serious, had now turned somber. The senior military leaders assembled knew that the coming days and weeks would see huge numbers of military personnel, equipment, and logistics moving around the western Pacific. It would be the largest deployment of US military forces since the buildup to the first Gulf War back in 1990–91.

Leonard spoke a final time to those in the room.

"Team, we all know what we need to do here. We have been preparing for this for years. The president has given us clear direction on deterring a PLA invasion of Taiwan. Forget this is an election year if you can. Our mission is to defend Taiwan. While the physical movement of our forces will be vital, so too will be the operational and strategic information ops, cyber support, and space operations. Winning the strategic narrative will be vital, as will be the maintenance of our alliances and regional partnerships."

Leonard then paused, sitting back in his seat. He considered the words he would use to conclude the meeting, and then sighed softly before continuing.

"We know from history that wars don't just start through detailed military planning and calculations. They often begin because of *mis*calculation—on both sides. Let us all pray that what we are doing will be enough to prevent a terrible miscalculation that could see us all descend into the hell of a war it will be difficult to walk away from."

AUTHOR'S NOTE (I)

Contained on this page is a slide from the strategic situation briefing conducted at the headquarters of Indo-Pacific Command on 5 May. It is one of the millions of declassified documents that were released to the US National Archives in early 2035.

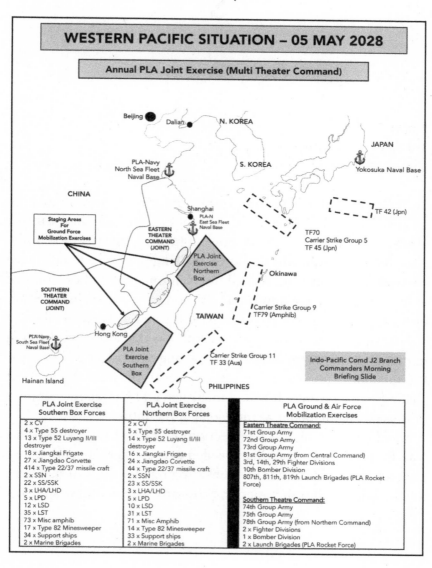

8

Grey Wizard

7 May 2028
3rd Space Operations Squadron
United States Space Force

Tech Sergeant Kara Hickling re-ran the zero-latency simulation in her VR set. It was about the twentieth time she had run the after-action review. The recent capture of the Chinese *Jinan 1* satellite, while not without some challenges, had eventually been successful. The mission, and all the planning that had contributed to its completion, was now used by the other operators in her Space Delta as a training aide to prepare for future recovery missions.

For Hickling, however, it was a reminder that even with the best of preparation, things could still go wrong that might compromise the mission. And where she could learn from these shortfalls or challenges, she would. It would make her, and her fellow members of the command, better at their jobs in the future.

Hickling, after all, was a perfectionist. She had always been that way. Even growing up she had needed to get top grades and perfect the other elements of her life, including relationships. It had been tough on her, and sometimes on those around her. But despite her infrequent failures, she had found that this mindset had generally served her well. Especially in this assignment.

She had reached the part of the after-action review where the grappling hand, at full extension from the cargo bay of the S-38 *Stiletto* spacecraft, had touched the Chinese quantum technology test satellite. Everything immediately went black.

"What the hell ...?" she had heard Captain Marcus murmur in her headset. He was monitoring the operation from another VR headset.

Her immediate reaction was to pull back the grappling hand on the assumption that the Chinese satellite had deployed an electronic counter-tampering device. These devices had been deployed on many satellites in the past decade to prevent on-orbit tampering of the kind that Hickling was an expert in.

Checking the telemetry from the *Stiletto*, Hickling saw that the power outage had been the result of an internal problem with the American spacecraft. Within a couple of seconds, backup power had been restored. After that, the recovery mission had continued exactly like Hickling and her teammates had rehearsed.

The *Jinan 1* satellite had been seized by the grappling hand controlled by Hickling through her VR set, and then drawn into the cargo bay of the *Stiletto* spacecraft. After the Chinese satellite was secured, several radar reflectors had been released. The bay doors had been closed and locked, and the spacecraft had made a rapid ascent in altitude. Shortly afterwards, the "debris" from the old American satellite has passed through the region where the Chinese quantum satellite had been orbiting.

Monitoring Chinese communications in the days that followed indicated that they strongly suspected the Americans had stolen their "bird." But with more evidence that it may have exploded, provided by the radar reflectors, the embarrassed PLA Strategic Support Force had quietly let the matter go. For now.

But there would probably be a price to pay for the Americans. The PLA, with its confidence in its highly advanced space capabilities, hated being bested. They were quick learners, and unlike the more bureaucratic, committee-based systems in Western military organizations, the Chinese would learn from this setback and improve their space operations and the design of their orbiting satellites and spacecraft. The Americans could be sure that every future Chinese satellite launched into orbit would contain more effective countermeasures to prevent satellite heists in orbit. But for this mission, Hickling and her team had pulled off a heroic and well-planned "acquisition operation."

For several days, at least among those who had the security clearance to know about the mission, Hickling and other members of her Delta had been feted. Senior officers had dropped by her team's work pod, and she had even been awarded one of the new Space Force commendations. It had confirmed her decision to move to the command. Not only was the work rewarding and challenging, but it was also recognized by those above her. It gave her purpose, and once again reassured her that she had made the right decision to transfer from the Air Force into the Space Force.

The successful mission had also boosted her confidence. Which was why she had just re-watched the after-action VR simulation. Her Space Delta was about to commence a new mission. And her part in the mission would require all the stealth, planning, imagination, and conviction she could muster.

Hickling's team were about to do a magic trick in space and on earth. They were going to make a military unit disappear.

Hickling sat in Captain Marcus' office—a small, utilitarian space that her boss kept spotlessly clean. The walls were adorned with framed pictures, certificates, and flags from his previous military assignments. A single row of challenge coins lined the front edge of his narrow desk.

"For most observers of military operations, and of the Space Force's activities, the rockets, satellites, and communications networks are the focus of attention. And why wouldn't they be? The United States, despite our declining technological advantage, still has some of the finest satellite and rocket engineers in the world. We also have decades of experience in building, launching, maintaining, and employing satellites for the full breadth of civil and military applications," Marcus began.

He paused, glancing at a folder on his desk, before looking up at Hickling again. "But it is the ingenuity of our people that is our true advantage in space. American industry takes risks that few other nations are willing, or capable, of taking. This ensures that, despite some early malfunctions and accidents, space technologies developed by our industry are at the cutting edge. Along with decades of institutional knowledge in the field, it permits us to sustain our lead over nations such as Russia and China, despite the breathless and often uninformed reporting of some in the news world and blogosphere."

Hickling appreciated what Marcus was talking about. Ingenuity and imagination also magnified the impact of these magnificent satellites, rockets, and the communications networks that joined it all together. The use of clever on-orbit operations to maximize the coverage of satellites on the earth's surface, minimize their chances of being hit by orbital debris, and reduce the capacity for interference by adversaries was an art in itself. Entire sections of the most brilliant lateral-thinking Space Force personnel were dedicated to the cunning application of space operations. This extended into both defensive and offensive operations, and often blended both. These teams of adroit, strategically and technologically minded people were known in the Space Force as "Black Herons."

The Black Heron was an African waterbird, known for its unique predatory tactic of canopy feeding. The birds would use their wings to form an improvised umbrella over the water, to simulate night. The fish, thinking they were now safe from predation, would poke their heads out of the water, and the Black Heron would use its sharp beak to stab their prey.

Hickling was drawn from her thoughts as Marcus continued his dialogue.

"The Space Force Black Heron teams have been busy in the past 24 hours." Marcus' face had transitioned to a grimmer countenance. "The president has ordered the quiet movement of a Marine Littoral Regiment to Taiwan. He intends to unveil its presence to the world once it has established itself ashore. The first MLR will be followed by two more in the coming weeks, with additional follow-on by ground, air, logistics, and headquarters after that."

Hickling instantly understood the implications of this change in American policy toward Taiwan and its defense. They had to get the first regiment ashore and established without Chinese interference.

"The planners at INDOPACOM headquarters have developed a simple deception plan to enable this. The 3rd Marine Littoral Regiment currently training in Guam will publicly embark, notionally to deploy to Okinawa for an exercise with other US and Japanese Marine Corps units. Just short of Okinawa, the high-speed vessels that are deploying the Marine Littoral Regiment will swing to the west and move at maximum speed for the port of Toucheng on Taiwan's northeast coast. The rest is in this top-secret ops plan."

Marcus slid a thin red folder across the desk. Hickling pulled it toward her and glanced through it. The most important part of the operation was deceiving the Chinese, Russian, and other adversary satellites about this turn to the west.

Cyber Command would support INDOPACOM through spoofing what the Chinese satellite downlink computers were seeing. Essentially, the actual western track of the embarked Marine force would be erased, and a new track to Okinawa inserted. At the same time, the classified operations plan described how Space Force—Hickling and her team—were to activate small devices they were to attach to multiple Chinese and Russian satellites using the S-38 *Stiletto*. These devices would generate a burst of energy that would temporarily disable the satellite. As Hickling read, Marcus continued speaking.

"A second element of the plan involves space weather."

While she didn't want to ignore her boss, Hickling was absorbed in the contents of the folder. Space weather. It was something Hickling had become very familiar with during her time in Space Command. It underpinned almost all of their activities.

The sun possessed an 11-year cycle, known in the scientific community as the solar cycle. This cycle saw variation in the numbers of sunspots and terrestrial phenomena such as auroras. Around the halfway point of each cycle, sunspot numbers reached their maximum. During this "solar maximum," coronal mass ejections became much more frequent. These coronal mass ejections produced cosmic rays that could damage the electronics and solar power arrays on satellites.

The current cycle, imaginatively called Cycle 25 by scientists, was approaching its peak. Relying on reports from the National Oceanic and Atmospheric Administration's Space Weather Prediction Center, the Space Force personnel knew that this cycle would last until 2030. Reports early in the cycle had predicted upwards of 130 sunspots during the peak, accompanied by much more frequent coronal mass ejections.

The sun had not disappointed. And while these ejections at times played havoc with space-based satellites and other spacecraft, Space

Command could also use this space weather to cover its tracks when engaged in more malign activities.

"Aided by Cyber Command," Marcus continued, "you and your team are to inject spoofed reports of coronal mass ejections into the Chinese and Russian solar observatory satellites. Then, several hours later, your team is to activate the small electromagnetic pulse devices, stealthily placed on the Chinese and Russian earth-observing satellites. These would cause a temporary loss of the satellites, probably for a period of no more than a day or two."

Hickling was barely listening as she absorbed the contents of the red folder in front of her. The ops plan also described how the American government would report the loss of several satellites due to the coronal mass ejection at the same time. The planners at INDOPACOM were betting that the temporary blindness of the Chinese and Russian satellites would last long enough to cover the westward turn of the naval task force carrying the Marines, and their unloading at Toucheng. Hopefully, the Chinese and Russians would not suspect American subterfuge—at least, not until it was too late.

A day later, Hickling and her team were connected through a VR construct, which they accessed with the new-generation headsets. The construct, viewed in very high resolution, showed the western Pacific from Medium Earth Orbit, at an altitude of approximately 8,000 kilometers. Overlaid with this was the planned route of the naval task force carrying the Marines, as well as the dummy route to Okinawa.

At the top of her display was the capitalized name that Hickling and her team—most of whom were fans of Lord of the Rings—had given to this mission.

Operation Grey Wizard.

The next layer in Hickling's VR display was the constellation of Chinese and Russian satellites that would be in a position to observe the naval task force's transit to Taiwan after its turn west. Both the

Chinese and Russians would have a mix of ocean surveillance, optical reconnaissance, and radar reconnaissance satellites that would have to be targeted.

The satellites at the lowest altitude were generally the optical reconnaissance satellites. These were found in orbits between 400 and 500 kilometers above the earth, and their tracks were shown in red on Hickling's VR display. At around 600 kilometers' altitude were the radar reconnaissance satellites. These used synthetic aperture radar to spy on ground and sea movements by military forces. These satellites and their orbits were shown in blue.

Next were the ocean surveillance satellites. The Russians, Chinese, and Americans all possessed these satellites, which contained passive electronic intelligence collectors, to triangulate large electronic emissions at sea. For the most part, the biggest electronic emitters at sea were naval vessels, so constellations of these satellites were parked in orbits between 1,000 and 1,200 kilometers above the earth. Hickling viewed these as green orbital tracks in her display. By this point, her display was quite crowded with the different orbital tracks of Chinese and Russian satellites.

With a quick finger gesture, she was able to highlight the much smaller number of satellites that would be in a position to detect the westward turn of the task force or detect it during its rapid move to Toucheng after the turn. She had run this simulation multiple times with her team in the 72 hours beforehand. They had then fed the resulting data to the Space Force mission planners in a different Space Delta. This other Delta was responsible for launch operations and assured access to space for the American military.

Over a period of 12 hours, they had been able to prepare and launch two of the S-38 *Stiletto* spacecraft. Each had its cargo bay stocked with small electromagnetic charges that were designed to temporarily disable satellites from close proximity. Hickling and her team had then spent the next two days in almost nonstop operations controlling the two *Stilettos* as they approached the targeted satellites, attached the charges, and then shifted orbits for their next targets. It had been exhausting work. But they had managed to finish several hours early, allowing Hickling and her fellow team members a few hours of rest before commencing the mission.

After leaving her workspace, Hickling had been worried that they had missed something in their planning due to the rushed nature of the mission. Any number of things could go wrong, including mission satellites that would observe the turn, misfiring charges, having the *Stilettos* detected as they approached the Chinese and Russian satellites, a misunderstanding in timings between the different combatant commands, or other scenarios that the Black Heron teams had failed to foresee.

These thoughts had consumed her as she walked back to her dormitory building to get some sleep before beginning this important mission. To allay these fears and relax her troubled mind, Hickling had engaged in meditation on arriving back at her room. She had often found this a good way of removing from her thoughts those things that were impacting on her physical or mental wellbeing. Most days, she practiced some form of meditation in the evening. It worked for her. Hickling's general wellbeing had improved since she had started meditating, and she was able to get a full night's sleep. And despite the demands of her responsibilities in the 3rd Space Operations Squadron, she found that the combination of meditation, exercise, and a good night's sleep had greatly improved her efficiency and effectiveness at work.

With just a few hours before the start of the mission, the meditation had once again done the trick for Hickling. She had no sooner placed her head on her pillow before succumbing to a deep slumber for several hours.

Hickling, now awake and with caffeine coursing through her veins, was ready. Her VR display, with the targeted satellites flashing in red, also showed numbers counting down in the top right of her field of view. This was the synchronized countdown that was being used at Cyber Command, INDOPACOM, Space Command, and on the naval task force carrying the Marines on their journey to Taiwan. The counter, ticking off numbers in its bright yellow figures, had just passed H minus one minute.

Hickling, her team, and the chain of command all the way up to the Space Force chief, watched the seconds count down. It would be the largest single operation that the Space Force had participated in since its formation. Timing and precision targeting were vital. All of Hickling's training, and that of those around her, had come down to this single moment.

The counter was in its final seconds. Tech Sergeant Hickling found herself holding her breath. As the numerals changed to a line of zeroes, Hickling exhaled. And while the actions that would now take place had been auto queued and would be executed by an intricate and bespoke algorithm, she felt the need to speak anyway, if for no other reason than to feel some sense of human control. It was right that humans should control the many algorithms and computer systems that would be involved in the deception of the Chinese and the Russians to allow the Marines to safely make it ashore. Hickling opened her mouth and uttered four words.

"Initiate Operation *Grey Wizard*."

9

Overall Defense Concept

14 May 2028
Northern Taiwan

Dana Lee looked down at her arm display. She double checked the locations of her people, as well as the status of her unit's fuel, ammunition, rations, and water. These statistics were compiled automatically every six hours by their logistic algorithm, which was embedded in the command-and-control system that connected all of her vehicles. No longer did the troop non-comms have to manually compile the status of their logistics. But Lee still checked it at least once each day to verify that the algorithms tally was the same as her approximation of their status. Old habits die hard.

And while she generally trusted the various algorithms that supported the operations of her unit, Lee also believed in the old saying "trust but verify." AI was still only as smart as its designers. Like humans, it needed to be checked every now and then.

The Army version of the logistics AI was similar, but not the same, as the Marine version. It had been an issue for the first few days after Lee and her troop had been detached from their Army brigade and assigned to the Marine Littoral Regiment. However, her unit IT specialists had put their heads together with the geeks from the Marine regiment and developed a solution that was both effective and secure. It was working. At least for now.

The difficulties with the logistics AI had only been the start of the integration challenges with the Marines in the last few months. Lee was canny enough to do her research as soon as she was informed her troop would be detached to support the new Marine Littoral Regiment. She had heard stories about bad blood between Marines and the Army. It was in the history files of the *Encyclopedia Militaria* on her arm screen that she found one of the great sources of Army–Marine tensions. Smith versus Smith.

It had been the subject of a conversation between herself and Sergeant James on the evening before they reported to the headquarters of the Marine regiment.

"So, let me get this right. The Marine three-star, in the middle of a battle on Saipan in 1944, sacks the Army commander of the 27th Division? How does that happen, Ma'am?" James had asked.

"Well, the Marine general—named Howlin' Mad Smith—already had ill feelings about the aggressiveness of Army troops in previous battles. So, when Major General Smith, who was leading the Army troops, had a couple days where he failed to smash through Japanese lines, Marine Smith removed him from command," Lee responded.

James, one of the most thoughtful non-comms that Lee had ever worked with, nodded.

"Well, boss, I am sure that upset the Army powers that be. How did that impact on joint relationships?"

"Sarge, they didn't think about joint operations in those days like we do now. The military services were still really parochial. The Army convened an inquiry which found that their divisional commander was removed without cause by Howlin' Mad Smith. It was a scandal that made its way into the press and even all the way to General Marshall in Washington, DC. Both sides remained pretty pissed at each other. The outcome was decades of ill feeling between soldiers and Marines. It saw them operate separately as much as possible in Korea and Vietnam, as well as in Iraq and Afghanistan," Lee continued.

"That's just dumb, boss. I know we haven't had much to do with the Marines until now, but we are on the same team, right?" muttered James. He was still shaking his head and pondering the idiocy of some general officers.

"We surely are, Sergeant James," Lee replied.

It had not quite turned out that way. At least not at first.

Lee's initial meeting with the regimental commander, a colonel named Furness, had been professional and productive. Furness appeared to appreciate that his unit had a shortfall in combat power. The Marines lacked the ability to counter enemy autonomous systems in the air and on the ground. He had welcomed her to the unit and assigned her directly under his command as an asset that would be used on the most important missions of the Littoral Regiment.

It was the Marine Infantry Battalion, one of Furness' units, that was more challenging. Their commanding officer and senior leaders were a tight group and had all been together in the Pacific for the previous 18 months. Many were skeptical of the Army's ability to move and fight as aggressively as the Marines. Others expressed open derision at the ability of the autonomous systems to be anything other than tools for surveillance or logistic support. And, as always, there were that small few who did not like having a woman in charge of a combat unit.

Lee and Sergeant James had spent several days working their way around the regiment, providing briefings to the leadership of its component units on what her cavalry troop was capable of. The Anti-Air Battalion, the Logistics Battalion, and the Regimental Headquarters were all enthusiastic about the new unit. They hosted productive tabletop exercises and AI-supported wargames to ensure that the Army newcomers could move, fight, and be supported like any other Marine unit.

The infantry battalion only went through the motions of playing nice—until a regimental exercise where Colonel Furness had Lee and her cavalry troop act as the red force against the infantry battalion. In both live and simulated exercises, her soldiers, vehicles, and autonomous systems had systematically mapped out and then destroyed two of the infantry battalion's rifle companies. Eventually, Furness had called off the exercise early, understanding that the commanding officer of the infantry battalion had been taught a lesson. There was no need to further humiliate him in the process of learning about the future of close combat.

The evening after the exercise, the commanding officer of the infantry battalion had appeared outside Lee's room back at their barracks.

"I was wrong. You were right," the Marine battalion commander had begun.

He then held up a bottle of 12-year-old scotch and two glasses. He also had with him his tactical sim-board—an enlarged version of Lee's arm screen. The Marine had graciously apologized for her initial reception by his battalion. He then poured scotch and grilled her about every aspect of her unit's capabilities.

Lee grinned, thinking back on that evening, as she conducted a survey of her battle positions here in northern Taiwan. It had been a hectic few days. After receiving the warning order that they would be the leading regiment of an American deployment to Taiwan, her days were a blur of producing load plans, equipment inspections, intelligence briefings, Taiwan and PLA familiarization briefs. She also spent time ensuring the personal administration of her people and their families was squared away before they deployed to a possible combat zone.

Their small naval task force, comprising two LPD-17 amphibious ships, two of the new light amphibious warships, as well as two Aegis-class destroyers, was protected by an extensive deception plan and air cover from a supporting carrier task group. The period on board the ships had been well used, with continuous briefings on the Taiwanese concept of defense for their island, their capabilities, and how the Marine Littoral Regiment would fit in with the Taiwanese military.

Their small fleet had eventually arrived at Toucheng port and offloaded over a period of 24 hours. The sailors were in a rush to offload. They had to return to their homeport to load up another Marine Littoral Regiment that would soon deploy to southern Taiwan. Other elements of the US Navy's amphibious fleet were rapidly embarking Marines, Army units, and their headquarters in case follow-on forces were ordered to Taiwan by the president.

An initial briefing by Colonel Furness, after they disembarked, confirmed their mission.

"Our regiment has been assigned to the Taiwanese Army's 6th Army Corps, which is responsible for the defense of northern Taiwan. Containing a mix of armor, mechanized infantry, light infantry, artillery, chemical warfare, communications, and engineers, it is the equivalent of the US Army Corps," Furness had said.

"Integration with the Taiwanese will not be without its frustrations. While Taiwanese and Americans have been training together for decades, never before has a large American unit been assigned under the command of the Taiwanese commander. The language barrier will be overcome by both sides using the auto-translate functions on the arm screens and other smart devices that the Taiwanese and Americans have issued to all of their officers and non-comms."

Lee, having completed her survey of her unit's battle positions, pondered other issues that had needed resolution since their arrival.

The differences in equipment, weapons, ammunition, and combat clothing were not significant issues. It might complicate logistic support for the Americans, but a logistic chain was already being established from the northern Taiwanese port, through a new base at Ishigaki to the east of Taiwan and all the way back to Guam, Hawaii, and the US west coast.

No, it was the operational approach to defending the island that caused most challenges. In many respects, it was something that Lee, Furness, and their senior leaders should have anticipated. Two nights ago, the issue had come to a head. Colonel Furness had discussed it with his leadership team, which now included Lee.

"We need to understand the history of the defense debate in Taiwan if we are to appreciate the nature of the Taiwanese defensive concept—and how we fit within that concept," Furness had begun. It had been early evening, after dinner, and the regimental commander had assembled them in his command post just to the north of the Toucheng township.

"In the 1950s, '60s, and even into the '70s, it made some sense for the Taiwanese to embrace a conventional approach to the defense of their nation. The PLA back then still possessed limited advanced weaponry or amphibious lift. However, once the Chinese economy began to grow from the 1990s onwards, and they started modernizing their equipment, training, as well as command and control, it demanded that the much smaller Taiwanese force rethink their concept of national defense," Furness continued, speaking confidently among his Marines and Army leaders.

"By about 2018 or 2019, the Taiwanese decided to pursue a more asymmetric approach to defense. Meeting Chinese invaders head-on with like-for-like capabilities would not work against a PLA that was now a more technologically advanced and joint force, and which possessed a budget 20 times the size of Taiwan's. So, they produced what they called the Overall Defense Concept. It focused firstly on force protection to ensure that the Taiwanese forces could survive the opening phase of any strikes conducted by the PLA. Secondly, it would use a range of conventional capabilities as well as large numbers of cheaper weapons such as mines, drones, coastal cruise missiles, electronic warfare, and short-range air defense to conduct a decisive battle in the littoral."

Heads around the room had nodded. Everything the colonel was describing made perfect sense for the defense force of a small island nation such as Taiwan. Furness then continued.

"The third and final aspect of the Overall Defense Concept was to be the destruction of the surviving PLA landing forces on or near the beaches. As this was taking place, reserve units would be mobilized to provide subsequent defensive lines along defensible terrain to attrit and destroy the Chinese invaders."

Lee, looking around the room before interrupting, asked what she had thought was the obvious question.

"Sir, what is the issue, then? That seems like a reasonable defense strategy given the size of the Taiwanese military and geography of the island."

Furness nodded, acknowledging Captain Lee's interjection with a smile.

"Institutional politics, Captain Lee," Furness answered. "Unfortunately, a change in the leadership of the Taiwanese military around a few years ago saw this concept shelved, left to gather dust. New senior military leaders, worried that a more asymmetric strategy would deny them funds for high-profile, prestigious conventional military capabilities, reverted back to the old doctrine of tackling the PLA head-on.

"Fortunately, enough of those who understood the Overall Defense Concept are still around. Among them is the commander of the northern ground forces in Taiwan. He was a senior planner for the asymmetric strategy and understands well what will happen if they try to take the PLA head-on. Our regiment, with its deployments around the northeastern parts of the island, fits in well with how the commander wants to fight—if it comes to that."

Lee, sensing this went higher, interjected again.

"But his boss doesn't see it that way," she offered.

Used to Lee's insights and manner of interjecting at times, Furness paused for a moment before responding. *If only you had been a Marine*, the expression on Furness' face appeared to convey.

"That's correct. His boss is a contender for the next Chief of General Staff and is an advocate of the older ways. It has caused some stress in the relationship. Our Taiwanese commander thinks he can apply an asymmetric approach within his current guidance. He doesn't describe it as such, instead calling it 'evolved conventional defense.' But he is walking on eggshells with his boss at the moment. I just thought you should know the context for some of the interesting redeployments we have had across northern Taiwan in the last few days."

Lee nodded. *Fucking politics*, she had thought. *No matter where you go, it always seems to raise its disgusting head.*

Her contemplations returned to the present—to her deployment position in northern Taiwan. On her arm screen, and the screens in the armored vehicle in which she sat, the dispositions of her cavalry troop were overlayed on a three-dimensional representation of the northeastern part of Taiwan.

Her crewed cavalry vehicles, the "gun cars," were dispersed and camouflaged—physically and electronically—in almost textbook fashion. For the entire history of human conflict, there had existed a race between lethality and dispersion of military forces. As lethality improved, military units always found one of the best ways to survive was to disperse more and to provide a smaller target for the enemy.

So it was in the 21st century. The profusion of military and civil sensor networks, fused with command-and-control networks into highly lethal kill chains, meant Lee had to disperse her troop over multiple grid squares. All her crewed and autonomous systems possessed physical camouflage. That was a given. But they were all also designed to have low noise and exhaust emissions as well as minimal electronic signatures. There was no way to be invisible on the modern battlefield, but you could reduce all your different signatures to make yourself a low-priority target for an adversary.

Lee had given a lot of consideration to such issues over the last couple of years. In fact, it had led her to start up a blog, which she called *Advance!*, that explored the interaction of humans and robotic systems in 21st-century ground warfare. She had become part of an active community of officers and non-comms who networked online and shared good ideas and best practice on land combat, training, and leadership.

One of the issues that Lee and her network constantly returned to was secure communications. Given the advances in network analysis over the previous decades, communications between the different vehicles and command nodes utilized different secure systems. The old voice-command networks were now rarely used. After all, the Americans and their allies had spent nearly two decades finding and killing insurgents by intercepting their conversations on the radio networks over which they spoke. Now, communications were largely kept to short, highly secure bursts of text. Or face-to-face communication. Which was just about to happen to Lee.

A short, secure text burst appeared on her arm screen from Sergeant James: "REGT COMD IN BOUND OUR LOC. ETA 2 MINS." This translated to "Colonel Furness will be visiting us shortly."

It was not unusual for Colonel Furness to visit Captain Lee's unit while deployed. Furness was an old-school combat leader. He liked to circulate among his Marines and soldiers to build his own picture of the situation on the ground. He would often be found in those elements of the regiment that had been designated as "main effort"—or where things were most uncoordinated and messed up, and required his direct intervention and prioritization.

As Lee's unit was directly commanded by Furness and was not attached to one of his subordinate battalions, the regimental commander also made a habit of regularly checking in on Lee and her soldiers. It made her feel part of the team, and her soldiers had noticed and commented upon Furness' concern for their welfare.

"What are you seeing, Captain?"

Furness had poked his head in through the rear combat door of her vehicle. His face, like the rest of the regiment, had been painted with the dark green, brown, and black mix of colors that was the normal camouflage for this part of the island. But his smile, and the white teeth behind the cam cream on his face, was hard to disguise.

Lee pulled down a folding seat in the back of her vehicle as Furness entered the back of her "car."

"Let me show you our latest dispositions, Sir."

Over the next five minutes, Lee briefed her regimental commander on the dispositions of her troop. She showed on her displays where she had programmed in waypoints for patrolling swarms of autonomous aerial vehicles and the patrol paths for her smaller uncrewed ground vehicles. Finally, she described her layout for the caches of currently unused autonomous vehicles, her logistic echelon, and her communications links within the troop and back into the regiment.

Furness nodded, satisfied with the troop situation.

"Looks good. How about your links with the Taiwanese Army units to your north and west?" Furness then inquired.

"Sir, we are tied in with the 269th Mechanized Infantry Brigade to our north. I have a daily liaison video conference, and we have a communications link established to share our locations, surveillance data both ways, and our ammunition status. The brigade is deployed around Keelung City. Their mission is to destroy any landing forces that come ashore in the Jinshan District to the northwest of the city." Lee then swiveled slightly to point to another screen to her left before continuing. "To our west, we are tied into the 584th Armor Brigade. It is deployed around the eastern and northeastern periphery of Taipei. It is the reserve brigade for the 6th Army, which as you know, is responsible for defending northern Taiwan. We have visibility of Taiwanese units further west and within Taipei itself, but don't have comms links with them—yet."

Lee concluded her brief. While her primary mission was to support the operations of the Marine Littoral Regiment, and its denial of northern landing zones in cooperation with the Taiwanese, her rules of engagement also allowed for support to the Taiwanese. At the moment, this support was the sharing of information. But she was also permitted in the rules of engagement to provide lethal support where she deemed necessary.

"Thanks, Dana. Good brief," Furness responded. "As of 30 minutes ago, it looks like the Chinese joint exercise in the strait and to the north and south of the island is winding down. They completed a live-fire exercise today, including firing several missiles over the island. It has upset the Taiwanese government, and they have issued some forthright responses about refusing to be intimidated or coerced by the Chinese Communist Party. With a little luck, our presence here has acted as a deterrent, and we can redeploy home in a few weeks."

Lee, her face illuminated by the red-light interior of her vehicle, acknowledged this with a nod. She was about to open her mouth to respond when a flash message lit up several of her screens.

Furness, whose attention was also drawn to the screen, spent a moment reading the full message. His expression remained neutral, but Lee knew exactly how he felt. She felt the same. Furness turned to look at Lee before he spoke.

"Well … heck. It appears we may not be going home anytime soon."

10

The Beetles

15 May 2028
269th Mechanized Brigade
Tainan Coast, southern Taiwan
0330 hours (Taipei Standard Time)

Private First Class Wei-ting Chen checked his Insta for what seemed like the hundredth time. The feed was going crazy with chat about the PLA exercise that was underway in the waters of the Taiwan Strait. Another trending topic online was the reactions to the American president's speech of the previous day where he had announced the arrival of the US Marines and Army in Taiwan. The American deployment of forces to the island for the first time was causing huge issues with the few Taiwanese who still thought that their nation should rejoin mainland China. The Chinese Communist Party, as expected, was enraged at the Americans, the Taiwanese, and anyone who was supporting them.

No surprise there, thought Chen. Every now and then, he also sneaked a look at what his girlfriend was up to. Mei-Hua, as far as Chen was concerned, was the love of his life. In Chen's eyes, she was movie-star beautiful, and the kindest person he had ever met. They had been introduced by mutual friends in high school and been dating for the past three years. When Chen entered the Army for his compulsory service, Mei had continued on to attend university in Taipei. Mei was studying veterinary medicine. She was now a student at the National Taiwan University, close to the center of Taipei. While they had not been able to see each other as frequently as they had at school, the young couple had been able to spend weekends together whenever Chen was released on leave from his unit.

This is very slow, Chen thought as he refreshed the screen on his smartphone. Normally, his service was lightning fast. *Perhaps the PLA is messing with us as part of their exercise*, he pondered. With a quick final look at a cached photo of Mei, he turned off his phone and turned back to the screen at his workstation.

On it was displayed a map of northern Taiwan overlaid with the dispositions of his brigade, as well as other units of the 6th Army Corps. The American ground units, adjacent to Chen's brigade, were also displayed using light blue symbols. All this visibility of unit locations, orientations, and other data had been made possible in the last couple of years by the new Integrated Battle Command System. Provided by the US Army and designed to provide better inter-operability between the ground forces of the two nations, it now featured in the command posts of most Taiwanese Army formations.

Theoretically, Chen understood the Chinese problem with the deployment of the American forces. But for the entirety of his year of service thus far, there had been small groups of Americans that had visited the headquarters where he worked. The Americans had assisted in the training of the various armor and mechanized infantry units that were part of the 269th Mechanized Infantry Brigade he belonged to.

But it wasn't only Americans. There had also been a contingent from the Ukrainian Army that had visited last year to pass on their lessons from fighting the Russians.

Just this morning, he had even been able to visit the newly established American headquarters with his commander during one of their daily liaison visits. The American unit, a new regiment that they called a "Marine Littoral Regiment," was deployed to their south. It was equipped with all kinds of advanced sensors, radars, and missile systems and acted as a supporting element to Chen's brigade and several others to the west. But, given the area of responsibility of Chen's brigade extended all the way to the coast from Keelung City to Jinshan, it was likely that it would be his brigade that would benefit most from the presence of the Marines and US Army soldiers.

When he had first joined the Army, Chen had been allocated to the armor branch. After basic training, he had progressed to training as a driver of one of the Army's M60A3 main battle tanks. The Army knew and trusted in this old warhorse, even if its main gun was no longer a match for some of the newer and more advanced Chinese main battle tanks. It was still a lethal and effective armored fighting vehicle, able to complement infantry, artillery, and engineers, in the close fight. The M60 was also less likely to place a strain on the island's roads and bridges like the heavier M1 Abrams that were beginning to be introduced.

After completing his basic driver training for the tank, he had been dispatched to the 269th Brigade. He had been excited about this assignment. Not only was it a front-line brigade, but its location would allow him to visit Mei in Taipei regularly. And, unlike his predecessors in the unit just a few years before, they had significant quantities of ammunition and fuel for training, courtesy of their American friends.

Chen had enjoyed an easy camaraderie with the other members of his tank crew. They lived together in the barracks, ate together at mealtimes, and spent long hours "buttoned up" in their tank during training maneuvers and gunnery practice. The few months as part of the tank crew had been fulfilling ones. It had come to an end so quickly. It was such a silly thing.

After completing gunnery training one afternoon, Chen and the crew of his tank had returned to their barracks and parked their vehicle alongside the other tanks of their platoon. He and the other members of the crew had been engaged in the usual banter, normally about the accuracy of their shooting, or what they would be doing during their next leave pass in Taipei. Chen had been laughing and distracted as he crawled out of the tank's driver hole. Taking off his headset and placing it over the back of his seat, he had been thinking of his next meeting with Mei as he leapt from the vehicle to the ground. Next Chen knew, he was on the ground, in terrible agony.

Not paying full attention to what he was doing, he had landed awkwardly and twisted his knee while dismounting. His crewmates had assisted him to the aid post to see a medic. It was not good news. He had torn the anterior cruciate ligament in his right knee and was placed on light duties for the next several weeks while he underwent treatment. A subsequent review had found him unfit to return to full duty as a tank crewman. But his injury was not so serious that he could not be of some continuing use to the Army.

And thus, he was sent to brigade headquarters to work in administration. As part of his duties, he had been trained as an operator on the Integrated Battle Management System in the brigade command post.

For the past two months, the brigade headquarters of the 269th Brigade had been deployed to its wartime battle positions. This had become the norm while the People's Liberation Army conducted their annual large-scale exercises in the Taiwan Strait. It would allow the Taiwanese military to survive any surprise attack and give them a head start in preparing for any potential invasion.

For the headquarters, its primary location was in one of the underground tunnel complexes that had been constructed by the Army over the last three decades. This intricate network of tunnels, storage warehouses, garages, hospitals, headquarters and even aircraft hangars, was an important part of the Taiwanese military's strategy for surviving any initial Chinese onslaught.

However, in the past 48 hours, it had become clear that the PLA exercise was nearing its conclusion and some units were returning to their home bases. And while there were more rumors than normal about Chinese saboteurs and assassins lurking about the Taiwanese capital, the threat of an invasion this year seemed to be passing. Because of this, Chen's brigade headquarters had moved to an alternative location outside the bunker complex. Now, Chen and the other members of the brigade headquarters were operating out of the back of armored command vehicles and small tents to command and control the units of the 269th. Currently, he was in one of the tent extensions behind his armored command vehicle, seated before his monitor.

Chen felt a presence behind him.

"What is that, Private Chen?"

The brigade operations officer, Major Lin, stood at Chen's right shoulder. Lin had his arm extended and was pointing at a red cross on the screen. As Chen moved to zoom in on the red cross, a short tactical report popped up. And then another. And another. Major Lin leaned over Chen to read the messages.

The first one was ominous: "SMALL AMPHIBIOUS VEHICLES EMERGING ACROSS SURF ZONE AT SHIMEN AND JINSHAN."

Where have these come from? thought Chen. While Shimen was west of their area of operations, Jinshan and its beaches were the responsibility of the 269th Brigade in northern Taiwan. He looked up at Major Lin's face to see it rapidly draining of all color. Chen had never seen the major like this before. He was one of the toughest officers on the headquarters. *This cannot be good*, Chen thought.

Messages continued to pile into Chen's queue on the screen: "MULTIPLE SMALL AMPHIBIOUS VEHICLES LANDING AT BEACH. APPEAR TO BE AUTONOMOUS."

"AERIAL SWARMS LAUNCHING FROM LARGER AUTONOMOUS AMPHIBIOUS VEHICLES. SMALLER VEHICLES APPROACHING VEHICLES AND BUNKERS AND EXPLODING."

"SUSPECT AUTONOMOUS AMPHIBIOUS VEHICLES DEPLOYING ELECTRONIC WARFARE AND JAMMING."

"BEACH OBSTACLES BEING DESTROYED BY AMPIBIOUS DRONES."

And then, different kinds of reports started to appear:

"LARGE CIVILIAN CARGO SHIP HAS EXPLODED IN CHANNEL TO ZUOYING NAVAL BASE."

"AUTONOMOUS SWARM ATTACKING AIRCRAFT AT ZUOYING NAVAL AIR BASE."

"AUTONOMOUS SWARM AND ELECTRONIC WARFARE ATTACK AT TAINAN AIR BASE."

Chen forwarded the messages to his sergeant, although he knew that he was probably receiving many similar notes. He turned to look at the map again. Many of the later reports were from areas far removed from where Chen's brigade was located. He needed to reset the filters on his battle map display so that he could provide the most relevant information to the staff and the commander of this brigade.

The battle map on Chen's screen had changed significantly since he had last glanced at it. The left-hand side of the screen, standing for the western parts of the island and well out to the Taiwan Strait, was now a sea of red. And instead of the red icons heading west as they had been several hours before, they were moving in a different direction. Every single red icon that represented the ships of the PLA Navy and aircraft of the Air Force was moving east. They were streaming east in a massive horde toward Taiwan.

Toward Chen's home.

Verbal and visual cues from the battle management system were beginning to overwhelm Chen and the other staff in the command post. The officers, normally a calming presence, were moving quickly and shouting at the battle management system operators for updates. In the distance, Chen could hear the power packs of tanks and other armored vehicles starting up, a sound he knew (and missed) from his time as a tank crewman. In addition to the sound of the units of the brigade coming to life, Chen now heard explosions.

Scores of them. And eventually hundreds. So many, it was difficult to distinguish individual detonations, or the direction from which they originated.

Then, all of the battle management systems, all of the different monitors in the command post, went blank. It was as if some giant hand had quickly pulled the power plug from a socket, depriving the screens and their hardened computers and communications network of the essential life force that underpinned how modern armies stayed connected.

For a moment, the cacophony of hectic activity in Chen's command post ceased. They all understood what this meant.

The People's Liberation Army had worked for decades to hone its operational concepts to break down the cohesion of enemy forces. It was something that Chen and all the personnel on the headquarters understood. One of the first things the PLA would do, if it actually came to a real, shooting war, would be destroy the Taiwanese command and control systems.

The PLA called it "systems destruction warfare." For years they had been publishing articles in their professional military journals about 21st-century warfare being about the confrontation between systems. It was a method of splitting large joint military forces down into smaller and smaller parcels that could be more easily attacked and destroyed. These foundational concepts had guided the development of new PLA organizations, tactics, as well as evolved kinetic and non-kinetic weapons.

Information warfare. Cyber and space operations. Deception and misinformation. Hard kill missile systems. These were orchestrated by the PLA in their operational system of systems. For Chen and his fellow soldiers, they had been schooled in these ideas as part of understanding their adversary. If systems destruction warfare was the PLA's theory of victory, the military forces of Taiwan needed to be able to counter it. They needed to survive, remain a cohesive joint force, and repel the onslaught of electronic warfare, cyber operations, and information operations. And destroy the invaders in their transit to the landing beaches in Taiwan.

All of this passed through Chen's thoughts in the seconds after the screens went blank.

Major Lin was back, standing beside him. Chen felt Lin's breath across the top of his head.

"It is finally happening, Private Chen. While we have been preparing for this eventuality for decades, none of us thought it would really come. Now is our chance to show what our brigade is made of."

Lin paused for a moment, looking around the command post. People were starting to rise, and to prepare to redeploy to another location. They all understand that moving and keeping a low signature was the key to survival for the headquarters, as well as the cohesion and operational effectiveness of their brigade.

Lin then spoke again. "Private Chen, pack up. We move in five minutes."

It was then that the air attack alarm blared throughout the command post. It was not a piercing screech like the sirens used by the Civil Defense Office in public areas around the country. The sound was more like an alarm from Chen's mobile phone. But it was instantly recognizable.

It meant that missiles and PLA aircraft were now inbound toward the 269th Brigade, and most probably, targeted on this very command post. Chen thought briefly of Mei. And before he could even stand to begin the evacuation process, everything went black.

Phase II

11

Tiger of the Land, Dragon of the Sea

10 June 2028
Off Tainan coast, southern Taiwan
PLA Navy Amphibious ship *Longhu Shan*

"Thirty minutes to embarkation, Sir."

The words of the runner, who had passed the message from his command post afloat, were expected by the man leaning against the ship's railing. He had a thin sheen of sea spray on his cheeks and a half-finished cigarette in his hand.

Colonel Bo Zhen peered across the waves, hoping to catch a glimpse of the shoreline. But, this far from the landing beach, the shore remained just beyond the horizon. He stood on one of the new generations of PLA Navy amphibious ships, a Type 071 amphibious transport dock. Launched in 2018, the *Longhu Shan* could carry one of his combined arms battalions as well as vehicles, helicopters, and supplies for his Marines once they had landed ashore. It was a vessel that Bo had spent much of the previous two years on, rehearsing and preparing for such a day.

The operations in the south, so far, had proceeded in accordance with the sequence that had been planned and rehearsed endlessly. Landing areas had been selected, subject to intensive intelligence collection, and then subject to preparation. "Preparation" was a euphemism for bombardment by electronic warfare, precision missiles, lethal drone swarms, naval gunfire, and aircraft-delivered weapons. Part of the preparation had also been the detailed strategic deception operations that had been put in train long before Bo had assumed command of his brigade.

The annual exercises in and around the Taiwan Strait were another segment of these preparations to deceive the military forces of this rebel province. But there had also been careful subterfuge conducted by CCP politicians, diplomats, and industrial leaders in the past year. Additionally, as part of the pre-landing softening up of defending forces, the PLA had attacked many more defensive positions in the different beach landing zones than they intended to use. It was all part of a massive shell game to keep the Taiwanese defenders off-balance. The aim was to achieve tactical surprise in the locations and timings of the landings by the liberating PLA Marines, Army, and airborne forces.

Bo's formation, the 2nd Marine Brigade, was normally based in the Southern Theater Command. His family still resided in a lovely house at their base near Hainan. He knew his wife and young son would be anxious for his welfare. But they understood that this was Bo's duty. His wife understood well the life of a military family. She had been the daughter of a senior PLA ground forces officer who had retired as a lieutenant general just a few short years before. She and her family had moved often throughout her childhood. This did not make Bo's absences any easier on his small family, however.

Bo dragged his thoughts away from his family and back to the deck of the landing ship upon which he now stood. His Marines were due to go ashore in the next few hours, as part of the second wave of troops that was responsible for seizing the southern parts of the island. The honor of first landings went to PLA Marines from the Eastern Theater Command.

But even these elite PLA Marines were not really the first wave. That was a mission that had been assigned not to the Marines, or even the Army. The first wave of combatants to land on the beaches of north, central, and southern Taiwan were not even traditional military units.

Bo pondered this new way of fighting, which he had assisted to bring to fruition before his current assignment as commander of the 2nd Marine Brigade. As part of the reforms to the PLA education and training system, Bo had been sent to the National Defense University in Beijing. It had been an intellectually stimulating year, and a good year for learning and socializing with old friends. It had also allowed him to spend more time with his wife and young son.

Importantly, he had been able to think and write about future warfare in a way he had not been able to before. The National Defense University had a first-rate library that was stocked with professional journals and books from all over the world. While Bo's English skills were rudimentary, there was a capable AI-based translation service available. This had allowed him to keep up with the latest developments in many advanced technologies with military applications being developed in America, Europe, Britain, and Japan.

More importantly, he had the time to consider the implications of some of the new technologies appearing in military and civil institutions, and what they might mean for how the PLA thought about war. He had the opportunity to ponder how the PLA might organize its fighting units on the ground, at sea, in the air, as well as in space and the cyber domain.

Much of the intellectual work had already been done. The concepts of "intelligentization" and "systems attack" were foundational ideas which all students studied during their time at the National Defense University. While these were important doctrinal concepts, endorsed by the Central Military Commission, Bo and his fellow students had also been encouraged to think of new and evolved ways to implement such ideas.

For Colonel Bo, this had culminated in a paper he had written on new way of teaming soldiers, Marines, sailors, and airmen with some of the new and highly advanced robotic systems that were being developed and deployed by Chinese defense industrial companies. He had focused on the most important operational problem there was for the PLA: Taiwan.

The key challenge was assembling, shipping, and disembarking a sufficiently large landing force—from the sea and air—to overwhelm the large defensive forces that were deployed by the Taiwanese. Not only did they have to defeat the Taiwanese military, but they would also have to do so before their American and Japanese allies could interfere with the Chinese operations and build a coalition to repulse such an invasion of the rebel province. The rapid defeat of Taiwan, and elimination of its government leadership, was an important lesson that the Chinese had learned from Russia's experience in Ukraine.

Surprise and deception were central to the problem. These principles always had been essential to success in war and were taught at every military academy around the world. Bo had studied the writings of the great Chinese warrior-philosophers such as Sun Tzu, Wu Qi, Cao Cao, Bai Qi, Han Xin, and Emperor Taizhong of Tang, among many others. The study of more recent successful military leaders, such as Zhukov, Eisenhower, Nimitz, and Schwarzkopf, had also supplied important insights for Bo's research.

It had taken him months, and many working drafts, but he had finally completed his thesis. His academic supervisors had grilled him for over two hours to defend the findings of this final paper, which had focused on human–robot–algorithmic teams in military operational art. They had questioned him on a range of topics, from doctrinal purity to technological readiness levels of the new doctrine, organizations, logistical support, intelligence preparation, deception, and the technological readiness of systems with which he had proposed to solve the operational problem of Taiwan. After the grilling, he had been invited to leave the room, and his academic supervisors had discussed his paper in private. They had given Bo no indication whether his year of study had been successful, or a complete waste of time.

That evening, he had received a knock at the front door of the small apartment he shared with his family. A PLA Navy lieutenant commander had informed a startled Bo that he had been ordered to accompany the naval officer immediately and report to a general at the PLA Academy of Science in Beijing. Upon reporting to the general, he had been informed that he had "passed" his final paper at the National Defense University. Further, Bo was being reassigned at short notice to the academy to oversee a new special project. The project would be based on the ideas contained in his thesis, well-resourced, and highly classified.

The following two years had been a whirlwind of writing, building, directing, and experimenting with the new capabilities that Bo had theorized in his National Defense University Paper. There had been two key operational challenges which had been the focus of Bo's thesis. He had proposed that autonomous systems should not just support the military services in solving these problems. Uncrewed swarming systems in the air, land, and sea domains, guided and connected by clever algorithms, could actually be at the leading edge of the solutions. According to Bo's hypothesis, a different conception of how these new technologies were used—involving new tactics, unit organizations, training, and command systems—would present a greatly improved chance of success for Chinese military units invading Taiwan.

The first operational problem that Bo had examined was how the PLA could generate the ability to successfully cross the Taiwan Strait for the first combat landing waves, follow-on forces, and a massive logistic tail. It was true that this operational challenge had been the focus of the Navy and the Air Force in the preceding decades. The PLA planners had developed a complex interwoven web of sensors, missiles, aircraft, ships, and submarines to overcome the difficulties posed by the Taiwan Strait. All of these were integrated within the new joint command and control approach that had been implemented in the late 2010s and early 2020s. But still there remained chinks in the armor of this advanced military expeditionary system that the Chinese leaders hoped would forcefully return their rebellious province to the fold.

The problem was that despite the massive investment in ships, aircraft, sensors, missiles, and command support systems in the previous years, they were all visible. Each individual capability, as well as their aggregation, could be easily seen by the watching eyes of the Americans, Japanese, and their other Pacific allies. This meant that none of these advanced capabilities would be surprising. It also resulted in years spent by their adversaries developing counter-methods to combat their most sophisticated systems.

This was not unusual in the history of warfare. It had always been difficult for large-scale invasion forces to be assembled without tipping off the target of such offensives. Sometimes, invading forces were fortunate enough that their target was either unprepared or had deluded themselves into thinking that an invasion was beyond comprehension.

This was not the case with the Taiwanese. They had spent decades preparing for such an eventuality. If the PLA was to successfully cross the strait and lodge forces, something else was required beyond their current equipment, massed forces, strategic deception, and operational concepts.

Bo had a potential solution. But his solution would need to be designed, built, and tested. And to achieve the element of surprise in a future conflict, it had to be done without the Americans or the Taiwanese knowing.

Bo had assembled the manufacturers of several of the PLA's small autonomous underwater vehicles and tasked them to design, develop, and test a mini submarine. This vessel would have to be more capable than the small unmanned underwater systems that had been captured by the Americans and Indonesians in the previous years. This mini submarine, which could be produced in large numbers, and totally in secret, would be networked with the PLA Navy's undersea sensor system, as well as with their submarine fleet. The small submersibles would be armed with four torpedoes and have just one mission—provide underwater security to turn the Taiwan Strait into a Chinese lake.

His next act as the leader of the new secret program at the academy had been to set up a field laboratory on the Yuan River in Hunan Province. Many of his superiors had initially been a little skeptical about whether Bo's approach would succeed. But as testing continued, and difficulties were ironed out, they had all become enthusiastic supporters of Bo's secret program.

The secrecy of the program was extraordinary. With the exception of Bo and several other senior military officers and scientists, all of the personnel involved in designing, building, and testing the craft were housed in the remote secure compound on the Yuan River. This was far enough from any other military or industrial complex that might otherwise interest the Americans. To further confuse their enemies, it was disguised to appear as a pig farm from the air and from the ground.

This was treated as a crash program by the senior leadership of the PLA and lavishly resourced with people and funding. Within a year (and after many failed attempts) a working prototype had been launched and tested on multiple occasions. The key tests had been centered on range and endurance. Given the length, width, and depth of the Yuan River—and the lakes it connected to in the north and west—this had been the ideal location for such a sensitive and important program.

Just over a year ago, the new autonomous submarine—named the *Mao Yu*, or spearfish—had begun to be manufactured in large numbers and shipped to coastal locations from where it might be discreetly deployed into the Taiwan Strait. None were permitted to be launched until the beginning of the joint exercise which had provided the cover story for the assembly of the invasion fleet.

Bo, looking across the water at the other ships of the amphibious task force on the way to Taiwan, smiled as he remembered both the disappointments and successes of the program. There were many, but his superiors had been tolerant of failure—as long as Bo and his scientists learned and improved next time.

If the *Mao Yu* were being employed in the invasion as he had envisaged, he was certain that there would be dozens of them within a few miles of the ship upon which he now stood. But that would be just a small proportion of the fleet. The vast majority of the *Mao Yu*, of which there were now several hundred, would be concentrated at the northern and southern parts of the strait, forming a line of invisible but lethal underwater guardians. Along with the other naval units and sensors, this would create an impenetrable barrier for the ships and submarines of the Americans and their allies. This maritime protective barrier was then supplemented with constant air cover provided by hundreds of manned and unmanned combat aircraft. Importantly, it would hopefully give Chinese naval and merchant vessels the best chance of successfully crossing the strait. Their simulated wargames in the past two years indicated that this was very likely.

Bo then thought about the second operational problem that he had worked on solving before his appointment to command his Marine brigade. It was a challenge that was at least as difficult as the smooth transit across the Taiwan Strait: the successful landing of the waves of combat troops on the invasion beaches on the west coast of Taiwan.

And not just landing. The PLA needed to rapidly get sufficient quantities of ground forces beyond the beach to engage in land combat, defeat the Taiwanese forces, and seize strategic targets such as ports, airports, and communications facilities. A final strategic target were the Taiwanese technology hubs in the Tainan, Taichung, and Taipei areas. If they could secure the design and manufacturing facilities for the world-leading semiconductors developed by the Taiwanese, China would dominate the world in the development of the most advanced semiconductors. It would place China in an enviable position for the coming decades.

The problem of successfully landing amphibious forces had no easy solution. Whether it was the amphibious operations attempted by the Persians and Greeks over two thousand years ago, Caesar's cross-channel transit to invade Britain, or the American landings at islands across the Pacific Theater in the Second World War, it was something that had bedeviled military leaders for millennia.

Assembling a naval fleet and loading the ground forces on the ships was difficult enough. However, the challenge did not stop with the successful arrival at a landing beach. No, troops had to be offloaded in a way that guaranteed enough of them were still alive to fight and to seize ground. And then fight again. And again, until the ultimate goal, supported by the amphibious landing, had been achieved.

At the same time, supporting forces also had to be landed. These included artillery, engineers, and logistics to both keep the landing site functioning as a pseudo arrival port for the invading force, and also to support the conduct of land combat. While all this was happening, the landing site—or sites—had to be protected against attack from the sea, ground, air, and in the electromagnetic spectrum. Wounded troops had to be treated and evacuated. A continuous feed of new troops had to be landed.

For the British and Americans in Europe, they had been fortunate to have to cross just 30 miles of water to get to their Normandy objectives in 1944. In the Pacific, the challenge had been much greater due to the enormous size of the operational theater. For the invasion of Okinawa in 1945, the American forces had transited from Guam, Ulithi, and locations much further afield.

So, if the PLA was able to construct the massive fleet of ships and aircraft to cross the strait, they still needed to fight their way ashore. To successfully do this in Taiwan, there were two issues. First, there were very few beaches capable of supporting the large-scale landings required to bring ashore sufficient troops to defeat the Taiwanese military forces. On the south western shore, there were only three or four suitable areas, and a similar number in the north west. Not only did this limit the options available to the Chinese, but it also allowed the Taiwanese to focus their defensive scheme of maneuver on just a few locations.

And the Taiwanese had prepared well. This resulted in a second issue for Bo's work: heavily defended landing beaches. All of the beaches that might be suitable for an amphibious assault by the PLA had been subject to decades of work to make them easier to defend. Physical obstacles had been constructed, with the intention of damaging landing craft and further channeling the landing forces into areas in which the Taiwanese could focus their firepower.

Beneath the water, extending well out to sea, were various types of "smart" and "dumb" sea mines. The Taiwanese, up until the last few years, had not made significant investments in these weapons.

However, the past three years had seen an energetic push from the government result in large minefields off beaches that might provide suitable landing sites for Chinese Marines and other amphibious forces.

Bo, and every other competent military planner, knew that Chinese forces landing at these beaches in the first waves would suffer massive casualties. Not only would this slow down the operation, but it would be a major blow to Chinese morale. Even in China, families had little tolerance for large human losses when most still only had a single child.

PLA doctrine stipulated there should be a preparatory phase before every landing, which would include large-scale bombardment by missiles, ground-attack aircraft, naval bombardment, and electronic warfare. However, this would still see significant defensive capabilities remaining under the water and from the waterline back up the beach and well inland.

But what if the first wave didn't need this preparation and was therefore able to achieve surprise? What if, as Bo had theorized in his paper, the first wave was entirely made up of low-signature autonomous systems that could aggregate to swarm and disaggregate when required? Systems that, together or by themselves, could destroy underwater mines, beach obstacles, bunkers, and military vehicles well before the first waves of humans landed in their more vulnerable landing craft?

Thus were born what Bo's scientists had named *Jia Chong*. Beetles.

So, in parallel with his oversight in developing the *Mao Yu*, Bo also led the design and development of a suite of small and mid-sized autonomous vehicles unlike any others deployed by military organizations around the world. They were amphibious and designed to be launched well offshore from ship decks, submarine torpedo tubes, and dropped in large quantities from low-flying cargo aircraft.

And they were stealthy. The craft were designed to have a very low profile in the water—in effect, the top of each vehicle would sit flush with the surface of the ocean. The only protuberance was a small marinized antenna which allowed it to orient itself using the BeiDou Navigational Satellite System, the Chinese equivalent of the American Global Positioning System. As a backup, in case the Americans destroyed the Chinese space-based navigation constellation, they were also able to use the Russian GLONASS or European GALILEO systems for navigation.

Some of the craft were small enough to be lifted by a single person and thrown off the stern of a ship. These smaller beetles were primarily designed to hunt and destroy mines in the surf zone off invasion beaches. With their various sensors, they were effective and very maneuverable.

These smart machines were fitted with clever algorithms that allowed them to swim, walk, avoid, or cross obstacles, as well as recognize and attack adversary systems. The first generation of beetles were quadrupeds. Modeled on developments in the West, they also utilized the best research and development in military and civil industry from China.

But these robotic quadrupeds were single-use entities. Once they found a mine, they were designed to self-destruct, destroying the mine and the beetle. It was a useful tool. But Bo would need more flexible robotic systems to fully realize his aspirations of a much more lethal human–robot force for the PLA.

The second generation of the new autonomous robots was larger. Because of the missions they would conduct, they needed to have better range and endurance. To improve their ability to carry heavy loads and more armor, and to better navigate over difficult landscapes, these were hexapods.

Called the *Beetle II*, or Jiakechong 2, these were designed to transit through the water and destroy obstacles on beaches. They were similar to the anti-mine beetles, in that they self-destructed in the process of clearing obstacles. The *Beetle II*s were also dual-use—effective against the armored vehicles as well as the bunkers that protected the Taiwanese soldiers waiting to mow down the landing PLA forces with machine guns and other heavy weapons.

Another model, based on the *Beetle II* chassis, was a UAV carrier. Essentially, once the *Beetle II* was ashore, it could launch a modest fleet of armed autonomous flying vehicles that could swarm and destroy soft targets with their small warheads. These were programmed to seek out radio transmitters—it didn't matter if they were military or civilian.

Finally, there was an electronic attack version of the vehicle, also based on the *Beetle II* chassis. It could conduct electronic reconnaissance and transmit data to a home station offshore that could collate the feeds from dozens of the autonomous vehicles. This data would then be analyzed by specially designed algorithms, and without requiring any human input or supervision, fed back into the beetle network ashore for hard kill where required. These beetles could also undertake localized jamming of enemy forces' communications.

Importantly, Bo and his colleagues had spent time ensuring that these new technologies could be integrated into the PLA's operational concepts. Key ideas, such as the "Informatized Local Wars" doctrine released in 2015, "Active Defense, system-of-system operations," and the recently released "Fifth Generation Operational Manual" were vital guides for his work. He was confident that his efforts of the last two years would contribute to the PLA's operations in Taiwan. At the same time, Bo hoped that this was only the beginning, and his research would drive further evolution in these important doctrinal publications for the PLA.

Bo understood that he was, as a Marine brigade commander, also the beneficiary of both inventions. They had been integrated into the

PLA's operational plans and used extensively since the beginning of the invasion. He understood that he, and the thousands of Marines that he commanded, now had a better chance of surviving long enough to land on the beach that had been assigned to his brigade.

Bo's attention shifted back to the present. He returned to thinking about the coming hours, and the mission of his brigade after they landed in Taiwan.

An hour ago Bo's staff had provided him with an update on the operational situation. The first wave of Chinese landing troops had been able to establish a beachhead line in accordance with the pre-landing plans. It had not been without opposition from the Taiwanese military. But the weight of PLA firepower, coupled with the successful use of the beetles on these southern landing beaches, had been sufficient to allow the Chinese to establish themselves ashore and begin advancing further inland toward their designated objectives.

Bo knew that the larger plan called for a series of long-range strikes. These would be conducted against a multitude of targets in Taiwan to degrade their air defense systems. American, Japanese, and other countries would also be targeted across the region. Airfields, fuel and ammunition storage facilities, major warships, and other establishments that might support any interference with the Chinese operations had all been battered as Bo's ship made its way across the strait.

The Chinese brigade commander, looking out across the water at the accompanying ships in this large naval task force carrying his marines, pondered how they had achieved this. For decades, the Chinese military had invested in short-, medium-, and long-range missile systems for just such a scenario. After the humiliation of the two aircraft carriers transiting the Taiwan Strait during the Clinton administration, the PLA had vowed to never again be found helpless in the face of American aggression.

A variety of tactical, theater, and intermediate-range ballistic missiles had been fielded by the PLA Rocket Force. These weapons, which supported the theater commands, focused on overwhelming Taiwanese defenses, as well as executing anti-access strategies to deny the Americans and their allies the opportunity to interfere with Chinese operations in the first and even second island chain.

The ballistic missiles were difficult to intercept. And despite the efforts of the Americans to develop defensive systems, if enough missiles were fired, some were going to penetrate a defensive shield and hit their targets. Likewise, the hypersonic missiles that would be fired by the Rocket Force were hard to intercept and gave defenders very little time to make decisions.

Bo smiled. *These strikes must have gone well*, he thought. The political officer had provided them with a summary during the operational update. Shortly afterwards, a message had been piped around the ship from the captain.

"Landing forces make ready. Prepare to land second-wave units."

Now, the second wave of troops was about to be put ashore. A second wave that included Bo's Marine brigade. He and his men had trained for this mission for the past two years. He understood that, despite the successful lodgment here in the south, there would be many days of hard fighting ahead. There would be death, destruction, pain, and sorrow. On both sides. But it was the destiny of the people of this island to return to the protection of China. Whether they knew it or not.

Bo stole one final look to the east, toward the island that would soon become part of China once again. The horizon was aglow with red and orange. There would clearly be a tough fight ahead. As he turned to make his way to the temporary command post aboard the ship, a junior Marine from his headquarters approached him. Out of breath, the man must have sprinted to find his brigade commander. He was sweating, and not from exertion. By the look on the Marine's face, something had happened that necessitated this message be passed verbally.

"Speak. What has happened?" Bo said.

Standing stiffly at attention, the Marine passed a short written message to Bo.

Bo looked down at the paper, reading quickly about how the Chinese task force to the north had been repulsed by the Americans and Japanese. Wanting to ponder the ramifications of what he had just read, Bo dismissed the young Marine.

Not everything had gone to plan for this massive PLA operation. In the north, despite some initial success, the first wave of the landing force had been repulsed by the defending Taiwanese and American forces. For some reason, a high proportion of the beetles there had either malfunctioned or navigated away from Taiwan instead of toward it. Enough American and Japanese naval vessels had survived the Rocket Force strikes to sortie south from Japanese waters and strike at the invasion fleet.

The first wave in the north, which had been assigned landing beaches around Taoyuan City, had failed. The initial landing forces, following on from the robotic beetles, had been slaughtered by Taiwanese and American long-range missiles, Air Force bombers and ground attack aircraft, and finally, by the defending troops on the ground.

Bo sighed. He knew this was not an auspicious start to the operation.

The simulations before the war had indicated that two different landing zones, one in the north and one in the south, gave the best chance of Chinese success in the invasion. Bo also knew that many of the simulation models were several years old, and had not been updated recently.

But there was an operational branch plan if this occurred. The theater commander had re-routed the remnants of the northern task force to reinforce the successful landings in the south. It meant that instead of a pincer movement from the north and the south, the PLA would now have to concentrate in the south and then advance north. It would have to fight all the way, across rivers, through cities, and over mountains.

Another inauspicious omen was the weather. A heavy rain squall had just passed over the fleet. Normally, this far south, the heaviest monsoon rains held off until June or July. But it looked like the rains in the south were coming early. Weather around the world was changing, and even the typhoon season around Taiwan and coastal China was much longer than it had been throughout recorded history. He should not see the early rains as an ill omen, but he could not help doing so. Military people were suspicious about such things, Bo contemplated.

As he turned and walked away from the railing, Bo had a final thought. *This is going to be a much harder fight, and take much longer, than we believed. I wonder how much of my brigade will be left when this is all over?*

12

Butcher's Bill

The ground forces were running out of most types of precision weapons and many of the types of ammunition for artillery, attack UAVs and UGVs, and tanks. Both the Taiwanese and the American ground forces had been fighting constantly. The Americans, working with their Japanese allies, had established secure sea and air lines of communications into Taiwan. It had taken two significant naval battles against the PLA Navy to achieve this. But the additional supply route would allow the flow in of reinforcements and logistic support.

The Chinese had gained a foothold in the south of the country. They had established air and sea lanes of supply across the strait, and this flow of logistics and personnel was allowing them to rapidly advance on key objectives in the Tainan–Linyuan area on the western coast.

The Taiwanese had proved to be tough opponents for the Chinese. But despite this, the Chinese were forcing the Taiwanese to retreat north along the coastal plain. At the same time, reserves of missiles and precision weapons for air and naval platforms were being run down at twice the rate of prewar estimates. Ship losses were also slightly more than prewar estimates.

"Cease the simulation, please," Admiral Leonard directed.

The 180-degree screen, which dominated the small conference room, froze. The thousands of red, blue, and green icons, previously moving at different speeds, appearing and disappearing, were now motionless. The room, part of a small complex that formed a secure underground alternate headquarters facility under the hills of Oahu's Waimanalo Forest Reserve, was silent. Originally begun during the Second World War, the facility had never been completed. After the Battle of Midway, it had become clear that the threat to Hawaii—from sea and air—had been significantly reduced. Scarce resources in the Pacific could be used more effectively than for building a large underground complex that was unlikely to be required to defeat the Japanese forces.

But a decade ago, with the realization of the importance of INDOPACOM in the 21st century, Congress had funded an expensive enlargement of the old tunnels so that the headquarters had a robust capacity to survive any long-range missile strike on Hawaii. The Army Engineers, working with their contractors, had finished the project in early 2022. The headquarters had regularly practiced operating out of the subterranean facility, just in case.

A week ago, those precautions had paid off—but there was a price. The smoking ruins of his headquarters building, under which still lay the bodies of dozens of his staff, were testament to the wisdom of those preparations. The shelter occupied by Leonard and his staff in the hills was of little consolation to those who had not been able to evacuate before the attack, however. Or their families who lived in the surrounding area, and who were reminded each day of their loss by the ribbons of smoke swirling into the clear Hawaii skies.

The smoke, although reducing each day, was visible from across Honolulu.

Leonard looked across the table at the briefing officer before speaking again.

"How many of these near-future planning simulations have we conducted over the past 24 hours?" he asked.

Simulations like these, with thousands of real-time data inputs from across the command and beyond, and driven by very specialized artificial intelligence algorithms, were an important part of decision making at the headquarters of the Indo-Pacific Command. The computers didn't make decisions themselves, but they had become a more important part of informed, evidence-based prioritization and command and control.

Opposite Leonard sat Mike Swadling, the Director of the J4 Branch at the headquarters. He was responsible for logistics and engineering across the theater. A US Army brigadier general, he had spent much of his career in the Pacific region.

"Sir, we have run several thousand iterations of the simulation, including multiple potential branch plans and sequels. We have also changed some of the variables, including contributions from allies, and degrees of air and maritime security over the island and the region between Japan, Taiwan, and Hawaii," Swadling responded. "The simulation runs forward in hourly increments through to three months from now. The results you are seeing are not the situation now, but as we project the worst-case logistic situation may be in three months' time."

Swadling paused for a moment. He knew that this was not the news that Leonard, and the other staff around the table, had been expecting.

"So, Mike, despite our higher-than-expected usage rates, we still have sufficient stocks of key weapons, ammunition, and fuel for at least the next three months?" Leonard responded. He had been expecting worse news from this meeting. It also went against many of the academic studies of conflict in the Pacific that had been conducted in the last few years.

"Sir, the quiet mobilization of industry in the past year, especially in the last few months, has seen a significant surge in production. It has meant that our production is almost meeting demand. The Japanese have also been able to increase production, and they have been able to provide some excess stock to us. It is the same with the Aussies. Their government's decision a couple of years ago to develop their own munitions production capability has taken a liability away from our industry, and they have been able to provide additional stocks into an alliance reserve munitions and precision weapons arsenal that we have built up at several locations."

The large screen at the head of the room went blank for a moment. It then came to life with a view of the Pacific, which stretched from the American west coast all the way to the Taiwanese east coast. Overlaid on this were old and new supply depots, as well as shipping routes that transported their precious cargoes from manufacturers to warehouses and all the way to theater storage locations.

"What about shipping and other transport to ensure there is a sufficient flow of materials from factories all the way to our theater logistics hubs?" Leonard asked.

It had been a constant challenge in this conflict, as it had been in every war since the first industrial revolution had permitted the large-scale manufacture of standardized military supplies. It was one matter to be able to build all the war materiel required by commanders in a theater of war. But there was also the accompanying challenge of being able to move that material to where it was needed, in the quantities required, by a specified time.

"So far," Swadling replied, "it appears that the Chinese have largely refrained from kinetic targeting of our supply chain. If they target our supply lines all the way back to the United States, they might

139

believe that we will respond in kind with stepped-up attacks on Chinese soil. That would not play well with their domestic audience. Such kinetic attacks would also quickly deplete their holdings of long-range missiles.

"It has not, however, stopped them from conducting misinformation campaigns and cyber-attacks on industry and some civilian infrastructure in our homeland."

Leonard nodded. In his daily update to the secretary of defense, the chairman of the Joint Chiefs, and the president, he had been kept abreast of these events back in the United States. While they had not made a major impact on the manufacturing side of his country's war-making potential, the psychological impact on government leaders and the population had been profound.

Despite this, the Congress had actually come together in the past week. It had been acting in a more unified way than Leonard could remember, at least since the immediate aftermath of the 9/11 attacks. It had been a shame that it had taken the death and destruction of the last month to drive such bipartisan action.

Developments in other segments of the American community had not been as positive. The tech community had taken a largely neutral stance on many of the Chinese and Russian cyber activities against the American people online. Much had been done over the last few years to secure networks in government, academia, and industry. But there were, and would always be, weaknesses that their adversaries could exploit. The tech industry, despite some notable exceptions, preferred to remain on the sidelines and sell its software.

Academia had been split over the new conflict. Many had immediately supported the administration and the defense of a small democracy in the western Pacific. There were important values at stake in defending Taiwan. And there were practical realities as well. If America's allies in the region watched it stand by and not help Taiwan, it would undermine the entire alliance framework in the western Pacific.

Not all were as pragmatic. A strong isolationist sentiment had emerged in some elements of academia, the media, and even some parts of Congress. They were not a loud voice, but they made the administration's job to fund the war effort, manage allies, and reallocate resources in the economy just that little bit more difficult. All of these divisions had been exacerbated by a bitterly contested presidential election year.

These thoughts all passed through Leonard's mind in a matter of seconds. They were part of a new normal that had been established in the last few weeks. But there was little he could do about the situation back home, other than keep his superiors informed and continue to seek resources to win the fight out here in the Pacific. There was not much to be gained by worrying about things he had no control over. His attention returned to the room and the briefing session he was part of.

It was time for an operations update. The pace of operations had been more rapid than anything Leonard had experienced before. Even though they had tested their operational tempo in large-scale wargames over the past several years, the pace of military activity had outstripped even his expectations.

There were several factors driving this. First, the new hypersonic weapons that had been deployed by the Chinese had condensed the time available to commanders to make decisions. They were difficult weapons to detect, and when there were several hypersonic missiles headed toward a major base, important decisions on defense and evacuation had to be made very quickly.

The pace of operational tempo had also been sped up by decision making that was now supported by very good artificial intelligence. Both the Americans and the Chinese had worked hard to corral their military data over the last few years. This had made their use of military algorithmic support more efficient and effective. It had helped them to think and act much faster at the tactical level. The increased tempo of American activities had overwhelmed the Taiwanese at certain times in the past few days. And it had challenged government ministers in Taiwan and the United States to reassess their traditionally slow and orderly strategic decision-making processes and committees.

But the American application of AI had also allowed for rapid joint activities where hundreds of concurrent actions could be better coordinated and deconflicted. On multiple occasions in the past week, the Chinese had learned that their concept of intelligentization applied to both sides of war. And the Chinese had paid dearly for it.

Leonard looked across the table at the officer responsible for joint operations across INDOPACOM, also known as the J3. A US Navy two-star officer, Rear Admiral Jane Davis was a naval aviator who had risen to command her own Carrier Strike Group prior to this appointment. A fit, petite woman with a permanent scowl, she was responsible for the coordination and orchestration of a complex range of military operations across all the domains. Like Leonard, she had also spent a large proportion of her career in billets at sea in the Pacific or in staff jobs in the Pentagon.

Davis understood the Pacific theater. She had spent years on deployments in the western Pacific and knew well the intricacies of working alongside their allies. The challenges of a contested air and maritime environment that extended for hundreds of miles beyond the Chinese coastline were clearly understood by Davis and her large staff.

Rear Admiral Davis, while running operations, also needed to coordinate operations with subordinate commands in Japan and Korea, as well as the different component commands that worked with the INDOPACOM headquarters. It required an open mind, a deft touch with people, and the ability to compromise. She had developed a balanced approach during her time as the J3, which focused on achieving her commanders' outcomes while also seeking to meet the needs of subordinate commands. It wasn't always easy, and at times her job required her to engage in some clever horse trading about time, resources, and priorities. But the investment in relationships that Davis had made in the preceding years was now paying off. The trust between senior leaders in the command was able to overcome the stress of combat, the extreme challenge of meeting the tactical and logistic needs of forward deployed units, and the pressure emanating from Washington, DC.

Davis looked up at the screen first to ensure the diagram that supported her update was showing. "Admiral, over the past month, we have been able to significantly attrit the PLA Navy surface fleet as well as their Air Force. So far, we have sunk or badly damaged 30 percent of their Type 55s, 40 percent of their Luyang destroyers and around 20 percent of their frigates. We have also been plinking their corvettes and Coast Guard vessels, and we believe we have inflicted serious losses—approximately 50 percent—on this part of their fleet.

"This is having an impact on their capacity to undertake operations beyond securing the Taiwan Strait. They have been able to sortie a second carrier attack group, based on the *Shandong*, after we sank the *Liaoning*. While we have been able to leverage the sinking for our info ops, the Chinese have been successful at the deception operations around this second carrier group. We are yet to confirm its location."

Leonard nodded. American and Japanese vessels had been spectacularly successful in the opening days of the war in taking a significant portion of the Chinese fleet off the board. So much for the armchair experts' predictions, he thought, peering at the diagram on the screen as Davis continued her update briefing.

"The strait unfortunately remains a no-go zone for our maritime and air assets. The combination of their conventional subs and their new UUVs has ensured that penetrating the strait has become almost impossible for friendly submarines. Both the Japanese and Australians have lost boats in the past 72 hours trying to sneak around a defensive line of Chinese crewed and autonomous submarines. One of our Virginia-class boats that was operating in the strait before the invasion remains unaccounted for."

Davis continued speaking for several minutes. She outlined a more detailed list of Chinese warships and support vessels that had been sunk in the past week. It was an impressive list, Leonard thought. Davis then outlined the American and allied vessels lost since the Chinese had commenced their invasion. It was a shorter list, but still sobering. And not all vessels had been sunk or damaged on the high seas. A significant proportion had been sunk alongside their piers before they had been able to put to sea in the ports of Yokosuka, Guam, Darwin, and elsewhere.

"The Chinese DF-ZF hypersonic missile and the DF-21 anti-ship ballistic missiles have been very effective. The DF-ZF is a hypersonic missile delivery system that can carry both nuclear and conventional payloads. Travelling at speeds between Mach 5 and Mach 10, it is hard to track and difficult to kill. Fitted to the DF-21 missile, such a hypersonic warhead has a range of nearly 2,000 miles. But not all of them have been able to penetrate American and Japanese anti-ballistic missile shields."

The CIA, which had been collecting intelligence on these missiles for many years, had briefed Leonard and his most senior commanders that there were limited numbers of the missiles in stock. The CIA had several excellent sources inside the PLA's strategic rocket force. More importantly, over the last decade it had also developed sources inside the China Changfeng Mechanics and Electronics

Technology Academy—manufacturers of these missiles that were crucial to Chinese war plans.

Leonard had also asked his plans and cyber staffs to collaborate with the strategic Cyber Command and the CIA to develop a strategic interruption plan for the manufacturers of key Chinese missiles and their components. It had long been a contingency, but because of other priorities, had not been given sufficient attention. Until now.

Leonard hoped that, within the week, there would be a comprehensive plan that he could endorse and launch to shut down the Chinese missile industry. Much of the cyber reconnaissance, planning, and analysis on the different networks had been conducted in the last decade. However, the security on both military and industrial networks continued to evolve and improve. Friendly cyber teams needed to understand changes in the Chinese protocols, while also preparing for an orchestrated and simultaneous strike to destroy the Chinese capacity to continue producing these missiles. Even with the urgency demanded by Leonard and the secretary of defense, it would take time to pull it all together.

But that was for the future. And while future plans were important, there were multiple priorities that were demanding his attention now. And there was one in particular concerning Leonard. The fight on the ground.

He returned his focus to Rear Admiral Davis, who had waited for him to look up. She was quickly checking her notes before continuing. Sensing Leonard's attention on her again, she looked up.

"Jane, where are we with the Taiwanese ground campaign?"

A grim look replaced her normal scowl.

"Sir, the latest update is not good. It is now clear that the fight for the possession of the island will be a slug fest until the end. The Taiwanese, despite some successes, are conducting a deliberate and orderly withdrawal north. The assassinations of key political and military figures in the first days of the Chinese campaign have had some impact on their operations as well. Demonstrations in several cities, some of them fostered by Chinese sympathizers as well as social media, are occupying police, as well as delaying the mobilization of reserve forces."

Leonard nodded. He had expected this news, even if it wasn't welcome.

Rear Admiral Davis continued speaking.

"The rainy season is also in full force. These rains, which we expected and planned for, are causing some delays in offloading ships and with tactical resupply operations."

She paused for a moment and then delivered a final piece of information.

"We expect the typhoon season to begin, as normal, in mid-July and continue through to October. Sir, that concludes my briefing, and I am happy to answer any questions."

Leonard nodded. The discussion about ground operations and weather had sparked an idea. However, almost as quickly as it had raised itself in his consciousness, it was gone again. He would need to think about that. But Leonard had one final question.

"What is the tactical situation with our American ground forces?"

Davis had not been looking forward to this part of her briefing. Beginning her update on the American ground forces engaged in combat in Taiwan, she uttered just a single word.

"Dire."

AUTHOR'S NOTE (II)

Contained on this page is a map that has been recreated using the data from the tactical arm screen of (then) Colonel Jack Furness. It shows the situation on 14 June 2028.

TAIWAN SITUATION: DIGITAL OVERLAY

141130ZJUN 2028
SOURCE: FURNESS, J, COL USMC (TACTICAL ARM SCREEN)

Chinese Beach Landing Zone A
(Unsuccessful)

KEELUNG CITY

Chinese Beach Landing Zone B
(Unsuccessful)

TAIPEI

TOUCHENG

HSINCHU CITY

ZHUDONG

TAICHUNG CITY

HUALIEN

Forward Line of Chinese Troops

CHIAYI CITY

Chinese Advance

Chinese Beach Landing Zone C
(Actual)

TAINAN CITY

KAOHSIUNG CITY

Chinese Beach Landing Zone D
(Actual)

DECLASSIFIED MAY 2035

13

Retreat, Hell

14 June 2028
Near Zhudong
Northwestern Taiwan

"Thank goodness that is over. These are only getting harder."

Colonel Jack Furness slowly lowered his right hand, ensuring the completion of his salute was in accordance with Marine Corps regulations. It was the least he could do. The final salute accorded to fallen Marines, as they were farewelled from their unit, should be by the book, Furness thought. As he concluded his salute, he turned briefly to look at his segreant major, standing off to his left.

"Roger that, Sir. Worse than Afghanistan."

They had both farewelled Marines killed in combat before.

"This is the absolute worst part of command," Furness replied. "No matter how many times we lose our Marines—in combat, during training, and even in car accidents back home—it is always a kick in the guts. It is the one thing that I truly despise about this job."

Military leaders, especially those who had lost people in combat, used many ways to console themselves at times like this. For Furness, his salve was poetry. Growing up, his father had imbued the younger Furness with a love of reading, and this included verse. While for many years he hadn't had much opportunity to read poetry—there were too many books on future conflict and politics to absorb—in the last two years he had returned to it.

At moments such as this, when he was about as low as it was possible to be, he had kept with him a poem, written by a New York priest called Charles Fink who had served in Vietnam. It was as poignant a poem as Furness could imagine. While it might induce deep melancholy in some people, for Jack Furness, reading it was a way of rebounding from the sadness of the deaths of young Marines in his charge.

Over the last two weeks, he had used Fink's words so many times over the bodies of his fallen that he no longer needed to read the words. They had been etched into his memory. He concluded the small ceremony by speaking part of Fink's poem quietly:

> The troops I know were commonplace;
> They didn't want the war
> They fought because their fathers and
> Their father's fathers had before.
> They cursed and killed and wept—
> God knows they're easy to deride—
> But bury me with men like these;
> They faced the guns and died.

The godawful thing was, Furness knew he would be doing this again. And again, and again, before this was all over.

These kicks in the guts, the terrible sickening feeling he always got when losing his Marines, would not be going away anytime in the near future. It was a rolling wave of sorrow that he, his sergeant major, and everyone else in his unit would need huge reservoirs of resilience to bear—and to continue on with their mission.

"You know, Sergeant Major, this is nothing like Afghanistan."

For Furness, his crucible had been the dusty, hot river valleys of Helmand Province. It had been his generation of Marines' baptism of fire.

"Many of us just missed deploying to Iraq. But all of us deployed on multiple tours of Helmand Province."

They had worked alongside the British and Afghan National Army, to bring some sense of stability and security to the local people.

Furness' senior non-commissioned officer stood silently, knowing his regimental commander was in a reflective mood. Furness would speak when he was ready.

That Afghanistan had all been for naught, given the catastrophe of 2021, did not play on Furness' mind. He, like all those that had served there, had done their duty. The fact that the Afghan government had eventually collapsed due to its own corruption and ineptitude was not a judgment on Furness or any of the other tens of thousands of military personnel who had served and sacrificed in that graveyard of empires over a two-decade period.

In Afghanistan, farewelling fallen Marines (and Navy Corpsmen) had been a very different affair. There was the security and time to have memorial services and proper ramp ceremonies involving all members of the fallen Marine's unit. What had made that experience even worse, if there was something worse than losing Marines, was the death of his fiancée Maria while he was deployed.

They had met while he was at the academy, and she was at college training as a medical intern in a small hospital close to the Marine base. Almost from the first day, they had been inseparable. Furness would often pick up his tired fiancée after long shifts at the hospital. But while he had been in Afghanistan, she had not had anyone to pick her up after these exhausting, hours-long shifts at the hospital. It had been after one of these shifts, exhausted and slow in her reactions, that she had driven under a semi-trailer truck.

Furness did not, and never would, forgive himself. He had not been there.

At least he had been there for his Marines in Helmand. He had been able to honor them appropriately and spend time with the men and women of his platoon to comfort them and listen to their heartache and questions.

But here, it was nothing like that. Here, where America did not own the skies and units could be attacked by PLA fighter-bombers, high-flying autonomous "bomb trucks" or swarms of lethal autonomous ground and aerial vehicles, and constant electronic warfare, life was very different. Standing out in the open meant you would be detected very quickly by the sensor network that the PLA had deployed to Taiwan.

Therefore, the farewell for these fallen Marines had been a small affair, with just Furness and several others conducting a solemn but short ceremony. Furness imagined that this was like what his forebears had endured at places such as Tarawa, Iwo Jima, and Okinawa. It was an unceasing maelstrom of death, suffering, and blood.

One's end here could come silently and quickly, or it might involve long, drawn-out suffering. Either way, fatalism had sunk in with the Marines. Most assumed it was only a matter of time before death or disfigurement came their way. Even Furness.

He looked up at the layers of camouflage above them as he walked away from the small assembly of his people. The use of such signature reduction measures to reduce their detectability was now the norm. Using an assortment of flying and ground-based autonomous systems, all kinds of signatures could be detected and fed into the Chinese military kill net. Smells (especially vehicle exhaust), noise of any kind, light, heat, and other signatures all made the American and Taiwanese vulnerable to detection. And if they could be detected, they could be targeted and killed.

151

Of course, they had known this when they deployed to the island. But the reality was very different. And the five Marines that Furness had just attended a ceremony for had joined the growing number who had learned the ultimate lesson of signature management.

It was the first time in nearly a century that American ground forces had had to be concerned about attack from the air. The early years of the Second World War had seen both Japanese and German air fleets used very effectively against US military targets. But eventually, as the joint might of the American and Russian war machines ground down the Axis powers, the threat from the air receded.

The wars of the second half of the 20th century had largely been absent of air threats. While the North Koreans and Chinese (with Soviet aid) had put up a solid fight in the air during the Korean War, it had not been decisive. The war in the air in Vietnam had been one-sided, as had Iraq and Afghanistan in the early 20th century.

But despite the preponderance of American airpower, those wars had still been lost.

The skies of Taiwan had been flooded with PLA fighters, fighter-bombers, bombers, and UAVs of all kinds and sizes. American and Taiwanese aircraft and ground-based air defense systems, however, had shot hundreds of Chinese aircraft out of the sky in the preceding weeks.

And the Americans, including the 1st Marine Air Wing which was now forward deployed and supporting Furness and other Marine units, had lost dozens of fixed- and rotary-wing aircraft in the past week alone. A situation the airpower theorists called "air parity" now existed over the island. Neither side could gain a permanent advantage or dominance in the air. They could, however, seize on situations where they might achieve a temporary advantage.

Two days before, Furness' unit had been deployed from its locations in the north of Taiwan to new positions in the western portion of the island nation. The city of Zhudong, to the southwest of Taipei, had been the location of a large-scale airborne assault by Chinese forces as part of the initial invasion. They had hoped to conduct a coup de main, cutting off supply lines between Taiwanese forces in the north and south, while also opening an airbridge that might support an advance on Taipei. These airborne forces were then to link up with ground forces landing over the beaches in the north of the country. It had not worked out that way.

The amphibious force had been mauled by a joint US–Taiwanese–Japanese air-sea task force. The Marine Littoral Regiment, commanded by Furness, had accounted for many of the sunk and damaged Chinese vessels. Most had been the Type 72 amphibious landing ship variants and Type 74 medium landing ships. They had, however, been credited with a shared kill, with the Taiwanese coastal defense forces, of one of the new Type 71 amphibious landing docks, similar to the US Navy's San Antonio-class ships.

It had only been possible because Furness' regiment's anti-ship missile battery had been integrated within the defensive scheme for northern Taiwan early in its deployment. The integration of the command, control, and sensor elements of the US and Taiwanese systems would normally not have occurred during exercises for security reasons. But, given the problem at hand, Americans and Taiwanese technical folks had found a workaround that allowed Furness' anti-ship battery to work as a sub-element of the Taiwanese coastal defense network.

It had been satisfying to know that those who had hypothesized about the lethality of a unit like the one commanded by Furness had been thinking along the right pathways about future warfare. There had been many doubters. But, given their contribution to repelling the Chinese in their attempts at northern amphibious landings, Furness considered the matter settled.

Those few Chinese vessels that had gotten close to the northern Taiwanese landing beaches had been sunk or turned away by smart mines and coastal defense missiles. Weeks later, the bodies of Chinese sailors, Marines, soldiers, and even Coast Guard forces continued to wash up on the beaches of Taiwan's northwestern coastline. And while the local municipal authorities had been diligent in collecting and burying bodies, the sheer numbers involved still overwhelmed their capacity. The awful, putrid smell of rotting human bodies was a feature of many social media posts by people who lived in the area.

But while the amphibious force had suffered and been repulsed, the Chinese airborne forces had been able to successfully lodge a large force numbering several thousand. The PLA had maintained an Airborne Corps at high readiness long before the current war. With six airborne brigades and a special force unit, it was a highly lethal and fast-moving force that was perfect for what the Chinese had attempted in the Zhudong area.

The Chinese had hoped that the airborne forces would cause significant confusion in the northern parts of Taiwan, allowing the amphibious troops to establish themselves ashore. Most of the paratroopers had landed in an area between Zhudong and Hsinchu City. Captured maps indicated that their primary objectives had been the Taiwanese Air Force base at Hsinchu City, the major bridges that crossed the Touchien River, and the Taiwan Semiconductor Manufacturing Company fabrication factories in Hsinchu.

They had succeeded in the first two objectives. At least initially. After the shock of the airborne assault had worn off, the Taiwanese Army had launched ground and air attacks over a three-day period that had retaken the airfield and the bridges. The semiconductor factory was a different story. The Taiwanese had decided not to waste troops on retaking the factory. They had dispatched several dozen suicide drones which had destroyed the building within hours of its being seized by the Chinese paratroopers.

These actions from the previous weeks were weighing on Furness' mind as he entered his regimental command post outside Zhudong. It was small and designed to be highly mobile. It could be broken down and packed up in vehicles in under ten minutes. If they suspected that they had been discovered by the enemy, it was unlikely they would have much more time than that before suicide drones, UGVs, or even long-range precision missiles might be dispatched their way.

It was also a useful shelter from the rain. The monsoon had arrived in full force, and rains were now a daily occurrence. Often, these were torrential downpours that would soak Furness' Marines to the skin in a matter of seconds.

It was raining again as Furness walked toward his small headquarters. Greeted by his executive officer and intelligence officer, Furness strode directly into a small annex of his field headquarters that was used as a briefing room. It was a tiny group of his senior staff, representing each of his subordinate units. The air in the small tent was thick with moisture. Some of the participants were wet, having been caught out in the open without their rain ponchos.

Jack Furness looked at the faces of his command team. Each was clearly weary. Their uniforms and body armor were uniformly filthy—bathing had not exactly been a high-priority item on their agendas in the previous days. But the men were all shaven and all of them—male and female—had freshly applied camouflage paint on their faces.

As Furness turned to speak with them, several of them smiled. *There is not much to smile about*, he thought. Especially for the infantry battalion. With losses approaching 20 percent of their strength in the last week alone, it had been a tough war since mid-May.

"Good morning, team. It is good to see you all. I have just returned from farewelling our casualties from yesterday."

Furness looked at the commander of his logistics battalion. The dead Marines that he had farewelled today had been from a maintenance and repair team that had been killed when several Chinese autonomous ground combat vehicles had discovered the Marines' camouflaged vehicle maintenance location the previous evening. Furness' regiment had been in the area for less than 24 hours.

"How are your folks doing?" Furness asked soberly.

The logistics battalion commander, who by now had become used to an almost daily casualty toll, responded with a nod and then a brief update on the status of his unit. He finished with what had become the normal conclusion to unit updates for the regimental commander over the last few days: "Despite that, we remain mission capable."

Furness nodded.

The definition of "mission capable" now was very different to what it had been a few months ago. Then, it had been a function of how many of their personnel billets were filled, how much of their stockholdings were on hand, and where they were in their training program. Now, it was solely about being able to complete the task at hand. With whatever people and resources were available.

Furness began his update. It was why he had assembled his senior commanders in person, instead of issuing orders over the encrypted digital command system.

"The commander of the 3rd Marine Division has just confirmed that we will now be transferred under his command. His headquarters, despite the significant casualties and material losses they experienced just after offloading at the port, are now in place and operational. Our division will be the center division for the Taiwanese northern Army Corps. While they have had a little respite because the amphibious lodgment did not occur in the north, the

Corps has been tasked with a clear-and-destroy mission. We are to assist in finding and destroying the remainder of the Chinese parachute corps. We will also retain our guard mission to detect and attack any maritime and air targets to the west."

With the deployment of the entirety of the 3rd Marine Division to the island, Furness' unit had come back under the operational control of an American two-star general. The general had been a clever and courageous leader who had given his subordinate division commanders a lot of latitude in the conduct of their missions. His Taiwanese boss had also been a fine proponent of mission orders, which provided clear intent and boundaries and then allowed subordinates to achieve missions in the best manner they saw fit. He would miss his Taiwanese commander.

But it was inevitable that his regiment would eventually come back under the command of an American general. American politicians and military leaders were by nature uncomfortable having their combat forces under the command of other nations. Even close allies. But given how the situation in the war had evolved, it had been appropriate for Furness' regiment to shift from working for the Taiwanese 6th Corps back to an American formation.

Furness looked up from the notes in his arm computer to see a young corporal run into the briefing tent. Instinctively he knew that something bad had happened. The look on the corporal's face said it all.

"What is it Corporal?"

The corporal, who was fit and hardly out of breath, did not hesitate to respond to his commander.

"Sir, our attached Army cavalry company. And Captain Lee. They're gone."

14

Adaptation Battle

14 June 2028
Near Zhudong
Northern Taiwan

These fucking beetles, Lee thought, *although they look more like spiders.*

She stood alongside her squadron sergeant major, as well as several other troopers from her unit. Sergeant James was also present. Lee squinted against the bright sun as she peered down the rough hillside. Dominating her view was a wide river valley that cut across the western part of the island from east to west. About half a mile down the hill were the remains of several dozens of the Chinese mid-sized autonomous ground combat vehicles. Most had been wrecked beyond all hope of repair. Several had self-destructed, as they had been programmed to do, if they were within a lethal radius of an American or Taiwanese armored vehicle.

Whoever designed these things really knew their shit, Lee thought.

Ever since the initial Chinese onslaught against Taiwan back in May, these autonomous ground vehicles, which the intelligence folks had begun to call "beetles," had been all over their area of operations. Crawling out of the ocean across Taiwan's western shore, they had

158

caused massive damage to beach obstacles and defensive positions from the beach line and well inshore.

Sergeant James broke the silence as the small group stared collectively at the carnage before them lower down the hillside.

"Ma'am, the latest intelligence update has just arrived. I can read out the highlights if you would like."

Lee turned and nodded, watching as James scrolled through layers of information on his arm screen. James began speaking.

"In the north, an American and Japanese naval task force destroyed most Chinese naval forces aiming to land in the area of operations where we were operating until a few days ago. It sounds like it has been a decisive naval battle. Both sides have lost frigates and destroyers. Even some of the PLA's new Type 55 Renhai destroyers with their 112 vertical launch systems were sunk."

This brought an ugly smile to some of the faces of those present. Not Lee. She took no pleasure in the deaths of thousands of naval personnel in the waters off Taiwan. Even if it did mean her troopers now had a better chance of survival. She remained silent, contemplative, as James continued his short update to the group.

"Apparently, some of our vessels were able to use a new laser defense system as well as swarms of marinized versions of the Phoenix Ghost killer drone developed for Ukraine. The report assesses that because of this, American and Japanese ships have been able to survive and hit back; the Chinese have not."

James paused again, waiting for any questions. There were none.

"The media are now calling it the Battle of North Taiwan Strait. Over the last couple of weeks, the info ops communities on both sides have been fighting to gain the initiative in the global analysis of what happened and what the impacts might be on the wider Taiwan War."

Lee, silent until now, interrupted.

"It will be like every other naval battle in history. And I expect that, just like the debate over the roles of Admirals Jellicoe and Beatty after the Battle of Jutland, this naval battle would be argued over by generations of historians who will fight about who turned when, and who should have signaled what."

Lee's sergeant major, a gruff 20-year veteran, then joined the discussion.

"I suppose that is good news. But it hasn't stopped the fucking beetles."

Unlike the tens of thousands of Chinese Marines aboard the sunken ships, thousands of the robotic beetles had made it ashore. They had continued to wreak havoc for the last few weeks. The beetles had been a major technological and tactical surprise. Their appearance had stunned Taiwanese defenders. While the use of autonomous systems had been anticipated, the beetles and their ability to stealthily approach the Taiwanese mainland before carrying out a range of different missions had resulted in considerable shock and confusion in the initial days of the invasion.

At the same time that the northern Chinese amphibious task force was being annihilated, a Chinese airborne assault force had managed to land several brigades' worth of troops in the northwest of the country. And the airborne troops were not just good fighters and hardy soldiers. They were apparently well trained in partnering with the beetles. Another surprise. As Lee's unit had found out in the past several hours.

Yesterday had begun with the Marine Littoral Regiment, including Lee's cavalry squadron, moving from the north to the vicinity of Zhudong. The Littoral Regiment had been given a mission to conduct maritime attacks against any Chinese vessels approaching Hsinchu City from the west. For Lee, her unit was responsible for reconnaissance tasks and providing early warning of enemy ground and air attacks against the Littoral Regiment.

Intelligence reports that they had received before moving south indicated that there would be significant enemy activity in the vicinity of Hsinchu and Zhudong. Hsinchu was a major city on the west coast. They hoped to avoid entanglement in its urban sprawl. Instead, the Marines and soldiers would deploy to the east of the city, in and around the smaller townships of the Zhudong area.

On arrival, they discovered that, for once, the intelligence reports were exactly right. Covering an area on the far east of the regiment's area of responsibility, Lee's UGV and UAV sentinels had shortly thereafter detected a large Chinese formation of airborne troops that had teamed with beetles and autonomous aerial swarms. The Chinese, moving from the south and obviously headed toward Hsinchu City, had made contact with Lee's troops around 20 minutes after the first reports from their autonomous sentinels.

The Chinese had initially launched a hasty attack in an attempt to brush past Lee's unit and continue its advance into Hsinchu City. This demonstrated a level of desperation from the Chinese. They were cut off from the Chinese forces in the south and had yet to achieve any of their tactical objectives in the north.

The ability of the PLA airborne troops to effectively orchestrate humans and robots in the encounter battle had shocked many of Lee's troopers. In a brutal but brief exchange, several of Lee's armored vehicles—and their crews—had been lost, along with multiple UGVs. But Lee's troopers had held their ground. And their autonomous systems in the air and on the ground had performed well.

Throughout the short, sharp action, they had been without any kind of air support. They had become used to that. After several generations of owning the skies, US ground troops were slowly getting used to Chinese aircraft owning the skies for significant portions of each day. There were increasing periods when American and Taiwanese air defense systems, autonomous aerial patrol planes, and crewed aircraft were able to gain primacy. But the battle between Lee's troops and the Chinese had occurred when allied air support had been unavailable.

They had been able to work around this. However, if not for the artillery support provided by Colonel Furness and his attached artillery unit, there might have been a different outcome. The resistance provided by Lee's squadron, with the artillery support, had been enough for the Chinese to disengage and withdraw. After the battle, the junior officers and non-commissioned officers had rapidly shared observations about the tactics, and human–machine teaming approaches, of their Chinese attackers.

Before the deployment, Lee had discovered a couple of papers in the military professional journals about learning and adapting during combat. One thing had led to another, and pretty soon she was devouring books, papers, and blog posts on the topic. In essence, she wanted to ensure that her squadron was not only better trained and more capable than the enemy, but also that they learned more quickly and adapted more effectively based on what they learned in combat.

She had studied how military organizations, regardless of era or service, invariably got the next war wrong. However, as American scholar Williamson Murray had written, "One of the foremost attributes of military effectiveness must lie in the ability to recognize and adapt to the actual conditions of combat, as well as to the new challenges that war inevitably throws up." It was probably one of her favorite quotes. She often pondered this idea. Lee had also used the core idea to evolve their pre-deployment training, and in her discussions with her senior leaders in the squadron, to discuss how they might best recognize changes in combat and other tactical operations, and then adapt to them.

This approach had paid off. Several hours later, the Chinese had come again. This time the enemy had coordinated their assault with attacks on the ground, from the air, and in the electromagnetic spectrum. It was this battle, and its aftermath, that Lee and her squadron senior leaders had gathered to discuss as they looked down the hillside.

They had also maximized the impact of a heavy rainstorm that was passing through the area. Not only did it make it difficult for the enemy to see them from their positions on the ground; it was also a challenge for their UAVs to pick out the heat signatures of humans amid the rain.

"That was an interesting night. I'm not sure any of our preparations at the National Training Center really prepared us for how the Chinese fought last night. We will need to do more analysis on their human–machine teaming, networking, and the emergent tactics from that teaming."

"Ma'am," Sergeant James said, "as you taught us and as we have been discussing over the last few weeks, we are in an adaptation battle with the PLA. We need to fight better, but also think better and faster."

Lee was now used to his observations. They had shared an armored vehicle for several months now. She appreciated his intelligence and his willingness to make insightful observations. Even when they might be seen as critical of different leaders in the squadron.

"Apparently this was the site of a glorious Chinese victory," Lee responded.

The gathered soldiers all looked at her. The carnage downhill was obvious proof to the contrary.

"I just received a short update from the regimental intelligence officer. She informs me that the battle here is already being represented as a major victory on Chinese social media. They even have footage of one of our destroyed vehicles."

She stopped there. Even though it was clear that the Chinese had received a beating here, the professional satisfaction of the small group was muted by their own losses. Good men and women, who just yesterday had been living. Vibrant human beings, and all the relationships and aspirations they embodied, were now charred husks in burned-out armored vehicles. It was enough to drive one crazy if one thought about it too much.

There was much to do, however. There would be time at some point to reminisce about such events. For those who did eventually get off this island, they would have the rest of their lives to ponder the lives they had already lost in the past month.

James spoke again.

"Well, give them credit, they are fast. No way our info ops teams could turn product and messaging around that quickly for an audience back at home."

While there had been major changes in how allied information operations had been conducted since the beginning of the invasion, they still had much to learn from how the Chinese operated.

"I once read that it was impossible to be a good democracy and good at information operations at the same time," replied Lee. "And the Chinese do have a preference for more indirect approaches, what they call 'winning without fighting'. We on the other hand have historically been reticent to invest too much in info ops. That is going to have to change, and fast, if we want to win this fucking thing."

She looked away from the mess downhill and at the officers and non-commissioned officers that were the senior leadership of her squadron. It was the first time in several days they had been able to assemble like this. Either they were on the move, or the tactical situation predicated against getting together like this. But not today.

Intelligence reports indicated that the remaining Chinese airborne troops had changed their focus to areas further west. This was expected to be a relatively quiet sector for several days. Lee had decided to take the risk and exploit the opportunity to compare notes by getting her folks together this morning. The sergeant major had other ideas.

"Ma'am, this sharing of lessons is important. But look at us. We are a grimy, dirty bunch. We haven't had a chance to change or shower for several weeks now. The accumulated sweat and dirt, combined with the normal grime of living and operating out of our armored vehicles, means our clothes and skin now an almost uniform brown-black color."

Lee nodded, acknowledging the advice of her most senior soldier.

"Everyone is tired," she replied. "The last few weeks have taken their toll on our troopers. The combination of constant moving, several small-scale battles, as well as the death and wounding of their buddies has been exhausting." While she had yet to see any cases, Lee knew that psychological challenges would begin to appear soon. It would begin to impact their troopers, NCOs, and officers. She needed to give her people an opportunity to rest. Even if it was short-lived. "We have an opportunity, at least for the next couple of days, to slow down a little. Our people are strung out. They need a break, even if it is for just a few hours."

She looked at the faces of her people. Most were grim but nodding their heads in agreement.

"For the next 48 hours, we will conduct low-tempo operations. I have discussed it with Colonel Furness, and he is keen to rest us. At the same time, he will be moving forward with the replacement plan. We will be receiving around 40 new troopers to replace our losses. The Marines are receiving over a hundred replacements for their regiment. Despite this, we will still have responsibility for part of the regimental defensive perimeter. The Marines will take over some of the area we are responsible for defending," Lee continued.

That generated some smiles.

"At the same time, I need you all to record initial observations of our operations in the last week. Especially those last two fights. We can then discuss how we might adapt our own tactics. It will also be important to share this with the Marines, as well as the Army headquarters in Hawaii. These lessons could save a lot of lives if they are shared with incoming Army units that are preparing to deploy to Taiwan."

She paused, waiting for comments. Her sergeant major spoke first.

"Ma'am, we will absolutely do that," he started. "But we also need the leaders here to get some shut-eye. Tired leaders make bad decisions. I recommend we create time so those of us here can also get some rest. We will all need it for whatever comes next."

There was general agreement among the small group. Several nodded, while a couple of the junior officers used it as an opportunity to smack talk the sergeant major's endurance.

"OK, OK, that'll do," interjected a smiling Lee. Before she could say anything else, her sergeant major spoke again.

"And Ma'am, you also need to get rest. I know you want to be all over the squadron while also remaining up-to-date with what is going on with our higher headquarters, but we need you sharp."

The sergeant major looked around the group.

"You all need to leave the captain alone for a couple of hours to allow her to rest. It is good for all of us if we can do this."

The sergeant major nodded at his squadron commander.

"Thanks Sergeant Major," responded Lee. "I appreciate it."

She reached into a pocket on her trouser leg to extract her green notebook, in which she had written some notes from her most recent discussion with Colonel Furness. She wanted to share the information with her team. Even in the age of hardened computers, clever AI, secure quantum encrypted networks, and hypersonic weapons, there was still a need for low-tech communications solutions like the Army's green field notebooks. And pencils.

She opened the notebook and looked down to read her almost indecipherable handwriting.

Jesus, she thought, *what a mess. I must have been half asleep when I wrote this.*

And that was when it happened.

15

The High Ground

14 June 2028
3rd Space Operations Squadron
United States Space Force

"Whoa, what the hell was that?" exclaimed Hickling.

Before she had even scrolled through the AI analytics in her VR headset, she heard a voice through her headphones.

"EMP detected in northwestern Taiwan."

EMP. Electromagnetic Pulse. *No. Fucking. Way.* Hickling's mind was roiling.

"There is no way they just used an EMP in Taiwan. What are they trying to do? Start a nuclear exchange?" Hickling's boss. He was almost yelling in her headset.

She took a breath and waited. While she had detected the electromagnetic pulse, Hickling also knew that it would have been detected by the Deltas that focused on earth-monitoring functions. The Americans, as well as the Chinese and Russians, all had satellite constellations designed to detect such events on earth and in its atmosphere.

Captain Marcus was speaking in her ear again.

"OK everyone, listen up. The first order issue is to conduct analysis to ascertain what has generated the pulse. If it was a non-nuclear electromagnetic pulse, it may be a Chinese portable, or missile-mounted, EMP weapon."

However, Hickling pondered, if it was a nuclear-generated EMP, that would change everything. It would mean that humans had used a nuclear weapon against other humans for the first time since August 1945. The use of the first atomic weapons at Hiroshima and Nagasaki over a four-day period in August 1945 had stunned the world. The destructive power of the new weapons had caused political and military leaders to reflect that warfare would never be the same.

Since then, the variety of nuclear weapons, the multitude of delivery means, and their destructive capacity had only grown exponentially. But if this was an EMP resulting from a nuclear detonation, numerous atmospheric monitoring stations as well as an international network of seismic stations would verify that quickly.

Hickling, now absorbed by analyzing the pulse, chewed her lip. She knew that each day could bring new surprises. But she had not expected this surprising development. The task she had been working on in the VR environment before the EMP event now subsided into the background.

As if reading her mind, Marcus spoke again, his voice coming through her headphones.

"Everything else is now a lower priority in Space Command. Hickling, I need you and your team to understand the nature of this EMP event in northwestern Taiwan. It could fundamentally change our space operations if a nuclear warhead has been used. And we need to protect our satellites that detect these events."

Surely the Chinese could not have been so stupid to use tactical nuclear weapons in Taiwan? Hickling thought. She knew that their invasion was not going as well as they might have planned. They had lost tens of thousands of troops on the ships sunk in the northern Taiwan Strait alone. And their advance north from their landing beaches was becoming increasingly bogged down. But going nuclear even in these circumstances? It seemed an insane decision to her. It could very easily escalate to something much, much worse.

A whole range of thoughts then flashed through her mind. What if the worst did happen, and the US and China ended up in a much more extensive and widespread exchange of nuclear weapons beyond Taiwan? She thought of her mother. She lived in Seattle and had done so since the death of her husband, Kara's father, several years back. Living in a small apartment not far from the center of the city, Hickling's mom led an active life with community groups and her book club. The city and its surrounding areas were home to a number of military bases and a concentration of naval forces. It was certain to be a target. The naval base at Kitsap, the Bremerton naval yards, Joint Base Lewis-McChord, the Whidbey Island Naval Air Station, and the Coast Guard station in Puget Sound provided a rich concentration of targets. *They will probably use several weapons to target them all*, Hickling pondered. *Just to be sure.*

She decided to bone up on EMP weapons just in case her team became involved in planning a response. EMP weapons used a brief burst of electromagnetic energy, according to the database she was directed to. This energy, generated through both nuclear and non-nuclear events, could be employed to damage electronic equipment and disrupt communications over various distances. While naturally occurring EMP such as lightning could damage aircraft or other equipment, the EMP weapons that had been developed by the US, China, and other nations over the last few decades were not that powerful.

But they were of sufficient concern for key elements of the military to be hardened against them. It had been a significant challenge during the Cold War. The use of tactical nuclear weapons in any conflict between the US and the Soviet Union was certain to have also generated multiple destructive electromagnetic pulse events. As a consequence, many aircraft, ships, and communications systems had been provided with hardening against EMP. But that had fallen into abeyance during the great peace after the end of the Cold War.

It was the natural world that thereafter had driven a resurgence in interest in research about the effects of EMP. Between the 1970s and the 1990s, scientific research into Coronal Mass Ejections enhanced understanding of naturally created EMP. A March 1989 geomagnetic storm that caused a nine-hour outage of Quebec's electricity distribution system heightened interest even further. It also had a severe impact on military communications in many places around the world, including an Australian Army deployment to Namibia that had its communications impacted for weeks afterwards.

It became clear from the 2000s onwards that a re-emerging China was investing in these weapons. The new weapons could potentially be used to destroy or significantly damage US power grids and other national infrastructure. As a consequence of both the natural and Chinese threats, a more proactive range of capabilities to harden the US military against EMP weapons was initiated. These efforts had been sped up by a 2019 Executive Order which had clarified for the federal government its responsibilities. Hickling pulled down the data on the order, perusing the first paragraph.

Human-made or naturally occurring EMPs can affect large geo-graphic areas, disrupting elements critical to the Nation's security and economic prosperity, and could adversely affect global commerce and stability. The Federal Government must foster sustainable, efficient, and cost-effective approaches to improving the Nation's resilience to the effects of EMPs.

The whole aim of this directive was to enhance the resilience of military and civilian infrastructure. Almost every key decision or event in the military or civilian spheres was now reliant on digital communications and computer chips. A major EMP event, or multiples of such pulses, could send them all back several hundred years. She was not sure that anyone, except maybe some of the crazies who didn't recognize federal government authority, wanted to go back to the days before wireless communications, internal combustion engines, and the benefits of a global trade market. Back to the days when there was no way that women would be doing jobs like the one she was currently doing.

The last five years had seen a flurry of activity to neutralize the impacts of an EMP event. Most new military hardware in the last two years had been hardened against the threat of an electromagnetic pulse. This included the different spacecraft used by the Space Force.

She was about to move to the next part of the electronic document about EMP when another "all hands" broadcast broke through into her headset. It was accompanied by a text alert, which appeared in the top right of her vision in bright red letters.

"EMP IN NW TAIWAN NOT NATURALLY OCCURING. EVENT WAS A NON-NUCLEAR EMP."

Not natural. Well, no shit, Hickling thought. The chances of some un-forecast solar activity causing an EMP event at that location right now were vanishingly small. She should know. Solar weather was one of the things that her Delta were focused on every day for its impact on their orbital warfare mission. And they had even faked some solar weather for the mission to recover the Chinese quantum satellite earlier in the year.

Non-nuclear. That was the key term that she and everyone else had been waiting for. Hickling discovered she had been holding her breath when the alert had come through. And why wouldn't she? Discovering that she could be incinerated in an exchange of nuclear-armed intercontinental ballistic missiles was enough to elevate the heart rate of anyone.

Reading the term "non-nuclear" had resulted in her breathing out and relaxing just a fraction. There would be no nuclear annihilation. Not today anyway. *I really hope there are some adults, on both sides, making sure that this does not get out of control*, Hickling thought as she turned back to her main task for the day: patrolling cis-lunar space.

It still sounded weird to her. Cis-lunar space was the volume of space between geostationary orbits above earth, and the orbit of the moon. The 2020s had seen a rush to transport spacecraft to the moon for a variety of different scientific and national aims. South Korea, the United Arab Emirates, Japan, China, America, and others had all sought to explore and exploit the moon. And the enormous volume of space that encompassed the orbit of the moon around the earth.

After some delays, the Americans and Europeans had placed a small space station called Lunar Gateway in orbit around the moon back in 2025. It was assisting in providing space awareness between the earth and the moon, as well as facilitating access to the surface of the moon. And that was the where the real game was for business and the military.

America and China were the key players, competing over the potential resources contained in the lunar regolith as well as ice deposits. Both were playing the long game, taking careful scientific and technological steps aimed at dominating the ultimate high ground in this patch of the solar system. The surface of earth's moon.

At the same time, gaining awareness of cis-lunar space helped to ensure that the Chinese did not place some form of space-based weapon beyond geosynchronous orbit around earth. Not only would it be difficult to find, it would be very hard to intercept or destroy. And of course, they did not want anyone to find some of the advanced and stealthy satellites that the Americans had lodged out there. Hickling shut *that* particular thought down immediately.

Even with her security clearance, she wasn't supposed to know about that black program.

Therefore, Hickling and her orbital warfare team had been charged with conducting a cis-lunar highway patrol in addition to their other missions in earth's orbit. They needed to deny the Chinese the ability to use that volume of space or interfere with friendly spacecraft headed to the moon.

Her VR display, shared with the other members of her team, showed a three-dimensional slice of cis-lunar space. It currently showed the region that was directly between the earth and the moon as it swung around on its 27.32-day-long orbit of the earth. Overlayed on this were hundreds of satellites and large pieces of space junk.

Finally, a bright blue icon represented their *Stiletto* spacecraft. It had been designed for missions well beyond the earth's orbit. Launched 36 hours before, it was on a lunar trajectory and would conduct a lunar orbit insertion maneuver before undertaking several orbits of the moon. These orbits would be used to verify Chinese activities on the moon. The *Stiletto* would then return from the moon and be placed into a parking orbit several hundred miles above the earth.

Hickling was comfortable with the progress of the mission. They had simulated it dozens of times before launch. And it was the second live patrol that they had conducted this month. After the first mission—the first time they had conducted a cis-lunar mission—her team had Space Patrol uniform patches fabricated in one of her headquarters' 3D printers. One of the patches was stuck next to her name badge above her cubicle. The other was attached to her uniform with Velcro on her upper left arm. They could not wear them outside the building, of course. The mission remained a highly classified one, and the last thing they wanted was the Chinese knowing about this highly sensitive American space capability.

But it did bring a momentary smile to her face. As a young child, her father had often read her a story that she remembered well. In it, the main character was told a story by her parents, who told her that they "loved her to the moon and back." Now, Hickling was able to monitor and mess with the Chinese all the way "to the moon and back."

After the hectic activity of the past few hours, she now had a few quiet minutes. While the cis-lunar work was overseen by others in her team, Hickling pulled up a folder which displayed in her VR headset.

It was the genesis of a plan she had been working on quietly in the last few days. After a discussion with Marcus about deception operations, an idea—or the beginning of one—had just popped into her head. It was probably a silly idea, but she wanted to do some research on it anyway. Perhaps there was something to it.

With a double blink of her left eye, she opened the folder titled "Morakot".

16

Break In

15 June 2028
Near Zhudong
Northern Taiwan

"Jesus, here they come again!" James screamed as he turned and sprinted back to their command vehicle.

Lee, while not quite as spry on her feet as the sprinting James in front of her, was only just behind her sergeant as he leapt on their Bradley armored vehicle and into the turret. He was quickly down through his hatch in the top of the turret and into his commander's seat, headset on. He ordered the vehicle driver to start up, and then slewed the turret toward the threat.

As the turret began to move, Lee leapt in through the open combat door at the back of the vehicle. They had done this dozens of times before, so she was able to quickly move over her pack just inside the combat door, and then turn and close the door behind her. She then swiftly inserted herself into her commander's pod in the rear of the vehicle.

With her helmet, containing embedded headset and microphone, now on, she spoke rapidly into the mic. "All callsigns, contact to the southeast in the vicinity of 1st Platoon. 2nd and 3rd Platoons, start up and stand by."

James called down from his turret, not using the vehicles intercom. "Ma'am, I think we got hit with an EMP. Our system was resetting when I started up, and our electronic warfare folks just sent me a flash message about an EMP event."

Lee looked down at her screen. Near her 1st Platoon, an electronic warfare icon was pulsing. A localized EMP event. It had temporarily disrupted communications and might have killed some of their smaller UAVs in the swarm providing flank security out to her east.

"What the fuck are they thinking?" she murmured.

Lee might be a junior officer, but even she knew that an EMP event could be misinterpreted in the friction and pace of battle as a nuclear event. And that was bad. Fortunately, this looked like something akin to a suitcase EMP. It had a small, localized effect only. And there had been no blast. *They must be desperate*, she thought. Lee then switched her attention to one of the screens in front of her, and rapidly tapped out a brief message to Colonel Furness and the headquarters of the Marine Littoral Regiment.

"CAV CALLSIGN IN CONTACT. ENEMY ADVANCING FROM SOUTHEAST. HAS USED AT LEAST ONE EMP WEAPON. REQUEST FIRES AND EW SUPPORT. MORE TO FOLLOW. OVER."

She had completed her most urgent actions. Lee's unit was now aware an enemy attack was developing and understood which direction it was most likely emanating from. Additionally, her superior headquarters now knew that one of its units was in contact with the enemy.

Lee then scrolled the 3D map on the screen in front of her to reorient herself with the ground. Her troop had only been in this location for a short time. She had familiarized herself with it on arrival yesterday. But she'd had only had a couple of hours of daylight and then had been fully occupied in leading her unit during the two previous Chinese attacks.

Her unit was located to the north of a wide river valley that swept down out of the heavily vegetated hills to the east and meandered in a westerly direction all the way to Hsinchu City and the Taiwan Strait. Most of her troop was located on a large hill that overlooked a small town on the northern banks of the river.

However, to the east, the hill dropped away into a shallow valley which rose again to a small series of hills. One of her platoons—the 1st Platoon—was occupying two of these hills. The southern hill and the ground down to the river was being patrolled by UGVs, while to the east, UAV swarms were providing flank security for Lee's troop. Beyond that, another Marine regiment was deployed to secure several large hills in the more heavily vegetated eastern parts of the Zhudong region.

To her west was the remainder of the Marine regiment to which her unit was attached. They were deployed in a thin band that stretched to the outer suburbs of Hsinchu City and paralleled the northern banks of the wide, slow-moving river.

Lee's headset and screen were starting to fill up with chatter from her platoon leaders. They, like their commander, were passing on their situational awareness about enemy movements and any changes they were making in their own dispositions. Several of the vehicles in her unit were still missing from her battle display, however. The EMP had clearly had a more significant impact on some of the older vehicles that had not received the full electronic hardening upgrades that most of the Army's vehicles had been put through in the past two years.

The Tactical AI, embedded in the battle command system in front of her, had quickly analyzed the initial reports. It had drawn a wide red arrow on the map in front of her that emerged from the southeast, just beyond her easternmost platoon. The arrow then continued up the boundary line between her unit and the Marine regiment further east. The solid red point of the arrow then turned west, crossing the hill where the 1st Platoon was located and was then pointed directly at her position.

"All callsigns. Enemy is advancing along our eastern boundary with the Marines to the east. TAC AI predicts it will turn west, through 1st Platoon and into our main defensive position."

She paused, staring at a new feature on her combat display before her. The Tactical AI had just drawn a second arrow. It was wider than the first one and was emerging from a southwesterly direction. The arrow was pointing up over the western side of her position, and into the rear of her position. This new arrow also had two letters embedded within it: M.E. Main effort.

The Tactical AI had assessed the initial assault to the east as a secondary effort and a feint. The main effort, where the enemy sought decision, was the attack coming up from the southwest and into Lee's main defensive position.

Shit, Lee thought. *Fuckers are trying an envelopment of our position by moving along the boundaries between our units.* It was a clever move, and one she would ponder more later. She recalled then the old saying that the enemy always attacks at the joins in your maps!

The only problem for the enemy in this instance was that instead of placing their strength against Lee's weakest position in the east, they were actually attacking straight into her strongest tactical location. *That is some fog of war shit right there.* The Chinese might have overestimated the impact of the EMP device and miscalculated, she quickly thought before turning back to commanding her squadron.

"All callsigns, new TAC AI overlay with enemy attack template has just been distributed."

Then, static in her headphones. "Dammit, now what?" Lee murmured to herself.

James was yelling down from the turret again into her command pod. The vehicle intercom was out again. "Another EMP. This one to the southwest."

Lee looked back at her screen. There it was. A new, pulsing icon showing the circular effect area of the latest EMP weapon.

She was now receiving contact reports from her 1st Platoon to the east and her forward-most platoon on this hill, the 3rd Platoon. The screen also showed that UAVs to the east had detected enemy UGVs and dismounted troops. The UGVs' security force to the south of the 1st Platoon was already engaging Chinese soldiers and their beetle UGVs. The American Ripsaw autonomous weapon systems in Lee's unit were well armored, deadly, and equipped with the latest tactical AI. They would be taking a toll on the Chinese airborne soldiers and beetles that were attacking her 1st Platoon.

"All callsigns. Forward platoons as well as flank security UAVs and UGVs are now in contact. 2nd Platoon remains out of contact and is designated as squadron reserve. No move without my command. Squadron headquarters will move to our designated alternate location in two minutes."

She then heard the vehicle's engine rev. James had heard her over the command network and was getting ready to move. She needed to say something else.

"All callsigns. Remember, we are the far eastern flank for our Marine regiment. If the enemy goes through us, they will be able to assault directly into the main body of the Littoral Regiment. And those Marines are protecting the skies and seas in all directions. We can't let the Chinese through. We must hold this position at all costs. Out."

She switched to the vehicle's intercom and directed James to move their vehicle to the location they had surveyed earlier in the day as an alternate command post. It provided good connectivity with her high headquarters as well as her platoons. Her vehicle was also located in a depression so it was not visible to enemy troops advancing from the south and the direction of the river, providing a modicum of protection against direct enemy fire.

During their rehearsal of this move earlier in the day, it had taken about ten minutes to move to their alternate command location. During what was turning out to be a fairly significant battle with the Chinese airborne troops and their autonomous systems, it took longer. Their vehicle had temporarily stopped and then restarted and rebooted after the last EMP device was used. Shortly afterwards, a small swarm of Chinese beetles had broken through the 3rd Platoon and had attacked the vehicles in Lee's headquarters.

Sergeant James had engaged and destroyed several of the beetles, while their Bradley's automatic defense system had also accounted for a few. Unfortunately, a sole remaining UGV had been able to approach the vehicle her squadron sergeant major was traveling in. The Chinese UGV, one of the large hexapod beetles, had exploded, setting off secondary explosions inside the sergeant major's vehicle within seconds and quickly overwhelming the internal fire suppression system. The armored vehicle, now burning at a temperature of hundreds of degrees, burned everything inside it. Ammunition, electronics, fuel, and crew.

James spoke into the Bradley's intercom in the rapid patter that was normal for the crew in armored vehicles.

"Sergeant Major is down. Vehicle is K-Kill."

Lee, knowing a "K-Kill" meant a catastrophic loss of the vehicle, understood straight away that there nothing they could do to save the vehicle or its crew. They were gone. She responded almost instantaneously.

"Roger. Carry on to the alternate headquarters location."

There was still a battle to command and win. Her sergeant major's vehicle was left behind as they moved on after the short skirmish, a burned-out hulk sitting forlorn and alone on the hillside several hundred meters away from their final destination.

A few minutes later, they arrived at their new location. The headquarters of her troop had drilled endlessly at occupying a new battle position and getting set up rapidly.

During the short skirmish, Lee had been distracted from what was going on in her two forward platoons. She looked down at her screens to quickly reorient herself on the battle and its progress.

The Chinese had continued their attack in the east and isolated her 1st Platoon. It was still fighting hard but was being assaulted from three directions by dismounted Chinese troops, their robotic beetles, and swarms of lethal UAV suicide drones. They were also receiving moderate amounts of artillery and large-caliber mortar fire. The 1st Platoon, according to the lieutenant in command, could hold out for now but would require reinforcement and relief in the next hour or so.

The situation on her own hill, with the 3rd Platoon just to her south, was more dire. The Chinese had massed a large number of troops and beetles for this assault and were slowly pushing her 3rd platoon back up the hillside. Losses in her platoon so far had been small, but they had lost over half of their UGVs and almost all of the UAVs.

Where the hell is our artillery and air support from the Marines? she thought. Lee placed her fingers on the screen and tapped out a quick secure text message to Furness.

"ARTILLERY AND AIR SUPPORT NEEDED ASAP. FORMAL REQUESTS HAVE BEEN REPEATED ON BATTLE COMMAND NET. PRIORITY IS SUPPORT TO CALLSIGNS TO MY IMMEDIATE SOUTH."

The sounds of the fight were quite distinct through the side of the armored vehicle and her helmet headphones—a cacophony of explosions, buzzing drones, sonic booms from various caliber small arms, and the infrequent flyby of missiles traveling in both directions.

And to top everything off, Lee thought, it had begun to rain. *Again.*

The vehicle, besides its highly advanced command systems, also had a series of high-resolution cameras that allowed her and James to see through the armor. There was even a telescoping mast she could elevate to get a bird's eye view as well as several small UAVs she could launch for the same purpose. She decided on the UAVs. They were less likely to give away her position.

Her immediate impression on receiving the first vision from the UAV was that she could not tell friend from foe. In the visible spectrum, with all the precipitation, smoke, and god knows what else was blowing around, it was difficult to recognize her own troops. Fortunately, the embedded AI in the UAV and her command screen was able to rapidly classify each human, vehicle, UGV, and UAV. It used a red designator for those that were enemy and blue for own forces and allied units.

"Holy shit, this is just a mess," she said into her microphone, not expecting a response from James or any of her other squadron callsigns. It was a statement of the obvious.

Even with the red and blue icons, the battle had become a confused mess of interspersed enemy and friendly vehicles, people, and autonomous systems. All the technology in the world was not going to help sort that out.

She quickly pressed a button on the screen that highlighted the locations of her platoon leaders. The 1st Platoon was still holding out on the eastern hill, but even as she looked at the screen, the number of its icons was steadily decreasing. 3rd Platoon was slowly moving back up the hillside, and similarly losing vehicles and autonomous systems. 2nd Platoon, her only reserve, was still deployed on a reverse slope of a hill to the north. It was not yet engaged with the enemy.

She made the call to deploy her reserve. Army doctrine taught that her reserve was that portion of her troops "withheld from action at the beginning of an engagement to be available for a decisive movement." Now was that decisive moment, she thought.

"2nd Platoon. On my order, you are to advance south and engage the enemy and support 3rd Platoon. Your axis of advance is the ridge running southwest down this hill. You are to destroy all enemy to your front and clear all the way to the northern riverbank. Acknowledge. Over."

The commander of the 2nd platoon, an experienced leader who had been expecting the call, came back immediately. "Roger. Ready to go, over."

Lee did not delay the order. "Move now. Out."

She glanced at the battle command system in front of her. The blue icons representing her final unit had begun a rapid move south. Leading was a deep line of the Cavalry Unit's UGVs, followed by the manned vehicles. Swinging around the west was another group of UGVs and beyond them, a massive swarm of UAVs. She looked at the text box for a response from Furness.

Nothing.

"Shit, the EMP must have messed up the communications link again," she murmured. *Well, I hope 2nd Platoon are on their game,* she thought. *They are our last hope now.* Suddenly, the text box on the screen blinked to life.

"ROGER THAT, CAV. EMP MESSED WITH OUR SYSTEMS BUT WE ARE BACK ONLINE. WE ARE ON THE WAY. AIR AND ARTY SUPPORT ALSO INBOUND. HOLD ON, ARMY."

Furness.

She repeated the message to James and passed it along to her beleaguered commanders.

"I thought we were supposed to be the cavalry that came to the rescue," James said over the vehicle intercom.

It brought a grim smile to Lee's face. The Marines had come through. Finally. She only hoped it would be in time.

17

Resolve

16 June 2028
Zhongnanhai, Beijing

President Zhang Xi should have had a spring in his step.

He was the leader of one of the oldest civilizations on earth—the world's most populous nation and one that had worked hard to enrich itself and stand astride the globe. For decades, the people of China, ably led by the Chinese Communist Party, had slowly but surely been dragged out of the mire of poverty, and from under the yoke of the arrogant Western powers.

In theory, Zhang and his Party, as well as the billion people he led, had much to celebrate. Unfortunately, that foolish Admiral He had ruined the president's day.

Zhang, while accustomed to purging competitors and untrustworthy subordinates, nonetheless had found signing the execution order for the admiral in charge of the Eastern Theater Command unsettling. Their public information operations campaign over the last month had showcased the admiral as an exemplar military commander and member of the Party.

It had all started so well. The PLA had, at least in the first few hours, achieved total surprise in their move against their rebellious province. Additionally, they had been successful in minimizing American interference by striking at military bases across the western Pacific region, northern Australia, and even in Hawaii.

The American media, as usual, had been split between condemning Chinese aggression and calling for a ceasefire before all-out nuclear war broke out. The Western media—a shallow lot, Zhang thought—could always be relied on to help. As Zhang had predicted, the fractious relationship between the American people and its media had played out largely to China's advantage.

Of course, the massive cyber and influence campaign being waged online and through social media in Western nations also assisted China. Zhang did not fully understand all the technical details, or even why people used social media. To him, it seemed to be the tool of self-obsessed and narcissistic movie stars and what the young people called "influencers." But Zhang understood enough to know that it was a powerful tool that could create division and destroy societal cohesion in America and other open societies.

But then had come that awful naval battle in the northern part of the Taiwan Strait. He knew that, in the West, it was being compared by some to the 1944 Battle of Leyte Gulf. That battle, perhaps the largest naval battle in history, had finished off the Imperial Japanese Navy as an effective fighting fleet.

The PLA influence operations were working hard to ensure that this narrative did not gain wide traction in the wake of the disaster in the Taiwan Strait. Not only might this influence those reticent to support Taiwan, but it could also cause domestic difficulties for Zhang and the Party.

Even now, Zhang could hardly bear to ponder what had occurred there. A fleet of American and Japanese warships, which had somehow escaped the rain of missiles on their bases in places such as Yokosuka in Japan, had decimated the northern amphibious fleet. Also sunk or badly damaged had been many of the warships that had been tasked with protecting the amphibious vessels in their transit to Taiwan. If it had not been for the thousands of robotic beetles that had been able to get ashore, the landings of the airborne troops in the north, and the underwater autonomous vessels in the strait, it may well have been an even larger catastrophe.

As it was, tens of thousands of Marines, soldiers, and sailors now lay in watery graves at the bottom of that body of water that separated China from its rebel province. Fortunately, only the most senior military and Party leaders knew the true cost of that fiasco. And so it would remain. Zhang could not afford panic or defeatist talk among Chinese citizens or within the leadership of the Party.

There were many benefits of exercising a tight leash on the people's access to information through the internet, social media, blogs, and the newspapers. And just as he had always been judicious with the release of information, so too would he be with that battle. There would be a cover story of course. The PLA Navy had provided excellent footage from other areas of the military campaign which could be spliced together to distract the Chinese people. They would only ever know that there had been a minor battle, the PLA Navy had lost some ships, but had eventually prevailed over the Americans in the face of overwhelming odds.

A few new heroes had been nominated. Medals had been pinned on chests. And then, the news cycle and release of information about the war had been subtly moved on to other parts of the military operations being conducted in, and around, Taiwan. Any hint of something more disastrous, particularly from the Americans and Japanese, could easily be censored online.

They had done so for a third of a century in the wake of the events in Tiananmen Square. There was no reason they could not do the same for a battle at sea, far from the eyes of most Chinese citizens.

The news from the south of that damned island was somewhat better. The PLA had managed to successfully cross the southern part of the strait and land tens of thousands of troops. The Taiwanese, aided by the Americans, had fought in the south like devils, however. It meant that the PLA had absorbed far more casualties than expected. There was now a steady flow of troop ships across the strait, full of PLA ground forces troops to feed what had become a mincing machine. Despite their horrendous losses, though, there was no shortage of PLA soldiers. And they were continuing a slow advance north.

From what he could decipher from the multitude of briefings he had received since the landings, it was actually the short- and medium-range missiles, as well as cyber operations and autonomous systems, that were giving the PLA an advantage on the ground, in the air, and on the sea. That had been some consolation.

But then, yesterday, Admiral He had updated him on a slowing advance north, and escalating casualty figures. He then described the use of small EMP weapons in the north. Apparently, they had been used without higher authority by an isolated PLA unit of paratroopers. This was met with deep concern around the table. It was important that they seize the island but not do anything that might lead the Americans to escalate the situation. The use of an EMP weapon, no matter how small, could be misinterpreted as a tactical nuclear weapon by some American hothead. While the fractious American Congress had been to their advantage until now, an event like that in the north might unify the Americans. *That would be very challenging*, Zhang mused.

Zhang, who thought this was yet another indication of the sloppy command culture nurtured by Admiral He in the Eastern Theater, was appalled. How could such a low-ranking soldier be issued with, and use, such a strategically problematic weapon? Zhang had cut off discussion by ordering that no further EMP weapons were to be used without clearance from the PLA's joint headquarters in Beijing.

Admiral He had then proposed—Zhang could still not believe this—that perhaps an armistice might be in order. Perhaps the Americans would accept a partition of the island. China could have the south, and the rebellious province could be contained to only half the island. At some point in the future, the PLA might then surge north and complete its conquest.

The suggestion had stunned the meeting. Literally. The room was quiet for a long time. And then Zhang had exploded.

"How could you propose such a cowardly act?" Zhang had raged at the admiral. "The Chinese people have sacrificed much in the last several decades to build this mighty, technologically advanced military machine that is finally being used. You assured all of us in this very room, before the campaign started, that your planning, wargames, and careful preparations would lead to success. And that Taiwan would be returned to the Chinese nation in a matter of weeks."

Zhang, feeling his heart rate elevating, took a short pause before continuing to vent his fury at the silent naval officer.

"How could I, the president and chairman of the Military Commission, give up now that we are so close to our objective? It is an outrageous and preposterous suggestion, Admiral. After so much blood of Chinese soldiers and sailors had been shed on the high seas and in the rebel province? No," Zhang roared, "there will be no armistice."

He sat back in his chair for a moment, pondering a range of different actions that he might take in the wake of Admiral He's gross arrogance and military negligence. After a moment of consideration, his blood pressure finally subsiding, he spoke calmly at the screen on which Admiral He appeared.

"Admiral He, you are relieved of your duties. I expect that you will be investigated for military incompetence, disloyalty to the Party, and corruption."

Zhang then turned to the vice chairman of the Military Commission, sitting to his right, and spoke a single sentence. "Find a suitably courageous and loyal replacement immediately."

The president of the People's Republic of China then stood and left the room.

Now, as he walked toward the same meeting room 24 hours later, he confirmed in his mind that he had taken the correct action in removing Admiral He from command of the Taiwan operation. The inevitable investigation had found, within hours, that Admiral He had been professionally corrupt and negligent in his military responsibilities. And there was only one punishment for such a finding during a time of war: death. A sentence that president Zhang had personally endorsed and ensured was carried out this morning before he left his office for the coming meeting. It was to be another of his regular updates on the situation in Taiwan and the wider Pacific region.

The doors to the meeting room were opened by the two military guards who permanently stood sentinel there. Zhang noticed that both were armed with their normal sidearms, in black pistol holsters on their right hips. Given that their nation was at war, the two guards were also wearing body armor and helmets instead of their normal ceremonial dress.

They held open the engraved timber doors as Zhang entered. The other members of the Central Military Commission were all standing at their places around the table. They, too, instead of their normal service dress uniforms, were wearing camouflage uniforms and highly polished black boots. The room was silent. Each of the men around the table, and the aides sitting against the walls, were grim-faced. They had all heard of the outcome of the Admiral He investigation. And that the execution of the failed military commander had already taken place, just 24 hours after he had dared propose his spineless course of action at this same daily briefing.

Zhang took a moment to look around the room. He glanced at the faces of those assembled. *They are wondering who might be next,* Zhang thought. *That is a good thing. It might keep their attention focused on their duties and their own survival, and not whether there may be an opportunity to replace me as president.*

Zhang sat, and the others in the room followed. He had decided not to mention Admiral He. As far as he, and the others in the room were concerned, the former commander of the Eastern Theater no longer existed.

He looked at the screens before him. As usual, one contained a depiction of Taiwan and the western Pacific region. The second screen had a face, which peered back at him. Zhang spoke at the second screen.

"General Zhao, you have assumed your responsibilities as commander of the Eastern Theater as well as commander of the campaign to return our eastern province. Do you understand your responsibilities and what is expected of you?"

Zhao, a member of the PLA ground forces, had been rapidly dispatched from his senior appointment in Beijing the previous night to assume command from Admiral He. His immense new responsibilities did not show on his face, however.

"Yes, Chairman Zhang. I have been fully briefed and have assumed responsibility for our operations. You can be assured that our forces are fighting hard and will successfully return control of the island to the Chinese people. And while our aircraft, rocket forces, influence campaigns, and Navy are performing extraordinary feats, it is a campaign that can only be won on the ground. That is where the people are. We will place our boots on the necks of the secessionists. We will embrace our returned citizens in the coming month."

Zhang nodded and then looked down at the piece of paper on the table before him to confirm the first agenda item for the meeting.

"Update on American politics and their support for Taiwan," Zhang barked at the briefing officer. The briefer, a senior major general from the Joint Staff in Beijing, was standing at attention behind a small lectern at the head of the room. "What is the status of the main coalition partners for the Americans and the Taiwanese?"

"Their most significant ally, Japan, is demonstrating strong political will to support the Americans and to assist the Taiwanese in resisting our resumption of governance on the island. Their parliament is currently debating major changes to their constitution which would legalize their offensive military operations of the past month, as well as future military adventurism in China's region.

"Despite our missile attacks on their bases, they continue to support their own and American military operations and logistic support. Their naval, air, and space forces are advanced and very capable. We were surprised at their level of participation in the naval battle in the northern part of the Taiwan Strait during the initial phase of the operation. They were able to deploy almost all of their warships that escaped our initial missile strikes.

"The Japanese are also an important partner for the Americans in the conduct of information operations throughout the western Pacific. They have increased foreign assistance to many Asian and Pacific nations and are actively supporting cyber and psyops campaigns against China and our military forces.

"Finally, they have now landed forces in the Senkaku Islands, including long-range air and sea missiles. We are building a sea and air task force to eject them, but that will be dependent on the release of some assets from the strategic rocket force and the Eastern Theater Command."

The general paused, looking up at the screen to confirm that new data was being displayed before he continued.

"The Australians, like the Americans and Japanese, have begun a rapid national mobilization. They have deployed air and naval task forces into the western Pacific. We also have reports that they intend to deploy a mechanized division, with significant rocket artillery, to Taiwan as part of an American corps.

"The Australians, in partnership with the government in Port Moresby, have established a large joint task force base on Manus Island with long-range missiles. They have also formed a coalition with the Indonesians and based missiles on Christmas, Natuna, and Cocos islands, essentially shutting most archipelagic sea lanes to the Indian Ocean.

"Politically, however, the Australians are torn between external issues such as Taiwan on one hand, and on the other, dealing with the big domestic issue of the secession of its Western Australia state earlier this year."

Zhang smiled at this last comment. They had worked hard over the years to buy off business and some provincial political leaders in the west of Australia. It was a bet that had paid off handsomely. Once again, the briefing officer paused.

"The Koreans have mobilized but are yet to participate in offensive operations. They have offered open political support to the Taiwanese and the Americans. However, they appear to be prioritizing defense against any North Korean attempt to exploit the current situation.

"The Philippines, Vietnam, Malaysia, and Singapore have all offered statements in support of the Americans and their resolutions in the United Nations Security Council. The Russians have been very supportive of us in that body, however, and it remains largely a toothless tiger at this stage."

The screen changed once again as the general looked down to check his notes on the lectern.

"The Indians are interesting. They too have offered political support to the Taiwanese and the Americans. They have not yet mobilized. But given the size of their military, they do not really need to. Even with their standing regular forces, they could sustain large-scale operations at sea and in our border region at short notice. The Indians are also assisting the Americans and Australians to interdict ships that are leaving the Arabian Gulf. This is having a significant impact on our petroleum imports, although we forecast that this would be the case and we are able to use our reserves for some months to come."

The general paused once again.

Zhang, who had observed this particular officer brief on multiple occasions in the past month, understood this as the general's "tell" that he was about to deliver bad news. He did not disappoint.

"We believe the Indians may be moving forces north for an operation along the border regions. Our forces in Xinjiang and Tibet, as well as our strategic intelligence gathering, have detected strategic signatures that indicate the Indians might launch a major offensive in those areas. We believe they would do so to exploit our focus elsewhere. It would also test our capacity to deal with more than one major military campaign at once."

Zhang nodded. They had anticipated this in the planning over the past year. Unfortunately, a large proportion of the forces that had been apportioned to deal with the Indian threat in these areas had been redeployed from the Western Theater Command to support the operations in Taiwan. It was yet another outcome of the longer duration, and the larger than predicted casualties, of the Taiwan military campaign. *Even with the most careful and detailed planning, there are so many unknowns in war*, Zhang thought. However, he had been pondering options on this Indian problem over the past few days. He spoke to those assembled.

"I have cleared the release of ground, cyber, rocket, and air forces from our strategic reserve. As such, the Central and Northern Theater Commands will deploy their forces south over the coming days."

The general nodded and then left the lectern to sit at a chair that was unoccupied along the wall of the room.

There was one final item that Zhang wished to discuss. He looked up to see the general in charge of the Political Work Department of the Central Military Commission, General Liu Hua, take his place at the lectern.

"Chairman, you requested an update on our strategic influence activities, especially against the Americans?"

Zhang merely nodded, allowing the general to begin his presentation.

"Chairman, our integrated influence campaign against the Americans continues to support our military activities in Taiwan. We continue to measure the outcomes of our actions in this regard, while also closely collaborating with the Joint Staff Department and the Eastern Theater Command.

"While there was an upsurge in American political unity in the immediate aftermath of our commencement of operations, after a month we are starting to see signs of a return to more partisan politics. We are also seeing corrosion of the national unity we witnessed a year ago. The proximate causes include American casualties and the lack of a clear political narrative to link these sacrifices with critical American national interests."

Zhang interrupted.

"How could they not have a powerful narrative at this point? I am continually amazed at their inability to master this. My apologies. Please continue."

General Liu, still standing at the lectern, nodded before continuing.

"We are using proxies to deepen the fractures in society on this issue. Their social media remains a powerful tool for us in this regard. They still are unable to reach any consensus on controlling it. And of course, the aggressive political environment of the presidential election year has been most beneficial to us. We have also been able to leverage our diaspora communities, some willingly, some not so willingly, to contribute to our influence campaigns. We have ensured that they are active in lobbying their local politicians to end the fighting because there are more important priorities within America.

"Part of our messaging is that once the question of Taiwan is settled, that is the end of Chinese interest in territory beyond its shores. Some American commentators on the far right and far left of their political system have begun to use this narrative as a justification to minimize the involvement of the United States."

Zhang smiled. He loved it. What a clever subterfuge. But the Americans were nothing but gullible when it came to such matters.

"Do you think the Americans will believe it?" he asked.

Liu nodded.

"Chairman, we only need enough of them to believe it to sow discord in their media, political system, and society."

Zhang nodded and smiled, as the general then concluded his briefing.

"Finally, we continue to influence several prominent journalists and media entities to broadcast information that breaks down political unity. We have also been able to highlight atrocities against Taiwanese civilians by American and Taiwanese forces."

"I was not aware of any atrocities carried out by the Americans," Zhang replied.

"There haven't been," responded the general, "but the world now believes that there have been."

Zhang, satisfied with the operations of the Political Work Department, merely nodded. The update briefing, at least that part where information flowed from senior military officials to the president, was finished. It was time for Zhang to speak before closing this daily meeting of his most important advisors and military leaders.

"Thank you. That was quite comprehensive," Zhang said. He looked at those assembled and then began to speak again. "We miscalculated American resolve and their ability to quickly resource this fight. We may also have underestimated the will of the governments of several regional nations as well. But we must keep fighting. The Westerners are fundamentally weaker societies than ours. They lack our vision, and our resolve.

"Since the formation of our Party, it has been our fondest hope that we should reunite our nation as one indivisible entity again. For decades, those rogues in Taiwan have resisted our good offers of reunification. Well, they have brought this war upon themselves. We will reunify our nation."

Zhang's face then took on a much more serious countenance.

"But we do not have much time. We are racing the clock to conclude our campaign before the nations of the world can unify their political and economic efforts against us. And, as you know, the typhoon season will soon be upon us. We must take back that island as quickly as we can!"

Zhang placed his hands on the table. He paused, and then glared at the screen upon which the image of General Zhao was projected.

"General, you understand the importance and urgency of this campaign. You are to clear our adversaries from the island, and you are to take the remainder of that rebellious province as quickly as possible. You are to deploy to Taiwan and personally take command of our military campaign on the ground."

Zhang paused for a moment before concluding.

"Continue your operations until that is done ... or do not come back at all."

18

Courage and Wisdom

17 June 2028
Near Zhudong
Northern Taiwan

Jack Furness stood at the peak of the hill, looking down to the south. The ground between the top of this geographical feature and the river was churned up, charred black, and broken. Even two days after the battle, the outline of what had occurred was still obvious.

"What a goddamn mess," he murmured softly.

His sergeant major, standing impassively to the left of Furness, merely nodded. But then, as an afterthought, the gruff old Marine responded.

"Maybe so, Sir. But I have never seen anyone fight like those soldiers last night. And that young captain? Colonel, she is probably the best combat leader I have seen—except you of course!"

Furness nodded before replying.

"We have to get her citation perfect. She will only be the second one."

Without waiting for a response, he then returned his attention to the hillside below, pondering just how lucky they had been.

Post battle, it had become clear that the largest concentration of PLA ground troops in the north had been responsible for the attack. The airborne troops of the PLA were the only force that had successfully landed in northern Taiwan during the initial phases of invasion. Well, the only human ones. Thousands of the robotic beetles had made it ashore, and many of them had teamed with the airborne troops during the battle.

They had been fortunate that they had been fighting airborne troops. While the ability to parachute forces into enemy territory was an important one, it was only decisive if it was used in cooperation with the arrival of other ground and air forces to support and reinforce them. And, by nature, airborne forces were light. They possessed none of the armored vehicles or heavy artillery that were vital in a combined arms ground fight.

And because they did not have many tracked or wheeled vehicles, their communications, battle command systems, and electronic warfare capacity were reliant on what men could carry. And how many batteries they could physically haul around in their packs. Which was not much over a sustained period of combat.

What had buttressed the enemy here were those elements that were not normally integral to PLA Air Force Airborne Corps. The autonomous beetles. Clearly, in the years leading up to the invasion, the Chinese had invested in thinking about how their soldiers and robots would work, and fight, together. The PLA appeared to have moved from a culture that saw robots as tools to one that embraced a full partnership with them. It was a powerful combination, and they had stolen a march on the Americans in this regard.

The heavy rains, now almost constant, had assisted the PLA troops by covering their movements and impacting on many of the heat and optical sensors that the Americans used to detect the enemy. That the Chinese had also been able to use EMP weapons and call for support from crewed and uncrewed ground attack aircraft had also assisted them in their series of attacks on this position.

Furness had already had his intelligence staff—and key personnel from the attached cavalry troop—carefully analyze how the Chinese had fought by teaming their ground soldiers with their aerial and ground robotic systems. While the Marine Littoral Regiment had learned from its relationship with the attached US Army Cavalry Troop, there were obviously other tactical teaming approaches that they could "appropriate" from the Chinese.

It was one of the reasons that the commander of the attached Army troops, Captain Lee, was standing next to him now. After Furness had presented several medals to her troopers that morning, they had begun a wide-ranging conversation about Chinese tactics. After a month of combat on the island, they were still learning about fighting with some of the new technologies that had been introduced into the US military in the preceding years.

That was not a bad thing. It was often difficult to simulate the full range of combat effects and outcomes in training exercises. Even with some of the most advanced AI simulations, and live training, it was only the crucible of real combat that highlighted where their preparations had worked. *And where they failed*, Furness thought.

"We would have been pretty screwed if your infantry battalion hadn't have come over that hill when they did," Lee said.

Furness, in his mental meanderings, had almost forgotten she was also standing beside him.

"We were being badly chewed up. My reserve might have been able to turn things around, but it was your Marines that were really decisive."

Lee was silent then.

She and Furness had discussed the battle several times in the last few days. He sensed there was something else she wanted to discuss but was leading into it with small talk.

"What's up, Dana?" he asked, turning to face her as she peered down the hillside. "I think I know you well enough to see that you didn't walk me over here to go through something we have already discussed several times in our after-action reviews and regimental adaptation meetings."

Lee was silent, continuing to stare down the hill. It had been the scene of the most significant combat in the north of the country for the past few days. That it was only a minor skirmish compared with the large-scale combined arms air-land battles that were taking place almost constantly in the south was of little consequence to Lee. Or Furness.

Lee, still not looking at him, then spoke.

"How do you do it, Sir?"

Furness, sensing where this was going, responded briefly.

"Do what, Dana?"

"Sir, how do you continue functioning and commanding each day, losing soldiers and Marines constantly, while not losing your cool or questioning our purpose here? How do you not feel fear?"

So, it is what I thought she wanted to discuss, Furness thought.

It was the same conversation that he had held with his battalion commander while serving in Helmand Province in Afghanistan. *That* conversation had taken place after a particularly brutal contact where he had lost several Marines. It was still a painful memory for Furness, even after all these years.

This was not the first time he had had this conversation with one of his subordinate commanders in the past month. It would probably not be the last time either. Furness sighed.

"You will never *not* be scared in these situations, Dana. It is part of command. Whether it is fear of losing your Marines or soldiers, fear of failing in a mission that has greater consequences for your organization, or just fear for your own life, it is something that does not go away. Ever."

He could see Lee looking at him, waiting for him to continue.

"You do, however, get used to it. You deal with it by keeping busy circulating among your people, talking with them, and encouraging them. You keep busy by collecting the status of your information and ensuring your command post is on top of the battle."

He paused. There was more he wanted to share.

"You prepare for it by reading about how others throughout history have dealt with it. Commanders have been dealing with fear, friction, and uncertainty ever since humans have fought. Many of the good ones have spoken about it or written about it. You need to read their memoires and see how they have felt and handled the weight of command during combat."

Dana was now nodding.

"Part of reading about our predecessors in this profession is building an understanding that how you feel is entirely normal. In fact, that you feel fear is a good sign. It means you are human, and that you are good leader."

He decided to finish with a little bit of philosophy.

"Have you ever heard of Zeno?"

Lee looked at him, shaking her head.

"No, Sir. Sounds like an alien," she said, trying to add a touch of levity to what was otherwise a pretty heavy conversation.

Furness chuckled softly. "No, Lee, he wasn't an alien. At least not that we know of."

Furness paused, turning to Lee as he continued his advice to the young Army officer.

"Zeno was one of the first philosophers who wrote and spoke about stoicism. He lived around 300 BC and was originally from Cyprus but eventually ended up settling in Athens. It was there that he dedicated himself to thinking about and studying how to live a smooth flow of life. And he helped codify the key principles of Stoic thought."

Lee, still looking at Furness, asked the obvious question.

"And they are?"

"They are, Captain Lee, the virtues of temperance and justice, courage and wisdom. I have read about them, although I would not call myself an expert. Still, I think there is enough in these ideas that we, as military leaders, can ponder. I think they are a good framework for how to live our lives, achieve balance, and be better military leaders. I keep a couple of paperbacks about it in my command vehicle, and will bring one over for you the next time I visit."

Lee nodded. She felt a little better, having shared her feelings with her boss. He had responded well and had reinforced her confidence. But Lee also knew that it was time to change the topic of discussion. They needed to discuss the immediate future.

"Sir, what's next? I have heard that the fighting down south is very tough. That casualties are high. I have also heard a rumor that we are moving south."

Furness nodded but didn't say anything for a moment. He wanted to take in the vista before him before responding. The burned-out armored vehicles, broken robotic beetles, and smashed American UGVs which littered the hillside were like a miniature harbinger of their future. Torn, muddy earth, shattered trees, discarded bandages and used medical supplies, splinters from exploded ordnance, as well as fallen vegetation, completed the picture of devastation.

He knew that the burned-out armored vehicles before him were much more than black, smoking hulks. They represented the tombs of men and women, previously living, breathing, loving, and loyal, who now rested charred and absent within their last duty post. It was the most awful way to perish, burned alive in a metal sarcophagus from which there was no escape. Fortunately, the bodies of the dead American soldiers, and their Chinese adversaries, had already been removed. But nonetheless it was still an unpleasant sight.

He pushed away these mournful thoughts. It was nothing compared with what Furness was hearing about the combat in the south. They would be moving there. But not yet.

"We will be here for a little longer. Our regiment, and the Marine regiments on both our flanks, will be refitting and taking on reinforcements over the next few days. We will also be receiving a large shipment of UGVs, UAVs, and precision strike missiles. But among the Marine regiments, we are a lower priority."

Lee could not help but question this last comment. After the battle here, surely they would have priority for reinforcements.

"Who in the division is a higher priority?" she asked.

Furness, who had seen a range of different reports from his fellow regimental commanders, was well informed about priorities.

"We are second in priority. The 5th Marines to our east are priority one in the division for reinforcements. They have had some tough fighting in the hills over the last few days. They also undertook a series of subterranean operations to dig out some remnant Chinese airborne forces that had managed to seize a couple of Taiwanese underground storage depots out east. Division headquarters, as well as the Taiwanese senior leadership, wanted the bunkers cleared out before we continued our advance south."

"Subterranean operations, Sir?" Lee asked. She had not heard of the term. It did not sound like something she would be keen to take part in. At least, not without preparation and rehearsals.

"We always thought this would be a possibility, given the Taiwanese Army's penchant for digging underground redoubts. It was only a matter of time before the PLA were able to get into one and cause a nuisance. We even employ the recent US Army doctrine and tactics on these kinds of operations. It was issued in 2019 and is quite good. But don't tell anyone a Marine complimented the Army doctrine!"

He smiled briefly before proceeding with his update of the tactical situation in their area.

"Unfortunately, even with the best preparation, these are operations that are expensive in terms of lives. Eventually, the 5th Marines were able to clear their objectives, but they lost a lot of Marines and pretty much all of the UGVs and autonomous recon vehicles in the fight. Therefore, they rightly get priority for reinforcements in the next few days. Then, it is our turn."

That made sense, Lee thought. This was despite the fact she would need to wait a bit longer to have her new soldiers and robotic systems arrive to reinforce her depleted squadron. Since arriving on the island a month ago, the squadron had lost nearly 30 percent of its strength through accumulated combat losses, other injuries, and psych assessments. And they had lost over 50 percent of the squadron's total autonomous systems. Reinforcements would be very welcome.

"Roger that, Sir. Understood."

Furness looked at her before he continued his update.

"We will need every person and every robot we can get our hands on. We will be heading south next week. It is a different war down there. Unlike the north, the Chinese were able to land amphibious forces and get armor, long-range artillery, rockets, and tens of thousands more autonomous systems. It is a combined-arms, air-land, human-robot team fight down there. And it is fast. The tactical-level combat is occurring so quickly that it is now robotic systems and missiles that are doing a lot of the fighting. The situation is the same on the ground as well at sea and in the air."

Jesus, Lee thought. *I knew that our teaming with UAVs and UGVs would continue to develop. But who would have thought that they would do more of the fighting than humans?*

"I suppose it was inevitable," Furness said. "We have been working toward this day for years, decades actually. But that Rubicon has been crossed. Our robots are now doing the larger proportion of fighting. I am not sure it will reduce our casualties. It will probably prolong the fighting because this war is going to become a slug fest to see who can produce the most robots and missiles with the greatest capacity to kill and destroy other robots and humans. And both sides are developing better and more lethal combat robots—for air, sea, and land operations—on a monthly basis."

He paused. It was a sobering thought. He knew the Marines back in the United States, at places like Camp Lejeune and Camp

Pendleton, were rapidly adapting their infantry units by incorporating hundreds more ground and aerial combat vehicles in each battalion. This included suicide drones fired from mortars as well as a variety of counter-autonomous systems. New tactics were being developed, and the old platoon and company structures were being ripped apart and reformed for a new age of human-robot combat. In some respects, it scared him. He was not sure where it would all end. And then, as if by afterthought, he spoke to Lee again.

"No, this is going to get worse before it gets better. I worry that the overuse of these robots will deprive this war of the humanity it so desperately needs. So much for Asimov's three fucking laws."

Lee was less shocked by the revelation about the evolved form of combat than she was by Furness using a curse word. It was the first time she had heard him swear in the entire time she had worked for him. It was clearly a topic he had strong feelings about.

She looked away, once again peering down the slope of the hill on which they stood. At the base of the hill was a small village that contoured the valley and lay at the northern bend of the wide, slow-flowing river beyond. Much of it had been destroyed or damaged during the battle two days before.

Hopefully the residents were able to get away before the worst of the fighting, Lee thought. She would hate to have their blood on her hands as well. It might be war, but that didn't mean the indiscriminate killing of civilians—of any nationality—was necessary or justified.

Lee had a final question for her commander.

"Sir, I have been meaning to ask, because it isn't marked on the battle command system. What is the name of that town down there?"

Furness looked down the hill before turning back to her.

"Captain, that is the township of Hengshan. Back home, that fight two days ago has been christened the Battle of Hengshan. It is all over the news."

"Congratulations Captain, you're famous!"

AUTHOR'S NOTE (III)

Contained on this page is a map that has been drawn from Colonel Jack Furness' tactical arm screen from an after-action review conducted in the immediate wake of the 16 June 2028 Battle of Hengshan.

The map shows the locations of the Cavalry Squadron, the 3rd Marine Littoral Regiment, and the direction of the Chinese attacks on their positions north of Hengshan.

It was declassified as part of the 2035 release of documents relating to the 1st Taiwan War.

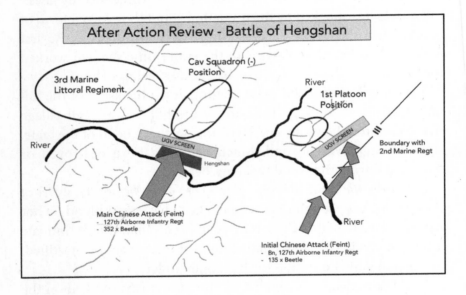

19

Remote War

18 June 2028
Just south of Chiayi City
Taiwan

The explosion obliterated his brigade command post.

Colonel Bo Zhen, who had been meeting with one of his combined arms battalion commanders several hundred meters away, heard for a split second the sound of the incoming missile before the deafening explosion rolled across the two blocks of demolished buildings that separated him from the explosion. He did not need to get a closer look at the site of the missile strike to know it had probably destroyed his headquarters. And the majority of his headquarters staff within. The heat and blast wave he felt, even at this distance, told him everything he needed to know.

It was probably one of the new US Army precision strike missiles, which was colloquially known as a "Prism." These had been manufactured in large numbers and were routinely used in the north. Increasingly, given the kind of fight in which they were engaged in the south, the Taiwanese had been given access to the missiles as well. Launched from either tracked or wheeled launcher vehicles,

207

the missile had a range out to nearly 500 kilometers. It was very precise. And quite lethal.

Not that it mattered, Bo thought. His men were just as dead regardless of which weapon had landed among them. There would be little remaining of them, or the vehicles, communications equipment, and tents that had comprised his headquarters.

Fortunately, Bo had recently split his headquarters into two: a larger, less mobile main headquarters and a lighter, more deployable tactical headquarters. It was the doctrine of the Western armies to split their brigade headquarters in such a way. While the PLA had not copied this approach before the war, many of Bo's fellow brigade commanders—Marines and Army—were now doing so. If you wanted to live, you did what you needed to do. Even if it meant stealing good tactics or ideas off their enemy.

Such was the nature of adaptation in war, Bo pondered. He had been given the opportunity to study military adaptation during his time at War College. Bo recalled one particularly compelling narrative from a book he had studied by American scholars Cohen and Gooch.

"The requirement to adapt to unexpected circumstances tests both organization and system, revealing weaknesses that are partly structural and partly functional, whose full potential for disaster may not previously have been noticed."

There had been plenty of opportunities for learning and adaptation since the landings last month. Not that there had been many opportunities to fight or learn from the Americans this far south. No, for Bo and his Marines, the Taiwanese Army had been the principal foe—the Taiwanese, supported by American and Japanese ground-attack drones, uncrewed aerial bomb trucks circling at 30,000 feet, and long-range strike missiles.

The Taiwanese, defending their homes and their families, had been tough and retained their organizational cohesion. They possessed excellent fighting spirit and engaged in combat like tigers.

Every meter of ground was disputed, and the PLA had paid in blood for every kilometer it had advanced from the beachheads.

So much for the briefings from their political officers on the weaknesses of Taiwanese society!

Their adversary had also made excellent use of urban terrain to delay the Chinese ground forces. It was an environment which Bo had trained in before; however, it was something that was very difficult to excel in. And the nature of urban combat was different from previous wars.

Bo pondered how cities now had become so much larger. Even with the entire PLA, it would be very difficult to surround and seize all of Taiwan's major cities. Instead, critical nodes were selected which would then become the focal point for tactical operations. Cities then became a series of localized engagements. Understanding the anatomy of a city, and what were its most vital points to possess, was critical before launching any form of urban operation.

The precise nature of new weapon systems had also changed urban combat. If you could be found, you would be targeted. If you were targeted, you would be hit by any one of the numerous precision direct and indirect munitions used by the Taiwanese and supplied through their American allies. And this could often be done while minimizing civilian casualties, an important factor if the Chinese were to rule this island once combat operations were finished. *At least, that was the theory*, Bo thought. It was somewhat harder in practice.

One feature of urban combat was the proliferation of autonomous systems. It was far from the first time that robots had been used in cities. The Americans had used many different types during their operations in Iraq. However, the new robotic systems featured higher levels of autonomous capability. They also had the ability to aggregate into swarms or disaggregate, depending on the threat and mission parameters.

These autonomous vehicles operated in the sky at different altitudes, and on the ground. Some variants of the autonomous ground combat vehicles were also able to work underground; this subterranean capability had come in handy on more than one occasion. In this campaign, both the Taiwanese and Chinese forces had used them for combat and engineering reconnaissance, longer term surveillance, electronic warfare, logistic resupply of forward troops, medical evacuation, as well the more lethal range of assignments they were capable of.

Both sides had also learned ever-improving tactics for mixing humans and robots in the combat and combat-support functions of ground and aerial operations. The Taiwanese and Chinese were in a battle to out-adapt each other and to learn more quickly, to gain a tactical edge.

The versatility of the autonomous vehicles in the air, as well as on and under the ground, had also evolved. Some of the UAVs had been tasked as hunter-killers that would only target the Taiwanese (and American) autonomous reconnaissance vehicles or electronic warfare vehicles. Others on the ground had been adapted to function as lethal and patient anti-UAV platforms.

This cycle of adaptation, learning, and changing tactics was operating at a vicious pace. Indeed, many of the small engagements between Taiwanese and Chinese forces in the past week had been between robotic systems only. The autonomous platforms, with their clever targeting algorithms and lethally accurate weapon systems, were able to function at a speed beyond that at which humans could think, move, and fight. And then regenerate and do it all over again. And again and again.

Given the western shore of Taiwan was a flat coastal plain dominated by a succession of cities and large towns, much of Bo's time on the island had been spent in urban combat missions. But not all.

As a Marine unit, they lacked many of the heavier vehicles and weapon systems possessed by the conventional Army brigades in the Group Armies that had been landing with such rapidity over the past month. Bo's brigade was equipped with the ZTD-05 amphibious tank, an amphibious infantry fighting vehicle, and a battalion of artillery. But these were no match for the heavier (though older) armored vehicles of the Taiwanese Army.

Therefore, Bo's brigade and the other surviving Marine brigades were on the far-right flank of the advancing PLA force. This way, they would be fighting against lighter Taiwanese forces that deployed in the interface between the towns and mountains to the east. It involved some urban combat and some fighting in the eastern hills.

It had been christened "peri-urban combat" by some clever staff officer. Peri-urban, a term that described hybrid landscapes with urban and rural characteristics, was a perfect description for the environment in which Bo and his brigade had been operating. The term had stuck and was now used widely, at least in this part of the advancing Chinese horde.

While seizing the small port at Tainan, the liberating force had been able to commence a rapid offload of two Group Armies in the south. The priority had been given to the operational units, and therefore the logistic supply train was still fighting to offload sufficient supplies to keep these Group Armies fighting and moving north.

That situation would hopefully improve once they secured the southern port at Kaohsiung. Part of the Third Group Army was still involved in vicious close combat operations to seize the port and the airfield in that Taiwanese city. It had been hard going, and the Taiwanese had maximized the use of obstacles, landmines, cluster munitions, precision strikes, autonomous systems, and their combined arms forces to delay the Chinese takeover in that area. That was of little concern to Bo, however. He was focused on their advance north.

Bo bade his battalion commander farewell. They had been discussing the next phase of the advance north, and the part of

Bo's Marine brigade in that advance. One of three combined arms battalions in the brigade, this one would be the vanguard of their advance north. The next phase of the PLA operations, after a month of heavy fighting from the Tainan landing beaches all the way north to Chiayi City, would see them as part of the major operation to surround and then seize a major city in west-central Taiwan.

But before they could do that, there was a succession of towns and rivers that they had to advance across and through. It was a linear distance of 80 kilometers. But Colonel Bo knew that he and his men would be fighting every step of the way.

While the information had been kept from his men, Bo knew that not all the Chinese landings had gone to plan. There had been some kind of disaster in the northern part of the Taiwan Strait. Consequently, the PLA had shifted its main effort to the landings in the south. After building up and breaking out of the beachhead, the campaign plan had thereafter featured this advance north along the heavily populated western coastal plain.

The next phase, according to Bo's commander, would be operations to secure the main city of Taichung in central Taiwan. Not only did it possess an excellent port that would shorten their supply lines, but it would also be an important symbolic victory for the PLA. *It might convince the government of this rebellious island to finally come to the negotiating table*, Bo thought.

During this phase, commencing in the coming days, another PLA Group Army would advance across the eastern mountains and fight its way north along the narrow strip of land on the eastern edge of the island. *That is the plan at least*, Bo thought. *Those mountains are very difficult terrain*. And just as their forces had prepared for fighting in the cities, the Taiwanese would be well prepared to defend the key terrain that allowed movement across those mountains.

Bo was rudely drawn out of his contemplations by one of his Marines yelling. He was being urgently waved over to his command vehicle by an agitated, and scared, Marine in charge of Bo's personal protection detail. He too had seen the missile strike on Bo's headquarters and knew he had to move his commander away quickly. While it was likely they would have been struck at the same time if they too had been detected, Bo ran over and crawled into the back of the vehicle. On entering, he was passed a headset by his adjutant. Bo seated himself in front of his command screen. It portrayed an area of 50 square kilometers, all of Bo's units, as well as those PLA units adjacent to his.

There were 3D domes at various locations, showing where both friendly and enemy jamming against precision navigation and timing systems was occurring. Or where there was an active electronic attack or air defense threat. These were analyzed by AI that was integral to the digital command system that prioritized the threats according to their proximity to Bo's troops. And the screen showed a series of red icons to the east and the north. The enemy.

"Send a detachment for search and rescue at the main headquarters site. I doubt there will be much left, but we must evacuate any wounded," Bo ordered into his command network. His words were auto-transcribed into secure texts that were then transmitted across encrypted networks to the surviving elements of the headquarters company for his brigade.

Now that he was again in front of his command screen, he realized that he had a series of messages and reports awaiting his attention. Normally his operations officer would have brought these to his attention. Unfortunately, the operations officer had been visiting the main brigade headquarters when it had been struck by the American missile. He would not be providing updates to Colonel Bo again.

One message in particular caught Bo's attention.

"NEW THEATER COMMANDER TO TAKE COMMAND IMMEDIATELY. PROVIDE LATEST STATUS ON YOUR BRIGADE STRENGTH AND MISSION CAPABILITY FOR NEXT PHASE OF CURRENT OPERATION."

So there was a new theater commander. Bo was unsurprised by this. Even to the most biased observer, it was clear that the PLA's campaign in Taiwan had become bogged down in the south. The debacle in the northern Taiwan Strait had resulted in thousands of deaths that would have to be explained somehow by the Party. That would be difficult enough.

But the slow, rain-sodden advance north from the landing beaches around Tainan had become an even greater problem for the leadership of the PLA and the Central Military Commission. The lengthy casualty lists—not that they would ever be published in China—were becoming more difficult for the PLA to explain to the president.

The time it was taking to return this rebellious province to the homeland was the biggest problem. It had always been a gamble. The PLA leadership needed to ensure that they could retake the island before the Americans could assemble an international coalition and conduct operations to interfere with the PLA campaign. There was still time, clearly, but they did not have all year.

While Bo was denied access to international news reporting of the campaign on their military communications networks, he and his men had often discovered Taiwanese newspapers and other digital media that did contain reporting from different parts of the world. The Americans had taken some serious damage at various bases across the western Pacific. However, their capacity to surge forces back into the theater, and combine them with the Japanese, Australians, and others had occurred much more quickly than Chinese planners had anticipated.

And, according to the foreign news reports that Bo had surreptitiously read in the rear of his command vehicle, Western military commentators and academics had also been surprised. Surprised by the level of American resilience in the face of the massive onslaught from the People's Liberation Army Rocket Force against

214

American, Japanese, and Australian bases. And surprised that the Chinese invasion was not the rapid *fait accompli* that many had been predicting over the previous decade.

We have all been surprised by different aspects of this campaign, Bo pondered as he continued scrolling through the succession of messages on his screen.

Suddenly his vehicle crew commander screamed into the vehicle's intercom system.

"Incoming, brace, moving now!"

They were coming under fire. From where, he would ascertain shortly. But if he was to guess, someone had broken their restrictive emissions policy and the Americans had detected some kind of electronic leakage that allowed them to target Bo's unit.

Bo did not need to give any orders. They had drilled the basic response under such circumstances: close up and move out to a pre-designated rendezvous point. There was always an alternate headquarters position for situations like this.

He was shaken by several explosions that were closer than he would have liked. The vehicle, moving quickly around and over the rubble of the town, rocked violently from side to side. Bo, knowing the vehicle commander was doing his job, now spoke into his encrypted command net.

"Headquarters moving to alternate location. Contact from indirect fire. Source unknown."

He didn't need to say much more. His artillery battalion possessed fire direction radars that would pinpoint the source of the incoming fire if it was from a ground-based source. This battalion was digitally linked to other artillery battalions across southern Taiwan, as well as their liaison with the PLA Air Force. If the source could be pinpointed, it would be allocated a target priority in the joint-target list and then attacked by the most suitable Air Force, Army, or Navy unit.

Like much of the ground combat now, it was an automatic process requiring minimal human input. Indeed, PLA military doctrine reinforced that humans should not interfere in this process to ensure that it occurred as rapidly as possible. Bo knew that this differed from Western organizations, which still preferred to have what they called "human on the loop" to make final decisions about killing other humans. *They will learn the hard way that such an approach is foolish and will cost them lives and battlefield success,* Bo thought.

After 15 minutes of a rough-and-tumble journey to their new location, the vehicle finally slowed and then halted. They had not experienced any explosions near the vehicle since the initial fusillade of fire.

Bo breathed a sigh of relief. As he did, he looked down at his command screen once more to verify how much of his headquarters had managed to escape. He was gratified to see that the entire complement of vehicles and Marines from his headquarters had managed to safely extricate themselves and arrive at this new location unscathed. Bo also noticed a new message had appeared at the top of the multitude of incoming secure texts.

"TOP SECRET. PHASE 2 OPERATIONAL PLAN."

This message required a password on top of the normal encryption that it was subject to. Quickly entering the text password and verifying his identity with a retinal scan, Bo was able to open the message. It was the orders for the next phase of their advance north.

They would cross their line of departure for this next phase in 48 hours. The three Group Armies of the Eastern Theater—the 71st, 72nd, and 73rd—would advance as a solid line of ground forces. Another Group Army, the 81st, would be held in reserve and would reinforce whichever of the leading Group Armies was experiencing success.

Bo's brigade remained attached to the easternmost Group Army, the 72nd. Because they were lighter in firepower than normal

PLA brigades, Bo's brigade would continue to be employed on the eastern flank of the advance north. They would provide security from attack out of the mountains, and feed early warning of any enemy activity on the far-right flank of the advancing Chinese. *More peri-urban operations*, Bo considered.

To conduct this mission, Bo's brigade had its normal strength of three combined arms battalions (now considerably weakened by casualties), an artillery battalion, air defense, and other support organizations. Over the past month, instead of human reinforcements, his brigade had been issued with hundreds of new autonomous ground combat vehicles and aerial recon and strike vehicles.

It had taken his Marines some time to get used to teaming with these robotic combatants. However, after several trials and unsuccessful tactical actions, they had eventually worked out satisfactory ways to use and fight with the machines.

The robots were slowly taking over the fighting. In this campaign, he and his men could still die. But as the attack they had just escaped from had showed, they just wouldn't do it in hand-to-hand combat or fighting against other soldiers or Marines. *It truly is a remote war*, Bo thought.

There was much to do between now and the commencement of the renewed advance north by the PLA forces. He perused the details of the operational plan. It contained an estimate of enemy strength, movements, and likely future intentions. And it appeared that they were both seeking the same thing—a major city that dominated the central-western coast of Taiwan. Site of airfields, ports, and a major urban concentration, it would be a significant propaganda coup for whichever side managed to seize or hold it.

The city would also provide an excellent logistics hub for subsequent operations. Whether they were moving north or south, whoever owned the city would have a superb foundation from which to conduct operations to secure the remainder of the island.

Bo nodded, now understanding the next objective for the PLA and for his brigade. It would be a hard fight all the way north. While the PLA missiles, cyber warriors, electronic warfare, and Air Force would be providing support every meter of the way, this was a ground fight. The success or failure of this next phase would be determined by the actions of the soldiers and Marines on the ground. *Like war all through history always has been*, Bo thought.

He then spoke on the vehicle intercom to his driver.

"Private Zi, it appears that all roads now lead to Taichung. Advance."

20

What Happens in Nevada

19 June 2028
Classified US Air Force facility
Somewhere in the American Southwest

The heavy hangar door rolled open on its metal tracks to reveal the last rays of a sun setting on the western horizon. The hangar, one of several at the remote facility in the western United States, was less a traditional metal-framed structure and more of a subterranean hideout. The entire structure had been constructed in a large excavation inside a mountain that was roughly in the center of the Nevada test range. It was an undeclared facility, even though the test range was marked on all civilian maps and well known to aviators, military and civil.

Air Force General Mary-Ann Scott peered out the doorway at the flat desert floor. The evening air was still and cool. She pondered what it might be like to be back at the controls of an F-22 in such lovely flying conditions before quickly pushing these ideas from her mind. She was here for much more important things on her first visit to this subterranean wonder.

The officer beside her began to speak.

"The facility was constructed during the 1980s and 1990s out of funds appropriated by Congress within the Pentagon's black budget. The black budget consumes just under 10 percent of the total budget for the American military. It's used to fund all kinds of highly classified programs that we hope will provide us with a winning edge in future conflicts. The facility you are standing in has accounted for a good proportion of the black budget over the past 30 years."

For most civilians, this was a world that was entirely unknown. Only a few journalists and think-tank academics tracked this aspect of America's military spending. And those that did were normally drawn to exotic aircraft or space-based capabilities that sold magazines or solicited thousands of clicks on webpages and likes on social media.

But the black budget was so much more. As was this facility, Scott thought. So far, what she had seen had not only surprised her, but it had also been a pleasant shock after the events of the past month.

Scott had been appointed the vice chairman of the Joint Chiefs only six weeks before the war with China had broken out. In the wake of the Taiwan invasion scare the previous year, her priority had been to quietly but quickly ramp up industrial production and personnel training across the US military services.

Scott had been an Air Force academy graduate and spent most of her career flying fighter jets. Her last flying command had been in charge of the F-22 Raptor air superiority fighter. A technological marvel, it had been a joy to fly and fight with. And while it was now getting to the point where foreign aircraft were beginning to catch up, a continuous series of upgrades had kept it at the leading edge of air combat.

None of her previous experiences as a fighter pilot, or her staff appointments, had prepared her for what she had seen so far during her afternoon and evening "under the mountain." It was a stunning facility.

For decades the United States Government, and its military leaders, had carefully prevented the world from knowing about this place or what it did. In some respects, it represented a final option in the use of conventional forces before any resort to nuclear weapons. Therein lay its importance to the national security, and global standing, of the United States.

During the Cold War, despite the many new technologies and operational concepts such as Assault Breaker, US and NATO military planners knew there was a reasonable chance that they might have to resort to nuclear weapons as a final option to blunt a Warsaw Pact invasion of Europe. That would have been pointless. They might have defeated the Soviets, but it would have been a pyrrhic victory. They would have left a radioactive legacy for generations to come.

Post-Cold War, planners developed a new and highly secretive program to provide another "final option" that did not involve killing millions of civilians and making portions of the earth uninhabitable for thousands of years. In the mid-1980s, this facility had begun to be constructed. Even when the Soviet Union collapsed, forward-thinking leaders in Washington, DC had decided that they would continue to invest in this final conventional option. Despite the claims of some that humans now existed at "the end of history," more sober heads knew better. History demonstrated that there was always another adversary who could rise up. Even if such an adversary was not yet obvious, there was always one just beyond the horizon.

Long-range planning from the net assessment team in the Pentagon, working directly for the secretary of defense, had provided a variety of strategic analyses that reinforced the need for the capabilities that this facility provided. And so, the facility was quietly and continuously expanded, and the best minds from the

United States and beyond were recruited to work in an assortment of classified programs.

Every now and then, there were sightings of strange aircraft being flown along America's west coast. Most were not actually products of this facility but were test beds from the many aviation companies that resided in California. But some were, so with careful information operations and subversion of certain publishers in the news industry, little remained known of what occurred here or what it produced.

The Gulf Wars in 1991 and 2003 had not been seen as significant enough to call on the capabilities developed under this Nevada mountain range. These conflicts were neither existential nor likely to result in a catastrophic loss of American forces. And then there were insurgencies of the first two decades of the 21st century, which hardly gained the attention of those toiling away in this facility.

No, until now, nothing had really justified the application of the technologies here that the United States had held so close to its chest. And even if the military wanted to, only the president could approve such use. If the capabilities here were to be unveiled, they needed to be used decisively and with strategic effect because other nations would quickly seek to acquire and copy them.

This place had even been given a top-secret codename, known to only a few of the most senior military and government people in Washington: DIAMOND GRAM. "Gram," after the sword wielded by the Norse god Odin. And "Diamond," because of its precious and costly contents.

The DIAMOND GRAM capabilities had never been used in anger before. There had never been a crisis that demanded the deployment of its uniquely lethal capabilities. That had all changed in the past month, Scott thought. She was visiting to ensure that the facility and its contents were ready for war. Her discussions with the chairman, the secretary, and the president in the past

48 hours indicated that they were considering the use of what lay beneath the mountain.

Had things really become so dire? Yes, they had, she thought. *They really had.* Scott turned and began to walk back into the depths of the mountain.

If one was to walk through the camouflaged hangar doors into this mountainside shelter, as she had this afternoon, they would find that the hangar itself extended for nearly 300 feet before leading to an even larger lateral tunnel that joined several other mountainside entrances to the underground facility. The tunnel included workshop space for maintenance on the advanced vehicles that were housed within.

In turn, the lateral passage led to another complex of large underground spaces that contained something that the black project followers and conspiracy theorists had never shown any interest in. Something that had remained unimagined by all except a few visionaries deep within the bowels of the Joint Chiefs of Staff. A capability so important that only a few in Washington knew of its existence. Of course, those who worked in the hangar were well aware of its existence. But even few of them understood the full capability of this facility.

It was a factory. A massive subterranean factory, where robotic assembly machines and additive manufacturing machines—also known as 3D printers—were capable of churning out all kinds of exotic military designs. With its massive reserves of metal feedstock, and covert procurement of subassemblies, this one-of-a-kind manufacturing facility could assemble the most advanced designs for flying machines ever imagined. And it could build them fast. Lightning fast.

The current generation F-35A joint strike fighter took an average of just over 41,000 human hours to assemble. In the 1980s, an F-16 took about 29,000 hours to assemble. Much of this time was absorbed by the tens of thousands of fasteners, and their testing, for each aircraft. It was a fiddly, difficult task requiring time and precision. Not anymore.

With the advent of additive manufacturing in the 1980s, a deep black program was initiated by the US Air Force that could assemble different military vehicles in a faster time than traditional manufacturing. As the science of additive manufacturing developing into the 2000s and 2010s, the secret facility here was continuously upgraded and expanded.

It now had the capacity for all forms of 3D printing of components and sub-assemblies for very sophisticated test aircraft. The ability to undertake binder jetting, directed energy deposition, material extrusion, material jetting, as well as assembly by large and small robots was all contained within the massive secret caverns beneath this Nevada mountain. Large reserves of different materials were also held in warehouses under the mountain just in case the US ever needed to shift to full-scale production of those test aircraft.

A new aircraft could now be assembled in the secret factory in just over 5,000 hours. Not linear hours—total hours. With three parallel lines, the facility could produce six aircraft every day if it needed to. It was a revolutionary capability for the US military and one that could be quickly adapted as lessons were learned from flying and combat operations—which made it one of the jewels in the crown of US defense manufacturing. A secret one, but an enormously valuable capability for the military, nonetheless. And it was a secret that none of America's allies knew about.

The first major test of the facility had been the X-44 program back in the late 1990s and early 2000s. A tailless, manta-shaped aircraft, it featured high levels of automation and cutting-edge stealth technology. While publicly the program had been canceled in 2000, the reality was that it had continued as an experimental program well into the 2000s. Several airframes had been constructed in the secret Nevada facility. These had been used, and sometimes sighted by civilian plane spotters, in test flights over the American Midwest and off the California coast.

Late in the test program, one of the aircraft had even been used to probe the edges of the Russian and Chinese Air Defense Identification Zones to ascertain just how stealthy the X-44 was. These experiments showed that it was very stealthy indeed. Cyber monitoring of Russian and Chinese air defense networks showed that the X-44 had never been detected. The results of these tests were then fed into the design of a successor.

That successor, a long-range stealth strike fighter, was what currently occupied the subterranean hangars under the mountain. Larger even than the Chinese J-20 heavy stealth fighter, the F/A-48 Super Corsair had a range, weapons payload, and stealthiness that was beyond any aircraft flying in any air force in the world. Its impressive and unique capabilities were why the US Air Force had decided in the 2010s to keep the super secretive aircraft—and its exquisitely trained crews—in the black world.

To complement this aircraft was a family of autonomous air and ground vehicles. Using the technologies developed for the X-44, these stealthy, swarming, lethal machines could operate either as loyal wingmen to the Super Corsair manned aircraft, or as entirely independent swarms and individual platforms. The swarms were guided by brilliant AI, which had also been developed under the mountain. Collectively, the Super Corsairs, UAVs, AI, and humans—at least in all the simulations that had been run—were unbeatable by any military entity on earth.

Upon her arrival at the mountain hideout earlier that afternoon, Scott had been briefed in detail on these simulations. Contrary to the overly pessimistic assessments of think tanks in Washington that always scored Chinese wins in Taiwan scenarios, the introduction of the capabilities developed in Nevada—such as the Super

Corsair—were game changers. In the same scenarios in which American forces were defeated a large proportion of the time, the inclusion of the secretive capabilities reversed outcomes and saw a near 100 percent success rate for friendly forces.

I hope they are right, Scott thought at the end of the session. Given how size and geography assisted the Chinese, the US military and its allies would need every advantage it could muster.

It was these scenarios that she was pondering when her escort officer, an Air Force brigadier general, intruded on her thoughts. "Ma'am, you have a flash secure message from the chairman. There have been some developments."

He paused while noting the reaction from Scott. She had only come here to verify the readiness of the facility and its products for employment in the coming weeks or months. She had not expected this. Nor the full potential of the aircraft within. She would need to find a secure connection to join the meeting. And she would need to call Admiral Leonard at INDOPACOM as soon as possible.

Phase III

21

Save Our Dream

5 July 2028
Underground aircraft hangar
Hualien
Eastern coast of Taiwan

Private First Class Chen touched the bandage around his head for what was probably the hundredth time that morning. The small patch, one of the new ones with smart-clotting and healing technology, was a far cry from the more extensive older-style field dressings that had been the mainstay on his head in the previous weeks.

He had awoken several hours after the attack on the command post back in May, being jostled around in the back of an Army ambulance vehicle. The ancient American M113 tracked armored personnel carrier had been converted to an upgraded Taiwanese version that was known locally as a CM21. In the last two years, as the PLA threat had become more imminent, several had been converted to transport combat casualties on the battlefield. The vehicles were old, much older than the humans who drove them or who were carried within. But as ambulances they were useful enough to protect wounded soldiers and transport them out of harm's way to the closest aid station or field hospital.

Chen had been lying down, with a drip inserted into his left arm and massive bandages that swaddled almost his entire head. The medic wearily turned around from tending another casualty in the triple racks of stretchers that lined the two sides of the rear of the vehicle. She looked at Chen with a mixture of empathy and concern.

This particular Army medic had clearly experienced a very hectic day. Chen thought that she must have been exhausted from spreading her attention and care between so many casualties in the close quarters of the ambulance.

"Private Chen, welcome back. You are on your way to the divisional aid station at Yilan. What do you remember?"

Yilan township, Chen had thought. *That is on the east coast. Why are we going in that direction, rather than down the western plain where the enemy was more likely to be?*

And where was the rest of his unit?

"I see you are confused. That is normal with a head injury of this type. But don't worry. It is not a major injury—it is just a concussion with several large contusions which bled quite a lot," the medic said.

Chen, beginning to get his bearings and to remember what had occurred back at the command post, was finally able to open his mouth to speak. His voice was raspy from lack of hydration.

"Where is the rest of my unit, and the soldiers from my headquarters?"

The medic nodded slowly before responding. This was a common question from soldiers emerging from unconsciousness in strange surroundings. She spoke quietly, wanting to soften the blow of the bad news she was about to share.

"Our medical detachment was close by, and we were able to get to your headquarters quickly after the strike. It was a mess. I am afraid that most of those in your headquarters were either killed or severely wounded. You and a couple of the less seriously wounded were treated on site and are in this ambulance and two others ahead of us. Fortunately, your commander and a small tactical party were absent. They have established a new, low-signature brigade command post to the south of Yilan. We are on our way there now."

In the days and weeks that followed, Chen and the rest of the soldiers that remained from his brigade headquarters had moved several times to respond to reported PLA incursions on the east coast. In nearly every case, these had been false alarms.

But on one occasion last week, a small group of PLA robotic combat systems had broken through into a large logistic supply dump in the northeast of the country. Normally, such affairs would be taken care of by the infantry or armor troops of the brigade. Not this time.

The robots, commonly known by his fellow soldiers as beetles, had been discovered in a section of a large military supply depot that was less than 500 meters from Chen's brigade headquarters. Chen and several of his fellow soldiers had been rapidly formed into squads and dispatched to deal with the beetles and keep them busy until other troops could be deployed to dispatch them. It was mountainous terrain, and it would be hard going to get there quickly on foot. However, the dense surrounding vegetation would also delay vehicles. It would be a dismounted operation.

Chen recalled the terror he had felt in the short march through the thick foliage to where the beetles had last been spotted. He had hoped that these were just dumb autonomous ground combat vehicles that could be quickly destroyed with small arms and light anti-armor weapons. Chen thought that he and his fellow soldiers would be able to destroy these stupid machines quickly. He had been disabused of that notion very quickly.

Chen and his squad had been ambushed by several of the PLA robots before they had even arrived at the supply dump. The beetles, armed with small-caliber automatic weapon appendages, had killed two of Chen's fellow soldiers almost immediately.

After conducting a counter-ambush drill that had been beaten into them in basic training, Chen and the surviving members of the squad had fought their way out of the ambush. They had then counterattacked the beetles, calling in artillery first to suppress the lethal mechanical killing machines. Chen and the other soldiers had then cleared the area where the beetles had been located, finding only smashed metallic carapaces and appendages. The artillery, thank goodness, had done all the killing. *Thank god for the gunners,* he thought.

Chen remembered, however, the lightning reflexes of the beetles when he and his fellow troops had initially been ambushed. The beetles had been able to fire, move, and re-engage at a speed that he had never seen from human troops. But when Chen and the surviving soldiers had leapt onto the ground to find cover, the firing had ceased. It was almost like the beetles had only been programmed to kill humans that were standing, walking, or running. Lying on the ground seemed to either confuse them, or their sensors were not able to sufficiently discern dirty, cold humans lying in a heavily vegetated area.

That had been two weeks ago.

Since then, Chen had not had to display his martial skills. He had been kept busy in the running of the command post and monitoring brigade operations. Private First Class Chen, now one of the most experienced members of the headquarters, also had two other important responsibilities.

First, he was responsible for welcoming and inducting reinforcements for the headquarters. The Chinese missile attack on their headquarters back in May had killed many of his fellow soldiers. Over the past few weeks, replacements from the national mobilization program had begun to arrive. Chen would ensure that they arrived at the correct location, would check their personal equipment and weapons, and then assign them to the highest priority vacancies in one of the three elements of the distributed brigade command post.

His second new responsibility was providing summarized updates to the brigade's operations officer. These updates incorporated the activities of their own brigade—the 269th—as well as those units adjacent to the brigade. As part of the update, he also had to compile a list of new American and allied units arriving in Taiwan in each 24-hour period.

There were many new combat and support units from other countries arriving. Some directly supported the Taiwanese forces in areas such as algorithmic analysis, air defense, and offensive strikes. Others were allocated to fight as part of the coalition's new corps, led by the Americans. All of the updates provided by Chen would then be further summarized for the brigade commander's regular briefing sessions.

It was a hectic existence. But it kept his mind off his family. And Mei.

In the past month, he had only received one brief electronic transmission from Mei. She had been sheltering with Chen's parents in Taipei. Power and internet access were intermittent. They still had running water, although food was being rationed. Even now, the PLA was conducting regular missile and cyber strikes on radio and TV networks, as well as government buildings. But the American missile defense units, including the new laser defense systems, were also shooting down many of the Chinese missiles, so the damage to the capital was not as bad as Chinese propaganda was portraying. It was a grim situation, to be sure. But Mei and Chen's parents were safe.

That sole message had come through nearly two weeks ago, in one of the regular secure email downloads that Chen's brigade received for its soldiers. He had received nothing since then. He could not use Insta to communicate with Mei. Social media was totally off limits. It was a sure-fire way to give away the location of military units. All members of the Taiwanese military had been prohibited from any usage of social media since the beginning of June. Chen had even heard quiet rumors of transgressors being shot, although he had not personally witnessed such things. Perhaps it was just another Chinese propaganda lie.

However, Chen was not going to risk finding out. He knew what the military police were like. He was not going to mess with them in wartime. Chen took his hand away from the small dressing on his head. Yes, it had been an awful few weeks, much worse than he had ever imagined he might experience.

With the threat of a Chinese invasion of his home becoming a reality, he now fully understood the mandatory military service, the beach obstacles, and other military investments that his nation had made in the preceding decades. Before his compulsory national service, and even at times before the Chinese invasion, Chen had been skeptical about whether all this military equipment and posturing was necessary. Surely the Chinese had other concerns than invading Chen's homeland? Had not the last several decades, with the massive Taiwanese investments in Chinese mainland businesses, ensured a more peaceful coexistence?

He appreciated that these efforts had not prevented Chinese aggression against his homeland. He understood many things now.

Chen looked up at the roof above his head. It was carved out of the solid granite beneath a mountain range that ran down the length of the eastern Taiwan coastline. The ceiling was lofty. Since the 1950s, the Taiwanese government had funded many large-scale projects to burrow into the hills and mountains of their island home to ensure their military could survive and fight back after any Chinese attempt at a surprise attack.

The offshore islands, particularly those closest to China, were underground warrens crisscrossed with subterranean bunkers and tunnels that stored equipment, weapons, ammunition, fuel, food, and water. These bunkers also contained barracks for soldiers, headquarters, and hospitals to tend to the inevitable casualties of any war against China.

In major population centers, the military had also constructed large underground complexes. One of the most impressive was the Hengshan Military Command Centre beneath the capital Taipei. A sprawling complex that stretched for hundreds of meters in all directions, this large, hardened bunker provided a command center for the Taiwanese military as well as an alternative site for the national government of the island. It was stocked with sufficient provisions for thousands of people to work and live deep beneath the streets of the capital for months at a time.

A similar complex, hollowed out of a mountain in Taiwan's south, was still holding out against Chinese attackers despite large parts of the south now being held by the PLA. They could hold out against the Chinese for months. But if they were not relieved by Taiwanese forces after that, it was inevitable that this southern redoubt would fall to the invaders.

But probably the most impressive of the Taiwanese tunneling projects were the subterranean airfields on the east coast. It was the largest of these, just outside the town of Hualien, in which Chen now stood. Built in the 1980s, it had been constantly upgraded to improve its resistance against Chinese missile attacks, and to expand the number of aircraft that it could host. Facilities for fuel storage and alternate runways had also been built, all protected by multiple layers of air defense missiles, cyber defenses, camouflage, and millions of tons of steel-reinforced concrete and stone. And now, part of that protection on the ground was Chen's brigade.

After their move from the north, the 269th had been tasked with defending the southern approaches of the massive underground complex and its connected runways. They also provided a ready reaction force that could be moved anywhere within several miles to counter any incursion by beetles or crewed-system PLA attacks. Chen, and the rest of the headquarters for the brigade, were located at the side of one of the large subterranean hangars in the Hualien complex.

It was a massive structure, with few like it anywhere in the world. Along with its air and ground defenses, it was one of the most impregnable locations on the face of the earth. Even after repeated barrages of Chinese missiles, the base under the mountain had remained operable. PLA attempts to destroy runways had been quickly repaired by Taiwanese engineers. It was something that they had rehearsed and trained for in the decades before the war.

In the past month, with the arrival of the Americans, the base had been renamed Joint Base Hualien. They brought with them their batteries of Patriot anti-missile defenses, as well as units of the Iron Dome anti-missile systems that had been provided by the Israelis. Hundreds of experts in cyber defense, power and fuel management, and airfield damage repair also arrived.

According to Chen's brigade commander, it was one of the new strategic bastions that were being created by the allies in Taiwan, and overseas. It was from these bastions that American, Taiwanese, Japanese, and other forces could project offensive power against the PLA in Taiwan and beyond.

The mountain base had once been a highly restricted location, with only Taiwanese military personnel with the highest security clearances being allowed to enter. But that had all changed. As Chen looked around him, he could see many different uniforms from not just Taiwan, but also from the military forces of the United States, Japan, Canada, and even some Australians.

Chen's boss, the brigade operations officer Major Lin, had also survived the attack on their command post in the north. He stood beside Chen now.

"Private Chen, I bet you never thought you would see such a sight," Lin mused.

Chen nodded. The major was correct. Chen, even after the days he had spent in this cavern, and others like it, still struggled to comprehend the magnitude of the underground base.

"Sir, it is like something from a movie. Even with everything that has happened in the past two months, this seems surreal," Chen responded.

He then asked the question to Lin that had been on his mind all morning.

"Sir, last night, those new American aircraft that arrived—they are not like anything I have ever seen before. They are not shaped like anything in our own Air Force and made almost no noise at all. And their color—it seemed like it was constantly changing. I could not tell you what color they were."

Lin nodded and looked at Chen. He had a serious look on his face.

"Private Chen, you had best not ask questions like that. Those aircraft are apparently part of some super-secret American project. I have heard that they have moved similar aircraft to another base located on the Ishigaki Islands bastion off our eastern coast. However, even our brigade commander has been told very little about what they are and what they are here for."

Major Lin looked across the hangar. It was more densely packed with Taiwanese, American, and Japanese aircraft than normal. Clearly the newly arrived secret aircraft had displaced many aircraft from their normal locations.

Lin then turned back to Chen.

"But it would make sense, Private Chen, that if the Americans are sending us their most secret and advanced aircraft, either things are worse than we thought or there is something big coming up soon."

Chen nodded, and then to his surprise, Lin's voice softened, and he changed the subject of their conversation.

"Have you heard anymore from your girlfriend or family?"

Chen, his mind having to shift from what he was looking at, responded quietly, "No sir. And you?"

Chen knew that Major Lin's wife and two children had been in the south of the country, staying with her parents when the war had begun.

Lin was quiet for a moment. When he spoke, it was a voice that somehow managed to convey both heartache and conviction.

"Nothing for the past six weeks. They tried to escape the city when the Chinese came. The last I heard, they were on the road north of Hengchun. But given how we have lost all communications with the south, I don't expect to hear much until we win—and take back our country from the Chinese."

Lin was quiet for a moment, and then spoke again.

"You understand what we are fighting for here, Chen? We cannot afford to lose. Because if we do, the Chinese will take away everything we have built in the past seventy years. Like Tibet, and Hong Kong, we will become another slave state, prostrate at the feet of heartless, ruthless old men in Beijing."

Chen nodded. He understood the importance of the way of life that they had built in Taiwan. More than ever, he appreciated their ability in this small country to speak their minds and live their lives how they wished to, free from some political party dictating large elements of their lives.

To some, it was just a dream. But it was a dream worth saving, Chen thought.

22

New Strategy, Old Strategy

6 July 2028
Headquarters INDOPACOM

"Sir, the actual words of the declaration, which was actually a tweet rather than a formal statement, are as follows: 'After 52 years it is time for the United States to fully recognize Israel's Sovereignty over the Golan Heights, which is of critical strategic and security importance to the State of Israel and Regional Stability!'"

The statement, issued during the previous administration, had been formalized in a presidential proclamation signed on 25 March 2019. The previous president had signed it in the presence of the Israeli prime minister. And while the proclamation had been criticized by many nations, including some of America's closest allies, the current president had upheld the recognition in 2021.

Admiral Leonard nodded his head, thanking Rear Admiral Jane Davis. She had begun the latest update on the Taiwan situation with a piece of information he had asked for earlier that morning—a statement, issued in March 2019, recognizing Israel's annexation of the Golan Heights. *The Chinese are going to continue to beat us over the head with that one*, thought Leonard.

"So, the latest Chinese maneuvers in the United Nations have continued using the statement by a previous administration to justify their invasion of Taiwan. Two months of bloodshed and violence all justified in their view because they seek to return what they see as a rebellious province to the fold?"

Davis nodded. So too did Leonard's political advisor in the head-quarters, James Sturten. He was a regular at these briefing sessions for Admiral Leonard. Sturten took his cue to join the discussion.

"Admiral, the 2019 statement has not helped us, but most governments are seeing this invasion for what it is—an old-school land grab, based on the shakiest of foundations. And of course, a lot have changed their views on such issues since Ukraine."

Leonard acknowledged Sturten with a curt nod. *These political advisers are getting younger and younger*, Leonard thought. And for once, he wished they would tell him something that he hadn't read in a news journal last month.

"Mr. Sturten, can you please provide us with the latest updates on where major nations are leaning on this conflict, and the key diplomatic initiatives that aim to end the war?"

At least the answer to that should provide something new, Leonard mused.

Sturten bobbed his head quickly and then began to speak in his measured northeastern accent.

Out of the corner of his left eye, Leonard could see the body language of several of his senior staff change. Most of them had little time for Sturten. He was well known around the headquarters for quoting his academic qualifications and his connections within the Department of State main building back in Foggy Bottom. He was less well known for the provision of informed and insightful advice. Davis even went as far as to roll her eyes.

While Leonard might agree that Sturten was an arrogant little shit, he was also not keen on deliberate displays of disrespect from his senior staff. Leonard gave Davis a subtle hand signal to cut it out. There was no need to antagonize the guy. Or the Department of State.

"Admiral, most of the African nations are continuing to sit on the fence. While none will come out and actively support China, especially after the revelations about atrocities in the south, many national leaders have been recipients of sufficient Chinese largesse that they will probably not support the alliance either. While that makes things a little tricky in the United Nations General Assembly, it does not change anything in the Security Council. It remains, as it has for the past three months, gridlocked. The Russians, Chinese, and three African non-permanent members continue to prevent any significant action from that body." Sturten paused. He briefly looked down at his secure, SCIF-compliant electronic notepad on the table in front of him, and then continued.

"South American nations are more of a mixed bag. The largest economy, Brazil, has remained mainly neutral. Its export trade with China is about three times that with the United States. However, most trade has ceased over the last three months with the blockade of Chinese ports by the alliance, and the Chinese using food reserves instead of imports. In foreign direct investment, most of the foreign investment in Brazil is from the Netherlands, the US, Canada, France, and Japan. We, and some of our allies, have reminded the Brazilians of that, particularly as their export earnings are down. Therefore, they are leaning our way without committing to the provision of combat troops. It is a similar case with Argentina. So, despite their previous trade relationships with China, neither appear to want to assist the Chinese in any way."

Sturten continued his toneless and sleep-inducing description of Latin American nations for another five minutes before halting his brief and looking around the table for questions. There were none.

Davis, who seemed to be taking a nap with her eyes open, simply stared at the slides on the screen that had accompanied the brief by the young Department of State's representative.

"Thank you, Mr. Sturten," Leonard interjected. "An excellent brief ... as always."

Sturten acknowledged the faint praise and then slouched back into his chair. It was another habit that seemed to rankle Davis and the other senior military officers in the room.

Leonard consulted his secure electronic notepad to confirm the next briefer on the agenda. It was Rear Admiral Davis again. She and her staff would be providing an update on the entire Taiwan campaign. Once that was complete, Admiral Leonard had some new and interesting information to share with the team assembled around the table. But that could wait for the moment.

Davis, as usual, was on her game. Leonard had rarely worked with an officer who understood not just her own service but maintained a deep professional knowledge of the other four services as well.

"Admiral, our alliance activities across the western Pacific continue to develop and broaden. The program to establish special strategic bastions in Japan, northern Australia, Manus Island, and the Ishigaki Islands to the east of Taiwan are well advanced. Each of these bastions features multilayered sensor and missile defense systems, as well as cyber and electronic attack security capabilities. All these locations now have ground and air-delivered long-range strike capabilities based within them. This includes missiles as well as detachments of the new B-21 bombers. The contractor is rushing these new aircraft and their accompanying drones off the production line. The accelerated production of the B-21 bombers, as you know, is now one of the Big Seven in our new alliance war production strategy."

Davis paused for a moment as she again called for the display screen to update.

"These offensive strike capabilities provide us with operational depth, and a second cordon to keep the Chinese Navy pinned inside the first island chain. We can then begin to squeeze them and eventually cut off their logistics lifeline to their forces in Taiwan."

Davis gestured at the screen with a red laser pointer. It displayed a map of the western Pacific with large 3D domes over the locations that she had just listed. Each of the domes was connected by bright lines, with other lines extending back to Hawaii and CONUS.

"These bastions are also major logistic hubs for the alliance. They provide trans-shipment points for all kinds of weapons, ammunition, fuels, food, you name it. They are also holding depots for units entering the theater and for the large numbers of reinforcements for units already in combat on the island."

The screen changed. This time, the image was focused on the chain of islands south of Kyushu in Japan that extended down through Okinawa, to Taiwan, and thence to the Philippines.

"We have been able to contain the PLA Navy within this strategic cordon. Frankly, with the losses they took early on, and their efforts to keep a secure sea passage between the mainland and Taiwan, they have limited capacity to break out. The vast majority of their fleet has always been frigates and corvettes with minimal blue water capacity. Our allies, particularly the Indonesians, Australians, and Indians, have contributed air and sea assets to keep the Chinese in, and their trade vessels out."

Davis paused for a moment and glanced at the screen and then back to Leonard.

"It has got to be hurting them. I know they have established continental trade routes and are being helped by their own reserves and trade through Russia, but still. They can't keep this up for the long term."

Leonard nodded, before he responded.

"That is true, Admiral Davis. But it is also true of our own forces. Alliances, particularly in wartime, have a shelf life. We must ensure that the shelf life of this alliance we have assembled is just that little bit longer than what the Chinese can stand."

"Indeed, Sir," Davis replied. "Now, influence operations."

An Air Force colonel, who had been sitting against the wall silently, stood and walked to the small lectern at the front of the small, secure conference room.

"Good morning, Admiral. The Chinese influence strikes on Western social media platforms have continued to evolve, based on what they have learned from our reactions over the past two months. We are seeing very sophisticated information operations out of their military and civilian organizations. The Chinese have also co-opted many criminal organizations, and these are only magnifying their reach. Their content mills are working at what seems like hyper speed. The Russians are also aiding, with data analysis as well as in the operational conduct of influence missions."

He paused for a moment and then continued.

"Counter-influence operations have received massive investment from all nations in the alliance in the past two months. This has included new transparency initiatives, public education campaigns and school programs, as well as investment in new AI-based analytical and counter-influence algorithms. It also appears, at long last, that the major social media companies have finally taken our side. Fortunately—for them and us—they are now active participants in alliance counter-influence operations."

This resulted in murmuring around the table. Many of the senior officers in the room had expressed their concern about how major technology companies had been sitting on the fence for years on this issue. Leonard quietened down the room and then asked the Air Force colonel to continue his briefing.

The colonel pressed a small button on the lectern in front of him. The screen at the front of the room changed again. This time, it was a map of the world, a version of the live cyber-attack maps that had been publicly available on the internet for years. However, this one was obviously backed up with data from across the alliance and many sensitive sources. The level of detail, and the granularity of targets portrayed on the map, impressed even Leonard.

"Admiral, what you can see is the live attack and defense map of the world. This is a 'to and fro' battle that is measured in micro-seconds but with impacts that are strategic and potentially long lasting. Every major piece of public infrastructure, military and civilian manufacturing, civil and military communications, and the entire transportation architecture of the United States and its allies has been targeted.

"We have also seen the conduct of the full range of hybrid attacks against civilians and military families in the homeland. This has included sending threats to the families of military personnel, racial and religious disinformation to cause societal division, theft of personal data, promotion of peace movements, and false information about poor morale in our military forces.

"At the same time, we have made significant inroads into targeting Chinese infrastructure networks. This is a new strategy for us. Unlike the Russians and the Chinese, we have always sought—at least publicly—to take the high ground in conducting cyber actions against public infrastructure. But because the Chinese are assessed as more vulnerable to these kinds of attacks during hostilities, we believe that this may have a moderating effect on Chinese and Russian cyber-attacks against us."

Leonard pondered this last comment for a moment before responding.

"Colonel, is that an assessment or a hope?"

The colonel, unfazed by the question from Admiral Leonard, was quick to respond.

"Sir, this is a strategy that has been developed by Cyber Command and coordinated across all the military cyber agencies, as well as those in other federal agencies and our allies. It has been extensively wargamed by humans, and this has been supported by thousands of iterations of an AI simulation that looks at various moves and countermoves the Chinese may take. Therefore, confidence is high that these actions on our part will at least have a moderating effect on Chinese and Russian cyber-attacks against our civilian infrastructure."

Leonard, remaining silent, looked around the table at his senior staff to see if there were any comments. There were none.

"Thank you, Colonel. Admiral Davis, let's move on with the updates please."

Davis nodded to the colonel, who resumed his seat against the wall.

"Sir, the final element of the normal update is ground operations. Currently, Taiwanese and American ground forces hold the western plain along a line from Taichung City across to the eastern mountain range. We expect that this is the next operational objective for the Chinese, and they have at least two and potentially up to four Group Armies postured to commence an advance north to seize the city and its surrounds. It would be a significant logistic hub for them if they can hold it. It would also be a major propaganda coup, and probably a trigger point for the Chinese to seek a negotiated surrender of the island from the Government of Taiwan."

Throughout the war, Leonard had been watching ground operations on the western plains closely. While he was no soldier, he had studied the Chinese and knew that they would want to win the battle for Taiwan on the ground. It was where the people lived, and it was the most difficult achievement to reverse if they were successful. Taichung City, with its major ports and airfields, high-tech fabrication plants, and its decisive position in the center of the island, would be a very important element of what came next in the military campaign. For both sides.

Leonard had a sense of approaching destiny. He looked over to Davis and dipped his head slightly, indicating she should continue.

"Sir, the Taiwanese still own portions of Kaohsiung City in the south. The fighting there has been vicious. It is causing the Chinese a major headache; having this large force of Taiwanese in their rear areas is creating havoc for their logistic support and is tying up large numbers of ground forces they would prefer to use in the advance north.

"There has also been a large-scale deployment of unmanned ground combat vehicles in these operations, in addition to a surge in UAVs and loitering munitions. The Russians have provided the PLA with several large shipments of the latest generation unmanned ground combat vehicle, the Uran-9. This thing is a beast; it packs a 30mm cannon, a 7.62mm machine gun, as well as anti-tank guided missiles or Shmel-M thermobaric flamethrowers. The thermobaric weapons in particular have been effective in urban areas, although they have caused many civilian casualties as well."

Leonard had been briefed on the urban operations in the south. City fighting was about the hardest kind of military operations there were. But, with more than half of the world's population now living in large urban areas, it was almost impossible to avoid conducting military operations in these environments and their immediate surrounds.

Leonard had previously been briefed on the civilian uprising in Kaohsiung City. Unable to escape before the PLA landings, many of the city's residents had joined local resistance groups which were causing all kinds of problems for the PLA. With the formation of the People's Armed Police a generation before, the PLA had lost many of its capabilities in suppressing the population short of full-on violence.

This had led to multiple atrocities against civilians by the PLA. The Chinese were becoming less disciplined in their interaction with the Taiwanese as each day progressed. The Taiwanese, Americans, and other members of the alliance had all been using reports and smuggled footage in their strategic influence campaigns to show the world what kind of governance awaited the Taiwanese if they were to capitulate.

"Please continue," Leonard said.

"Sir, the Taiwanese still hold much of the mountain range that runs up the central part of the island, as well as the narrow eastern plain. The Chinese have tried on several occasions to penetrate east through the mountains. There have been some bloody battles. So far, the Taiwanese, with our support, have been able to repulse these Chinese advances to the east. We believe that the PLA have now decided to focus on the western plain and securing the major cities before pursuing more operations in the east.

"Finally, the Taiwanese are racing in reinforcements to shore up the defensive line that crosses the western plain and defends Taichung City and its surrounding areas. Their 10th Army Corps is fully committed in the central part of the island and has been reinforced by the call out of all reservists. We are also providing air support, cyber and influence operations backing, and other logistic and resupply services.

"The Taiwanese 6th Army Corps from the north of the country is relocating most of its combat forces south now that the remnants of the Chinese airborne troops and most of the UGVs have been mopped up. Joining them is the US I Corps, which has Army and Marine Corps divisions. It also has an Australian division, which fortunately is equipped with equipment similar to the US Army's. All of the ground forces have been issued with tens of thousands of our new UGVs, UAVs, and loitering munitions. They have evolved their ground tactics based on our experiments, and combat lessons, of using autonomous systems."

Davis paused for a moment, checking her notes, and then continued.

"We have now assembled a large alliance Air Force consisting of Taiwanese, Japanese, American, Indonesian, Australian, British, and Canadian aircraft, autonomous aerial vehicles, missile defense and strike units, and other supporting elements. We also have every

B-21 and the new Loyal Wingman drones that have been accepted by the Air Force, which is still pitifully few. That said, the alliance air units are distributed across Taiwan and the wider region, primarily in our strategic bastion areas. The main effort for the alliance air forces is the destruction of the PLA Air Force, with supporting missions of destroying operational logistics hubs, missile launch sites, and ground close support for the land forces around Taichung City. We also have streamlined our integrated alliance logistics and communications networks. This has been useful as it has made our provision of assistance to the newly developing southern Taiwan insurgent networks a little smoother."

Over the last several weeks, an insurgency had emerged in the cities of southern Taiwan, as well as some of the more rural areas along the central mountain spine of the island. The Taiwanese, being generally well educated, had clearly studied the lessons of mainland Chinese during the Second World War, as well as more recent examples from Iraq and Ukraine.

"Do we have an estimate of how much combat power the Chinese Group Armies are having to hold back to deal with this emerging resistance movement?" Leonard asked.

"Each of the Group Armies has dedicated at least an entire brigade in their rear areas to deal with the insurgents. Their methods, brutal to say the least, don't appear to be working. Indeed, the estimate I read this morning indicates that the numbers involved in the insurgent groups are growing each day."

Davis, her update complete, sat back in her chair, ready for any questions from Leonard or the other staff.

There were few. All of the participants in the room had been part of the planning and execution of operations in and around Taiwan for several months. This daily update added another level of insight, but all of the senior staff were also constantly monitoring operational reports from the campaign.

"Thanks, J3," Leonard replied. "Just one question. How are we with the distribution of operational and tactical lessons, especially with the growing number of partnered autonomous systems in all the domains?"

It was a good question. Everyone around the table knew their military history. Those forces that dedicated effort to learning combat lessons and sharing widely throughout their military institutions were better at adapting quickly. And adapting quickly to changes in the situation, technology, terrain, and tactics was the key to victory.

Davis was quick to respond.

"Admiral, we have established hubs in Taiwan, Japan, Hawaii, and Australia where we are collecting, analyzing, and distributing lessons. These insights are going back into theater, but also to the training schools and educational establishments in all the alliance nations. Some of the training institutions are having trouble keeping up with the pace of change. However, the chairman and his fellow chiefs of defense have conducted some 'demonstration removals' of training and education leaders that have not been quick enough to adapt. That has ensured everyone else gets the message."

Leonard grinned at this last comment. He knew well that the training and education organizations in military institutions were often quite resistant to change. If some equivalent of the old Roman practice of decimation was needed to get them on board, then he was all for it.

"Thanks. That is all I have for now. Can we clear the room for the final item? It is a new compartment and I need to brief the senior staff from the intelligence, operations, logistics, cyber and plans branches only."

There was murmuring among those in the room as several staff rose to leave. Leonard understood that some would think they should remain behind for what he was about to unveil. But the sensitivity of what he was about to discuss could only be revealed to a select group.

Within moments, the noise had died down and there remained just six people in the room, including Leonard himself. Five expectant faces now looked directly at him. All of them had the highest security clearances. They were used to being briefed on the most sensitive American military capabilities and operations.

They will never have been briefed on something like this before, Leonard thought. He pondered, he hoped, that it would be a once-in-a-lifetime event for all of them. It was a risk, but if the alliance was able to orchestrate the five strands to this massive operation, it could potentially shorten the war significantly.

It was a big "if" though, Leonard thought. Already, the war had gone much longer than the clever academics and think-tank analysts had predicted in the preceding years. And longer than the Chinese leadership had probably hoped, as well.

"We humans are good at deluding ourselves that we can keep wars short," Leonard began. "Throughout modern history, we have searched for technologies, tactics, and organizations that might allow countries to go to war for only short times to achieve their national objectives. As the Schlieffen Plan, Blitzkrieg, and Shock and Awe have shown, this is a myth. I hope what I am about to brief you on is not another one of those myths but something that will truly result in a breakthrough that will either cause the operational collapse of the PLA or at least an armistice that will bring the CCP to the negotiating table."

This raised a couple of eyebrows. But the senior officers in the room were all experienced and hardened by combat in this war and others in the Middle East. They would wait for the details before offering any views on this new and highly classified plan.

Leonard then provided additional backstory to the operation.

"For decades now, we have been developing several highly classified military programs deep under a mountain range in the American Southwest. The result is that we now have a design, manufacturing, and deployable action capability that is entirely unique. It is an optionally crewed air and ground attack system that uses advanced AI, shaping, paints, cyber operations, laser systems, and some other technology even I don't understand to stay invisible and penetrate enemy sensor networks and conduct physical and cyber strikes.

"Some of you are aware of the arrival of the 1001st Special Action Wing in theater over the last week. This organization is able to rapidly regenerate lost airframes and munitions through advanced additive manufacturing techniques. Earlier this morning, the Wing was declared ready for its first missions and will be one of the five lines of effort in a massive alliance operation which will be launched very soon."

There was nodding around the table now. Leonard knew that all of them were impatient to learn the details.

"I can't tell you an exact launch date because that is reliant on some very specialized, highly classified capabilities required to predict and map weather in the Taiwan region. Believe me, weather—extreme weather—is an important part of the plan. But so are other operations by our allies—in the real world, the cyber domain, and in space.

"The new weapons of the 1001st will be vital. But they are not a silver bullet, and we cannot rely on advanced technology alone. The foundation of this plan rests on some very clever thinking and imagination—and guiding it all is the belief that we are doing the right thing to defend a fellow democracy."

Davis looked like she was ready to explode out of her skin. She certainly had a bad poker face. Leonard could see the anticipation in her body language, and to a lesser extent, on the faces of the others in the room.

"A whole lot of things have been coordinated by our strategic agencies, and not just those who we would normally be working with. From Australia to India and across to Japan, there has been agreement at the very highest political levels to proceed with this operation when the conditions are just right," Leonard continued.

He paused, looking down at the notes on his secure electronic notepad. He then glanced around the room once again, seeing eagerness in the faces of those around the small table.

"We have a lot to go through, and I need to brief you on the political context, who will be doing what in our command as well as what activities our partners in other agencies and countries will be undertaking. In the coming hours and days, you will have to do extensive planning and synchronization. But before I start with that, you should know the codename for this new operation."

Leonard, never one for the dramatic, nevertheless felt that this may one day be seen as a historic occasion. The name of the operation had been carefully chosen. While it did not in any way reveal what kind of operation was to be conducted, it did provide an indication of the high hopes that alliance governments and military leaders had placed in its successful completion. And Leonard himself liked the codename. To him, there was something auspicious about it.

"Ladies and Gentlemen, this grand event, one of the largest and most complex alliance military operations in history, will be called Operation *Chakra Rain*."

23

Liberators

8 July 2028
South of Taichung City

It wasn't supposed to go this way.

Everything they had been told about the Taiwanese people, and about how quickly they would defeat the poorly equipped and led Taiwanese military, had been wrong.

And this place smells like shit, Bo thought, surveying the urban sprawl that unfolded before him. He stood on the roof of a small three-story building currently being used as his brigade command post. Parked up against the side of the building was his armored command vehicle. It was permanently ready to move away quickly. The enemy had become skilled at locating headquarters and command posts over the course of the campaign in Taiwan. It did not pay to remain in one location too long. But, Bo thought, it felt good to be out of that smelly, noisy vehicle for even just a few hours. Next to him stood his new brigade operations officer, Major Chin. The officer had arrived after his predecessor had been killed in fighting several days before.

Chin held a mug of steaming hot tea in each hand. The dull metallic cups—recognizable to any soldier or Marine in most military institutions—bore the chips and scrapes of war. Bo accepted the tea from Chin and nodded, grateful for small gestures such as this.

It was clear that the destruction across the city sprawled before him, wreaked by the fighting over the past two months, had led to a breakdown of water and sanitation services. That was not supposed to happen, Bo thought, shaking his head. *Why target civilian infrastructure when we will only have to rebuild it after our eventual victory?* The locals would only hate them more when they installed a new Chinese government.

Bo sighed heavily, careful not to voice his mental meanderings. *Eventual victory.* It was a term that had been used before the landings and was still popular among the senior PLA leaders on the island. But for Bo, it was a mirage in his mind. Always something just beyond the reach of the Chinese soldiers and Marines on the ground. And the worst of it was that it was not just the Taiwanese Army and the Americans that Bo and his Marines now had to worry about. Over the past several weeks, urban rebellions were now occurring in almost every area where the PLA had taken over control in the south of Taiwan.

And in all this, the PLA leadership were pretending that it was not happening. Their information operations refused to acknowledge that many of the Taiwanese had now taken up arms against their invaders. Bo shook his head solemnly. No, it wasn't supposed to be this way.

Their political officer had been quite clear during his pre-landing briefings. While some of the people who lived on this island harbored a desire for separation from China, the vast majority of people still held a special regard for China. They liked being Taiwanese but were also proud to be Chinese.

It was the Taiwanese politicians, as usual, who were the most dangerous. Over the last two decades, these "elected" officials had stirred up animosity towards China in the Taiwanese press and in foreign countries such as the United States and Japan. The attention that these rebellious curs had received meant that most people in the world had a false view of what the majority of Taiwanese thought about their nation.

The political officer had been insistent that while the PLA might not be welcomed with garlands by the Taiwanese, the vast majority would be content to wait out combat operations and then readjust to their new rulers after the inevitable Chinese victory. The Taiwanese, after all, were a trading nation. Maintaining a profitable relationship with China and other countries was so much more important than notions of democracy and liberty. While the Taiwanese military was expected to put up a fight—and indeed they had—the civilians were expected largely to be docile and remain non-combatants. Or so they had all been assured before they moved to their boarding stations on the amphibious landing ship.

It had all been a lie, Bo thought. And if not a deliberate lie, it had been wishful thinking on the part of the political officers and senior leadership of the PLA. It was obvious now that the docile Taiwanese that the PLA had expected had not received the message. Docility and passivity were not the words that Bo, or his Marines, would have used to describe their interactions with the locals.

The Taiwanese were sullen in the presence of Chinese soldiers and Marines. Even if they could be induced to cooperate in the most minor task, they were slow and uncommunicative. And these were the easy dealings! Many of the Taiwanese had joined resistance networks that had sprung up all over the south of the island. Using mini-satellite terminals that were constantly dropped from American UAVs and high-altitude transport aircraft, these resistance fighters had managed to cobble together a loose command and control network to coordinate their operations and to share lessons about how to attack the Chinese.

They were adept at finding individual Chinese soldiers and Marines who might have been separated from their units and killing them—sometimes in the most gruesome ways. No amount of reprisal killings by Bo's Marines had halted these attacks.

The Taiwanese civilians had also perfected vehicle ambushes, especially on Chinese logistic convoys. Supporting a large military organization far from its own bases is always difficult, especially during an advance. But it was made almost impossible when fuel trucks and convoys with all kinds of ammunition, food, water, and other supplies were destroyed by these bandits.

Perhaps the worst were the damned hackers. Somehow, the Taiwanese had figured out how to break into their encrypted tactical networks. Fortunately, the cyber-defense algorithms were normally quick to detect and shut off network vulnerabilities. But not always. Sometimes the Taiwanese hackers had been able to make concentrations of enemy forces disappear from the PLA battle management systems. This had led to ambushes, and several units had been wiped out completely in the wake of such hackings.

Other times the hackers would change simple reports, such as personnel numbers or the requirements for food and other supplies. It would result in Bo's Marines going hungry or his brigade running desperately short on fuel for its vehicles or ammunition for their weapon systems. Sometimes they had even been able to break into the highly sophisticated algorithms that controlled their autonomous ground combat systems, the beetles. One evening, dozens of the beetles in Bo's brigade and an adjoining Army brigade had turned on their PLA masters. It had resulted in over a hundred casualties in the two units and had taken several hours of tough combat to destroy the affected beetles.

What also upset Bo and his Marines was the propaganda. The Taiwanese hackers would occasionally insert video compilations of Chinese airstrikes on civilian areas, or covert film footage of protests that were alleged to be occurring back in China. Many of Bo's Marines had been deeply disturbed by the videos. These films had had a definite effect on unit morale and were becoming corrosive for unit cohesion.

And while none of Bo's Marines would have access to external media feeds, Bo was aware that China was being constantly disparaged by governments and the press around the world. The continued feed of pictures and videos, through social media and satellite communications, allowed Western audiences a constant diet of what might be described as "war porn." But unfortunately, most of the videos were one sided, only showing Chinese troops at their worst. So, China was now finding itself on the backfoot with influence operations in almost every nation around the world.

Dragging himself out of his contemplations, Bo remembered his new operations officer was still standing beside him.

"Very well, Chin. Let's have it." Bo was expecting a short update on the disposition of the battalions in his brigade, as well as a status update on their logistic situation.

Chin retained his serious demeanor as he turned to Bo and began speaking.

"Sir, our 1st and 2nd battalions are occupying defensive positions to our north and northeast. The 3rd Battalion is just to our rear in a reserve location and is collocated with our engineers and logistic troops. Recon troops and beetles are conducting screening operations one kilometer to our north and northeast and to the east as well."

Pausing for a moment while Bo turned again to look at the city, Major Chin then continued with the briefing for his brigade commander.

"Sir, our supply situation continues to worsen. Two more convoys were destroyed last night. The attack helicopters and armored vehicles that were escorting them were also destroyed. We are now down to two days' food, and all our vehicles only have half-full fuel tanks. Ammunition is not yet an issue, but we will need a quick resupply if we are engaged in combat that is unanticipated or sustained in nature."

Chin paused, anticipating questions from his commander.

"*Unanticipated or sustained.* That sounds very much like the title of a book that might describe our campaign here," Bo responded. He raised his mug to his mouth, taking a sip of the rapidly cooling tea. Bo winced while he did so, immediately regretting his outburst in front of Major Chin. It would not help ease the already troubled mind of his operations officer and other staff to utter such intemperate language about the state of the campaign. Even if it was obvious to the most junior Marine that things were not going well with their reconquest of the rebellious province. And of course, there was always the risk that Major Chin might mention Bo's outburst to the political officer. That would probably not end well for Bo, even if he was well connected through his wife.

"Forgive my silly outburst, Chin. I am weary and should know better," Bo corrected himself.

Chin nodded. The young man wanted to plan and conduct operations. He had no interest in philosophical or political matters that were beyond him.

"So, Chin, how are our preparations for the advance into Taichung City?"

For the last several days, while enduring attacks from the resistance and continuing to act as flank security on the eastern flank of the Chinese advance, they had also been conducting final preparations for the operation that aimed to surround and then seize Taichung City. It had been an even more hectic time than normal for Bo's ever decreasing number of Marines as they rehearsed different urban-fighting techniques.

"Sir, our preparations have been impacted by the lack of rein-forcements over the last several weeks. We have not been able to keep up with our combat losses. Our current strength is 62 percent of normal establishment."

Chin stopped then. He had suddenly become reticent.

He was easy to read, thought Bo. There was bad news—or at least news that was bad compared to what he had just delivered.

"Speak freely, Major Chin."

Chin, who had yet to touch his own tea, looked at his commander.

"Sir, the Commander of 71st Group Army has directed we provide ten Marines for special duties in dealing with the Taiwanese resistance."

While not shocked, Bo was somewhat taken aback—not by a superior commander taking his men; that was normal in military operations. No, Bo was quietly disturbed by the term "special duties." Every man in his brigade knew exactly what it meant, even though there had been no formal order issued that used the term.

The PLA had begun implementing a very simple solution in dealing with the Taiwanese resistance fighters—that is, when they could catch them. Summary execution by firing squad. No trial. No mercy. "Special duties" was a euphemism for the small teams of Marines and soldiers that had been assembled by each of the PLA Group Armies in Taiwan to carry out summary executions of suspected insurgents.

Bo had first heard the term used during his last visit to the headquarters of the general in command of the 71st Group Army. As the brigade commander responsible for the flank security for the large group formation, Bo would regularly visit the headquarters and ensure he remained familiar with the future intentions of the commander of the army.

It was a term not uttered by the general. But the term had been whispered to him by the Chief of Staff of the Group Army headquarters, who just happened to be a classmate from their time at the National Defense University. Neither he, nor Bo, was comfortable with the direction the war had taken.

Bo pondered this as he stood on the rooftop, surveying the urban sprawl that meandered north towards Taichung City. Weren't they supposed to be the liberators here?

He decided to return to the subject at hand. It did no good to reflect on such issues at this point of the war. When they were victorious—*if* they were victorious—there would be all the time in the world to consider such weighty philosophical notions of right and wrong in war.

Bo had important matters to finalize before they moved into their jump-off positions for the next phase of their advance north.

Chin, sensing his commander wished to move on, continued his update.

"While we have not been able to get human replacements, we have received large numbers of the robotic vehicles. The majority of our brigade is now beetles. Each company has at least two hundred of the machines. And while we still have periodic maintenance issues, and hacking from the insurgents, they are almost all serviceable."

The balance of humans and machines had been shifting in most military organizations over the past decade. The American wars in Iraq and Afghanistan had accelerated such developments, particularly with uncrewed aerial vehicles. But these wars had also spawned new technological creations on the ground which had been further refined by the Americans, and the PLA, for this war.

"I wonder what the local people will think about being liberated by robots?" Bo wondered aloud, not expecting a reply from Chin. It was time to give his final orders for what was to come tomorrow morning.

"Major Chin, you may complete our final preparations today and then get yourself and the staff some rest. We have a busy few days of advancing and fighting ahead of us. But, with fortune smiling upon us, we will quickly capture the city and then give our Marines some respite."

Bo tried to smile but it came off more as a grimace. He then turned to look north once again at the massive cluster of humans and buildings that stretched beyond the horizon. It would be a very difficult fight through confined streets, with every building a potential defensive bunker for the Taiwanese. Every street was an ambush site and a potential death zone. And, at every moment, behind them were insurgents wanting to maim and kill Bo's Marines.

The hardest part of this fight is not yet behind us. It lies right there in front of us. The Taiwanese have proven to be stout defenders of their island. All of them now want to fight us, even their old people. Even if they are defending the lie that they are an independent nation, Bo contemplated.

The city that stood before them was a large one. The built-up areas alone took up over 500 square kilometers and contained over 2 million people. Even with displaced inhabitants streaming north to avoid the likely battle for their city, there would be many, many civilians remaining in the city. *It would make things difficult for both sides,* Bo thought.

And we cannot underestimate the determination or resourcefulness of the Taiwanese. Or the impact of the American forces that were now also approaching Taichung City from the north.

The forthcoming fight will be different from what we have experienced until now, Bo mused. So far, the Taiwanese had made their advance a bloody and expensive affair for the Chinese. But in central Taiwan, the Taiwanese had assembled a large proportion of its elite forces. It had had time to prepare, and it was now backed up by the massive American corps as well as the US Air Force and long-range strike missiles from across the Pacific. Regardless of their casualties up to this point, they would be much higher once they were in the city proper. *Well,* Bo thought, *there is nothing for it now. We have our orders, and there is no turning back.*

He turned back to face Chin. The young officer was eager to return to the command vehicle and transmit the order that he knew the brigade commander was about to give him.

"Major Chin, you may confirm the warning order that we issued last night. We will cross our line of departure and begin the advance on Taichung City at 0400 hours tomorrow."

24

Monsoon

21 July 2028
Outer Taichung City

"This fucking rain!"

It was probably the most common phrase in Captain Lee's unit. But not by a significant margin. The second most uttered phrase was "these fucking beetles!" Closely followed by "watch that building!"

Two weeks into their mission around the northern and north-eastern periphery of Taichung City, the rain had yet to let up. The constant downpours affected their communications and the serviceability of their vehicles and their autonomous systems. Some of the smaller recon UAVs were unable to launch in the heavier monsoonal rain. The driving water pellets ensured that any flight by the smaller aerial vehicles—some the size of large insects—was almost impossible.

Fortunately, the Chinese were fighting under the same restrictions, Lee thought as she fetched the steaming hot water off the burner to make a canteen of coffee for her and the crew of her vehicle. Normally her vehicle crew commander, Sergeant James, would do this. But this late at night, he was on duty in the turret, scanning their surroundings with thermal and other imaging devices for Chinese beetles and other enemy units.

They could all do with some caffeine. She poured the coffee sachet into the hot water, added multiple packets of sugar, and then moved forward to hand the coffee up to James sitting in the vehicle's turret.

"Thanks, Captain. I needed this." James cupped the steaming drink in his hands and blew on it to cool it down. He looked up, scanning an arc of about 180 degrees across their front.

James, as Lee knew, was not much of a talker. After handing the coffee to him, Lee looked down at her hands. They were grimy, covered in a mixture of dirt, grease, and lord knows what else. None of them had been able to bathe for the past two weeks. During their daily "morning routine," conducted before sunrise, they had the opportunity to perhaps quickly wash their face and maybe use a damp cloth to wipe other areas of their bodies. There just wasn't time to attend to such niceties at the moment. She turned back from the turret and sat in her seat in the command pod at the rear of the vehicle. *Jesus, I would hate to be the first clean person that walks by our vehicle*, she thought with a smile. It would not be a pleasant aroma.

Lee then turned back to her screens. They displayed an array of different views that integrated thermal, night vision, and other spectral scanners. It was all quiet, which was what she expected. Fortunately, they were no longer in forward positions, or as the Army called it, the "Forward Line of Own Troops."

Lee's troop, along with the infantry battalion from the Marine Littoral Regiment, were occupying a reserve position on the far-left flank of the allied advance down into Taichung City. This placed them in the east, operating hard up against the mountain range that ran the length of the island. It had taken a couple of weeks of moving, halting, scouting, fighting, and moving again to get to this point.

Not that there had been a lot of fighting north of Taichung City. The Taiwanese still controlled most of their territory in and around the city, as well as everything to the north. But, as the large Taiwanese and American corps-sized formations had moved south, they had to contend with small groups of isolated Chinese troops from the failed northern parachute drop. These PLA soldiers were taking it upon themselves to interfere with logistics convoys and other small military units. Lee peered out the open combat door at the rear of her vehicle. It looked like a quiet evening for once. There had been mercifully few of those in the past month.

A sudden squawk sounded through her headset. Voice communications were rare, with most interactions being via secure text chat on the battle command systems. It could only mean one thing. Almost simultaneously, she heard the callsign for her unit over the radio, followed by "Blue Ghost." It was the codeword for her unit to deploy immediately to deal with a Chinese penetration of their regiment's position. Called a counter-penetration mission, it was normally a task allocated to the regimental reserve force. Which, at the moment, was Lee and her troopers.

When Lee's unit had arrived here, they had planned deployment routes and counter-penetration drills with the staff of the Marine infantry battalion. She knew what was ahead of them. What she didn't know was the size of the Chinese force they would be up against in a matter of minutes.

Sergeant James, always monitoring the communications coming into the command pod, had already started up the armored command vehicle's power pack and passed a quick warning order to the remainder of the unit about the impending mission. Lee, over the noise of the radio, could faintly hear the sound of engines starting and vehicles jockeying, reading to move out to seal the breach in their defensive position.

Lee received a curt follow-up message, this time from Furness. That was normal. Generally, the deployment of his reserve force would only be ordered by him.

"Chinese beetles and infantry dismounts have broken through our outer perimeter at the five o'clock position. You are to advance south, destroy the enemy, and re-establish the outer perimeter. Move now, out."

Lee didn't need any more information than this. They had rehearsed this and other scenarios the previous afternoon. She issued a quick set of radio orders to her platoon leaders and then gave Sergeant James the word to start the vehicle moving south behind the lead platoon's vehicles. As the vehicle moved, Lee turned back to her command screens while monitoring her troop command radio net. There was minimal chatter. Her junior leaders knew their jobs, and also knew to keep the command net as free of unnecessary transmissions as possible. Still, the silence was slightly eerie.

Several red icons now appeared on her screens at the approximate positions that her regimental commander had described just moments ago. Lee felt her heart rate start to rise, and a thin veneer of sweet appeared on her grubby brow. It was always like this. While she had learned to deal with fear of her own mortality, Lee still worried for her troopers every time they found themselves about to make contact with the enemy. Sometimes, they were even lucky enough to not take casualties. But that was rare now.

The further south they moved, the more the allied forces came into contact with beetles and other Chinese autonomous systems on the ground and in the air. These pitiless Chinese machines did not hesitate to kill the Americans or target their vehicles. And the further south Lee and her troopers advanced, the more Chinese reconnaissance troops they had contact with. Especially now they were in the vicinity of Taichung City.

"Contact front," one of her platoon leaders yelled into the command net.

Lee peered down at her screen and saw that a red icon had merged with several blue icons from her leading platoon. They were several hundred yards to her south. If they were in contact, it was likely that her vehicle and the remainder of her headquarters would also be among the enemy very quickly.

Suddenly the command radio net was a cacophony of noise, with platoon leaders passing on details of the enemy and other details.

Fuck, Lee thought. *This is more than a small Chinese recon force. It looks like at least a battalion of troops, supported by hundreds of beetles, UAVs, and suicide drones.* The counter-UAV systems in her vehicle and those of her troops were starting to activate automatically, identifying and shooting down those that posed the greatest threat. She could hear her own vehicles' systems already targeting Chinese drones and could see that electronic jammers were activating constantly on her command screens.

At the same time, she started to hear James and other gunners from her troop engaging the Chinese. The constant hammering of the vehicle's main armament was added to by the explosion of what sounded like enemy mortars and artillery among the vehicles of her troop. Frequently, the outside of her vehicle was showered with fragmentation, sounding like heavy rain on a tin roof.

She needed to speak with Furness straight away. She changed nets and called him up on the regimental command net. His callsign, Cobra 6, was known to all.

"Cobra 6, this is Foxtrot actual. Looks like at least a battalion-sized force in front of us. Sending through a digital overlay now. Estimate this is the recon elements of a Chinese Group Army attempting to establish our eastern boundary. Request air and arty support."

Furness was quick to respond.

"Roger. On the way. We are piling up air support for your JTACs to use in five mikes. Divisional artillery is also at priority call for you. I will leave you to it while I see if we can get some more help on the way. Out."

Holy shit, he must be worried if he is allocating that much air and artillery support to us already, Lee thought. But she quickly turned to other, more important concerns. She forwarded the codes to her operations staff in the armored command vehicles adjacent to hers so they could coordinate the fire support being requested by all of her platoon leaders.

She looked down at her screens again. Her swarm of recon drones were rapidly collecting information on the advancing Chinese force and feeding it into her battle command system. Lee's quick glance only confirmed her assessment about the size of the enemy force and its likely mission. If it was the recon screen for a Chinese Group Army, it probably had orders not to become decisively engaged with the Americans. It would fight for information, but then probably withdraw to continue its reconnaissance mission while follow-on units engaged the Americans later. They had to smash the first echelon of the Chinese quickly. That was the way they would get the Chinese to withdraw. If they didn't, the Chinese would keep pushing. *Just like a bayonet that keeps penetrating a body until it hits something hard,* Lee thought grimly.

The noise outside seemed to increase. Several large explosions sounded forward of her position. At the same time, three icons that represented crewed combat vehicles from the forward platoon disappeared. But the blue icons for their unmanned systems remained.

"Fuck, Sergeant James, we lost most of 1st Platoon. I am going to call forward our rear platoon to plug the gap."

"Roger," James responded curtly before returning to command the vehicle and identifying more Chinese targets to engage with their vehicle's main gun.

Lee quickly passed the order over her command net. It was quicker in these circumstances than typing in a secure text.

"Roger, moving now," came the response from the commander of 3rd Platoon, which she had directed to hang back about 500 yards as they had moved south. She could hear the screaming of armored vehicle power packs as the platoon roared past her position to the south. Every man and woman in these vehicles knew that ahead of them was only fire, destruction, and possibly death. But they also knew that their friends needed help, and if they did not halt this Chinese penetration of the Marine regiment's position, someone else would have to.

Lee could hear the main armament of the platoon opening up on targets as they roared through her position. It only added to the maelstrom of noise that was coming through the thick armored hull of her vehicle.

By now Marine and Air Force aircraft were on station and beginning to drop their ordnance on targets identified by the Joint Tactical Air Controllers—JTACs—in Lee's unit. Looking down at her screens again, she could see that more blue icons had winked out in the past few minutes. But the number of red icons was also decreasing rapidly. Suddenly she heard James over the vehicle intercom system.

"Ma'am, turn on your through-armor sight system. You are not going to believe this."

The through-armor sight was a helmet-mounted system that used a series of cameras mounted on the outside of her vehicle to virtually see through its hull. It allowed a user to see outside without exposing themselves to enemy fire or inclement weather. James knew she rarely used it because the most valuable tactical information she received was from sensors operating at longer distances than she could see with her own eyes.

This must be something worth seeing, Lee thought. Glancing at one of her monitors, she pressed two buttons on the far-left screen that activated a small heads-up screen mounted on the inner edge of her helmet. Two small clear screens slid down just in front of her eyes. Almost instantly, the screens showed a stereo view of the outside world.

As she did so, the noise outside suddenly reduced markedly. It was not complete silence. The sound of her vehicle's rumbling engine was still in the background. Small explosions could also be heard. But compared to the tumult of the past hour, it was almost serene. She focused on the view on the small screens just in front of her eyeballs. What she saw astounded her.

It was as if she had been teleported into the center of a raging forest fire. All around her vehicle was fire, embers, and swirling currents of thick black smoke. Around her vehicle were the remains of Chinese armored vehicles and beetles. Once recognizable as military machines, they were now blackened and twisted, and red hot from the flames that consumed them.

Lee was at first confused. As the confusion began to fade, replaced by a measure of satisfaction that they might have halted the thrust of the Chinese into their position, her radio came to life again.

"Lee, this is Cobra 6. You are looking all clear from what we can see here."

She looked down at her monitors. The only red icons remaining were streaming east quickly. None remained within the perimeter.

After a short pause, Furness was back on the secure radio again.

"I know what you are thinking. It was something the Marine Air Wing is calling 'Mega-Blade'—a package of 100 Switchblade drones. And you were the first operational test of the system."

Lee knew what the Switchblade was, essentially an airborne drone with a small sensor package and a warhead that could be launched and loiter over an area before a target presented itself. It had several variants, including an anti-armor version. The drones had been used widely in Ukraine a few years before, and the lessons from that conflict had informed constant improvements to these important parts of the Marine Corps armory of uncrewed systems.

But a package that launched one hundred at once? No wonder outside her vehicle looked like Armageddon. It was likely that many of the Chinese beetles and vehicles had been targeted by at least one, and perhaps many more drones, given the number that would have been loitering overhead.

The next voice on her radio was unexpected. It was the platoon leader for her 1st Platoon. Lee had thought his platoon had been overrun by the initial Chinese attack.

"Ma'am, we are back. We lost comms for a while there but have now linked up with 2nd Platoon and are making some repairs to get back on the grid. I'll be back in your location for an after-action review in 20 mikes."

Lee grinned. It wasn't such a bad night after all, and it sounded as if their casualties had been kept to a minimum. Then something caught her eye. At the corner of her vision was a flashing red icon on her far-left screen. The regimental secure text channel. It was reserved for commanders within the Marine Littoral Regiment, and Lee had been added to the list after her cavalry troop had been assigned to the regiment. That felt like an age ago. Lee reached out with a grubby hand and touched the icon. A short text from Colonel Furness appeared on the screen.

"WELL DONE ON COUNTER-PENETRATION MISSION. HIGHER HQ IS REASSIGNING YOU. THEY HAVE A SPECIAL MISSION FOR YOUR CALLSIGN. BRIEFING IN MY LOC IN 10 MINS."

Lee sighed. Her troop had done well. It had successfully plugged the gap in the regiment's defensive perimeter. But there would be little time to celebrate.

This reassignment was interesting. And concerning. Lee had come to enjoy working with the serious, but very tough and professional, Marines. They were great fighters but also good thinkers. They fought smart, and despite her early misgivings, they had looked after her soldiers throughout the campaign. But obviously, there was now a higher priority mission for Captain Lee and her Army cavalry troopers. She hit the screen to acknowledge the message and then moved it to a cache.

"Sergeant James, prepare to move in five minutes. We have a meeting with the colonel. And it looks like we might be getting a new boss."

Shit, thought Lee. *Not again!*

25

The Pledge

2 August 2028
Secure Communications Facility
Washington, DC

No fucking way, Diane Keene thought as she pressed the "end" icon on the screen of her secure video conference facility.

She was sitting in the only room in her entire building that had been accredited for conversations of a classification of "secret" and above. It was actually a bit of a pain in the ass to have to walk down the several sets of stairs to the room, even for short conversations. And the room was small, had uncomfortable seats, and smelled like old farts.

She shifted in the hard-backed chair, pondering the information that had just been passed on through the secure video conference. After the discussion just completed on the secure VIDCON, she now understood the rationale for such rooms.

"Holy shit," she murmured as she wrote down a few lines in her notebook. While doing so, Keene took care to ensure that she committed the most sensitive information to memory rather than putting it on paper.

A month ago, her agency had been placed on a heightened alert for severe weather. That was no surprise. They were, after all, in the middle of the normal Atlantic hurricane season. And the catastrophic events of several months ago, from which the east and west coasts of the United States were still recovering, had given the politicians and senior bureaucrats a solemn lesson in the necessity of Keene's agency, FEMA. Over the last couple of months, the agency had been the recipient of a massive influx of federal funding. This was despite the increased demands on the resources and time of the president and his administration because of the war in Taiwan.

The president and his administration had managed to keep a relatively unified political front toward the war. Congress, despite a decade of rancorous and bipartisan arguments, had largely coalesced in their support for the president and the defense of Taiwan. Keene thought that many in Congress probably believed that the war with China had been inevitable. The fight over Taiwan, which they had managed to contain to that part of the world, was the culmination of a decade of tensions between the two superpowers.

Even though both nations had subjected each other to ongoing cyber-attacks against different elements of their national infra-structure, the American people had, by and large, supported the administration. Keene wondered how long that would last. While civilians would tolerate some inconvenience, they would only do so for so long. Combine that with the long casualty lists that were starting to be published online and in the few remaining newspapers that printed paper copies, and it was clear the administration would have to do everything it could to bring hostilities to a rapid conclusion.

Returning to the call from the Pentagon, Keene had another thought. *So, our federal government and its agencies really can focus on more than one thing at once*, she pondered.

Keene returned to the severe weather warning of a few weeks ago. What had made it stand out was that it was not for either the east, or even the west, coasts of the continental United States. The warning, direct from the National Military Command Center located deep beneath the Pentagon, was for typhoons—in the western Pacific.

To be more specific, the alert had requested that FEMA and the National Hurricane Center provide early warning (no less than 72 hours) of any typhoon that was likely to have a track out of the Pacific and up the Taiwan Strait. Not up the east coast of the beleaguered island. The typhoon had to possess a projected track that would take it to the west of the country.

At the time, Keene and the senior staff who were part of the small group scanning for such events had rolled their eyes. Even with the massive advances in weather prediction, severe weather detection, and preparation, it was still a tricky endeavor. Sometimes, these massive and destructive storms would veer off projected tracks in ways that befuddled even the most experienced weather experts and their advanced data analytics and algorithmic models.

The means to detect and track such events were very sophisticated indeed. In April 1960, NASA launched the very first low earth orbital weather satellite. Called the Television Infrared Observation Satellite, or TIROS, it proved the utility of weather observation from orbit as well as the various sensors, instruments, and communications equipment to make this a reality. Since then, successful generations of weather satellites had been launched by the United States, Russia, China, the European Space Agency, Japan, India, North Korea, Canada, and South Korea. A little over 100 weather satellites had been launched over the past 64 years.

Keene knew the rough numbers of current operational weather satellites that were in various orbits. She had one more secure call to make this morning, related to the operation that she had been briefed on during her previous VIDCON. There were a few minutes before it was to begin, so she pulled up a presentation on her computer from the previous month to confirm the number: 52. Fifty-two operational weather satellites owned by nine nations, some of which were friendly. They could collaborate with friendly nations. But the others would take some work.

And these were only part of the weather-reporting networks. The weather birds orbiting high above the surface of the earth were supported by satellite ground stations. Supplementing the information collected by the satellites was the data from thousands of ground stations, and the complex and ever-improving data analytics which provided predictions of rainfall, temperature, wind, snow, and severe weather.

Keene pondered all these elements of a weather-observation, analysis, and reporting system. It was extraordinarily complex. And that did not include the thousands of humans involved in making observations, undertaking analysis, writing reports on long-term weather trends and short-term predictions, all the way to the people who appeared on television, the internet, and radios around the world to keep people informed.

Normally Keene would not have given much time to such considerations. After all, she just assumed it all worked for the most part. Not now.

While she was sure that she had not been given the full picture, Keene had been told enough to appreciate the magnitude of what the Pentagon was planning in the coming days. It would be a hectic 72 hours for Keene and her staff, particularly those at the National Hurricane Center. But they would need to work closely with the national weather agencies in multiple nations across the western Pacific if they were going to successfully execute this unbelievably audacious plan.

But before she could speak with her senior staff and get the ball rolling, she had one more person to speak to. It would be an unusual call, because it was with an agency that Keene had not worked with in the past. But, for the task at hand, it was the designated lead organization, and it would be responsible for orchestrating the many different elements of this operation.

She looked at the screen before her and touched the connection for her scheduled secure conference call. The logo on the screen showed the badge for Space Force.

———————————————➤

Tech Sergeant Hickling looked at the small group of people around her and on the screen before them. She was participating in a discussion with other members of the Space Force as well as Director Keene from FEMA. The highly classified briefing session, conducted over ultra-secure, quantum encrypted computer networks, was being held to rapidly orchestrate one of the five elements of the alliance's Operation *Chakra Rain*. It was an apt name. If FEMA, the National Hurricane Center, Cyber Command, and the Space Force got this right, the rationale for the use of the word "rain" as part of the operational description would become very clear.

But they had little time. Weather in the western Pacific, inherently unpredictable at the best of times, was something they could only forecast 48 to 72 hours in advance. Especially the severe weather they were hoping to exploit for this plan.

The briefing had commenced with a round of introductions from all of the participants. All the key agencies and military services were represented. Also attending was a senior military staff member from the headquarters of Indo-Pacific Command. Currently working from a secure underground facility, the staff at Indo-PACOM were the lead planning and execution organization for Operation *Chakra Rain* and its five sub-plans.

Introductions complete, Hickling's immediate superior wasted no time getting to the point of the meeting. Captain Marcus cleared his throat before speaking.

"Ladies and Gentlemen, thank you for joining us this morning. I will hand over to the operational lead for this shortly. However, I wish to reinforce the importance of this sub-operation in the overall scheme of maneuver for Operation *Chakra Rain*." He paused, consulting his secure e-pad in front of him. After a moment, Marcus then looked up to address those in the room, as well as the attendees that were displayed on several screens at the head of the secure conference center.

"I know that some of you are not familiar with the full details of this operation. There are five distinct yet interconnected elements of *Chakra Rain*. Two lines of effort are focused on tactical and operational strikes on Chinese land and maritime forces in Taiwan and in staging areas on the Chinese mainland, by the 1001st Special Action Wing and by swarms of UAVs, medium-range strike missiles and loitering munitions. These two activities will be synchronized with activities on the Chinese periphery, from India and Russia."

He let that sink in with those joining the meeting. He knew that it would require careful planning to coordinate the nations in the alliance on such a massive scale.

"The fifth and final leg of this operation is what we are here to discuss. I will hand over now to my lead officer for the planning and execution of this aspect of *Chakra Rain*, Tech Sergeant Hickling." Marcus turned to his left and nodded at Hickling.

She had been preparing for this moment for the past month. It had been Hickling who had pitched the outlandish idea she was about to brief to the assembled small group. Almost two months ago, at their normal daily operations meeting with her boss and the rest of her team, she had speculated about whether Americans were creative enough to deceive the Chinese on a massive scale. When

Captain Marcus asked for an example, Hickling quickly described the outline of an idea she had been considering. Originally, her boss had been skeptical of the logistics and coordination required.

Hickling had therefore tasked her team to design and conduct multiple simulations of her idea. They had discreetly skimmed data on a range of subjects, including severe weather prediction and typhoon history in the western Pacific, to populate the data sets needed for their simulations. Eventually, after demonstrating the potential of her idea to Captain Marcus, and then Marcus' chain of command all the way up to the commander of Space Command, Hickling's idea had been embraced.

Not just embraced. It had been given a "high-priority" designation, and then continually honed and simulated while they waited for just the right circumstances to enact her plan. The call from the Director of FEMA two days ago was the final piece of this extraordinarily complex puzzle to fall into place.

"Ladies and gentlemen, every magic trick has three parts," Hickling began. "First, a magician shows their audience something quite ordinary, like a box or an animal. This is called 'the pledge.' Second, the ordinary object or animal is made to do something astonishing, like disappear. This is called 'the turn.' Finally, the magician goes beyond the disappearance and makes the object or animal reappear. This is known as 'the prestige.'"

She paused there. Hickling knew her audience had been given some details of what she was going to describe. But apart from her small team, no one had all the details. Until now.

"As the fifth leg of the alliance's Operation *Chakra Rain*, we are going to attempt a trick that has never been attempted before. We have had to wait for just the right conditions because it relies on nature to cooperate."

Hickling saw that some around the table were starting to catch on. But not all attendees were there yet.

"We are going to attempt the largest takeover of a system ever attempted. Orchestrated by the team here, we will be using Space Force as well as alliance cyber assets to gain discreet control of the dozens of active friendly and adversary weather and earth observation satellites over a 72-hour period. At the same time, we will be spoofing weather data reporting from hundreds of ground-based weather stations in Taiwan, the Philippines, China, and beyond.

"With the formation of what appears to be a strong tropical depression in the western Pacific over the past 48 hours, everything is set for us to begin the implementation of this highly sensitive and technically difficult operation."

A *ping* rang out across the room. It was the noise that normally accompanied one of the virtual participants raising their hand for either a question or a comment. Hickling paused, looking up at the screens arrayed at the front of the small conference facility. She settled on a secure video feed from Washington, DC. Director Keene from FEMA had raised her virtual hand in the corner of her screen.

"Director Keene," Hickling announced to the others assembled in the room.

"Thank you for that introduction. And I find this quite fascinating. I understand the broad outlines, based on my previous brief on this topic. But can you confirm the detailed execution of what we are trying to do here?" Keene asked.

Hickling, understanding that she had been deliberately mysterious in her introduction, merely nodded her head. She looked around the room and then back to the screen on which Keene's image was displayed.

"Yes, Director, I was just getting to that. We are going to attempt the greatest magic trick in history. We are going to make this typhoon disappear."

26

Wild Ride

2 August 2028
Eastern Taichung urban area

The explosions, all around now, sent clumps of concrete, steel, and dirt spewing into the air. Pieces of shrapnel from the artillery shells, both large and small, clattered against the sides and top of the armored hull. While the barrage lasted only a minute or two, their transit through it in Bo's armored command vehicle seemed an eternity.

The small convoy, comprising Bo's tactical brigade headquarters vehicles, was moving from where his brigade was deployed on the right flank of the advancing Chinese forces. He had been summoned again to the headquarters of the 71st Group Army, itself the far-right formation of three Group Armies that were advancing in line north into Taichung City.

Bo could hear the commander of his vehicle, perched in his turret, speaking on the command radio net. From what he could ascertain by listening in, one of the other vehicles in the convoy—an armored command vehicle similar to the one Bo was currently riding in—had taken a direct hit from either artillery or one of the American suicide drones. The vehicle, now stopped dead in its metal tracks, was brewing up with the white-hot flames of ammunition cooking off in the turret.

Given that it was already consumed by the flames, it was unlikely that the crew had been able to escape.

Bo interrupted the conversation. "Continue on to our objective. There is nothing we can do for them. And stopping in the midst of this barrage will only result in more casualties. Out."

After a second of silence, he heard several callsigns acknowledge his order. His vehicle was still rocking from side to side as the crew command and driver of the vehicle sought to travel an unpredictable pathway through the barrage. The noise of explosions from around them was still deafening, added to by the plinking noises on the side of the hull from shrapnel.

But this was hardly the first time they had endured such an attack. It would probably not be the last. Bo and his vehicle crew had long since resigned themselves to the likelihood of perishing in such an attack. But until then, there was work to be done and a brigade to command. Bo tuned out the conversation on the command net. He had other more important matters to consider.

Clearly, the Americans were now targeting moving command and control nodes, Bo thought. *That is a change, and a very dangerous one at that.* Until recently, it had mainly been static headquarters and concentrations of troops and logistic supply hubs that had received the most attention from the long-range artillery and strike missiles of the Americans and their Taiwanese lackeys. That they were now able to target command and control vehicles on the move meant a couple of things that concerned Bo.

First, it meant that they were able to triangulate the location of command vehicles down more quickly to Bo's level. Direction-finding radio transmissions was an old science. Normally it was most effective on static vehicles in the land environment, given just how many transmissions and vehicles there were. But it was about more than just detecting transmission; this was about detecting the central elements of communications networks.

This was a relatively simple undertaking for air and naval platforms; they operated in low densities. However, in the land environment where there were tens of thousands of platforms emitting at any one time, detecting important nodes in command-and-control networks was an exponentially more difficult proposition. Clearly, the Americans had developed new algorithms and deployable high-performance computing to solve this problem in real time. *That is going to be a problem*, Bo thought.

Adding to this problem was that the Americans and the Taiwanese now had sufficient firepower on the island to target even small moving convoys like Bo's. *This might be an even bigger challenge*, he pondered. For the past month, supplies of Chinese artillery and missiles had been limited. The impact of naval and air attacks on their 200-kilometer sea supply route from the mainland had begun to bite on the PLA forces in Taiwan. In particular, 155mm artillery ammunition and the 300mm rockets for the multi-barrel rocket launchers were in short supply. It meant that their advance north into the city had been slower than anticipated, and any attack had to be planned at the highest level to ensure an adequate supply of supporting firepower.

While the PLA Air Force was helping, it too was not large enough to provide all the ground support required. And it was having challenges of its own, Bo knew. The buildup of airpower from the Americans and others in the Taiwanese bases to the east had hurt the Air Force. Unlike the first couple of days of the invasion, where they had been able to generate air superiority over the landing beaches, the PLA Air Force was now fighting for its life. The Americans had excellent aircraft and very capable long-range missiles, all coordinated by their advanced air-battle management systems.

Bo knew this because he was now a regular at the operations briefings at the headquarters of the 71st Group Army. But even these briefings did not explore the full dimensions of the Chinese challenges in the air. It was only in whispered side discussions with Bo's Air Force colleagues during his walks around the headquarters that he was able to discover just how difficult the air war was.

Bo's attention was suddenly drawn back to the world around him. It had gotten very quiet. Their vehicle was still moving but the sounds of explosions had ceased. The normal sounds of his vehicle, a variant of the Chinese-designed ZBD amphibious infantry fighting vehicle, returned. The crew commander spoke on the intercom. As always, his report was succinct and devoid of emotion.

"Sir, the enemy barrage has ceased. We lost one vehicle—it was a catastrophic explosion. Several others have minor damage but remain serviceable and mobile. We are 15 minutes out from the headquarters. Over."

Bo quickly thanked the commander and allowed him to return to commanding the vehicle and scanning the terrain around them for other threats. As Bo well knew, even when they were not being attacked by artillery, long-range strike missiles or lethal autonomous drones, there was danger on the ground from multiple sources. They were currently traveling through Caotun, a built-up area that was a satellite township of Taichung. Most of the buildings were still standing. But here and there, houses and office blocks had collapsed, with some still burning from a recent battle or missile strike. The streets were mainly clear of rubble, but that was due largely to good mission planning before they departed to ensure they traveled through areas where they would not need engineer support to clear obstacles.

He had no sooner thought this when the vehicle command yelled into the intercom: "Contact right."

Bo looked down at his monitors. Already, one of the vehicle crews had placed a small red marker on the shared battle map to display where they thought the enemy was located. The marker showed the symbol for a man-portable anti-tank weapon. Bo felt sweat rise on his forehead and temple, even though the environmental control in the vehicle kept its internal temperature at 18 degrees centigrade.

In urban areas like this, a small team of soldiers with access to good battle management systems to share knowledge of enemy locations, and a few of the new Javelin II missiles, could cause carnage among Bo and his men. While they were mounted in armored vehicles, this was not a fighting patrol. It was supposed to be an administrative movement back to their headquarters. They could protect themselves, but fighting their way rearward for every briefing session would begin to seriously attrit what was left of his brigade.

Then, a sudden, shattering explosion rocked Bo's vehicle.

27

The Mission

3 August 2028
Taichung City

The through-armor vision system was playing up again, Lee thought. *This fucking rain.*

It had been incessant, and the approaching typhoon had only made things worse. Normally the through-armor vision provided a good view of the terrain and potential enemy positions in the urban environment. But the heavy rain, and buildup of moisture in almost everything, had degraded the performance of the system. Not that it mattered that much at present.

Lee and her soldiers, mounted in their vehicles and accompanied by hundreds of aerial and ground autonomous vehicles, were moving through a part of Taichung City where the streets were exceedingly narrow. Indeed, their vehicles were of a width that ensured they only just fitted down the narrow roads one at a time.

It was a deliberate choice to use these slender urban canyons. They had to mask their approach to their objective today. And it was just one layer of security around the mission Lee was leading. Multiple layers of ground and aerial recon drones protected their flanks, as well as their rear.

Lee continued to scan the command screens in front of her. "It's just like the briefing said," she said into the vehicle's intercom system to Sergeant James. "There is almost nothing in front of us. The intel staff and the division planners have threaded the needle for us. Two thousand meters to the objective."

It had been almost two weeks since they had been assigned to this "special duty" with the 3rd Marine Division. The divisional commander, a spry yet quiet man who was also Colonel Furness' direct superior, had taken Lee's unit under his command in the wake of their evening battle just north of Taichung City.

Since then, Lee and her company-sized cavalry organization had been dispatched on numerous special tasks by the divisional commander. Sometimes these tasks involved just a small element from her command; a platoon here, or even a half-platoon detachment there. But in every case, on every mission, the proportion of autonomous ground and aerial vehicles increased.

There was now a virtual flood of these systems flowing into theater from CONUS as well as from new advanced robotic factories established in Japan, Australia, New Zealand, and Canada. Robots were now building robots in the thousands. *Weird*, Lee thought. Robots were reproducing themselves in a never-ending stream.

The Ukraine War had driven a lot of new thinking in Western military organizations. Some of this thinking was applied to building more munitions and lethal drones at a much faster rate than ever before. Factories, already producing autonomous systems before the Chinese invasion, were now turning out drones like American factories turned out tanks and aircraft during the Second World War.

A 21st-century multinational Arsenal of Democracy had been constructed from the collaborative efforts of America and its allies. Lee had even heard rumors that the Taiwanese were churning out precision missiles and drones in several subterranean factories established deep beneath the mountains that ran down the eastern side of the island. But, as with many things, such knowledge was beyond her paygrade.

They had learned a lot from the Ukrainians after the Russian invasion of their country. The Ukrainian Army and Air Force had developed some very clever tactics for teaming humans and autonomous systems for various offensive and defensive mission sets. Lee and her troopers had studied these before their deployment and had gone back over some of the key lessons from the Russo-Ukraine War in the last couple of weeks as well.

Not that they hadn't engaged in their own learning during the fighting here in Taiwan. While studying lessons from other wars and conducting training exercises were one thing, combat was an entirely different learning opportunity. *At least for those that survived*, Lee considered. She and her troopers had proved to be great survivors and excellent learners so far during their time on the island.

They had learned the hard way about good tactics and how to beat the clever, well-equipped Chinese ground force they had been fighting for months now. And the more they learned, the more they shared with the Marines and their fellow soldiers about good tactics, techniques, and procedures for beating the Chinese.

One significant aspect of their learning had been subterranean operations. This island was riddled with underground caverns, tunnels, roads, and other infrastructure that had been built over the past six decades. The Taiwanese had been very industrious in constructing a complex, three-dimensional defensive layout to slow down and defeat any Chinese invasion.

Lee and her troopers, since their assignment to work directly for the divisional commander, had been dispatched on multiple missions that saw them fighting in the massive underground facilities that every city seemed to feature. Sometimes, they fought dismounted supported by smaller uncrewed ground combat vehicles. Other times, they had to fight their way through massive subterranean

289

passages that would swallow every vehicle in her unit as well as all of their ground and aerial drones.

This was one aspect of the situation that had surprised Lee. She had expected the tough, bloody combat. She had expected to lose soldiers. She had not expected to be spending so much time fighting the Chinese deep underground.

Lee's unit had devoured lessons from previous wars, including Vietnam, Iraq and Ukraine, in preparing for their first underground mission. She had no doubts it had kept many of her folks alive, and ensured that they had succeeded in that mission, and many others since. And it would help them with their current mission—which, according to Sergeant James, currently up in his turret commanding the vehicle and scanning his sectors, could only be described as "heroic." It was a more polite term than several other non-comms had used just within her hearing.

Batshit crazy.

Insane.

Fucking awesome.

Lee, if she had time to ponder it, would have agreed with all these comments. They were on a mission that, if she proposed it at command and general staff college, would probably see her given a "fail" grade and then booted off the course. But wars were like that. Sometimes it meant that soldiers were given a mission that made no sense even a few days before, but now was the most natural thing in the world.

They were going after a big fish. A really big fish.

For several days, the intel folks had suspected that the headquarters for an entire Chinese Group Army was hiding in a part of the city that Lee and her troopers might be able to infiltrate. The suspicion was that the Chinese headquarters had located itself in one of the many multi-story parking garages on the eastern side of the city. This gave it a very low signature and made it hard to detect from the air. It also ensured it would be almost impossible to attack from the air or the ground. The emphasis, of course, was on "almost," Lee thought.

The breakthrough had come in the past 24 hours. A Chinese Marine brigade was being withdrawn from the flank of the easternmost Group Army and re-tasked to protect the Chinese headquarters. Lee had not seen the raw communications intercept but had received a very thorough briefing on the Chinese Marine brigade, its composition, and key leaders. She had also been given a very interesting brief on how they had finally confirmed the location of the Chinese headquarters.

It was pretty sneaky, actually. *Typical of those intel fuckers*, Lee thought. The Americans had used an artillery barrage, while the Chinese brigade commander was moving from his eastern flank location, to drop swarms of small drones that had secure trackers embedded in them. Given all the Chinese armored vehicles had electronic drone killers now, they needed to drop the trackers onto the Chinese vehicles. Out of the hundreds dropped, only several had succeeded. But it had been enough.

The Marine Division headquarters intel staff had been able to track the Chinese Marine brigade commander all the way into a large suburban shopping mall parking garage. There had been no movement from that location in the hours afterwards. The division staff had assumed that their trackers had not been discovered.

The planners on the division headquarters had rapidly developed a plan to infiltrate along the same secure Chinese routes used by the Chinese Marine brigade commander. And then attack the Group Army headquarters.

Given the Chinese method of controlling their operations, it would cause considerable confusion among the Chinese divisions and brigades that were commanded by this eastern Group Army. Centralized control was the approach most Chinese military commanders used. Removing an important higher command node like a Group Army headquarters would cause a period of decision paralysis that the Americans could exploit. It was an excellent opportunity.

Lee's troopers, moving slowly in heavy rain through the cluttered alleys of this large city, were pivotal to ensuring they could make the most of it.

28

Battle for Taichung I

3 August 2028
Taichung City

The explosion that rocked his vehicle would have thrown Bo out of his seat had he not been strapped into his command pod chair.

It was a lesson that the Chinese had learned from observing the Americans and their allies operate in Iraq and Afghanistan. Wearing a safety harness while seated in an armored vehicle generally stopped people being blown around the cabin in the event they were attacked.

The vehicle intercom again.

"Foxtrot vehicle destroyed. Enemy engaged at 150m in white warehouse. Wait out."

Bo knew not to interrupt his vehicle crew commander. He had passed on what he knew, and now he was fighting to save their vehicle and their lives, while trying to eliminate the dismounted anti-tank team off to the right-hand side of the road. Bo followed the back and forth of short conversations on the command network. Information about range, locations, and weapon effects was passed quickly and efficiently. This was a well-drilled team.

Suddenly, a drone feed of the surrounding area appeared on Bo's far right command screen. Obviously one of the vehicles had launched a small surveillance UAV and it was sharing its feed among all the vehicles in the small convoy.

The drone would not fly directly over the suspected location of the enemy. The enemy probably had one of the advanced American counter-drone systems developed in the wake of the Russo-Ukraine War with them. And they would also want to ensure that the Taiwanese or American infantrymen and their missiles were not alerted to the presence of this airborne sensor. *Sneakiness matters, even when sensors can see almost all the battlefield*, Bo pondered.

The drone used a mix of different sensors, including thermal imagery. Using these sensors, it was obvious where they were being ambushed from. A small team, with two missile launchers, was spaced out on the first story of a warehouse approximately 150 meters down a wide alley way off to their right. Bo admired the beautifully sited ambush location, before remembering that this clever group of ambushers was trying to kill him.

There they are, thought Bo. Several flashes appeared on the image feed from the small surveillance drone in the next few seconds. These had been preceded by several streaks, indicating rounds from the 30mm cannon mounted on Bo's vehicle, as well as other vehicles in the convoy.

"Threat eliminated." A short report over the vehicle's intercom and they were on their way to the headquarters again.

The excitement of the ambush and explosions of the preceding day had not been replicated during the movement of Bo's small convoy to the headquarters today.

Bo was now perched on his normal seat in the main briefing tent of the headquarters complex for the 71st Group Army. This Group Army had been established in 2017 and was normally assigned to the Eastern Theater Command. It was the equivalent of a large Western corps, and for this campaign it commanded three infantry divisions, two motorized infantry divisions, and an armored division. It also possessed an array of artillery, air defense, intelligence, and logistics supporting forces.

Funny, thought Bo. *You wouldn't know it, even with all those additional logistic battalions and brigades assigned to each Group Army.*

Not only had Bo's brigade been attached to this Group Army, but it would soon be withdrawing from its eastern positions to replace the unit currently defending the headquarters of this large formation. Bo's visit, in addition to this briefing session, would include a meeting with the Chief of Staff of the headquarters to coordinate the relief in place of the current unit in 24 hours.

The headquarters, normally a highly mobile aggregation of armored vehicles, trucks, trailers, and communications systems, had been static for the past 72 hours. Being in such a static location made Bo nervous. Staying in one location not only made a headquarters easier to find, but it made the members of such an organization lazy. Better they move daily and keep their battle discipline than stay in one place and become comfortable and complacent.

He had to admit, though, they had found an interesting location for the headquarters. Sited in the middle levels of a multi-story parking garage and a large shopping center south of Taichung, they were shielded from overhead observation by the Taiwanese and American drones that were almost ubiquitous on the battlefield now. They also had several layers of concrete above and below them as protection. And all that concrete was excellent at minimizing the visual, heat, and electromagnetic signatures of the large headquarters.

It would be a difficult target to find, let alone attack, Bo pondered. But, the Americans are very clever, he remembered. And his nervousness returned.

His thoughts were interrupted by the entry into the room of the major general in command of the Group Army. Those awaiting his arrival rose to their feet in what seemed like an instant. But the commander, long used to such courtesies, merely motioned for everyone to sit and for the brief to begin. He had a reputation for impatience with formalities.

After a moment of speaking to his Chief of Staff, the commander turned his gaze to the front of the briefing tent and to the colonel standing there.

"Begin."

The colonel, long accustomed to such curt directives from the commander on this campaign, and long before, launched into his briefing.

"Sir, three Group Armies, including ours on the right, are advancing to Taichung City. A fourth army is in reserve to the south, and the new Group Army which has just completed offloading at southern ports is now in charge of rear area security. Taiwanese partisan activity remains high, and we are losing several convoys each day to dismounted anti-armor teams, suicide drones, and teams of autonomous ground combat vehicles. Instead of reinforcing us in the advance, Eastern Theater Command has reallocated this fifth Group Army to rear area security."

There was murmuring in the room. Most knew that the situation in rear areas was more dire than shown on the officially endorsed PLA information networks. While officially the local people had welcomed the invaders and were cooperating with the PLA, Bo and his fellow commanders knew nothing could be further from the truth. His brigade, like all the others, had dedicated disciplinary platoons responsible for meting out justice to the Taiwan resistance. It had not seemed to slow them down, however. Obviously this was an issue that was gaining attention at the highest levels.

The commander, known as a man of few words, merely nodded and indicated that the colonel at the front of the room should proceed.

"Sir, enemy activity in the south parts of the strait continues to interfere with our maritime resupply efforts. Over the past 72 hours, only 30 percent of our urgent logistic and supply demands have been fulfilled. We are already rationing artillery ammunition, tank ammunition, and precision missiles. Our units have captured sufficient fuel and food to last several weeks; however, those items unique to our equipment are running in short supply."

Bo, sitting several rows behind the commander, heard an almost inaudible grunt from the major general before he then waved his hand for the briefing to continue. The commander, like everyone else in the room, knew there was nothing their Group Army could do about the supply situation. There was no point dwelling on the matter. But it would slow down their advance in the coming days. *That will not go down well in Beijing*, thought Bo.

The colonel took his cue to continue.

"Sir, three of our divisions remain in contact with American and Taiwanese forces in the southeastern sector of Taichung. They have advanced several hundred meters in the past 24 hours. However, they are taking heavy casualties in people and beetles and will need to be relieved in place in the coming 72 hours.

"As you know, this is our first major ground combat operation where we have faced both the Taiwanese and Americans together. So far, they have constructed an effective unified command. We are seeking seams in their command-and-control network to exploit, but their networks and their command philosophy have proven quite resilient. Our best intelligence and cognitive warfare experts are developing a contingency plan, which they will brief to you this afternoon to try to break down the cohesion in the American–Taiwanese command structure."

Bo could see the commander smiling at this last comment. But he wasn't sure whether it was because he was excited about the prospect of breaking down the cooperation between his different adversaries, or because he thought it was more conceptual babble. The commander had made clear that he had little time for some of the unproven concepts such as "cognitive warfare" and "systems destruction" that had been discussed before this war. Like the Russian transformation program in the past two decades, the battlefield had tested these uniquely Chinese ideas to destruction in Taiwan.

The commander then spoke, surprising Bo.

"Let's just focus on finding and killing the enemy, thank you. All these fancy terms from before the war have not helped us so far. We must ensure we are truly brilliant at the basics of soldiering, shooting, supply, and command and control. It is when we are deficient in such basic parts of our profession that our forces have problems."

Bo, surprised that such a senior Chinese general would criticize PLA doctrine in public, was transfixed. He was certain that this would, at least, lead to stern words from the Group Army's senior political officer after the briefing. At worst, the commander might even be removed.

Each time he had visited the headquarters, Bo had heard quiet murmurings about how the Chinese campaign was progressing. While they had advanced to almost the center of the island, their northern landings had failed. The entire eastern part of the island also remained in Taiwanese hands. And, at least according to their intelligence briefings before the invasion, the Taiwanese kept their best units in the north and central parts of the island. To make things worse, the Americans, Japanese, Australians, and others were arriving in large numbers on the island, in the skies above it, and in the waters to the north, east, and south of Taiwan.

As he had feared before the advance on Taichung had commenced, the toughest fighting was still ahead of them. So, it was clear that the invasion force was in trouble. The Chinese supply lines to the island were slowly being choked by the enemy. This resulted in a lack of reinforcements and resupply of critical munitions. Already, nearly 60 percent of Bo's combat power was being provided by uncrewed ground combat systems. And he had heard of divisions in this Group Army where that percentage was even higher. No, things were not going well, Bo thought. But it was best to keep that opinion to himself. Even with his political connections due to his marriage, Bo knew that expressing "defeatist ideas" such as these could lead to removal from command, and potentially time in a labor camp in the western regions of China.

Before he could return his attention to the briefing, and the colonel, Bo was thrown from his seat. A massive concussion wave rolled through the room, followed by shrapnel and screams.

Then a second series of explosions, closer. He saw a brief vision of his wife.

And then Bo, already lying prone on the floor after the first explosion, tumbled into oblivion.

AUTHOR'S NOTE (IV)

Contained on this page is a copy of the battle situation overlay that was used as a backup in the headquarters of the 3rd Marine Division during the Battle of Taichung in 2028. It shows the advance north of the three Chinese Group Armies into Taichung, with a fourth Group Army as the operational reserve for the Chinese forces in Taiwan.

North of the Wu River, the Taiwanese 1st Corps and the US III Corps are deployed to defend against the Chinese advance. Among the combat divisions in the US III Corps are the 3rd Marine Division and the 1st Australian Division.

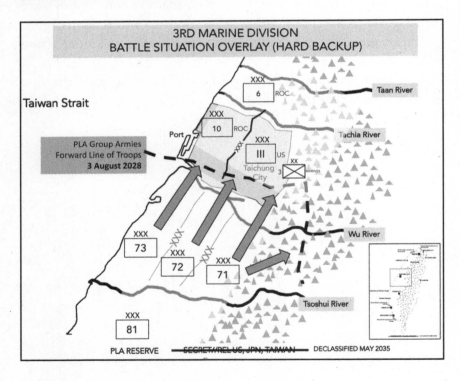

29

Battle for Taichung II

3 August 2028
Taichung City

Lee's vehicle continued its slow crawl towards her objective.

The two- and three-story buildings on each side were dark, deserted, and showed in a multi-hued grey color in her through-armor display googles. Pock marks from large-caliber machine-gun and cannon rounds marred many of the buildings. Others were missing parts of their facades or their roofs.

Lee's unit was operating in radio and electronic silence. They had to maintain a stealthy approach to the Chinese headquarters to have any chance at success. It was late and in the middle of a torrential downpour. Their visual, heat, and electromagnetic signatures would all be very difficult for the Chinese to discover. *Well, that was the plan*, Lee thought, continuing to scan her command screens.

But there was something else going on. Walking through the headquarters after the mission briefing for this mission, Lee had observed more activity than usual. And more covered maps and screens than was normally the case. This typically only happened when a major operation was being planned, and the staff were seeking to preserve operational security. So, her mission, as important as it was, was part of something larger.

"Contact front!" yelled James from his turret.

Her goggles briefly whited out with the intense heat of tracer rounds that were now crisscrossing her vision. She could hear the small-caliber machine guns and larger cannons that they had come to associate with the Chinese uncrewed ground combat systems. The beetles had become smarter and better armed over the last few months. But they were still no match for a human in an armored vehicle with good communications, weapons, and electronic attack capabilities. Individually, at least.

However, beetles never attacked as individuals. They operated in swarms of ten, twenty, and sometimes up to one hundred units at a time. The algorithms and machine learning that controlled them accepted a certain proportion of the individual beetles would be lost. Beetles were designed to overwhelm an enemy, not to be precision instruments of death.

"There are dozens of beetles, and we..." she heard the commander of 1st Platoon pass on the secure communications net before the transmission was suddenly cut off. The 1st Platoon of her unit was in the lead, and she had expected them to take the brunt of any initial attack by the Chinese if they were discovered.

It was a brutal calculus for any combat leader. Deciding who would lead an advance was often the same as deciding who would die first in combat. But for this mission, Lee had given the 1st Platoon dozens of additional ground and aerial drones. She had also ensured they were the priority for air and ground fire support that would be provided by the Marine division and its air wing. Fire support that was quick in arriving.

Already, artillery, rocket, and Switchblade II drones were being brought to bear against the Chinese beetles that were swarming out from beneath the massive, multi-story concrete parking lot where the Chinese headquarters was located. Lee turned back to her command screens, while listening in on her secure radio command network.

"The boss is gone. Taking over."

The platoon sergeant for 1st Platoon, new to Taiwan herself, was taking command of the leading element of her unit in this fight. After all they had been through, it was hard to believe the young lieutenant had finally been taken by combat. Lee pondered this for no more than a second.

"Roger, carry on. No change to mission orders. You have priority call for fire support." Lee then punched her finger on a different blue icon on her screen and spoke briefly into the command radio network. "2nd Platoon, be prepared to support 1st Platoon in fixing the Chinese defenses. 3rd Platoon, execute 'Rapier.' Over."

Two quick bursts of static indicated that her other callsigns had received her order. There was little to do now but monitor her three platoons while ensuring divisional headquarters provided them with the cyber, electronic, and fire support in the coming vital minutes.

Her codeword, *rapier*, was the signal for the 3rd Platoon to commence its infiltration of the parking garage while the other two platoons fixed and distracted the Chinese forces defending the headquarters. The 3rd Platoon would act like a vicious and violent stiletto to penetrate through to the central hub of the Chinese headquarters. Her command element would follow in due course, prepared to conduct a rapid exploitation of material found in the headquarters.

The noise from outside her vehicle continued to escalate. Both sides were hindered by the heavy rain and increasingly fierce winds sweeping across the island. Her command screen provided constant updates on the progress of the typhoon as it moved north from the Philippines Sea. She dreaded to think what it was like further south on the island.

Clearly the Chinese had a large force defending the headquarters. Heavy-caliber cannon and machine-gun fire continued to target her armored vehicles and uncrewed ground combat vehicles. At the same time, her forces were slowly pushing their way into the enormous concrete structure before them. They had to be careful though. They could not afford to become decisively committed. Once 3rd Platoon had completed its mission, the rest of the unit needed to be able to support its withdrawal and then disengage before other Chinese units in the area arrived.

This is not supposed to be a suicide mission, Lee thought for what must have been the hundredth time in the past few hours. But at the moment, the Chinese drones and their human teammates were fighting like demons. Lee knew that this was to be expected. It was only one of four Group Army headquarters that the Americans were aware of on the island. It was a very important command and control hub for the Chinese. And given how the Chinese disliked delegating, the loss of such a headquarters would have a paralyzing impact on all the units that belonged to this eastern Group Army.

The penetration of Lee's troopers into the Chinese headquarters was being aided by the geodata provided by the tracking device that had been placed on the Chinese Marine commander's vehicle. 3rd Platoon, while the Chinese defenders were being drawn away by the rest of Lee's unit, was making steady progress in its infiltration of the parking garage. There was some fighting, but generally the attention of the Chinese had been drawn by Lee's two other platoons off to her left.

"Time to move," James stated into the vehicle intercom.

"Roger," Lee responded. It was time to follow up 3rd Platoon as part of the entry into the parking garage. The vehicle power pack revved a couple of times and then they lurched forward, into the gloomy interior of the concrete structure. In her through-armor goggles, Lee could still see some of the fighting off to her left that had deceived the Chinese. *How long will that last?* she pondered. This had to be quick if they were to get in and get out without it really becoming a suicide mission.

Suddenly, multiple small explosions pounded the right side of her vehicle's hull. James swore and she heard the whining of the turret quickly slewing to the right. Looking through the armor, Lee could see several beetles—possibly a small reserve force—that had detected her vehicle and engaged it. But just as quickly, the gun on her vehicle and the two vehicles following hers dispatched the beetles. They only needed one or two rounds from the armor-piercing ammunition fired by James to become useless, smoking metal wrecks.

An eerie quiet descended. Lee's vehicle, following the trailing vehicle of the 3rd Platoon, was only just able to fit through the low-ceiling parking levels. It was dry in here. The heavy rain and winds outside were unable to penetrate deep into the concrete structure. She could still hear fighting and was able to track the movement of her forces on her command screen by the red and blue icons that moved and flashed out when vehicles or beetles were destroyed.

But here, at least for this moment, all was serene. It was odd. She could see the wreckage of Taiwanese and Chinese vehicles scattered throughout this ground level of the parking garage. Clearly, the Taiwanese had also established defensive positions here before being overwhelmed by the Chinese. But there were no people or active drones to be seen. They had caught the Chinese off guard.

Flashes to her front caught her attention. Sound waves then rolled over her vehicle, and she could hear the sounds of combat ahead. Sound carried differently in this low-ceilinged concrete maze than in the streets and open terrain she had become used to.

"Checkmate, checkmate," blasted through the earphones in her combat helmet. It was the commander of 3rd Platoon. She could hear a mix of tension and joy in her voice.

It was the codeword for the Chinese headquarters. They had found it. And if they could see it in this concrete mess, they could kill it. And maybe even capture some of their quantum encrypted communications systems for exploitation back at divisional headquarters.

"Contact front," she heard from James. Then their gun was firing at targets to their front and left. In her through-armor vision system, she could see multiple flashes around their vehicle.

A massive explosion sounded to her rear. She looked to her right, behind her vehicle. Her sergeant major's vehicle, which had been moving immediately behind them, was gone. Well, not totally gone. Some of its road wheels, attached to jagged pieces of metal that had once been a hull, remained in a darkened patch on the concrete floor of the parking garage. But everything else was gone.

Fuck it, Lee thought. *He was one of the originals from our unit. Here from day one and now gone. His entire life, existence, memories, experiences, and future now reduced to atoms in the stinking, dark concrete hell*, she pondered. *No time for that. There is still a fight to command*, Lee told herself as she turned back to her command screens.

"Where the fuck did they come from? Jesus, ma'am, I think we are going to be overrun..." she heard James scream.

The gun in the turret above her continued to hammer away at targets to the left of her vehicle. She could no longer see the vehicles of 3rd Platoon ahead of her. They had been drawn forward in their efforts to overrun and destroy the Chinese headquarters. And, given the last transmission from the platoon ahead of her, they were succeeding.

Thank goodness, Lee thought. *It looks like we might just pull this mission off.*

Suddenly, she was consumed by the most violent, loud, and hot feeling she had ever experienced. She was wrenched from her seat, despite the restraints, and slammed against the rear combat door.

Excruciating pain coursed through her brain and to the core of her body.

A brief sense of failure.

And then, nothing.

30

Morakot the Second

3 August 2028
3rd Space Operations Squadron
United States Space Force

"Look at the size of that thing."

Captain Marcus peered over Hickling's shoulder at the large flat screens at the front of the room that provided a common picture for the orbital warfare team conducting this mission. Swirling clouds of the typhoon were projected in high definition. It seemed to make them all the more threatening, even at this distance.

The vast rotating cloud bands of the storm already stretched several hundred kilometers across. Large rainbands spiraled slowly into the center of the typhoon as the storm slowly moved on its northwestern track. While in some typhoons these rainbands often appeared to be motionless, in this storm they were rotating around the eye of the storm.

The eye at the geometric center of the typhoon was almost perfectly circular; approximately 80 kilometers across, it appeared to be an oasis of calm amid the maelstrom around it. There were no clouds within. But it was here the lowest pressure would be reached. And within the eye, while it remained at sea, was where the most hazardous seas would be found. It was here that waves from every point of the compass converged. The result was highly erratic waves, which could build upon each other to reach massive wave heights.

"Heaven help any poor soul caught in that eye," Hickling murmured, not looking over her shoulder at Major Marcus. She knew he was lingering but understood. What they were witnessing was perhaps the most powerful typhoon recorded for decades in the western Pacific region. And they would be observing it live as it continued its northwestern track of destruction.

"Tech Sergeant, what are the maximum wind gusts being detected in the eye wall region?" Marcus asked.

Hickling had the data in an instant, using her augmented reality rig to call it up and then project it on the large wall screen before them.

"Sir, winds are already exceeding maximum recorded sustained gusts over the past three decades. Haiyan, one of the most powerful typhoons ever, had one-minute sustained winds of over 300 kilometers per hour. We just received data that recorded a gust that reached nearly 340 kilometers per hour. It's a real monster, Sir," Hickling responded.

"I guess that's what happens when there is more heat in the ocean," Marcus responded.

"More heat equals more potential energy for storms like this. At least that is what the weather folks explained yesterday during the final mission briefing. Over the past 40 years, upper ocean warming rates are thought to be responsible for more intense typhoons."

Another voice interrupted.

"Very good, Major. The science is reasonably clear on this now. Our modeling over the last few years suggests we should expect more Category 4 and 5 storms, which are individually more powerful and contain heavier rainfall."

Keene's image appeared in the right corner of Hickling's vision. Hickling threw the image onto the larger wall screen so that everyone could see it.

"Hickling, it's Keene. That's enough of the basic science behind what we are doing. I have a quick update from DC."

Hickling nodded, responding with a terse "send please" before returning to monitoring the storm and the multiple satellite feeds that she and her team had assumed control over in the past 12 hours.

"We can confirm the storm track continues to closely mirror the reference typhoon from 2009. After developing out in the Pacific, it has moved in a west-northwesterly direction over the past day or so," Keene described in an almost monotone voice. She was clearly weary, having been at work since the beginning of this mission almost a day ago. In the background, her military aide passed her a single sheet of paper and made a comment that was inaudible, at least to Hickling and her supervisor standing at her shoulder. Keene then looked up into the camera once again before continuing her update.

"According to the information I have just been provided by our Pentagon liaison officer, the Cyber Command operation that is working with our allies to gain access to ground weather stations throughout the western Pacific is proceeding as planned. Generally, these ground stations for collecting data—government and those at universities and private institutions—have low levels of security. Accessing them has not been a significant challenge, even the Chinese ones."

"What about the PLA weather units in Taiwan?" Marcus asked.

"Yes, those were a little more challenging, but several days ago, Cyber Command was able to insert themselves into their data feeds. The folks at Cyber Command have high confidence that they can control what is sent from these weather stations for analysis, regardless of what weather data they collect. In effect, we now have the power to change the weather—or at least change how people see it for the next day or so."

Hickling nodded.

"Thank you, Ma'am. We have the storm on the screen here. I can confirm we have control over the feeds from all our weather satellites. The Japanese, Canadians, Australians, and Singaporeans have all handed over control of their feeds to us for this operation. We have secured control of Chinese satellites, and those of several other nations. We are now providing the alternate feed which shows the storm tracking up the eastern coast of Taiwan. At least from their satellite feeds, they are only going to see what we want them to see."

Keene pondered this for a moment and recalled Hickling's statement when they had first discussed this operation: *We are going to make this typhoon disappear.* As a pragmatist and an American, Keene knew what they were doing was essential to the military operations being conducted to defend Taiwan against the Chinese. She understood that the path of the typhoon, having been hidden from the world by their subterfuge and manipulation of satellites, weather stations, and communications links, would undoubtedly have a significant impact on the Chinese forces on the ground, in the air, and at sea. She only hoped that it had the effect that the military planners, and their political masters in Washington and beyond, hoped for.

Because the other side of the potential military success of this operation was that thousands—probably tens of thousands of humans—would die because of the storm. It would pass over densely populated areas, and straight across the top of the main concentrations of the PLA in southern Taiwan. This included their principal logistics depots and their sea and air supply hubs.

Keene decided to describe what they would be seeing on their screens as the typhoon moved onto a more westerly track in the coming hours.

"You all have the projections for the typhoon track. We expect that it will make landfall on the western coast near Hengchun. It is likely to slow a little at that stage because it isn't drawing as much energy from the ocean. The storm will then track roughly in parallel to the southern coastline. Because part of the storm will remain over the ocean once it crosses the most southern tip of Taiwan, it will retain a lot of energy."

"We expect that it will move across Fangliao, Kaohsiung, and Tainan before moving out into the Taiwan Strait. This takes it over the key Chinese logistic hubs but also straight over the top of the major concentration of its shipping that moves between Taiwan and southern China.

"We are projecting catastrophic damage to the areas on land that this storm passes over. Buildings will likely suffer significant damage. Deployed military infrastructure, which normally uses tentage or portable huts and containers, will probably be totally destroyed due to the high winds," Keene noted to those assembled in the Space Command operations center.

Hickling, Marcus, and the others in the room nodded. There was little time to consider the ethical trade-offs that had to be made in such an operation. To them, they were achieving a mission and saving the lives of their fellow service personnel from America, Taiwan, and elsewhere. The loss of Taiwanese civilians, and PLA, was just part of the harsh reality that was at the heart of every war.

Hickling knew that Keene, with her hectic schedule, would need to sign off shortly. She would be in high demand in her role as Director of FEMA. *Especially in wartime*, thought Hickling.

"Ma'am, how about the winds? How much impact will they have on other phases of Operation *Chakra Rain*, particularly aerial operations for crewed and uncrewed aircraft?" asked Hickling.

Keene nodded.

"We modelled various storm strengths and tracks. The thing with typhoons is that their maximum winds occur at an altitude of

311

approximately 300 meters. Above that, the greater the altitude, the more the winds are weakened by the horizontal pressure-gradient force. I can send through a primer on this, but you can be assured that most of the aircraft and drone swarms in the strikes that are now taking place—and that will continue over the next few hours—will not be in any danger from the winds of this typhoon."

Keene looked away, ready to sign off, but then turned back to the camera. "Good luck to you all. Before I go, I wanted to share the name of this particular typhoon." She smiled slightly, her eyes creased with the wrinkles of fatigue, then continued. "In 2009, a massive typhoon swept out of the Pacific. It hit Taiwan and caused catastrophic damage and loss of life. It then moved over eastern China and then north to the Korean peninsula. It was the deadliest typhoon to ever hit Taiwan." Keene paused, puffing out her cheeks briefly before speaking again. "We have therefore named this storm after its predecessor. It is called Morakot the Second."

After a second, Keene's screen turned blank. Hickling, Marcus, and the others in the command center went back to monitoring their screens, providing an assured feed of data and analysis to INDOPACOM and ensuring they retained command of the various weather satellites.

31

One Heart, One Soul

4 August 2028
Underground aircraft hangar
Hualien

Private First Class Chen watched the aircraft steam back into the massive cavern. Several hours ago, he had watched as the Taiwanese, American, and a hodge-podge of other nations had taxied out of the gargantuan underground hangar for their various missions, their planes slung with missiles and precision bombs under their wings. But many of the aircraft, including the mysterious American stealth aircraft, carried their weapons in internal bays to reduce their radar cross sections.

He had known that a major operation was underway as he had watched them depart. His boss, Major Lin, had given him hints in the preceding days that a massive strike on the Chinese was about to take place. While he had not been able to piece together all the details, the number of aircraft involved in this single mission was much higher than any Chen had seen during his time in this subterranean fortress and airfield.

And there was good news on another front. Chen, just that morning, had finally received a message from his girlfriend, Mei.

She had been sheltering with her family for the previous month and had not been able to get a message to him. But she, and her family, were all well. Chen was overjoyed. Mei was alive. Now they both had to survive the coming days and weeks so they could be reunited.

While not usually a superstitious person, Chen took the message this morning, received as the aircraft were taxiing out of the underground hangar, as a good omen for the coming operation. He knew that this was silly. But he also wanted to hang onto any shred of hope that he could.

As he stood at the edge of the underground cavern, just outside the headquarters for his brigade, Major Lin walked up beside him. Despite the disparity in their military ranks, they had worked closely together in the last few weeks and had developed an easy rapport. Lin, with a small mug of tea in his hand, offered Chen a sip of the steaming hot brew.

Declining, Chen asked the one question that had been on his mind as he watched the returning aircraft.

"Sir, were they successful? I know I should not ask the details of their mission, but can you at least tell me that this aerial armada succeeded at what it set out to do?" He looked at Lin, whose face had initially been serious. However, his superior officer was now breaking out into a wide grin. *That probably tells me all I need to know*, Chen thought. *The major almost never smiles.*

Lin then surprised him again. He clapped a hand on Chen's shoulder and drew him into a tight embrace. Holding him for a moment, Lin then stepped back. The smile remained on his face.

"Chen, there is so much that has happened in the last few hours. A small team of us were permitted to monitor a feed from the different elements of a massive operation which has just concluded. These aircraft, and the large missile, cyber, and drone swarm strikes that accompanied them, were successful at decapitating the

PLA leadership and destroying many tactical headquarters across the south."

Chen opened his mouth to speak, but was quickly silenced by Lin.

"Wait—there is more, Chen. The Chinese in the south have been hit by a massive storm. That wind and rain of the last few days? Well, it was actually part of a typhoon. It has passed over our southern cities. The resistance movement was able to warn our people, so apparently the death toll among our own is low.

"But the Chinese were caught totally by surprise. The reports I have seen in the last hour or so indicate that all their major supply dumps have been destroyed, as have nearly all their aircraft on the ground. The Navy is also reporting that dozens of PLA amphibious ships and warships have also been sunk or badly damaged."

Chen, hardly believing what he had just been told, could not move. Could it really be true?

"Chen, it just came through the radio. The Chinese have accepted our demands for a ceasefire and to evacuate their remaining forces. You know what that means? We have won. We have defended our island. Our president will be making a national address shortly."

Lin, now overcome, embraced Chen again. While Chen briefly considered that it was inappropriate for an officer to give his subordinate a bear hug like this, the circumstances were exceptional. They had defeated the Chinese. And with that last thought, he felt the tears begin to stream down his cheeks.

3 2

The Bitter Plain

7 August 2028
Southwestern Taiwan

Bo lifted his head gently from the pillow.

Sunlight was streaming through the gaps in the canvas tent that was his hospital ward. The field hospital, located near their embarkation point at the port of Tainan, had over a dozen such tented hospital wards. And there were multiple field hospitals within a stone's throw of where Bo rested.

It was an older canvas tent, drawn from their reserve stores and erected after nearly all their more modern field hospitals had essentially disappeared in the awful typhoon several days before. Bo avoided thinking about what that must have been like for the hospital staff, and their thousands of patients. He had heard stories of bodies scattered by terrible winds like grains of rice.

The Chinese Marine colonel had not been here for that catastrophe. His motionless body had been recovered from underneath the parking garage to the north in the wake of an American assault on the headquarters he had been visiting at the time. The journey south had been a stop-start affair as his rescuers sought to avoid both the extreme weather and the swarms of enemy killer drones that had almost magically appeared in the previous 24 hours.

It was agonizing at times as the field ambulance swerved and bounced its way south. But as bad as his wounds were, he was fortunate. Fortunate because his brigade had not yet assumed responsibility for the defense of the Group Army headquarters. Bo's brigade had been scheduled to take over the defense of the location several hours after the attack had occurred. His predecessor, a pleasant enough Army colonel that Bo had met on several occasions, had been taken out and shot within an hour of the American assault which had killed the Group Army commander. The thieving Americans had also spent time looting the headquarters for secure communications equipment and other intelligence. It was a disaster. On any other day, this would have resulted in wholesale sackings, jailings, and executions of many senior officers.

That had all been overtaken by the typhoon.

One of his final recollections from the headquarters under the parking garage in Taichung City was the briefing about weather and environmental considerations for the next phase of their operations in central Taiwan. He recalled the information about a typhoon that had formed south of Taiwan, and how its projected track would take it up the eastern shoreline and out into the vast emptiness of the northern Pacific Ocean.

Bo even remembered one of the senior officers, who sat at the front briefing table with the Group Army commander, asking about the certainty of the projected typhoon track. The curious senior officer had been assured by the weather expert in the room that multiple reporting stations on the ground, and satellite data, confirmed their projections.

After waking here two days ago, Bo had initially been confused about what had occurred. Gradually, he pieced together a story of his rescue by survivors of the attack on the Group Army headquarters and the overnight journey through various aid stations. Throughout this journey, his rescuers had to avoid the terrible devastation wrought by the typhoon and its high-speed winds.

More difficult had been piecing together details about what else had transpired after the attack on the headquarters. Bo had been assisted in this by his brigade operations officer, Major Chin, who had played a key role in Bo's rescue. He had not left his brigade commander's side for the past several days. When Bo had questioned the young officer, he had explained their situation simply.

"Sir, we are all that remains from our brigade."

Bo had then tasked the young officer with finding out more about the events of the past several days. Information came in small pieces, based on a conversation here with a medical orderly, or a discussion there with another hospitalized senior officer. Bit by bit, the tenacious Major Chin got a fuller picture of what had occurred.

"The Americans orchestrated a vile, complex plan of attack against our forces," Bo's operations officer had begun one of their bedside conversations.

Bo had raised an eyebrow at that. It was not the Americans or their plan that had aroused concern. It was the word "vile." He had taught the young officer that such terms were superfluous in their discussions; he wanted facts only.

"My apologies, Sir," Chin had replied straight away, knowing he had overstepped the mark with his commander.

"Please continue, Chin. I understand that it has been a taxing few days. But we must stick with facts if we are to learn from this disaster. I assume by our presence here that our forces have experienced a catastrophe?"

"As you directed, I have been able to construct a rough chronology of the past four days. There remain many gaps, but from my various discussions with those who are withdrawing and embarking on the evacuation flights and ships, a great tragedy has befallen our army of liberation."

Chin paused and took a deep breath. Bo could see the anguish in the young officer's face. Chin would need to learn to deal with this trauma if he was to carry on and live a meaningful life, Bo thought to himself.

"The timing and sequencing was exquisite, Sir. You may recall that in the final briefing before the attack at the Group Headquarters, there was a short discussion about the Indians. Well, apparently, they mobilized their Northern and Eastern armies and began to move towards the border. This set off a minor panic in Beijing, given the pressures on the campaign here. Many of the reserve forces being sent here were redirected to the southern and western borders."

Bo nodded. The Indians were most unlikely to invade China, but it was a clever piece of subterfuge. Their very existence was threat enough. It was probable that they had been well compensated by the Americans for this ploy. They had not had to fight but had received the credit anyway.

"Please continue, Chin. I sense it only gets worse from here."

Chin nodded.

"We were subject to a massive strike across the entire front. Huge swarms of aerial hunter-killer drones—Switchblade II, Ghost Phoenix and several new types we had not seen before—attacked almost all of our command-and-control nodes at brigade level and below. Within an hour or two, nearly every one of our infantry, armor, artillery, and logistic battalions had lost their commanders and key staff."

Bo gasped at the audacity of the plan, and the ability required to execute it. He had never heard of such a decapitation strike. "Normally such strikes on command-and-control hubs are kept at division and above," Bo replied.

Chin, looking down at his notebook to double check his information, indicated there was more information to come.

"That is normally the case, Sir. And they did indeed strike Division and Group Army headquarters. These were carried out by long-range missiles from the Taiwanese, US, and Australian Army strike battalions. At the same time, we lost a majority of our aircraft flying combat air patrol over the island as well as every single air command-and-control, refueling and surveillance aircraft."

Bo, feeling his mouth drop in surprise, quickly snapped his lips together.

"Sir, I spoke to a classmate who escaped from the 72nd Group Army headquarters. He is an intelligence officer. He had heard rumors that the Americans had deployed some kind of new stealth aerial platform that was not detected by any of our sensors."

Bo acknowledged this information with a curt nod, then looked up at the ceiling. All those years of planning, development, and training had come to nothing. It would take the People's Liberation Army years to recover from this disaster. He looked back at Chin. The major had more to share.

"Sir, the final element of the American operational design was the storm."

Bo gave Chin a questioning look. How could the Americans incorporate an act of nature into a complicated military operation?

"I can see, Sir, that you are skeptical. I understand. But the Americans made the storm disappear from one place and appear in another."

At this, Bo raised his hand to stop the story that was spilling out of Chin's mouth. What outrageous nonsense. He was about to reprimand the young man when Chin began to speak again.

"Sir, it was not magic. Somehow, the Americans were able to predict the path of the storm and then take control of the feeds from every ground and satellite weather station and insert a different track. So, while we believed that the typhoon would move up the eastern coast of the island, this was just the deception plan inserted into every weather satellite in the region. In reality, the storm swept over the southern part of the island, catching us completely unprepared. Not only was the physical devastation enormous, but there was almost no senior leadership left to deal with the aftermath."

Chin paused again, checking his notes.

"Our northern defenses collapsed rapidly. The three Group Armies on the front line around Taichung were effectively destroyed or captured. Most of our logistic supply facilities between there and here in the south were either destroyed by the Americans or the typhoon that came afterwards. To add to the devastation, many of our small and medium-sized warships and amphibious vessels, without warning, were severely damaged or sunk in the storm."

Bo, stunned by this collection of disasters that had befallen the People's Liberation Army, placed his hand gently on Chin's forearm, bidding him to stop. He had heard enough for now. There would be much for him to ponder as his recovery progressed in the coming weeks.

I have to learn how to walk again, Bo thought, as he looked down at the flat bed where his legs would have normally rested. He closed his eyes a moment, and then remembered that even in his damaged, legless state, he remained a senior officer of the Chinese Marines. Even with just a single subordinate remaining, he must show composure and leadership.

"Major Chin, this has been a military failure for our country. I realize my words must sound distressing. However, if we are to learn from this, we must call this exactly what it is. Given my injuries, my time in the military is probably at an end. But you are a young man. You must study what has occurred here. It will assist you in the future. I am sure that we have not, as a nation, given up our desire to make China whole again."

Chin, who had his head bent toward the floor, looked up at his commander. He nodded briefly, and then glanced behind him.

"Yes, sir. I expect we will return here again."

Two orderlies stepped forward to Colonel Bo's bed. They carried a stretcher but held back while Chin spoke to his commander.

"Thank you, Sir. There is one final thing. As one of the last senior officers alive, you are being accorded a high priority for evacuation. These orderlies here will assist you to your aircraft, which departs ..." Chin looked down at his watch. "Sir, your flight leaves in one hour. It has been an honor to serve with you. But I must now leave you. I have volunteered to assist in coordinating the evacuation of our troops. To be honest, it is a bit of a mess and I think they could use my planning skills."

Bo, his energy spent, smiled and gave a weak salute to the final surviving member of his Marine brigade. Chin stood, returned the salute, and after a moment, turned about and left the ward.

Bo recalled, all those months ago, wondering how many of his Marines he would lose in the conquest of this island. He had never imagined that he would lose them all. The campaign for Taiwan had left the most bitter taste in his mouth. The destruction of the Chinese forces of liberation on Taiwan's western plain was a calamity. But China was a large nation, Bo thought. It had a great depth of resources.

Colonel Bo, now one of only two survivors of the PLA's 1st Marine Brigade, let his head drop onto the pillow. Sleep came quickly. He did not awake again until the announcement was made that his aircraft was descending into Beijing.

33

Mors Honesta

8 August 2028
South of Taichung City

Colonel Furness peered out across the sand dunes, beyond the old rock wall defenses, and out into the Taiwan Strait. The seas were still choppy, with sea spray blowing across Furness and his Marines, a leftover from the recent storm. A rain squall was slowly working its way across his line of vision, from north to south, on the distant horizon. The skies remained grey and surly, much like his mood.

The last four days had been the most extraordinary of the campaign—at least, from the perspective of Furness and his regiment. The fact that he was standing here, well south of Taichung City, unmolested by Chinese drones, beetles, or long-range artillery and missiles, was testament to the events of the previous few days. The locals were already describing it as a miracle.

Many Taiwanese believed what had occurred was akin to the "divine winds" that had saved Japan from two different Mongol invasion fleets dispatched by Kublai Khan in 1274 and 1281. Thousands of Mongol soldiers, embarked on large wooden ships, had departed for the Japanese islands. Massive typhoons had destroyed the Mongol fleets and spawned the legend of the Kamikaze—a legend that had been reborn during the Second World War and applied to the brave but futile efforts to use manned aircraft to target American naval vessels in the western Pacific and Japanese home waters.

Social media in Taiwan, and around the world, was already brimming with new memes and metaphors for the massive tropical storm that had roared up from the Philippine Sea, across southern Taiwan, and then up the Taiwan Strait. But it was not so much the storm as its effect on the Chinese invasion that had gripped the world's attention. While Furness and his Marines had limited access to news feeds, there had been a relaxation (only slight, of course) of internet access policies in the past couple of days. He and his men had been able to read about the reactions of many nations to the sudden and catastrophic Chinese capitulation.

For the most part, news feeds back home and in English-speaking nations were rapturous in their joy at what seemed to be a quick and decisive conclusion to the war over Taiwan. Casting a shadow over the victory was the triumphant and bellicose advice of a few to "finish them off with nukes." Fortunately, the American president had heeded wiser counsel.

The reaction from countries in the western Pacific was more mixed than Furness had expected. While generally the reporting and editorials were positive, there was a theme emerging that some countries were worried that a beaten China might actually be a more dangerous neighbor. The leaders of some regional nations now worried that, having failed at conquering its rebellious province, China might vent its rage on a closer nation. One with which it shared land borders.

The defeat of China had not permanently removed the threat to Taiwan or the rest of the democracies in the western Pacific. The Chinese might lie low for a few years, but eventually they might try again to forcefully bring the Taiwanese back into the People's

Republic. All these concerns, however, lay in the future and would be dealt with by people well above his paygrade, Furness thought. He had other, more immediate and pressing worries that would occupy him and his staff in the coming weeks.

There was battlefield clearance to be undertaken. The PLA had left all manner of equipment and weapons behind when it had been evacuated from the island. The ultimatum from the Taiwan–America joint command had given them two choices: evacuate personnel and leave behind their equipment, or continue fighting. It appeared that even the Chinese high command in Beijing, and their invasion headquarters at the southern tip of Taiwan, knew that to continue fighting would only result in the destruction of the entire invasion force.

Perhaps some visualized this as a Dunkirk moment, Furness thought. *Maybe the strategic planners in Beijing believed that if they saved enough of their people, they would be able to turn around in a couple of years to try this all over again. Maybe.*

But in the meantime, the territory between Taichung and the southern parts of Taiwan needed to be cleared of Chinese tanks, vehicles, weapons, and unexploded ordnance. It was a massive task, one that would involve multiple Taiwanese and American combat divisions.

While they were undertaking this mission, Furness also knew that they would need to plan their withdrawal from the island and send the Marines back home to their families. It would take time. There were only so many ships and aircraft available to send home the hundreds of thousands of US and coalition service personnel who were now stationed on Taiwan.

Furness had spoken to his Marines about it. While they were eager to get home, they also knew there was little they could do. They had been away for months and were battle weary, sick, and exhausted. Furness and his command team would have a tough

325

job keeping up morale—that is, for the Marines that were still alive.

He had lost several hundred killed and a thousand or so wounded during the campaign. While many commanders in Iraq and Afghanistan had memorized the names of their dead Marines or soldiers, the scale of the fighting and number of Marines who had been killed in action in Taiwan prevented that. He had tried, but the sheer numbers, as well as exhaustion as the weeks passed by, meant it had become an impossible task.

And this morning, it was time to farewell another one of them.

------------------------→

Furness peered at the casket. The end of fighting had allowed the regiment to finally conduct numerous memorial services and ramp ceremonies for their fallen Marines. Furness had attended dozens of such events in the last two days alone.

But this one was different. Lee.

The young Army captain had been killed while leading a special mission on the eve of the typhoon. Tasked by the Marine divisional commander, her cavalry troopers had been given the tough mission of infiltrating through the Chinese lines and destroying the headquarters of a PLA Group Army.

Furness turned to his executive officer.

"You know, when I first heard about this, I thought it was an insane mission. I mean, we do have Tomahawks and other precision missiles. But the more I looked into the parameters of the mission, the location of the headquarters, and who they were able to capture, it kind of made sense."

He looked back at the casket, draped in the American flag. His executive officer, Lieutenant Colonel Nick Eyre, nodded. While Lee had not been assigned to their regiment for the conduct of the mission on which she had been killed, Eyre had pulled some strings at division headquarters to ensure their regiment was given the responsibility to farewell her properly.

"She would have made a fantastic Marine, Sir."

Both knew that this was the ultimate compliment a Marine officer could make about a soldier. Old habits and rivalries die hard.

"That she would, Nick," replied Furness. He turned to his regimental chaplain and nodded his head as a signal that the upload process for Captain Lee, and the other soldiers killed on the mission, could be placed into the aircraft and begin their long journey home.

Furness felt his heart drop as Lee's casket, carried by some of the remnants of her cavalry troop, passed by his position. He, Eyre, and the others assembled in the long line to the rear of the aircraft slowly but precisely rendered final honors to the young captain and her fellow soldiers. They would hold a memorial service later in the day, but right now was about the formal farewell of these soldiers.

Furness watched as the caskets were reverentially loaded onto the aircraft. The loadmaster supervised the tying down of each casket. Earlier, he had ensured that a large American flag had been hung on the bulkhead that separated the aircraft cockpit from the cargo hold.

The loadmaster was well practiced in this procedure. Ramp ceremonies such as this one had been conducted every hour, around the clock, since the end of the war.

Eyre turned to his commander.

"Sir, they are all done. Lee and her soldiers are secure and ready to go home."

Eyre paused then before continuing.

"She was certainly one for the books, boss. I know you really admired her. She told me once that she thought you were the best boss she ever had. High praise from a soldier."

Furness nodded. He would miss Lee. She was smart, gutsy, and a hell of a fine leader. Furness turned his gaze back to Eyre.

"You know, Confederate General Lee is reputed to have said, 'It is well that war is so terrible—we should grow too fond of it.'" Furness paused on the edge of saying more.

"I don't know that I have seen much to be fond of here, XO. Our Marines have been magnificent of course, as have our soldiers. But overall, this war has left me with a huge sense of loss. Despite their courage, too many of our men and women have had promising futures destroyed. There has been so much suffering and destruction ..." His voice trailed off. "And how could the Chinese, who we have always looked at as master strategists, think they could execute some kind of short war without massive resistance from the Taiwanese, and the United States and Japan getting involved? I mean, when in history have major powers launched wars of this kind and the war has been over quickly? This is not just a war for Taiwan. It is a hegemonic war—a war over the future of global power and influence.

"Modern states are too big and too rich. They can afford to fight for a long time. How did a culture, with such a long history, overlook this? Or did they?"

Furness quietened for a moment, gazing at the destroyed Chinese aircraft and vehicles that still dotted the edge of the runway in places. He turned back to Eyre.

"No, we haven't beaten the Chinese here. They have suffered and lost a lot of people. But they are not going to give up on taking this island, or on their larger aspirations to stand astride the world, just as the United States has for the last few decades. This isn't over."

Furness paused for a moment before continuing.

"The divisional commander has endorsed my recommendation for the Medal of Honor. He is confident that it will get through the system."

Eyre nodded. Like Furness, he already missed Lee.

"I can't think of a more fitting recipient," replied Eyre. "It's time to go, boss. The aircraft is departing now, and the regiment will begin its move south in a couple of hours."

They moved to the edge of the airfield and watched as the aircraft taxied to the end of the runway. It was one of several others that were queued up on the taxiway, ready to depart. With a sudden crescendo, the aircraft's four engines increased power to propel the cargo plane down the runway. And then, it was airborne.

Lee, you are going home, Furness thought. *I'll come and visit you when I get back.*

Epilogue

20 August 2028
Zhongnanhai, Beijing

The pain in his knees was excruciating. At his age, kneeling was uncomfortable and quickly became painful if he had to do so for any length of time. He generally preferred to avoid it. Especially when it involved resting his ancient bones on stone floors. Not that he had any choice in the matter. The end of his reign, when it had come, was quite rapid, he mused to himself.

He had expected it, of course. The invasion was always going to be a gamble. Even after the Russian debacle, and the counsel of those who believed that a forcible reintegration of Taiwan was no longer possible, he had persisted. He had been insistent that it was their destiny to bring Taiwan back into China's embrace.

If only they had killed the rebellious government leaders and landed their forces quickly enough to forestall any American intervention. But that was not to be. A combination of events, including the naval disaster in the northern Taiwan Strait, had ensured their best laid plans had gone astray almost from the start of the invasion. *So much for a short, glorious war*, he huffed to himself.

And his proposal for tactical nuclear weapons to be used against the Americans had been rejected by other members of the Politburo. After that, it had only been a matter of time before they had come for him.

The disaster in their rebellious province had meant that 20 years of investing national treasure on new military forces, new ships and aircraft, missiles, and land combat equipment, had been squandered. Much of it now either sat on the floor of the Taiwan Strait or was locked up in cantonments in southern Taiwan after having been left behind during the withdrawal of their personnel. His precious Army was now largely gone, swept aside by weather, combat, and bad luck.

That the Taiwanese and Americans had allowed the Chinese to withdraw their people unhindered after the storm made the Chinese humiliation even worse. Every Chinese citizen knew, as every soldier on the ships on their way home from Taiwan knew, that they were only alive because the Americans allowed it.

Former President of the People's Republic of China, Zhang Xi, looked around. On his knees, he could only crane his neck so far as to observe the small courtyard. Of course, he was familiar with this small, walled space. Deep in the Zhongnanhai compound, he had stood behind the observation windows two stories above where he now knelt to watch the demise of many of his opponents.

They had come for him three days ago while he was taking his morning walk—the only time he had to himself before he commenced his duties for the day. He normally strolled in the private garden reserved for members of the Politburo. The leader of the mutiny, and a team of the special military unit that guarded Zhongnanhai, had approached him and quickly escorted him to a holding cell.

He had been formally charged with multiple crimes—all made up, of course. But, for the members of the Politburo, it helped them to justify what they were about to do.

He heard soft footsteps behind him. Zhang Xi knew exactly what would happen next. An officer of the elite guard force in this exclusive compound would have been chosen by ballot. The officer, briefed on his duties, would have awoken early that morning and prepared his weapon—and himself—for the duty he was about to perform. While Zhang Xi could not see the officer, he knew that the officer would be dressed in his best ceremonial uniform. It was considered an honor among the large guard force to be selected. After all, one rarely had the opportunity to execute an enemy of the state who also happens to be a former president.

He heard a slight rustling noise. That, Zhang Xi knew, would be the officer withdrawing his Chinese-designed and manufactured pistol from its holster. It would be the standard-issue PLA ground forces pistol with its 5.8mm armor-piercing bullets. Strange how such details came back to him now.

He looked down at the paved ground, then raised his head to steal a final glance at the sky. It was a grey and cloudy day. *Fitting*, Zhang Xi thought.

He felt something metallic touch the rear of his head.

------------------------➤

The assembled members of the Politburo heard the report of the pistol and saw the body of Zhang Xi drop to ground. Dominating the group was a man in a PLA ground forces uniform.

General Lin Weiguo had been the commander of the Central Military Command. Married to the daughter of a member of the Politburo, he had been carefully cultivating influence and relationships in Beijing for two decades. When the former president had directed that the invasion of Taiwan proceed just three months ago, Weiguo had made arrangements to take control of the government in the event of a failed invasion.

He knew, as a military veteran and a prolific reader of military history, that such an invasion would be almost impossible to conduct successfully, even with the massive investments in the PLA of the past two decades. Several years earlier, he had counseled caution to the Central Military Committee about invading Taiwan.

He had been listened to but ignored.

It had not hurt his career, given his contacts in the Politburo. But it had reinforced his belief that he would need to act to reassert Chinese dignity if there was a disaster. So, he had schemed and organized, waiting for his opportunity.

In the wake of the typhoon, what the Taiwanese were calling the "heavenly storm," he had acted. Within several days, he had the backing of most of the Politburo. It had then been a simple task to detain and place on trial the former president for crimes against the Chinese people.

Weiguo glanced back down at the corpse in the courtyard before again turning his gaze on the gathering of the most senior leaders of the Chinese Communist Party.

"Comrades and friends, thank you for your confidence. It is time for us to move beyond the short rule of Zhang Xi. There is much to do now that our reunification with Taiwan has been delayed again." He saw nodding heads in the assembled group. "We must reassure our people of China's greatness. That we are not beaten."

Weiguo paused for a moment. He knew that his next words would be welcome but would involve more struggle, more time, and more risk in the immediate future. They all knew that there was one obstinate and difficult challenge that had to be faced. It could no longer be put off.

"Comrades and friends, it remains our destiny to stand as first among nations. But to do that, we will need to deal with the American problem. Once and for all."

THE END

(MAYBE)

Author's Afterword

Ten Years After the War

The war in Taiwan was not the first time American and Chinese soldiers have fought each other. And as we have seen in the past decade, it was not the last. We have been witnesses to intermittent fighting in different regions across the globe over that time. However, the Taiwan campaign was the first time in the new grand strategic competition of the 21st century that the two massive protagonists went to war. They unleashed violence on each with much vigor, in many places, and in huge numbers.

It is proper, however, on this tenth anniversary of the beginning of this global conflict, that we explore where this destructive conflagration began. Born from a decade of mutual distrust and competition, it began where many expected. The war was fought in some ways that were predictable, and in other ways, a total surprise.

Strategists in the West expected, in the early 21st century, that naval and air power would be decisive in any conflict over Taiwan. Space and cyber power, coupled with information operations, would also play important parts. Land operations, while important, received much less attention.

As the war played out, it became rapidly apparent that all five domains were vital for warfighting. It was impossible to place one's main effort in just one or two areas like the coalition of forces had in Afghanistan or Iraq for nearly two decades. The protagonists, in seeking the advantage, had to invest massive resources in all domains concurrently. This should not have been a surprise.

Over the last few years, several excellent histories of the war in the western Pacific have been published. Doctor Nathan Finney's *Cataclysm in Formosa* has become the standard textbook on the early days of the Taiwan conflict. Doctor Steven Leonard's equally superb *Ghosts of Magong* unveils the desperate hand-to-hand combat of the Chinese, American, and Taiwanese combatants—and their supporting robots—on the tiny island of Magong in the Taiwan Strait.

Doctor Jessica Scott's study of information conflict in the 2020s, *Path to Glory: Information, Misinformation and Deception*, set a new standard for the examination of the role of info-cyber-psyops in 21st-century warfare. And finally, retired Australian Air Vice Marshal "Maz" Jovanovich's authoritative study of sub-surface attack in the maritime domain, *Sub Sea Attack*, sits on the bookshelves of every senior naval and Air Force officer that I interviewed for this project.

In the last two years, the United States government has commissioned the writing of an official history of this war, with the first two volumes to focus on the growing strategic competition of the 2010s and the outbreak of war in Taiwan. The United States has a wonderful tradition of producing such official histories. The well-known "green book" series produced by the US Army, which chronicles events in the Second World War, stands as a beacon of excellence and detail to historians who seek to research and write about the history of warfare.

Like earlier official histories, I expect that this new effort—to be released over the coming years—will provide historians, policy makers, and the public at large with unique and well-informed insights into what happened, who did what, and why, during this critical phase of 21st-century history. Like the war of 1939–1945, the past decade is an epoch that massively changed all that came afterwards. It has revealed to the people of not just the United States, but the entire world, a new era of savage conflict and competition across all dimensions of national endeavor.

There is a rich trove of paper and cyber resources about the war from military institutions and from individuals that fought in it or who contributed by serving in government and industry. Historians will undoubtedly study these sources for centuries to come.

Despite the excellent histories that we have already seen, there are many, many more to follow. Books on the US Civil War are still published over 170 years after it began. I expect we will see scholarship and publication of this conflict over Taiwan well into the future.

As readers will know, the failed first Chinese invasion of Taiwan did not curb the aspirations of the leadership of the Chinese Communist Party. Very shortly after the defeat of the Chinese in the wake of Operation *Chakra Rain*, the Chinese replaced their president with a much more militant and aggressive leader. Despite the enormous losses in people, materiel, and wealth that resulted from their first failed invasion of Taiwan, the Chinese Communist Party continued to attempt its expansion of influence throughout the western Pacific region and beyond. But this continued tale of heartbreak, destruction, and catastrophe is a story for another book.

What of the main protagonists in this story?

Technical Sergeant Hickling, after the stunning success of the operation that deceived the Chinese about the typhoon, was subsequently commissioned and eventually assumed the role in the Space Force that had previously been occupied by Captain Marcus.

Private Chen remained in the Republic of China Army. He transferred into a communications occupational specialty and fought in subsequent campaigns as an information warfare specialist. He remains in the Army as a first class master sergeant.

Colonel Furness was wounded in a vehicle accident a short time after the Chinese surrender in Taiwan. He gradually recuperated and returned to duty several months later. In due course, he was promoted and today commands the 7th Marine Division in the Philippines.

FEMA Director Keene retired from government service not long after the events portrayed in this book. A lifelong resident of Washington, DC, she now runs a boutique consulting agency with an office on K Street.

Colonel Bo of the Chinese Marines returned to China after the Chinese defeat in its first attempted invasion of Taiwan. Even though many of his fellow senior officers were sacked and demoted upon their return home, Bo somehow managed to avoid the purges that occurred in the PLA in the wake of the failed Taiwan operation. Several years after his return to his wife and family in Beijing, Bo defected to the United States. Interviews with Bo were critical in the development of this book, and he is now an active writer and public speaker in his new hometown of Boston.

Admiral Leonard, after the success of Operation *Chakra Rain*, returned to Washington, DC and was appointed as the Chairman of the Joint Chiefs of Staff by the next administration. An erudite yet humble man, he led the expansion and transformation of the American military over the next few years that underpinned its battlefield and strategic successes across the Indo-Pacific region in the wake of the campaign in Taiwan. He is now retired, and lives in his hometown of Savannah.

The body of Captain Dana Lee, perhaps the best known of the historical characters portrayed in this story, was returned to the United States and given a hero's burial at Arlington National Cemetery. Awarded the Medal of Honor at Zhudong, as well as a posthumous Army Distinguished Service Cross for the mission in Taichung City and multiple other awards for bravery, she is one of the most celebrated and adored combat leaders that emerged during the war. She is buried alongside Sergeant James and thousands of others killed in the war over Taiwan. I have included a copy of the citation for her Medal of Honor on the following page.

Her family, devastated by her loss, established a scholarship in her name at Columbia University.

Congressional Medal of Honor Citation

Captain Dana M. Lee, United States Army

For extraordinary heroism and conspicuous gallantry in action against enemy Chinese forces, above and beyond the call of duty, while serving with the 3rd Marine Littoral Regiment, 3rd Marine Division, in the Battle of Hengshan, Zhudong region, northern Taiwan. While the enemy was attacking at the defensive positions of her Army cavalry troop, Captain Lee, in command of her troop, fought valiantly to check the savage and determined assault. Captain Lee, commanding from a vulnerable position on the forward part of the battlefield, was constantly in motion directing her subordinate units and supporting fires from the Marine regiment and Air Force elements. A little while later, and personally leading her troops, she attacked directly into the Chinese forces, and under continual fire, personally led the destruction of hundreds of Chinese troops and robotic combat systems. Captain Lee gallantly led the coordination of holding this vital part of the defensive line throughout the battle until reinforcements arrived. At great risk to her life and in the face of continued enemy attack, Captain Lee successfully defended a strategically important part of northern Taiwan, and her actions contributed in large measure to the virtual annihilation of two Chinese airborne infantry battalions and hundreds of robotic combat vehicles. Her great personal valor, example, and courageous initiative are in keeping with the highest traditions of the US Army.